A QUESTION OF BETRAYAL

AN ELENA STANDISH NOVEL

A QUESTION OF BETRAYAL

ANNE PERRY

THORNDIKE PRESS
A part of Gale, a Cengage Company

Thorndike Press® Large Print Basic.
The text of this Large Print edition is unabridged.
Other aspects of the book may vary from the original edition.
Set in 16 pt. Plantin.

LIBRARY OF CONGRESS CIP DATA ON FILE.
CATALOGUING IN PUBLICATION FOR THIS BOOK
IS AVAILABLE FROM THE LIBRARY OF CONGRESS.

ISBN-13: 978-1-4328-8284-6 (hardcover alk. paper)

Published in 2020 by arrangement with Ballantine Books, an imprint of Random House, a division of Penguin Random House, LLC.

Printed in Mexico
Print Number: 01   Print Year: 2020

To Diana Howie

CHAPTER 1

"What did you say?" Elena asked incredulously. She could not believe what she had just heard. She was standing in the small sitting room of her London apartment, the September sun pouring in through the window and illuminating the ornaments she had collected in the few years she had been here: a carved ivory box, a gift from her mother; candlesticks from her grandparents; family photographs. But the light was the best thing about the place, the smooth lines and the shadows, a photographer's delight.

Peter Howard stood opposite her, a couple of yards away, his face calm, as if he had no grasp of the outrageousness of what he had asked her. He looked very ordinary in the clear morning air: a little taller than average, fairish hair, regular features. Forgettable. Only his eyes and mouth were remarkable. They showed both a touch of humor

7

and an awareness of pain — and of what it meant.

"I have an important job for you at last," he repeated. "Something that really matters."

He said "at last" because it had been four months since Elena's extraordinary adventure in Berlin, her baptism by fire. It had been her introduction to the truth about her own family and their connection with British Military Intelligence, kept secret from the public. Her tasks since then had been very occasional, and of no particular importance. Case markers, as it were, for a beginner, after the horror and the losses in Berlin. She felt she was capable of far more. Had she not proven that?

But what Peter was asking now was not a matter of skill or courage.

She shook her head. "Yes, but —"

"Are you saying you won't do it?" His face hardly changed, yet he managed to convey disappointment, even contempt.

"You don't know what you are asking —" she began.

"Yes, I do," he interrupted her, his voice still perfectly level. "One of our most important agents is embedded in Trieste, seeking vital information, and his cover has almost certainly been blown. We can't reach his handler, and we want you to go and find him. Tell him that he must leave immediately, with as much information as he has. Otherwise, he may be killed. We cannot lose him and all that he has learned over the last year. He has a list of names, and it's vital we know who is on it."

"He was a traitor!" Even saying the words almost choked her. It brought back memories, disillusion, and then humiliation.

"No," Peter said calmly, although there was a shadow in his eyes that suggested, for an instant, that he was aware of at least elements of the truth. Wasn't everybody? Elena's dismissal from the Foreign Office had been pretty public.

"He was . . ." She did not need to raise her voice. She wanted to sound in control, as if she no longer cared. She was twenty-eight; this had been six years ago.

"He betrayed you," Peter said quietly, and there was emotion in his voice now, some kind of sadness. "He did not betray Britain," he continued. "He went into Germany as a Nazi sympathizer to gain their trust. We gave him information the Germans would believe — his rite of passage, if you like — but, of course, we knew what they knew and could work around it. It was successful. He earned their trust. He became one of them."

Elena tried to process what he was saying. So, had Aiden Strother been loyal to Britain all the time? Could that be true? Even as she turned it over in her mind, she could see how it made sense. She had learned a bit in the few months since Berlin. Somewhere inside her, she had aged years and grasped a new reality. She had lived through the war, the privation, the constant fear, the grief of loss: most immediately of her brother, Mike, and her sister Margot's husband, Paul. Every family she knew had lost somebody, and a million men were left shells of who they had once been. There had been radical social changes; rank and privilege had melted away; all blood is scarlet in the trenches.

But there had been other changes as well. Women worked at jobs they would have had neither the wish nor the opportunity to do before the men went away. Social class distinctions were blurred, some even obliterated. Women wore short dresses now, not much below the knee. Many had short hair. The elegance, the sentimentality, the blind hope of the Edwardian era were gone. It was 1933, a new, brash, desperate age now, familiar with the Depression, jazz, moving pictures, and the brilliant music and haunting lyrics of songwriters such as Cole Porter.

No one wanted another war. Never again must such grief, such abomination of loss, be allowed. Whatever the cost.

Elena tried to say yes, she would do it. Peter was waiting.

She looked away. Aiden may not have betrayed Britain, but he had betrayed her. Used her, and then gone without a word. It still hurt.

Peter stood there in the sun . . . and silence.

She drew breath to say, "Isn't there someone else?" She met his eyes. Damn him! He was doing everything the right way: asking her, and then leaving her to realize how selfish it was to think of her own dismissal and ruined career, instead of the job at hand. No one wanted to go to war, but they went anyway. She thought of Mike, and how he had said goodbye that last time, almost as if he had known he would not come back. "Chin up, kiddo, we're almost there," he had said.

She refused to think of that any further. She glared at Peter Howard, her eyes filling with tears. What the hell did Aiden's betrayal of her matter, then . . . or now?

"Yes, of course I'll go," she said, then realized all it would involve and instantly regretted it. But it was too late to withdraw.

11

"Good," he said gently. "You are by far the best person because you know him by sight, and he knows you well enough to trust you."

She raised her eyebrows. "After what he did to me, do you think he would place his life in my hands? I should be the last person he'd trust, if he had any sense."

"Or, on the other hand," Peter replied, with a slight twist of humor in his eyes, "he might think you put the country and the Service before your own hurt feelings, to save the life of a man who has already given so much."

That took her breath away. For a moment she could think of no answer. Could Aiden really have sacrificed this much? Had he really loved her, but put service to the country, his duty, first? He was fifteen years older than she, old enough to have served in the war. He knew more of it, in reality, than she ever would. She breathed in and out slowly. Surely Aiden could have given her some indication: a word, a gesture? "Why didn't he . . . ?" she started.

"Why couldn't he have told you?" There was an edge to Peter's voice, patience and something else: disappointment. "And you would have felt better?" he asked. "You would not have been so wounded, so grieved?"

"Yes! It would have been just ordinary decency!" Now she was furious, with a lump in her throat that betrayed the tears so close to breaking through. "Just . . ." She stopped.

"Just have lessened the pain for you. Even allowed you to have kept your job, perhaps."

She glared at him. "Yes! Was I really expendable?"

"That's a harsh word, but . . . yes, you were, in that job. In this one, perhaps not, but you have a lot to learn, and quickly."

She did not answer. *Expendable.* What a terrible thing to admit of anyone. It hurt. It meant you could be done without.

"Elena." Peter spoke gently now. "If you had not been hurt, what would other people have thought? Honestly."

"I don't know. I . . . who? Who are you talking about?"

He raised his eyebrows very slightly. "Do you think there are no German agents watching us? Listening to us? Or even our own people, good but naïve, repeating office gossip?"

She blinked at the sudden humiliation. As if she were a moth pinned to a board and watched.

"Do you think no one sees you?" he asked. "Talks about you? You are a lovely woman;

13

in your own way, beautiful. But more than that, you have considerable intelligence, in spite of your occasional lapses of judgment, and you are Charles Standish's daughter and Lucas Standish's granddaughter. Of course people talk. And of course you have enemies. Think, Elena. If Aiden Strother had used you and damaged you, gone over to the enemy with no grief on your part, no sense of betrayal . . . if you were a German, what would you have thought? How much of what Strother said to you would you have believed? And don't pretend to be naïve. It's too late for that."

"I . . . see. It would've been . . ."

"Suicide." He said the word for her. "As well as a betrayal of all the connections he used to get information back to us."

Elena felt suddenly very stupid, and angry. She had thought she could do this. After all, with a little help, she had done pretty well in Berlin. She had survived in spite of the Gestapo and the Brownshirts being after her. She had even outwitted Peter himself — briefly.

"Which is why you will go to Trieste without visiting your family," he went on. "Your parents and your grandparents are not to know where you are. I will tell Lucas after you are gone. You are on a photo-

14

graphic assignment to Trieste. There are those who see Trieste as the most beautiful Italian city, which means more exquisite than Amalfi or Naples or the great Tuscan cities. My favorite used to be Florence, with its classical Renaissance history, more intimate than Rome. More full of the details of personal history and color than Milan, or Turin, more even than Rimini or Venice."

"That's ridiculous." She dismissed him impatiently. It was all irrelevant.

"It's the light," he continued, as if she had not spoken. "Go and take pictures that prove me right. Show everyone Trieste at its best. You can prove me wrong another time."

"The light?"

"You're a photographer. You know what a difference light makes to everything, most of all to photographs. To see things with a different eye, what is accentuated and how, what catches your imagination and takes it beyond what you see. That's your art; use it."

She was caught by surprise. She had no idea that he saw things in such detail, with such understanding of the emotional moods of light and darkness. "Yes," she affirmed, "yes, I will. I've got to have a reason for being there, for the authorities."

"Quite." He gave a slight smile. "You're

15

going as yourself: Elena Standish. Your recent successes will help."

"Successes?" She was startled that he should know about her photographic achievements: pictures published in magazines, even a large section in an exhibition. Her portraits of old people's faces filled with the tracery of lines, both triumph and tragedy, had earned some very pleasant comments. She was proud of the power and beauty of them. The backgrounds were autumn farmlands, suggesting a timelessness. The sharp angles of the stocks, curiously barbaric against the softer rolling, shaven fields, had won her a prize. Other faces stared at cloud racks full of brilliance and half shadows, or falling leaves in ever-changing patterns. The praise was sweet because she felt it was honest. There was no flattery. "I didn't know you knew of them," she said awkwardly.

"Of course I do. I can't send you undercover as a photographer if you aren't any good at it. Do you think I'm that incompetent? Quickest way to get killed . . ." He hesitated, then smiled with a sudden pleasure, like a shaft of sunlight. "But you are good!"

She was surprised by how much that pleased her. She hardly knew him, and their

16

few conversations had been less than pleasant. But outside the family, he was the closest friend her grandfather had, although she had learned that only since she had returned from Berlin in May. There was so much she had discovered since then, and she knew it was only a small part of the huge country of the past. Peter and Lucas had worked together, trusted each other with their lives, and grieved for the deaths of the same comrades. "Thank you," she accepted.

He shrugged one shoulder. "You will leave early in the morning the day after tomorrow. We will give you tickets for a flight to Paris, and the train from there to Trieste. You will have to change in Milan. We have an apartment in Trieste. I'll give you the address and the keys and some Italian currency, plus copies of some of your best work, in case you need to prove yourself to the authorities. You probably won't need them, but you don't know what you will encounter."

Elena listened without interruption. This was so different from her adventure in Berlin, where she had been a fugitive most of the time. Her purpose had been self-chosen. She had moved every few days, sometimes even daily. It had been terrifying, exhilarating, and she had discovered a

17

part of herself she did not know existed, a braver side that cared passionately for causes bigger than herself, that dared not stand aside from issues that would involve everyone, sooner or later.

"We can't give you any contacts," Peter went on. "Aiden Strother's handler was Max Klausner, who has disappeared with no trace that we can find. Discreet inquiries to the police have shown nothing, and we can't afford to draw attention to him in case he's still alive and the answers to our own questions lead them to Strother."

"Do you know who would have killed him?" Elena swallowed, but her mouth was dry. "Or who would try to kill Aiden?" Against her will she could see Aiden's face in her mind, the way he held his head high, his quick smile.

"No," Peter said. "Whether Aiden has any idea we can only guess. He may not have trusted any of the ways of getting information to us."

She started to speak, then realized she did not know what to say.

"If this task were easy, we could send anyone," Peter said bleakly. "You have the advantage of knowing Aiden by sight and knowing his mission in Trieste — at least, what it was to begin with. It's up to you to

18

remain enigmatic. You might even find it advantageous to pretend — if it is a pretense — that you still have feelings for him."

She stared at him in disbelief.

The shadow was over his eyes again. "This is real, Elena. Other people will live or die depending upon whether we succeed. But you understand that. Aiden's information is very important indeed, not only to Britain, but to all of Europe. Saving his life is important, too, but his mission matters above all."

"I don't suppose you'll tell me why." She was afraid. For the first time, Trieste sounded like enemy territory. The Italians had been on Britain's side in the war by the end of it, but now the answer was obvious: Benito Mussolini. Il Duce. He had taken an iron hand to the government of Italy. He was leading the way to social change with belligerence, and controlling people's beliefs, behaviors, even thoughts, and Hitler was on his heels, perhaps soon to overtake him.

"You will do whatever is necessary, whether it is comfortable or not," Peter said quietly. "Or else you'll tell me now that you can't do it, that you're not up to pretending, even to save other people's lives. But if you did say that, you would surprise me. I

19

remember in Berlin, you were rather . . . inventive." He let the details lie unspoken.

She could feel the color burn up her face at the memory. It was one she did not want to revisit. "I'll go! You don't have to pressure me into it. You imagine I care so much what you think of me? I care what's right and what's possible. The only person whose opinion matters to me, and to whom I could explain this, is my grandfather."

Peter's face hardened. "I have already told you, you will tell Lucas nothing whatsoever about this. In fact, you will not see him before you go."

Now she was angry. He was being unreasonable. "I'm going to say goodbye. For heaven's sake, you can't believe my grandfather would tell anyone. He knows more secrets than you do." She had been shattered at first when she learned that her elderly, dry-humored grandfather — who loved his books, his dog, the countryside, restoring old drawings and paintings — had once been the head of MI6. It had been a lot to take in then, but now she was actually proud of him. "I won't just walk out and not even tell him I'm going. It could be days."

"It almost certainly will be," Peter agreed. "Several days, at the very least. But you will

20

tell no one anything about it at all."

"I've got to tell —"

"No one!" he repeated sharply. "It is a photographic assignment in Italy. As I said, I shall tell Lucas after you have gone. You can drop a note to your parents to say a brief assignment has come up without warning, and you will see them again when you get back, which is the truth."

"But Lucas . . ." she protested.

"Would you lie to Lucas?" he asked, eyes wide.

"Well . . . I . . . I'm not sure that I could. I mean, get away with it."

"I'm sure," he said drily, "that you couldn't." Now there was an edge to his voice.

"But you'll lie to him," she said. "I can see it in your face!"

"I will tell him as much as he needs of the truth, the same as I will tell you." His shoulders were stiff, his eyes very direct, clear and shadowless blue.

Now she was afraid.

Chapter 2

Peter Howard walked down the stairs and out onto the street, into the sun. He had disliked having to ask Elena to undertake this task. He knew about her affair with Aiden Strother — most of the Foreign Office did, if not through office gossip before Strother had so dramatically defected, or appeared to have, then certainly afterward. It was Elena's own doing. Twenty-two and not long graduated from Cambridge with an excellent degree in classics, she had not been pushed into the affair. The languages essential to her Foreign Office job she already knew, having been with her parents while her father was ambassador in Madrid, Paris, and Berlin during her childhood. It did not take long to become proficient in a language that was spoken all around you, and she had a natural gift for it.

She had been left to shoulder at least some of the blame when Strother departed, ostensibly as a traitor, carrying many secrets to the Nazis. At least, that was what appeared to have happened. But now she knew the truth: that he could not tell anyone. Certainly not an emotional young woman with whom he was intimately involved. It had cost her her job. That was unfortunate, but the slightest sign that the situation was not as it appeared might have betrayed Aiden to the Nazis. After years of careful work, some of which had jeopardized lives, Aiden was risking his own life by appearing to defect, carrying carefully prepared secrets with him. Some had been current but most were old, out of date, and not dangerous anymore, even if by a hairsbreadth. A word of comfort to a young lover could have ruined it all: a thread to pull that could have unraveled everything, destroyed a plan carefully laid over years, and all the lives involved.

Peter reached a corner and crossed Tottenham Court Road, oblivious of the traffic increasing around him. He had not known Elena then. In fact, he did not really know her now. He had met her only a few months before, when she had accidentally become involved in that desperate affair in Berlin. She had acted with courage and, at times, great presence of mind. At other times, she

23

had betrayed amateur impulsiveness. But then, she *had been* an amateur, involved by chance and knowing very little. Heavens, at that time she had not even known that her beloved grandfather, Lucas Standish, had, during the war, been head of MI6, the existence of which was a secret from the general public. To everyone outside the intelligence organization, Lucas was a mild-mannered man who did something mathematical in the Civil Service. Supposedly, even his wife did not know his real job, except that Josephine Standish had been a decoder during the same war — Peter smiled at the memory — and brave, eccentric Josephine knew far more than even Lucas assumed. Peter had a great respect for her. He hoped he never knew the full extent of her abilities. It pleased him to have some mysteries left.

Lucas would not approve of Peter's having sent Elena to rescue Aiden Strother. Intellectually, he might understand why she was the best person to do so, inexperienced as she was. She spoke both Italian and German fluently. German would be an advantage because, of course, Trieste had been occupied by many different forces, and recently the German-speaking Austrian Empire. The danger they feared, and that

Aiden had gone to investigate, was inspired by Germany.

Elena had firsthand knowledge of how Hitler's rise to power in Germany at the beginning of this year had changed everything. Experience was a visceral part of understanding. She had proven that she had determination and, when pressed, a considerable imagination, and courage to act. Peter admired that. But was it enough?

This was still an operation he would rather not have given to someone so new to the Service, and so emotionally raw. Both were disadvantages, in that she lacked training, but more seriously, her feelings for Aiden would leave her vulnerable. Could they easily be reawakened, used against her, even fatally?

He turned the corner and walked more rapidly along the next street, the sun in his face.

There were also advantages. Elena was not a professional. No one in the service on the other side would know her. That was the best disguise of all. But by far the most important advantage was that she would know Aiden Strother by sight, no matter how his appearance had superficially changed. She would recognize the things one cannot disguise: the shape of his ears, the way he stood when casually waiting, the things that made him laugh or, more likely, irritated him. Some things are unchanged even when disillusion sours everything else. Peter knew that, too, but preferred not to remember.

Had Aiden loved Elena? Peter smiled at the thought of her. She had a turbulent face, vulnerable and full of emotion. And yet she was capable of great calm, as if she was searching for something and, every so often, found it. She was interesting, different.

He hoped profoundly that she would succeed, quite apart from the imperative of recovering Aiden Strother's information . . . and that was crucial. The other news he was receiving about the rising power of Hitler within resurgent Germany, gaining strength and casting his hungry eyes toward its neighbors, might be dismissed as fearmongering by some, but Peter took it very seriously.

Austria was particularly vulnerable. Its new young president, Engelbert Dollfuss, had come to power the year before. He was an unusual man who, though less than five feet tall, had managed to be accepted into the army, where he had served with some distinction. He was an ardent Catholic, and very right-wing politically. He was extremely sensitive about his height and punished anyone rash enough to make jokes about it. He was altogether heavy-handed in exercising his power.

It was Peter's job, as well as his nature, to foresee problems, and to know as much as possible about the players, their power and their interests. Aiden Strother's years in Germany, Austria, and northern Italy were fundamental to that.

Lucas Standish might understand his reasons, but he would still be angry that Peter had gone behind his back and sent Elena to find Strother. The knowledge of that was a growing darkness inside him. He cared what Lucas thought of him. It left him vulnerable, and yet he realized Lucas was the most important influence in his life, more important than his own father, whom it seemed he would never truly please, no matter how hard he tried. To begin with, he could not share any aspect of his work with his parents or, for that matter, with his wife, Pamela, but that was a whole other area that he preferred not to visit now.

He was walking quite automatically, passing people without seeing their faces. Everyone was hurrying, even in the mild September sun. Hurrying somewhere, toward something, or away from it. He smiled —

not at any of those passing, but just at the light and the warmth, at memories of friendship, shared discovery, successes . . . and the comfort of companionship in the face of failure. That, too, was a tight bond.

Had he broken it all by sending Lucas's granddaughter on a mission that could only be painful to her?

Peter went back to his office and completed all the travel arrangements for Elena under her own name. He booked a car to take her to the airport and one at the other end to take her into Paris and to the railway station. He already had the rail tickets to Milan and then on to Trieste. From that point, she would have to take care of her mission herself. He had city maps with notable places marked, specifically where she might like to photograph. She must keep that cover always.

He included the address of the three-room apartment rented for her. On balance, this was better than a hotel, more discreet. There was a landlord who would know how to watch and help, if necessary, and who would provide the basic food supplies for her arrival.

Peter reached the office and went upstairs. He knocked on Bradley's door. As soon as he heard the muffled order from inside, he went in.

Jerome Bradley, head of MI6, was sitting at his desk. He looked up with a bland expression on his face. He was immaculately dressed, as always, in a tailored pinstripe suit, white shirt, anonymous tie. His school was not one to boast about. His thick brown hair was brushed back off his forehead. "Yes?" he said, but he did not invite Peter to sit, even though there was a chair a few feet from the desk.

Peter stood straight, not quite at attention. "I'm sending someone to Trieste to find Aiden Strother and get him out —"

Bradley cut across him. "What's he doing there anyway? I don't remember sending him."

"You didn't," Peter replied. "You weren't in charge then. It was six years ago." It was surprising that Bradley, who had replaced Lucas Standish when he finally retired, had not read the confidential papers that would have told him about Aiden Strother.

"Strother?" Bradley's eyes narrowed. "Just a minute, wasn't he a traitor? Do you mean he's turned our way again?" His voice was heavy with doubt. "How?"

"He was always facing our way, sir," Peter said patiently. "We planted him, and he sent

29

back a great deal of information."

"Really." That was not a question, only an acknowledgment that Bradley had heard him. "I don't remember seeing his name on anything." His voice had a note of criticism.

"No, sir, we don't leave the names of our informers on things." Bradley should hardly have needed a reminder of something so obvious.

"What has he done that he's in danger?" Bradley changed tack. He looked skeptical. "Be careful who you bring back into the country, Howard. Think very hard about what you are doing. You have been known to let your enthusiasm mislead your judgment."

Peter felt the hot blood rise up his cheeks. Bradley knew far more about him than he knew about Bradley. Much of his experience had been in a different area, higher in administration, less in action. "You don't accomplish much by always playing within the bounds of safety, sir," Peter said, needle sharp. Peter had been active in intelligence during the war and shortly after. Bradley had not.

"You don't need to remind me of your accomplishments, Howard. At least not more than half a dozen times," Bradley responded with the ghost of a smile.

That was unfair. Peter never boasted. He abhorred braggarts. It was the surest sign of insecurity, a serious weakness in any officer. Bradley was baiting him deliberately. "Then you know the answer to your questioning, sir," he said between his teeth. "Strother was embedded six years ago, with the orders to go wherever his opportunities led him, and to report back anything he felt of interest, but with the greatest care and as seldom as possible. He sent his information . . ." He hesitated, reluctant to tell Bradley anything he did not have to.

"Yes?" Bradley said impatiently. "For God's sake, Howard, stop dancing around like a bloody ballerina *en pointe*. I know everything that you do, and a lot that you don't."

"I don't doubt it, sir," Peter replied. He knew a lot that he had not told Bradley, and did not intend to. Little things, day-to-day details, but that was how most pictures were created. Not in spills of paint, but one stroke at a time.

"What does this Aiden Strother know that is worth risking another man's life to get him out?" Bradley went on. "And if Strother is really any good, tell him to lie low for a while and find his own way out. Where is he? Germany? Austria?"

31

"Since his handler has disappeared, and we have no direct contact with him, how do you suggest we do that?" Peter tried to keep sarcasm out of his voice and failed.

Bradley asked the one question Peter had hoped he would not. "How do you know his contact has disappeared?" His eyebrows rose. "Who told you that? Let him tell Strother to get out, if he hasn't got enough sense to get out anyway. Since the line of communication has been cut, surely the man is bright enough to know that?"

This was settling into a battle of wills, no longer tied to the actual issues. Why? Personal dislike? Or was Bradley actually trying to provoke Peter into something more? An open insubordination, for which he could be dismissed? Was it all still about Lucas Standish and the ghost of his leadership that lingered on? Bradley wanted to put one of his own men in Peter's place. That was an open secret. Peter might even have wanted the same were their positions reversed.

How much of the truth should he tell Bradley? Certainly not that he had sent Lucas Standish's granddaughter, and yet he could not get the travel expenses passed if he did not clear them through the usual channels, which Bradley was bound to see. Damn Bradley. "I don't care if Strother stays or leaves," Peter answered, measuring his words. "But I want his information to date. In his last message, he implied it was very important."

"Oh!" Bradley's eyebrows shot up and his tone became sharper. "Such as what?"

"I don't know." That was partly true. Peter did know it had something to do with Dollfuss and the changing power in Austria. "But before he sinks back into the woodwork and we can't find him, alive or dead, I wanted to discover exactly what he has learned. If we bring Strother himself back, so much the better, but if not, then at least his information."

Bradley's face tightened with displeasure, but the argument was reasonable. "All right, if we must, but a messenger, that's all. And train, second class; he'll get there just as quickly. Is that everything?"

"Thank you." Peter took the authorization. He had just put out his hand to open the door when Bradley spoke again.

"Howard?"

He turned. "Yes, sir?"

"Lucas Standish is gone. You answer to me now, and only me. I want a report on Strother as soon as possible, do you understand? And if you succeed in getting him out, then I want to debrief him personally.

Is that understood?"

"Yes, sir."

"And you still see Lucas Standish?"

"I see him socially now and then, as you see your friends." Peter swallowed hard. "Lord Irwin, for example. I don't intend to criticize it, even though he has some extreme right-wing views. I would go so far as to say pro-Nazi. And, of course, there's Oswald Mosley . . ."

Bradley's face was filled with a sudden and powerful dislike. "As opposed to Churchill who, thank God, is out of office," he snapped back. His pen was clenched in his heavy hand as if he wished to stab something with it. "A forgotten man, who doesn't know when to keep his crazy and disruptive opinions to himself," he added bitterly. "You may want another war, Howard, but most decent people with any sense do not. Especially those of us who fought in the last one. I mean really fought, in the trenches. Who saw their friends and brothers blown to pieces, or caught in the wire and riddled with bullets, helpless to do anything about it. And there were plenty of us. You would do very well to remember that. And if you think I would throw you out the first legitimate chance I get, you're bloody well right. I would, so be very careful. Don't make the slightest mistake . . . and give me the chance."

"Sir —"

"Don't interrupt!" Bradley snapped. "You're good at your job, I'll give you that. I'd have got rid of you years ago if you weren't. But you're Lucas Standish's man. There, I've said it openly, though everyone knows it already. I hope you keep our other secrets better than you keep that."

Peter swallowed hard. "Since I served with him for fifteen years, it's hardly a secret, sir. If there's anyone who still doesn't know he was the best director we've had — and he taught me just about everything I know — then we need to get rid of them. They wouldn't find their own backsides with both hands and a map."

Bradley sat forward in his chair. "Get out, and bring back Strother's information. Whatever it is, give it to me. If it's any bloody use! Do you understand me?"

"Yes, sir."

"And if you give it to Lucas Standish, I'll have your head on a plate, and that's a promise."

"Yes, sir." Peter went out and resisted the impulse to slam the door. He closed it very quietly, not even allowing the latch to click. But he did wonder how much Bradley knew

35

about Aiden Strother that he was so keen to get the report. Was it just to make certain Peter obeyed him? Or did he know more of it than he admitted?

It was early in the evening when Peter went home. The anger from his interview with Bradley had subsided. There was something cathartic about having their differences out in the open, even though he could not afford to give Bradley even the ghost of a chance to fire him. He loved the work. It was the center of his life. It had been for twenty years, since he left university and joined the Service.

He loved the complexity of it, the intellectual rigor of working through all the possibilities. He dreaded and yet was excited by the unforeseen; the tragedies made the victories more precious. Some enemies he hated, some he despised, others he respected, on occasion even admired.

He was afraid of physical pain — he believed any sane person was — and yet it also made him acutely aware of the joy of being alive and what was to be valued: the smell of new-turned earth, the glory of a sunrise over cliffs on a clear day, the flowers of the hawthorn, the drift of cherry blossoms, scarlet poppies on the edge of a field

36

of corn. Poppies always reminded him of grief, as they did every Englishman he knew. They were the symbol of sacrifice: too many young men to count, leaving their blood and their bones in the fields of Flanders, as his elder brother, James, had done. He had that in common with Elena, though he had never mentioned it to her. It was still a raw pain because too many things had been left unsaid. Had he ever let James know how much he admired him? Wanted to be like him? Even though, to their parents' chagrin, nature had cast them utterly unalike.

He was moving more quickly without realizing it, his sense of purpose, whatever Bradley said, energizing him. Peter would rather not have had to fight against Bradley, but if the wretched man made it necessary, then so be it.

He turned in at his own gate at half past six. The sun was lowering and there was a shadow of dusk in the air, the noise of starlings coming home, a warmth in the light. It was comfortingly familiar, with the late roses in bloom or deadheaded, so nothing looked careless. He liked this time of year, a season of harvest, the survivors' scarlet and purple and rust, fulfillment of promises kept and anticipation of winter and sinking back into the earth.

He put his key into the front door lock, and it opened easily. He should thank Pamela for caring so meticulously that everything was cleaned, oiled . . . whatever it needed. Somehow it never seemed the right time to say so.

"Hello!" he called from the hallway. Absentmindedly he looked at the post lying on the silver tray, a memento of university days, some prize or other. There was nothing but the usual bills and receipts, a letter from an old acquaintance.

Pamela came into the hall. She looked exactly as she always did, cool and elegant. He had often thought she would be able to walk the length of a room with a pile of books on her head and not lose any of them. A useless attribute, but it gave her a degree of unthinking grace that never let her down.

He kissed her smooth cheek automatically. She smelled of something pleasant, a flower of some sort. "Have you seen this?" he asked, holding up the envelope.

"Yes, it's Ronald Dashworth, reminding you of the anniversary dinner, as if you'd forget."

He had forgotten, on purpose. "Oh, yes," he said noncommittally. "What night is it again?"

"Sunday," she said, moving a step away

from him. "Did you say you had something else on that night? Because you do not."

There was no answer that would not provoke an argument. He did not want to go, but he owed it to Pamela. It would be a full-dress affair, glamorous, very formal; he should make an effort.

"What are you going to wear?" He tried to sound interested as he admired her honey-colored hair, classic features, blemishless skin, even at forty-three, a year younger than he. They should have grown comfortable with each other. Why hadn't they? Because the most important thing in his life was his work. It had his interest, his loyalty, his triumphs and disasters, all his depth of emotion, and he could not share any of it with her.

Not that he had tried. Or would try. He could have told her at least the nature of it; he could have shared parts that were not secret. He could have let her know the pain of his failures. She did not need to know the exact cause, the names and faces of the men he had lost, the memories of those wounded most deeply. What could he have said? *I lost a friend today? Can't tell you the details, but it hurts? Terribly? I hurt, and I feel guilty? Even though I could not have prevented it?*

And beyond those failures, it was as if his elder brother, James, had walked out of the door last week, leaving Peter behind. He had understood what he did and why. Major James Howard was an officer at the head of his men, the first over the top. He died at the Somme in 1916, leaving behind a grieving mother, a father who covered his grief in pride, and a younger brother feeling desperately alone, working secretly.

No one was untouched by something of that sort, although it took people in different ways. Some could share very little of the pain inside. There was not much one could put into words. If you took the bandages off at all, it was in private.

Pamela had stopped talking. As had happened far too often, he had not heard what she said. "You will look beautiful." He tried to catch up.

She smiled blandly. "Peter, I could have said I would wear the sitting-room curtains and you would have said I would look beautiful."

He met her eyes this time. "You have a flair for it, and blue suits you."

"They're green," she told him, referring to the curtains.

"No, they're not, they're blue. Blue like the sea, not the sky." That was one thing he noticed, color. Shape was the bones of a thing, color was its spirit. He said so . . . again.

She looked at him with surprise. "Did you just think of that?" she asked. For once it was as if she wanted to know, beyond just filling a silence.

"No, I've always thought it. You can't capture color, can't hold it as you would a shape."

Suddenly her smile was natural, warming the classic perfection of her face. "Sometimes, you amaze me."

He smiled back, but it was tentative. He was afraid he had revealed too much.

CHAPTER 3

Lucas Standish sat in the familiar chair in his study, gazing through the French doors into the garden. The late roses were losing petals, but still rich and sweet-smelling in the motionless air. The low sun made bright patterns on the carpet, showing where it was worn from years of pacing back and forth, thinking, waiting. The walls were lined with bookshelves and, of course, family photographs, so many of people who were gone now.

Toby, Lucas's golden retriever, sat on his master's feet, leaning hard against him. It was what Josephine called his "heavy disobedience." Lucas put his hand on Toby's head. "You're too early," he said. Toby thumped his tail on the floor and leaned even harder.

"Are you arguing with me?" Lucas asked.

Toby thumped again, then stood up and lifted one foot, preparing to climb onto Lucas's lap.

"No!" Lucas said firmly.

Toby subsided, ears down, eyes reproachful.

Lucas rose to his feet. "Oh, come on, then. Doesn't matter if we're early. You can go and look for rabbits."

Toby started to jump and dance around. He knew a lot of words, and "rabbits" was definitely one of them.

"Down," Lucas said firmly. "Come on."

Toby followed him into the kitchen to fetch his lead, turning round and round like a dancer pirouetting.

Josephine was standing by the sink, fitting flowers one by one into a vase of water, mostly early bronze chrysanthemums but also a couple of yellow roses. She looked up at Lucas and smiled. She was not a big woman, of average height and still slender. Her hair was now completely silver, but she had kept it long, as it had been when she was a girl, and she knotted it at the back of her head. It looked totally casual, but Lucas knew it was not. He still enjoyed pulling the pins out and watching it uncoil and slip loose.

"Just going for a walk," he told her casually. "Toby's keen . . ."

"Of course he is," she agreed with a smile. "You've been watching the clock and fidget-

43

ing for the last hour. He can read you like a book, my dear."

"He's a clever dog, but he doesn't read books."

"You do, and no doubt you will tell him all he needs to know," she replied, unperturbed. She found one red rose and put it into the left side of the vase and stood back to regard it. "Right, Toby?"

He barked sharply.

Lucas held him still for a moment and fastened his lead. "Come on, you're getting too excited." He touched Josephine lightly on the shoulder, then went back into the hall and out the front door to the car, where it stood beside the curb. He opened the door to the backseat and Toby sprang in and sat down immediately, shivering with anticipation. He had heard the magic word: "rabbits." Anywhere was good.

Lucas got in behind the wheel and pulled the car out onto the road. He was going to meet Peter Howard, at Peter's request. They met every so often at their favorite places in the woods at any time of the year, but especially when the bluebells were flowering; across the fields when the hawthorn was as thick as snow in the hedges or in the harvest fields when, as now, they were shaven gold, edges grazed with scarlet pop-

44

pies, the stocks standing in barbaric splendor. No one needed an excuse to be walking, most of all a man with a dog.

Lucas was not as talkative as usual. He was happy with silence, apart from the rustle of the wind or the cry of birds. But he knew Toby liked to be spoken to, so every now and again he made a remark. He remembered when Elena was little. She, more than her sister, Margot, was always asking questions. *What is that? What is it doing? Well, why?* He smiled as he remembered her, aged about three, asking Josephine very seriously, "Well, if God made the world, what was he standing on when he did it?" It had taken Josephine a couple of moments of sober silence to come up with an answer. "God doesn't need to stand on anything. He can fly in the air." Elena had thought about this for a moment or two. "Oh . . . by himself?" When Josephine said, "Yes," Elena had said soberly, "I wouldn't like that." Josephine had agreed, "Of course not, you would have to have somebody to talk to." Elena knew that was funny, because Josephine had laughed, but she didn't know why.

Elena had demanded Lucas's love in a way that no one else had, and her constant interest in everything he said or did, her implicit trust that he loved her, had won his attention and kept it. She had listened solemn eyed to his explanations of war and peace, the nature of the stars, the logical perfection of mathematics, as if she understood all of it. That was when she was four. At twenty-eight, she probably didn't remember any of this, but he was certain she still knew unmistakably that he loved her. And not just as his grandchild, but as a person.

Toby began to fidget and whine. They were nearly there. Lucas pulled the car onto the gravel patch under the trees and climbed out. He let Toby out of the back and put his lead on again.

"Just till we're off the roadway," he explained, as if Toby did not know. Together they walked along the path to the edge of the trees, through the gate and into the sun again, and across the broad sweep of the field. There were cumulus clouds towering up into the air, like mountains of light too dazzling to look at, casting occasional shadows on the land. The land was dull gold, with occasional dark, plowed fields here and there. All the flowers were gone from the hedges, but their places were taken by berries. He could not see them, but little flurries of birds told him where they were.

He removed Toby's lead and the dog

began following his nose around in circles. When he looked up and saw the figure of a man far away, on the opposite corner of the field, he stood rigid, then suddenly leaned forward and started to run as fast as his legs could carry him, leaping a few stalks of corn still standing, like a surfer riding the waves.

"Toby, you don't even know it's him!" Lucas called out, but Toby took not the slightest notice. Lucas shook his head, smiling, then walked round the edge of the field toward the corner, where they would meet. He had gone at least another hundred yards before he could clearly recognize Peter Howard's figure, kneeling on the ground, arms around Toby, who was wriggling and jumping.

Then Toby saw Lucas again and turned and came careering back, Peter following after him. Peter was within a few yards of Lucas before Lucas noticed the pallor of his face and the lack of spring in his step. He did not immediately ask what had happened; Peter would tell him soon enough.

They started to walk gently up the slight slope of the ground. The wind carried the bleating of sheep from the distance. Other than that, there was silence. The skylarks belonged to the spring; this was autumn, the fulfilling of the year. Another month and the trees would begin to turn color, then one by one shed their leaves to stand with limbs naked against the sky. In some ways, Lucas found that the most beautiful time of all, the ever-enduring strength without the garment of leaves.

"The situation in Austria is getting worse," Peter remarked. His voice was casual enough. The men could have been mere acquaintances at a cocktail party.

"Dollfuss?" Lucas questioned.

"He's not up for this much pressure," Peter replied. "He's too new at the job, and he has no real grip on it. He's there rather more by chance than design. He's a very young man, and no one takes him seriously. It doesn't help that he's already beginning to be very ambitious with his authority. It's a sign of weakness, and his enemies know that. They smell fear, as a dog does."

"Give him time."

"I'm not sure we've got any time." Peter still faced forward, as if seeing something ahead in the bright distance. "I'm waiting for word from someone I have embedded. The Fatherland Front is getting stronger. I've lost my best news from there, at least most of it."

Lucas stopped. "What's happened?" He did not guess; it was too serious a matter to stab at in the dark.

"His handler has disappeared, so I can't reach my man."

"Do you know anything?" Lucas asked. It was a situation they had faced many times before. Too often, the answer was tragic.

"Very little," Peter answered. "I think he's still alive, but I have to assume his cover is blown, and I've got to get him out."

"Send someone . . ."

Peter stared across the shaven fields. There was a small place where the harvesters had missed the poppies, scarlet as a splash of blood. Perhaps they had fought in the trenches, and the poppies were left on purpose.

Lucas waited.

"If I send someone . . ." Peter began, watching where he was putting his feet, rather than facing Lucas.

"You'll have to be very discreet," Lucas thought aloud. "If your man's cover really is blown, it will be dangerous to contact him. Don't send anyone . . ." He was giving a warning he realized was too late. "I hope it isn't anyone who will draw even more attention to your man."

Peter walked in silence for a while.

Lucas kept pace with him, waiting for him to continue. "Why did you want to tell me?"

he asked finally. "I don't know that area very well. I don't think I've got anything useful to add. Are you expecting something bad to happen?"

Peter looked up at him quickly, surprise in his face.

Lucas shrugged. "I listen to the news. It wouldn't surprise me to learn that Hitler has his eyes on Austria. It would be natural. He is Austrian, isn't he? From Linz, or somewhere?"

"Yes, near Linz, but like anyone who doesn't really belong, he's more German than the Germans, God help us."

"You're evading the question, Peter."

"I sent Elena."

Lucas stopped walking, his body tense. "And how is she going to know this agent of yours, in deep cover?" He was puzzled. "Photographs are hardly enough. He should have altered his appearance to some degree. How long has he been there?" He resumed walking.

"About six years. Just after you left. He's good . . ."

Lucas frowned. "You're saying he wasn't clumsy? That he was betrayed somehow?"

"I don't know."

Lucas was concerned now. "Elena's bright, but she's had very little training. Aren't you

50

expecting too much of her?"

"She'll know him," Peter said with certainty. "And he'll know her, and trust her."

Lucas caught Peter's arm and forced him to a stop, causing him to turn round. "What are you not telling me, Peter?"

Peter met his eyes, unflinchingly now. "It's Aiden Strother. He was never a traitor to England. He was a deep plant when he left. We branded him a traitor and gave him steady information to leak to the Germans. Harmless, or false, but we got good material back, a little at a time. That's how we know how bad the situation is. There's a strong pro-German tide in Vienna that is rapidly getting stronger."

Lucas froze inside. "You . . . sent Elena to find and rescue Strother?" He could hardly believe what Peter was telling him. It was as if he had suddenly ripped off a mask and found somebody totally different underneath.

"She's the best person to do it," Peter said. He did not flinch; he looked straight at Lucas, but there was pain in his eyes. "It's very important that we get this information, even vital. It could have to do with the rise or fall of Dollfuss, and the fate of Austria. Not to mention getting him out safely. She's the only person we've got who knows him

51

by sight."

"She knows him as a traitor!" Lucas said hotly, his memory going back to that awful episode and Elena's grief that he could do nothing to ease. He would have taken on her suffering himself if he could, but that was never possible.

"She knows now that he is not," Peter interrupted his thoughts.

"And she's going to go?" Lucas could scarcely imagine it. He ached inside as if he could feel a physical pain, and he remembered how she had wept when Strother had fled in hideous disgrace. There had been no warning. Lucas had not liked Strother, but he had tried to accept him for Elena's sake. Now his feelings were mixed, surprised, and still angry.

Peter was talking but Lucas had not heard him.

". . . knows him," Peter was saying. "She has imagination and intelligence. She can warn him that he must get out, and bring with him any information he has about the Austrians. She speaks pretty fluent German and Italian —"

"Italian?" Lucas interrupted sharply.

"He's in Trieste."

"Why Trieste?" Lucas asked. "That's northern Italy."

"I know where Trieste is!" Peter said a little sharply.

Lucas cut him off: "I can see why Strother would be there, but . . ."

Peter faced him. "She wants a proper job, Lucas. No more filling in for someone else, and then leaving when it starts to make sense to her. You agreed to our using her after Berlin. She's brave, resourceful, intelligent, and above all, after her experiences in May, she cares intensely about what is happening in Europe. She's seen it up close, and she won't stand by and wring her hands, or believe what we all wish were true, but isn't." His eyes were intensely serious now; his voice dropped lower and became almost frantic. "Hitler's going to war, one step at a time. You know it, I know it, and perhaps Churchill does, but our government's playing the game of Statues. We played it as children, we all did: turn your back and it moves; look and it freezes, but it's closer, closer every time. You can't say you'll use her, but only for the small jobs that are safe. She doesn't deserve that, and she'd know, sooner or later. You never did that yourself, to protect Josephine, or anyone else."

Lucas felt the fury rise up inside him. "That's different —" he began.

"Why?" Peter interrupted. There was not anger in his face so much as distress. "We send the best person for the job. We always have. What am I going to say to others? Too close to me? Too precious? They might not come back? How can you ask another man to send his child to war, but you won't send your own?"

Lucas had never forgotten his only grandson. There were times when it hurt as if it had been yesterday. Or Margot's husband of one week. She had never remarried. But Lucas had, at least temporarily, forgotten Peter's older brother, James. When he spoke again, it was quietly, but his voice was still tight with pain. "I'm sorry, I had forgotten about James. But it wasn't the danger I was thinking of, it was the shame, the humiliation of Strother leaving. He seemed to have betrayed us all, but Elena far more than the rest of us. They blamed her, you know that, for having helped him, albeit unknowingly. They believed her, but she still lost her career." He remembered it so sharply. All the university education, her position in the Foreign Office for which she had worked so hard. He remembered her argument with a pain that was still very real, like a knife inside him, a long, curved blade. "That hurt less than the betrayal of love. Her father

54

doesn't mention it anymore, but he was so ashamed of her. He's never really let it go; it humiliated him, too."

"I'd forgotten about that," Peter admitted. "I wasn't here at the time. I was abroad when I heard about it."

"Why the hell do you think she left?" Lucas asked bitterly. "It was the career she worked so hard for, and she loved the bloody man. That would've hurt the most, but I think she's over that now." He took a deep breath. "But after Berlin, she needs . . ." He did not know what she needed, or what more to say. Everyone got hurt, if they were alive at all. The only way not to be wounded was not to care enough about anything, or anybody, for the loss to touch you. But then you might as well be dead. It's just that when it was Elena, it cut him more deeply. In some ways, she was still the eager child who trusted him so completely.

Peter was struggling to find words. "Even if I had known all that, I still might have sent her," he said quietly. "What would you have me do? Let Strother be killed and his information lost? Do you think that's what she would want? I'll do my job, as long as it isn't painful? Doesn't dig up old memories, and open old wounds to bleed again? Let somebody else do it?"

"No, of course not!" Lucas said angrily. "That's . . ." He lost the word, or perhaps never had it. "Is that what you came to tell me? That you sent Elena to Trieste to rescue Aiden Strother, of all people?" He was shouting now, and he could hear the anger in his voice, but not control it.

"Yes, would you rather I kept it from you?" There was defiance in Peter's face.

"I'd rather you bloody well hadn't done it!" Lucas snapped back. "But you have, and I won't be able to get in touch with her. You can at least tell me she's all right."

"No, I can't," Peter replied. "I won't know. You weren't listening. Our contact in Trieste has gone silent. I don't know if he's alive. I don't know what's gone wrong. I sent the best person I have, perhaps the only person. I didn't know how deep the Strother affair went. All I heard was that it was an affair."

"And if you had known, would you have sent her anyway?"

Peter met his eyes. "Yes, and so would you."

"Would I?"

"Yes," Peter said without hesitation.

Lucas wanted to tell him to go to hell, but instead he turned to walk away, slowly, leav-

56

ing Toby to realize he had gone and follow him over the rough earth and the cornstalks.

Lucas arrived home, took Toby's lead off, and let him run into the kitchen, where he was sure Josephine would have a biscuit for him. She always did. Just one, and Toby knew not to ask for another but would still sit there looking soulful and hungry. He was happy enough if she talked to him.

"What's for dinner?" Lucas asked, when he came into the kitchen to hang up Toby's lead. He was not interested, but he wanted to talk. He just did not know where to begin.

"I've no idea," Josephine answered with a slight smile.

He was completely wrong-footed. He stood in the middle of the floor, frowning.

"We're going to Charles and Katherine's." She smiled at him. "I thought you'd forgotten. You usually do."

"Oh." She was right, he had forgotten, on purpose, even though his relationship with his son was better than it had been for years. Events in May had forced Lucas at last to tell Charles about his position during the war. He had become so used to its being secret, he had not realized how totally he had shut out even those closest to him. Josephine had known what he did, but she had never mentioned it until then. He was startled that she knew and, when he thought about it, rather pleased. It gave him a sense of not being nearly as alone as he had imagined, and her silence meant that she understood him professionally as well as personally. He had been in love with her when they married over half a century ago. Now it was more than that: a companionship of the mind and spirit.

He was standing just out of her way, by the spice rack, where Toby's lead was hung and they kept a spare emergency flashlight. "I lost my temper with Peter Howard today," he said quietly. "I think I was wrong. But I can't change how angry I am."

Josephine looked at him steadily for a moment. Her eyes were solemn, as silver-gray as her hair. Her face was made for emotion. "Perhaps you should decide who you're really angry with," she said quietly. "Or what you are really afraid of."

"Afraid?" Instantly, he started to defend himself.

"Oh, Lucas, don't play games with me," she said mildly. "You know as well as I do that most anger is actually fear of something. Anger is so much easier."

He smiled with momentary amusement. "Are you saying I'm being cowardly?"

"What is it about, really?" she asked instead of answering.

He took a deep breath, but couldn't find the right words. They were too blunt, or else too evasive.

Josephine turned away from the bench, but she did not prompt him.

"He has sent Elena on a job," Peter admitted.

"Good, she was getting restless," Josephine said. "I think she was beginning to think she was not good enough."

"That's absurd!" he said immediately. "Berlin —"

"Could have been a fluke." She cut across him. "I don't think so and neither do you. But you know Elena: she questions herself; she always has. But more so since that miserable business with Strother."

"That's it." He grasped the opportunity to explain. "Peter has sent Elena to Trieste, to bring Strother back, with his information." There, it was out.

Josephine froze. For a moment her shock was perfectly plain, then she mastered it and looked calm again. Only a shadow in her eyes betrayed her emotions. "That's awkward. Are you afraid she's going to be so upset that she can't do the job properly?"

"No!" He denied it instantly. "I was thinking of how humiliated she would be because that bastard . . ."

"What? You aren't going to make any sense at all if you don't tell me whether she is rescuing him or bringing him back to be executed."

He was stunned. "Good God. You don't think I'd let Peter do that, do you? Anyway, if we were going to execute Strother, we would've done it years ago. A discreet accident somewhere." He paused. She already knew that. "Stop interrogating me, making me answer my own questions."

She gave him a soft sweet smile. "You are the one who knows the answers, my dear. Are you really saying that sending her was a good idea, as long as it remained only an idea? Or that she is competent, but she shouldn't have to face anything emotionally unpleasant or embarrassing?"

"No!"

"Good, because she wouldn't thank you for that." She walked past him to put the pruning shears away in the drawer used for small garden tools. She touched his arm on the way back to tidy the table. "You have to let children fall over, and then get up by themselves. Otherwise, they will think they can't. They don't always need help, and Elena is much stronger than you think. You play off each other, you know. She does what she thinks you want her to, and you do what you think she needs. Don't protect her from doing her best; she won't thank you for that, either." She gathered up the cut stalks and fallen leaves and put them in the rubbish bin. "And of course, if I'm wrong, you are going to have to work hard to forgive me." She gave him another bright smile, but there was a flush of anxiety in it, gone again so quickly he was not sure he had really seen it.

"Am I suffocating her?" he asked.

The sweet smile flickered across her face again. "I would rather say you're tipping her out of the nest." She pushed the last of the stalks down into the rubbish bin. "Now go and change for dinner; you're not going out like that. You look as if you've been playing with the dog out in the fields."

At the word "dog," Toby sat upright and cocked his ears.

"Not yet," Josephine told him. "But I won't forget you. Your suppertime is six o'clock." She avoided using the word "dinner." That was another word he knew.

"Lucas."

He looked at her.

"I know she needs a success," she explained, "but she needs to get it herself.

61

And, if you think about it, you know that as well as I do. For goodness' sake, let her believe you trust her, even if you don't."

"I do!" He was horrified.

"Good, so do I." And with that she gave him the vase of flowers to carry into the hall and put on the table next to the wall.

Charles Standish was Lucas and Josephine's only child. He was handsome in a traditional way: regular features, fine dark eyes, and a charming smile. But he had not inherited either Lucas's high intellect or Josephine's imagination or wit. Somewhere, unspoken, was his awareness of it.

But he had had an excellent education, and he maintained a sincerity that drew many people to trust him, a conviction he had never betrayed. He had a remarkable memory, especially for people, their names, their occupations, and very often their vulnerabilities, which he did not abuse. That must have taken some skill in the Foreign Office. He had been as successful as an ambassador could be in the highly danger- ous and constantly shifting world of post- war Europe, now lurching yet again toward violent change: Hitler in Germany, Musso- lini in Italy, and the dark shadow of com- munism spreading in from the east like a storm on the horizon.

It was Katherine Standish, Charles's wife, who welcomed Lucas and Josephine at the door. She was undoubtedly Charles's greatest asset. She was American, but she had become international in the best way: at ease with everyone, and without the imperial baggage that hampered many of the British. Whether she was beautiful was a matter of taste. She was a little lean, even angular, but she knew how to dress to flatter and charm, and above all to be individual. This evening she wore a silk crepe de chine dress of white with casual black splashes. It was crossed at the front, giving it some unaccountable fullness toward the hem, which fell well below her knees. Lucas knew at a glance that it was expensive, but she wore it with an ease that would have made anything look classic.

"Come in," she said with a wide smile, standing back to allow them past her. She kissed Josephine lightly on the cheek, then Lucas.

Charles met them in the withdrawing room, which was very formal and only redeemed in its comfort by the well-worn leather of the armchairs beside the fire. He offered them drinks. He had his father's favorite sherry and the lighter, drier one that Josephine preferred.

The other person in the room was Margot, Elena's elder sister. She was as dark as her father and as elegant as her mother, with the same spare figure and extraordinary grace. She wore a flame-red dress cut on the bias to fall in a cascade of silk from the hips.

"Grandmother." She gave Josephine an uninhibited hug and, a moment later, a hug of the same warmth to Lucas. That was new. After the Berlin episode, she, too, had learned of Lucas's position during the war, since events had made it impossible to exclude his family any longer. It had broken the brittle barrier between them of secrecy, blame, and grief over losses both universal and uniquely individual.

They exchanged news and spoke of small, comfortable things. Katherine was an excellent cook, although she had domestic help tonight so she could enjoy the company. When the chef informed Katherine that dinner was served, they went through to the dining room, with its formal dark blue velvet curtains and starkly beautiful photographs of bridges, symbols of other people and other times. They were one of the few things in Charles's house that Lucas loved, something that bridged gulfs in ways only imagined by dreamers.

They took their places at the long mahogany table, set with crystal and silver. There were two shallow bowls of scarlet leaves and floating white chrysanthemum heads set near the center, between the silver cruet sets. It was a typical Katherine touch.

Soup was served.

"Did I tell you, Grandpa, that I'm going to Cecily Cordell's wedding?" Margot asked casually, referring to the daughter of friends in Berlin.

"No," he said with surprise. "Is she getting married in London, then?"

"No, Berlin. She's marrying a young officer in the army."

"The German army?" Katherine looked startled. "You didn't mention that."

"I don't think it's exactly the army." Margot looked at her soup appreciatively and took an elegant spoonful. "This is good, Mother. Did you teach Cook how to make it?"

Katherine did not cook as often as she would like. Her social duties took up a great deal of her time, as Charles's position in the Foreign Office was still demanding. Neither of her daughters had inherited her talent. Margot might have, had she taken the trouble. Elena, so far as anyone knew, had never tried.

"What do you mean, *not exactly*?" Lucas asked, keeping his voice as level as possible.

Margot looked up. "I'm not sure. It's some special group doing more important work."

"I beg your pardon?" Charles's tone was suddenly cool.

"Sorry, Father, I think this only applies to Germans. They aren't supposed to have a proper army, are they?"

"What does he do?" Katherine asked.

"I have no idea. I'm just going to represent the family and take everyone's good wishes. I'm sure you wish her well."

"I think it will take more than good wishes to make her happy if she's to live in Germany," Katherine said doubtfully. "But yes, of course we do."

"I don't think you should go to Berlin at the moment," Charles said grimly. "It's in a state of unrest. Rather unpleasant, in fact."

"I'm only going socially, Father. There and back in a few days."

"Two days?" Charles suggested.

"Hardly worth going for that short of a time," Katherine pointed out. "She'll stay with the Cordells and it should be fine."

"I think she should send a really nice gift," Charles began.

"The gift Cecily will like is her friend turning up to support her, Father. On a day like your wedding, you want to see family and people you've known for years who love you," Margot told him.

"I didn't know you were so close to her," Charles said with a frown. "It must be years since you've seen her."

"Months," Margot corrected him. "We have exchanged letters, but that's all got nothing to do with being a friend now."

"Berlin is not —" Charles began again.

"Really, Charles, Berlin is a very civilized city," Katherine said. "And reasonably well disposed toward the English. Indeed, the people of Berlin have strong friendships with many notable people. And not only Mosley and the Mitford sisters, also some of them like Lady Colefax and the Duchess of . . . I forget, but she's very well connected."

"Half the royal family is German, my dear, and none of it makes any difference if you get in trouble in Berlin." Charles's face was grim. "Or in any other German city, or Austrian city, for that matter. I don't want you taking the risk. And even the profoundest apology won't help."

"You're exaggerating." Katherine smiled placatingly. "Margot's got enough sense to

67

be careful. She's not Elena, Charles."

"Elena did rather well." Charles looked as if the remark had surprised himself.

"With Margot's help," Katherine pointed out.

Margot looked from one to the other. "Mother, I'm over thirty. I'll go if I want to and not if I don't. Cecily Cordell is my friend, and I'm going to support her and be there to wish her happiness. I'll be a guest of the British embassy. Right now, that means quite a lot. As you point out, several of our rich and titled people are falling over their own feet to impress that appalling little man, Adolf whatever. The most they'll do is make me sick with their disgusting manners." She added, "And don't fuss, Father, I'm going to have fun and wish Cecily well. God knows, she needs it." She turned to Josephine, who so far had not spoken.

"Oh, I agree with you," Josephine said. "But that doesn't mean to say I would be right."

"Did you mean that?" Lucas asked in the car on the way home, driving slowly along the dark roads, which were darker still under trees.

"As far as I went, yes," Josephine replied, as if staring straight ahead of her, through the windscreen, might help her think.

"Do you think she'll be safe?" Lucas asked.

It was a question with many layers of meaning, some darker than others. Josephine took a few moments to choose how she would answer. "Margo will go if she wants to, and our arguments will only confirm her decision. She looks lovely. She's so full of life and occasionally laughter. But have you looked at her face in repose, Lucas?"

"I know. She still grieves for Paul," he answered. "Maybe she always will. And certainly she won't forget him; she would despise herself if she did. But she has no purpose. She needs something to fight for or against. All that intelligence and energy is being wasted, turning back against her."

"Let her go," said Josephine.

"Could I stop her?" There was self-deprecating amusement in his voice.

"You could probably stop her from going to Berlin, if you tried hard enough," Josephine answered. "You couldn't stop her fighting against herself, one way or another."

Lucas took his hand off the wheel for a moment and put it over hers.

She gripped it gently.

CHAPTER 4

Elena woke up the first morning in Trieste and wondered where on earth she was. The bed was comfortable enough, but a bit narrow. She felt that if she turned over, she might fall out.

The room was totally unfamiliar. There were no curtains on the window, only wooden shutters, but they were very effective at keeping the daylight out. There were only slight cracks around the edges allowing in enough light to see the outline of the simple furniture: a wardrobe into which she had unpacked her clothes, a chest of drawers for underwear and personal things, a basin on a handsome wooden stand, and a big ewer of water. The water was cold, of course. Hot water was in the bathroom . . . or was it the kitchen? She only dimly remembered the rest of the small apartment. She had the necessities and not a lot more.

She turned sideways to look at the alarm clock on the table beside the bed. It was nearly nine o'clock. How had she slept for so long? Then she remembered it had been midnight when she had finally arrived on the train from Milan and found a taxi at the station to bring her here.

She pulled the blankets more closely around her and lay back again. What on earth had she done? Why had she told Peter Howard that she would find Aiden and rescue him? She had no idea where he was; she had done everything she could to forget he ever existed — though, how could she? Hadn't he turned her life upside down, ruined her career, disgraced her both publicly and privately, and made her doubt herself in every way? Even worse, hadn't she willingly chosen that path? He had not forced her into anything. Yes, he had deceived her and lied to her, but it was her choice to believe him.

Elena had ached for Margot when the news had come of Paul's death, physically hurt for her. But Margot was better off than Elena, who had loved Aiden and discovered that the man she had cared for so profoundly had never even existed, and he certainly had not loved her. She knew that now, and so did everyone else, starting with her own family and extending . . . who knew how far? *Elena Standish? Oh yes, that stupid girl who was so infatuated with Aiden Strother that she couldn't see what he was, and so she let everyone down. Her poor father most of all, because he had got her the Foreign Office job.*

Peter Howard had made it seem like quite a good idea for her to be the one to rescue Aiden, now that she knew Aiden had been on their side all the time. In some ways it vindicated her belief in him, if not his behavior. She would do this casually and gracefully. She would accept his thanks with a smile and walk away. *It was nothing, just my job,* she would say. *Goodbye.* She must be professional. No thudding heart. No breath catching in her throat, no longing for his touch, his smile, the sound of his voice. She would wish him good luck and turn away without even glancing back to see if he was looking at her.

Only now she was lying in a narrow, rather hard bed with blankets that smelled strange — not unpleasant, but unfamiliar — in a bare room with nothing that belonged to her except her clothes and her suitcase. She had information that Peter Howard had given her to read, remember, and then destroy. It was confetti now, mixed in with the waste from the train's toilet, irretrievable to anybody.

There had been little enough to memorize: the name of Aiden's handler, Max Klausner, who had apparently disappeared. She knew roughly his description, and the places he had frequented, although that information was mostly secondhand and could be false. But Max was the only place to start. There were tens of thousands of people in Trieste. The city was filled with all nationalities, languages, and cultures. It had been occupied over several hundred years by many other countries. Its streets looked Austrian rather than Italian, with their high pale buildings of classical proportions. Most Italian cities had their ancient medieval and Renaissance history, and names famous for art, science, exploration, and ideas that had shaped the world.

Trieste was different, and there were those who said it was the most beautiful of all the cities in Italy. Which was irrelevant to Elena, except that she was a photographer and was supposed to be here to try to capture some of that beauty for those who might never see it for themselves. She must do that sufficiently well, at least to be believed. This meant she needed all her skill, as well as enough time, to do it justice, find something

73

new to say, as if a thousand people had not done it before her.

At the same time she must not lose sight of her mission to find Aiden, rescue him and whatever information he had. Why had he not sent it back himself? It could be helpful to know that. Had he only just compiled it? Was the information so sensitive that it could not be sent by post? Surely, he had the means to send information back regularly? Had that only been through Max Klausner? But what had happened to him?

The possibilities were not good. Was he dead? Or a prisoner somewhere, or too ill to send a message? Or injured, perhaps, in a hospital? That was not likely; MI6 could have ascertained that for themselves.

The worst possibility was that Max Klausner was a turncoat, in which case Aiden might well be dead and they had not yet discovered his body. If he had been taken out to sea, they never would.

There was no point in lying here thinking of the worst. She must get up, get breakfast, and begin to make plans. Go out and find a café. Have breakfast publicly, start talking to people and, above all, listening. Peter had made sure that MI6 provided Elena with an apartment in this area because, as far as they could tell, this was either where Max had worked or where he had lived. Most likely both.

She was going to lie, and of course her lies must be consistent. Peter had told her always to use as much of the truth as she could. She would be less likely to trip herself up if she didn't appear to be secretive. Share with people and they will feel at ease, and if they don't then share with her, she would need to figure out what they are covering up.

She rose and opened the shutters. The floor was made of stone, possibly low-grade marble, and cold under her bare feet. She looked out at the street below. She remembered now. She was on the third floor. The stairs were steep. She had lugged her suitcase up herself, after paying the taxi driver.

The street was narrow. As she stood at the window, the opposite side looked only a few yards away. She almost felt she could reach across and touch someone on the other side, except for the bright laundry hanging on ropes extending from one building to the next and fluttering now and again in the slight breeze. In the distance someone was singing, a man with a light tenor voice. Right below her, laughing children were playing some sort of game with stones.

Elena closed the window and clipped the

shutters back. Then she washed and put on a short-sleeved linen dress in an unusual shade of light blue-green. It had been recommended by Margot, whose advice Elena thought she should have taken years ago. She chose shoes that would be easy for walking.

Outside, the air in the street was warm already, and people were buying newspapers and hot rolls for breakfast and hurrying to work or school.

The first thing she did was find a café serving breakfast. She smiled as charmingly as she could and asked the waiter about the neighborhood. The coffee was excellent and the bread as good as any she could remember — but then, she had always loved crusty Italian bread still warm from the oven.

On the long journey from Paris, she had studied all the information Peter had given her. She marked in her street map the locations she knew to have any connection with Max Klausner: messages from him or left for him. Aiden was never mentioned in them, but the more she looked at them, the more she saw a pattern emerge. They were all restaurants of some sort or other, most of them small and out of the way. She imagined they were the sorts that residents would dine at regularly, rather than fashionable places for business meetings or to take a new friend or a romantic interest.

She could not afford to draw attention to herself by asking questions that could not easily be explained away. It seemed Aiden's cover was blown and that he was known by the enemy to be a British agent. But who was the enemy? Italians under Mussolini? Why? What plans or ambitions did Il Duce have that England might thwart? More likely, from what Peter Howard said, Aiden's interest was the Nazis, specifically the Germans, although she had been made aware of the increasing support for the Nazis in Austria. Klausner was Austrian rather than Italian, even though, apparently, he was born here in Trieste.

She sipped her coffee and watched the people passing by. What did Max Klausner do for a living? MI6 knew few facts. Klausner was deliberately elusive, but he must do something that offered him both a degree of freedom and anonymity. He needed to be unnoticed to do the job of a fixer and to pass on messages and give information.

The waiter poured Elena another cup of coffee and she thanked him. She asked him about one or two of the other restaurants in the area.

"What type of food do you like, signorina?" he inquired. "Tell me, and I will tell you the best places to go, apart from here, of course." He gave her a wide smile.

"I should come here every day for breakfast," she answered. "As long as you have that jam. What is it? It's lovely."

"Apricot," he answered with pride. "We make it ourselves."

"Then I will be your friend for life," she said. "Or until you run out of jam."

He raised his eyes and put his hand on his heart, then answered her questions with entertaining descriptions of all the restaurants within comfortable walking distance.

She thanked him, paid the bill, then went out into the street. She followed her marks on the map and by lunchtime she was listening to her fifth helpful waiter, and wanting never to drink another cup of coffee.

Where better to meet than a restaurant? The waiter spoke to you, it was his job. He brought you a menu, you gave it back to him with your order. You did not even need to look at him. You paid him at the end of your meal and left. Everybody did it, either alone or in company. It was so normal as to be entirely unnoticed.

She used the obvious excuse to explain her questions. She was going to write an article for a travel magazine on the best places to dine in Italy. She wanted to mention those specializing in local cuisines, as well as the glamorous ones with a reputation already established. She took some good photographs of them: colorful entrances, dining rooms with interesting views, unique décor. Possibly she would sell them to a travel magazine.

She had learned quite a lot about the different places, and what their specialties were, when she began to realize how alike the waiters all were. What one had said blended in her mind with all the others. They had written down notes for her on prices and recommendations. Then they had turned to the next customers and spoken as easily. In a way they were invisible. Customers were nurtured, people eating, talking, laughing, but a waiter in the traditional distinct black was not remarkable, not really seen, because you expected him to be there. He would only be noted if he were not. Nobody said, "What's that waiter doing here?" They only said, "Where's the waiter?" if he were not there.

It took Elena the best part of two days to discover where Max Klausner had worked. It was not in one restaurant, but three. He had had a small apartment, though no one had seen him there for more than a week. He had completely succeeded in being what Elena had deduced: an invisible man. He was good at his job, an expert on food, and imaginative in his descriptions, making anything sound delicious. Nobody could remember exactly what he looked like. Dark. Average height. A little plump. A wry smile. One person thought he had a chipped front tooth, but could not be certain. There were hundreds, if not thousands, of middle-aged, dark-haired men in Trieste. Only his knowledge of food, his ease in conversation, and the name Max made her think it was likely to be the same man at all three restaurants.

The thing that mattered was that it bound him to a certain area, and only those restaurants that specialized in Austrian dishes. If they had a large Austrian clientele, surely Aiden would be among them.

Elena disliked dining in restaurants alone. She felt conspicuous, because it seemed that everyone else dined with friends. But it was necessary. She saw few other women doing so. She had lain awake a good part of every night since she had accepted the job, wondering exactly what she would do when at last she found Aiden. Would she be casual? Or would seeing him again, remembering so vividly how they had parted, make that impossible? Would emotion drown out all her intentions? The betrayal still hurt. She had been prepared to give him everything of herself, and he had refused her. Yes, it was a blow to her self-respect, self-belief. Was rescuing him now an oblique kind of revenge? But in a way, that was still letting him win, because she would be behaving badly, in a manner that injured herself even more, in order to hurt him. And would it?

Peter Howard trusted her to fulfill her mission, to be far bigger, far better than that. And so would Lucas.

She would just do her job. She would not give Aiden Strother that power.

For all her preparation, she was not ready for it when it happened. She was sitting at a small table in one of the more fashionable restaurants where Max Klausner had worked, when a group of people came in. There seemed to be six of them, three men in dinner suits and three women in evening gowns. It was one of the women who caught Elena's eyes first. She was of average height, but she moved with such grace that she captured Elena's attention, even more than the blonde in silver sequins or the startling brunette in red. She had very dark brown hair and she wore a black silk dress with fluid lines that moved with her. She was laughing genuinely, not for show, and her face was beautiful. If she had worn hopsack, she would still have been beautiful.

Elena watched her for several minutes before a flood of heat filled her whole body. She recognized the man with her: Aiden. It was his profile, the angle of his head, the light on his fair hair. He was handsome and he knew it. She had forgotten until now how straight he stood, which gave him several inches he did not really need. She swallowed hard. Her heart was thumping so, she thought it must be visible to other people, shaking every part of her.

Fortunately, they were all totally absorbed in each other. Not one of them was looking at her. Aiden slipped his arm around the waist of the woman in black. She allowed it. In fact, she was smiling easily. They passed within a couple of feet of Elena. Aiden actually glanced at her, just to make sure they were not accidentally going to bump her table. There was nothing in his face. No flash of recognition, or wondering for an instant if she reminded him of anyone.

"Excuse us," he said casually. He spoke in German; the cadence of his voice was exactly as she remembered it.

Then he turned away and spoke to the

woman in black. "Gabrielle, do you want to face outwards?"

She smiled at him. "Of course. Don't we all?" But her tone was so light, she clearly did not care. "I've been here before." She gave a slight, very elegant shrug, and moved further ahead of him.

Elena knew that she was blushing. She could not control it. Thank goodness no one was looking at her! She was a stranger worthy of no attention at all. A woman dining alone. She watched them until they were out of sight behind a pillar.

Aiden had looked straight at her and seemed not to know her from any other stranger. Could the memory of their passion, laughter, intimacy all disappear so completely, so soon?

He looked much the same. A little heavier, maybe. His skin had more color. It must be from the Italian sun. It suited everyone.

She could remember everything about him. The obvious things . . . and the others. The feel of his skin, the thrill of his strength, how easily he moved, his laughter. The way he kissed her slowly, softly . . . at first.

She searched for the waiter. She would pay the bill and escape.

Then her own voice rang in her ears with contempt. *Elena, what the hell is the matter*

83

with you? You've found him. You have to stay here as long as he does, and then follow him. You have to give him vital information to save his life. And even more importantly, to get the information Peter Howard wants, needs. You let Aiden destroy your career once. Are you going to let him turn you into a coward now? You have been given a chance to redeem yourself. You can't get the past back, but you can influence the future. Don't let him do that to you!

The waiter came. She paid him and ordered more coffee, so she had an excuse to sit there until Aiden left.

It seemed like ages. Her coffee grew cold and she still sipped at it, as if it were delicious. Time seemed to stretch out endlessly. She only glanced at Aiden and his friends now and then. She should not be caught staring, although it would be natural enough to stare; they were anything but discreet. The woman in black, whom Aiden had called Gabrielle, apparently was vivid enough to draw the eyes of men in admiration, and of women in envy. And perhaps curiosity as to how she achieved it. Was it her hair? Her clothes? Her perfect features? Or did it lie in the grace of her movement?

It seemed like midnight when eventually they rose and made their way to the door, and Elena rose, too. Would they call taxis? There would have to be two, or possibly three. Would she lose the chance to get one also, and to follow the one with Aiden in it? Or on a fine night like this, would they walk?

She stood on the pavement as if she were waiting for someone. She had had some training in this, but now it seemed far too little. She had already spent two days in Trieste, and time was short. Why was she dithering? She was standing just yards from Aiden. Was she just going to watch him walk away? Was she being cautious or cowardly? She must speak to him now. He had to recognize her, for heaven's sake. Whatever his feelings, perhaps they were not as deep as hers. They had slept together for months! She had lain in his arms almost all night, woken to kiss one last time before he left in the dawn light. He might not acknowledge it, but he must know. It was impossible to forget such things.

She walked up to him casually, a cigarette in her hand. She had never smoked, but it was a useful pretense. "Excuse me, can you give me a light? My lighter seems empty." Did that sound like she was trying to pick him up? She could not let it matter now. Once he had recognized her, he would know that she had some message from MI6. That would be all she needed.

She was a couple of feet away, close enough to reach out and touch him. He looked at her and met her eyes. There was a look of puzzlement, then a flash of recognition, and an instant later it was gone, masked. But there was a stiffness in him, tiny, almost invisible. Did he know that he had been betrayed?

No, Peter had believed that he did not yet know. It was part of Elena's job to tell him. Peter had sent her because she and Aiden had known each other.

Aiden was looking into her eyes, waiting for her to catch a light to her cigarette, and they were blank. She was a passing stranger, possibly trying to scrape an acquaintance. Pathetic. Could anyone be desperate enough to approach a man who was already with a woman like Gabrielle?

Elena put the cigarette to her lips and took the light he held up. She drew in. She disliked the taste of tobacco. The minute he was out of sight, she would throw it away. "Thank you," she said softly. "It's a nice restaurant. Max Klausner recommended it to me."

He hesitated only a second, perhaps two. "Max, the waiter?"

"Are there two Max Klausners?" she asked.

"Probably half a dozen," Aiden said. His voice was light again, courteous, but uninterested.

Along the street, there was a shout rising in anger. A group of figures seemed to jostle each other, clumsily. One of them stumbled off the pavement into the street.

It was Gabrielle who broke the moment's tension. "Signorina, are you waiting for a taxi? I think perhaps you should wait inside the restaurant. It isn't really safe, alone in the street. Even in good areas like this, there's a certain unease."

"She might be —" one of the other women said with a slight sneer.

Gabrielle laughed, a rich, happy sound. "Don't be absurd, Sara. If she were looking for customers, she wouldn't be dressed like this. She's waiting for someone who stood her up. She's trying to act like a lady and still get out of it with some shred of dignity. Don't pretend that's never happened to you."

Elena seized the opportunity. "Is it so obvious?" she asked with a rueful smile. "I don't know Trieste very well. How easy will it be to find a taxi?"

"A woman alone, smoking a cigarette?

87

You'll look as if you're waiting for someone." Gabrielle shook her head. "You'd better come with us. We'll drop you off somewhere. Anton and I are going . . ." She stopped short of giving an address. "We can take you to a better district."

"Thank you," Elena accepted. She did not look at Aiden to see if he agreed. Anton? She knew he would not be using his own name: too easy to trace. Especially when he had been here for years. He could pass for German easily, even over a period of time, and the Germans themselves would know who he was, of course. That was his cover: a turncoat, a traitor to the country of his birth. He was supposedly loyal to the new order of Nazism.

Aiden had no gracious way of refusing to help a young woman in an awkward situation. A scuffle had broken out among the men along the street. They were clearly more than a little drunk, and coming closer. She would have had to go inside if Gabrielle had not offered her help.

"Anton Salinger," he introduced himself.

Aiden Strother? Close enough. "Elena," she said, her voice catching in her throat. She was committed. "Standish." In the artificial lighting of the streetlamps, color was distorted. All she could see in his face was a deepening of tone in his cheeks. His composure was perfect.

"How do you do, Miss Standish?" he said, this time in English. It was an acknowledgment that sounded like nothing, and yet in a way it was everything. He was warning her that they were strangers. The past did not exist.

Could he really imagine they had met by chance? No, of course not. She had mentioned Max Klausner's name. She had not quite suggested that in some way she had replaced Max, but he must at least consider it. "I live on Franz Josef Street," she said. "Thank you very much."

He did not reply, but she had done enough.

CHAPTER 5

Lucas drove home, parked the car, and went inside, Toby bumping against his legs. Surprisingly, Josephine was not in the kitchen.

"Jo," he called. Where was she? It was not alarm he felt, but discomfort, because it was unusual. He went into the hall and called again. "Jo."

The sitting-room door opened and Josephine came out, closing it gently behind her.

Lucas saw the gravity of her face. "What's wrong?" he asked immediately.

"Stoney is here to see you," she began.

"Stoney?"

"Stoney," she repeated very quietly.

Gladstone Canning was a mathematician Lucas had known at Cambridge. They had worked together quite a lot during the war. Over the years, their friendship had grown. Lucas had spoken of him often to Josephine,

90

because Stoney had been such an essential part of his youth and his war years, although he had never revealed just how important.

But now Stoney was here. Why? He had never once arrived without having been invited, or asking to see Lucas in his home.

"I haven't seen Stoney for months, maybe a year. Why is he here? Is he all right?" His concern became deeper as he spoke, and long-ago images came back. Stoney was in his mid-seventies, closer to eighty. When they had first met as young men more than half a century ago, Lucas had liked him instinctively. Stoney was quiet, steeped in his work, but loving it intensely. He still worked in the intelligence service, quietly, diligently, his skills unsurpassed by anyone of a younger generation. His commitment to accuracy showed in everything he did, from complicated mathematical calculations to trying to toss pancakes and catch them in the pan, correct side up — or even at all! He enjoyed a good conversation as much as anything in life, except perhaps a good joke. The shaggier and more absurd, the better. But why was he here? Now? "What's wrong?" Lucas asked.

"I don't know," Josephine admitted. "He seems to have trouble even finding the words for it. And, of course, he is not sure

whether to trust me or not." She smiled ruefully. "I think he is torn between not trusting me, because I am not MI6, and trying
not to upset me with ugly facts, because I
am a woman."

Lucas felt his anxiety increase, tension
suddenly ratcheted up. Stoney did not often
confide in people, but it was not out of a
lack of lucidity in his mind, or words to
express it; it was an extreme discretion with
secrets, something that was both natural and
taught in his position. Also, he would not
want to distress Josephine, if what he had to
say was an ugly fact. He had never married,
and so had no daughters. He had not
learned that women were as tough as men
any day, beginning with nannies and govern-
esses, going right through to army nurses
and women in the Resistance, or tougher
still, in espionage, embedded in enemy-held
territory.

"Lucas!"

"Yes!" He brought his attention back to
the present. "I'll talk to him. Perhaps we
can have a cup of tea?"

She rolled her eyes. "For heaven's sake,
do you think I set him down at teatime to
talk about his anxieties without tea? And
cake? Do you want some?" She looked at
Toby, now sitting at Lucas's heels and

sweeping his tail back and forth across the carpet to signal that he was being obedient and it was dinnertime.

"After I've seen Stoney . . . it sounds odd." He smiled. "But Toby's hungry."

"I'm sure he'd like a piece of cake," Josephine said drily. "But he's not getting any. Come on, Toby, dinner. Dog dinner."

He followed after her, happily. Anything she gave him was always good.

Lucas opened the sitting-room door and went in. Stoney Canning was leaning back on the sofa, but still managed to look uncomfortable. He was large, over six foot, broad-shouldered, and untidy. Even the best tailor in London could not make a suit that looked as if it fitted him. Not that any tailor could be blamed for the way he looked today. His tie was crooked, his shirt was clean but crumpled, and his jacket appeared to be mismatched with everything.

"Ah, Lucas." He made as if to stand up.

"Good to see you, Stoney." Lucas held out his hand and gestured for Stoney to stay seated. He himself sat in the chair opposite and leaned back. "How are you?"

Stoney pushed his hand through his long white hair. "Lucas, I've . . . I've got a bit of a problem." He trailed off into silence, but his eyes searched Lucas's face, as if he might help him somehow.

It was a typical Stoney understatement, as when, speaking to a German friend, he had referred, with a rueful smile, to the war as "the recent slight unpleasantness." It was a typical way of dealing with horror. His strength was mathematics; numbers were like music to him. He could see both form and beauty in the most complex calculations, and could not understand why they were not apparent to everyone, if only they would allow themselves to see them. Lucas recalled countless conversations that had begun like this one.

"What is it about, Stoney?"

"That's it," Stoney admitted. "I'm not sure. It seems to be figures, but it's what they represent that matters. It could be anything. Weapons, men, something we already possess, or that we will buy. Anything."

Lucas bit back his temptation to interrupt. Stoney was intensely serious.

"I think it's money," Stoney went on. "Very large amounts of it indeed." He stared at Lucas with wide, troubled eyes. "And what is unforgivable is that they are doing it through MI6!"

Lucas struggled to keep up. "Who is doing it? The government? What makes you think so? Go back to the beginning, Stoney."

"Money in the wrong place," Stoney said succinctly. "Money that moves around inexplicably, at least not by any ordinary cause that I can see. And I've been keeping books since Victoria was queen. It doesn't fit, Lucas. I know the pattern."

Lucas believed him about that, but there could be several explanations. "Theft?" he asked. "Embezzlement?"

"No," Stoney said without hesitation. "More like funneling money from one place to another. It's very cleverly hidden." His eyes showed reluctant respect for a skill he understood. "Not a few hundred here and there — that could be covered up — I'm talking about millions."

Lucas was troubled. It sounded exaggerated, even absurd. And yet there was fear in Stoney's face, and beneath it a steady, burning anger.

"What do you think it is?" he asked. "Your best ideas. Doesn't matter how ridiculous they sound, we've got to start with something."

Stoney hesitated.

It occurred to Lucas that he was afraid of being laughed at, of having the ideas that distressed him so clearly dismissed by a man

95

whose opinion mattered to him, perhaps more than Lucas had previously appreciated. "Tell me," he urged again. "If it's impossible, we can dismiss it."

"I wish we could," Stoney said earnestly. "I wish more than anything else I could think of. Please tell me I'm a fool, that I've lost my grip, and this isn't happening . . ."

At that moment there was a knock on the door. As soon as Lucas answered, Josephine came in with a tray of fresh tea and cake, Toby on her heels.

Lucas stood up to take the tray from her, and Toby rushed over to Stoney, who leaned forward and put both his hands out to shake his paw, then stroke his head. Toby was delighted. He sat on Stoney's feet and wagged his tail so hard his whole body swayed with it. He even ignored the cake when the tray was put on the side table, barely out of his reach. He ignored Josephine when she told him to come back with her into the kitchen.

Lucas looked at Stoney's face and his large hand resting gently on the dog's head. "Let him stay," he said to his wife. Their eyes met and she understood.

"Don't give him any cake," she instructed. "It really isn't good for him."

Stoney looked up at her, his hand still on

Toby's head. "Is there something he could have instead?"

"Of course," she answered. "I'll get him a rusk. It's really the attention he wants."

There was a look of rueful understanding in Stoney's face.

Josephine went out of the door, closing it softly behind her.

Toby moved a little further onto Stoney's feet and settled himself.

"I think someone is using MI6 to collect money for Hitler. Specifically, the Nazi-led Fatherland Front. They're the people who say we must never again fight a war, that we can't do it again, and half of us agree with them." He looked at Lucas. "But the other half don't. Not at the price they're prepared to pay. Not using MI6, without their knowledge, to finance it secretly, and —"

"Whose money is it?" Lucas interrupted.

"Donors," Stoney replied. "From all over. Some of them even British. People who think Hitler is the answer. Good men — and bad — who think we can appease our way out of another war." Stoney's voice cracked for a moment, and his hand tightened in Toby's thick fur. "But what I can't bear is that they are using the men of MI6 without their knowing it. At least, I think they are." He was pleading with Lucas to contradict him, only he could not say the words.

Lucas's mind raced. He did not have enough knowledge to confirm such a hideous thing, nor did he have sufficient cause to deny it.

"It's MI6, Lucas," Stoney said so quietly his voice was barely audible. "Our men." He stopped. The rest did not need to be said. The shared memories were there: the all-night planning sessions, the waiting for word, any news at all, whether they had succeeded, who was lost. Occasionally, they had gone on operations themselves. Lucas could recall the cold, the danger, the casualties, the endless waiting, and the grief for those who had been killed. The job of having to tell their families, the half-truths, the courage, the cost, but not the reason, not the details.

Josephine came back into the room and found them silent. Toby, in his own way, was also communicating with Stoney, leaning heavily against him. She glanced at Stoney, then at Lucas.

"Why don't you stay?" Lucas said to her. "You can use my cup. The cake's very good." It had nothing to do with tea or cake, and she understood that. Even Toby understood. He had heard the word "cake" but ignored it.

Josephine sat down without speaking.

"Then we must find out," Lucas continued, as if there had been no interruption. "Is it all in the figures? Or do you have something else?"

"Someone broke into my home," Stoney told him.

"What's missing?"

"Nothing I didn't have copies of," Stoney said, as if realizing that fact only now. "But they were searching for something, turning out my desk drawers and other places I keep books and papers. Bookcases and so on."

"But nothing is missing?" Lucas pressed.

"No, not that I've found . . . yet. They want to know what I have; they don't need to copy it."

Lucas wanted to be as gentle with him as possible, but so far there was nothing to grasp on to. "If nothing was missing, what makes you sure that it was searched? Couldn't you have caused a mess in your own search for something?" He did not add that Stoney was extremely untidy. It seemed unkind and would serve no purpose. Stoney knew his own faults.

"I . . . it's hard to explain." Stoney shook his head, as if that might clear his thoughts. "It doesn't look like it, but I do know what

99

I've done with things. I can always find them. Except now I can't." He leaned forward, frowning. "Lucas, I know I forget things. I tell jokes I've forgotten that I've told before. I forget people's birthdays, I even forget their addresses, but I know where the address book is. I pay my bills on time. I'm not . . . I'm not losing my grip. Somebody searched my things!"

Lucas felt a stab of pity, sudden and unexpectedly deep. Stoney was growing old, and he was painfully aware of it. Gradually, piece by piece, things were eluding his grasp. Would Lucas come to that himself soon? Had it already begun, and he had not noticed? Was Josephine protecting him from knowing it? There was no one to protect Stoney. "What would they be searching for?"

"Proof that I know about the money, who it came from, and where it is going to. Proof of the ways it is hidden, and who is doing it." He bit his lip, and his face was white.

Josephine moved a fraction forward and then stopped, knowing she should not interfere.

Lucas said nothing.

"Knowing who was implicated, who would be ruined if it came to light," Stoney finished. "I think the good and the bad are too hard to tell apart. If this matter is exposed,

100

it'll bring down the whole of MI6."

"And if it isn't?" Lucas asked.

"We'll be riddled with corruption, so we can't tell the good from the bad, and eventually we'll help stoke another war . . . which we may not win."

The enormity of it washed over Lucas like a wave with the weight of an endless ocean behind it.

Josephine spoke for the first time. "You came to Lucas because he would understand what it is you have seen?" she asked.

Stoney turned to look at her. "Yes. And because he might believe me . . . and . . . and I know he wouldn't be involved."

"Who else would understand it?" she went on.

He took her point immediately. "Not many. Of course, there is always the possibility that someone is a genius at figures and we didn't know it."

"And understands the entire system well enough to hide a very large amount of money in it?" she said. "Knows all the departments? Or are they not all implicated?"

Lucas looked at her, then at Stoney. He was beginning to understand why Stoney was so hurt. This was the Service that had been his family during the prime of his life.

Some of his friends had died for it, as had some of Lucas's. Perhaps, at the heart of it, that was the force behind his need to save it now. "What would you like me to do, if I can use so old-fashioned a word, for the sake of honor?" Lucas asked. "Whoever is leading this has to be someone high up. You've concluded that already, haven't you?" It was hardly a question.

"Yes," Stoney said quietly.

"What would you like me to do?" Lucas repeated gently. "Is there anyone else you trust?"

"Not really," Stoney began, then looked down at his large hand resting on Toby's head.

Suddenly, Lucas knew what Stoney was going to say, and it struck him like a dead weight. Stoney was not asking for protection. He was asking for Lucas to advise him, and if he failed, to pick up the burden he had let fall. He could not deny it.

"Would you like me to keep a copy of your work, in case you . . . can't finish it?" Lucas could hardly believe he had said it. Of course, he meant in case Stoney died. Someone had broken into his house once. Did they know Stoney had come to Lucas? Was it hard to work out? What about Josephine? If Stoney wasn't crazy, imagining things, then he had put them both in danger. But Lucas had offered, and he saw a flood of gratitude in Stoney's face. Then the light faded out of his eyes.

"No, thanks, Lucas. I appreciate it, but that would only put you and Josephine in the same trouble I'm in now, and it's not your problem. At least, not yet. I feel better for telling you about it. At least someone else knows. There's no one else I can trust, you see?"

"Yes, I do see," Lucas admitted. "But surely there are other people you can exclude from suspicion?" He sounded desperate, as if he were looking for a way out, but that was not what he meant. Like Stoney, he did not want to think that the people he had trusted could believe in appeasement, in joining the enemy rather than fighting. It changed everything. Too many of the pillars that held up what he loved were resting on sand. How much would it take to blow away the foundations, a little at a time? A word here, a belief there, something you took as true discarded, one lie at a time.

"Give me a copy of what you know," he said. "Even if we can't make anything of it yet, it will be a place to start."

"It's time for the truth, Lucas." Stoney shook his head. "The war's over, for the time being. At least the most physical part of it is. But it's still there, under the ground, like interconnected rats' nests, one leading into another."

"What a revolting analogy," Lucas said sharply. "Don't you believe we learn anything?"

"Frankly, not much," Stoney replied. "But the bit I believe I would die for, as would you."

The pattern in Lucas's mind made him feel faintly sick. Perhaps the more so because he knew it was true. He had not thought of it exactly like that, but he knew the German navy was being rebuilt far faster than the British. They were rearming, building tanks, planes, guns. Churchill was the only one who cried any warning, a voice in the wilderness, and nobody wanted to go into that wilderness again. Too many old wounds were still bleeding.

"What else do you know, Stoney? Even roughly."

"It has to do with Austria and the Nazis, of course. Everything has to do with them, lately."

"Everything?"

"Sooner or later. It all comes down to fear and greed. The easiest way to make that respectable is to call it nationalism, as you can't fault a man for loving his country."

Lucas answered with what came first to his mind. "Samuel Johnson said that patriotism is the last refuge of a scoundrel. I'm not quite sure what he meant, but by God we use it to excuse an entire army of sins. And some people get away with it. Despite the scar to the soul and the stain on history, tell anyone he's serving his country, and that excuses almost anything. We all want to belong. We have a view of the world that validates who we are. What we are. We need it to survive."

"I know," Stoney said quietly, "but I'll take care of these papers. For a moment there, I was prepared to share them with you, but I realize I don't need to. And it's an abuse of a friendship I value more than I've ever said. I find all I need is to be sure that you know and understand. We have to find the guilty and get rid of them. The innocent trust us, they always did. If MI6 is rotten, who is to protect us from the enemy we can't see?"

Pushing Toby away gently, he rose to his feet and turned to Josephine. "Thank you for the cake. And for listening."

Lucas stood up also, waiting.

Stoney shook his head. "Just take care." His smile faded and he held Lucas's hand for a moment, hard. Then he walked out through the French doors and across the lawn, toward the place his old car was parked.

"Will he be all right?" Josephine asked.

"No, I don't think so," Lucas replied, putting his arm around her shoulder. "I don't know. I don't know if he's onto something real or . . . ."

"Or just lonely." She filled in what he had not wanted to say. "And feeling frightened and old, and like he's rapidly becoming irrelevant."

"Yes, that, too," he agreed. He felt the coming twilight, soft, filling the air, hiding the things you know are there: trees, fences, the neighbor's wall. And in the twilight of the mind, old enemies rising again.

CHAPTER 6

Peter was sitting in the small hard-backed chair in front of Bradley's desk, answering his questions. He had clearly given the subject a lot of thought. Of course, Austria had lost badly in the war and, like everyone else, was slow to recover. It had been an old and powerful empire in 1914, and now Austria was struggling to find itself, to create a new identity, and it was with an anguish that was inevitable. The political mess from which the inexperienced Dollfuss had emerged as chancellor had only made it worse.

"Howard, I want an answer," Bradley snapped.

"Yes, sir. I've given you every report as I've received it. Dollfuss is becoming more authoritarian as he assumes more power to try to keep order. He's been sabotaged by factions —"

"I know that!" Bradley interrupted. "He's

chancellor of Austria, for heaven's sake! Has he got the power and the backing to succeed?"

Peter sat a little straighter and kept his temper with difficulty. They had covered this before, several times. "I don't know, sir. This June, the National Socialists — the Nazi party — began using live grenades against a group of auxiliary police. As a result, Dollfuss banned Austrian National Socialists from the country."

"You are repeating yourself, Howard!" Bradley said acidly. "You said the Nazis in Germany made them welcome. I suppose that was to be expected. Dollfuss doesn't seem to know which side he's on. Next thing we hear, he's in Rome, in Mussolini's lap, looking for support. We've got a man in Trieste, which is more or less one foot in Italy and the other in Austria. What does he say?"

"Very little, and he doesn't interpret it, he just says what he knows," Peter replied.

"Oh?" Bradley stiffened, his attention sharper. "What does he say? What's his name?"

Peter sidestepped the second question. Bradley did not need to know. "Nothing, for a while."

Bradley leaned forward in his chair. He

clenched his strong hands.

Peter's temper was slipping away.

"Have you contacted him?" Bradley demanded.

"Yes, I have. Haven't heard back yet," Peter replied quietly.

"So, you don't know what he has to say?"

"No."

"Ideas?" Bradley banged his closed hands on the desk.

Peter had considered this before he had arrived at the office. He had received a one-word telegram from Elena last night: *Contact.* He had stood in the kitchen with the paper in his hand, waiting until the delivery boy left before he opened it. His hands had been stiff. He had not realized how worried he was about her. Had he sent Elena too soon? Had her success in Berlin just been a series of coincidences? Perhaps she was never as brave or as clever as that had made her seem.

How would he face Lucas if she was hurt? Or worse? But he did not say those words, even allow those thoughts.

He had torn the telegram open, then read only *Contact.* So, she had found Aiden Strother and spoken to him already.

"Oh, wake up, man, and give me a straight answer!" Bradley said angrily.

109

Peter jerked back to attention. "I don't know. There are too many possibilities. We know where most of the main players are. We know Dollfuss is courting Mussolini. We expected it. Anyone would, in his place."

"I know that, Howard! Damn it, man!" Bradley cut in. "You are letting this slip out of your control! Strother is our only lead to the Nazis in Trieste; God knows what they're planning. It could lead eventually into Vienna and be the beginning of a takeover of the whole of Austria! Think, man! Stop letting your old loyalties to Standish and his damn family get in your way. You know better than that, don't you?" There was a question in Bradley's eyes. He was uncertain of Peter's answer.

"I was going to say they are gaining considerable financial backing . . ." Peter kept his temper with difficulty. He refused to answer the question about Lucas. Why did Bradley even ask? Was his jealousy so deep? Or was he covering something?

"From whom?" Bradley interrupted again, his face pinched with anxiety. "Is that a conclusion based on specific information, or just a general fear?"

Peter hesitated again. He had learned not to tell the whole truth where he did not need to. He disliked Bradley, and he profoundly believed it was mutual. "A large collection of small things, sir," he replied very formally. "We don't know the sources of all this money, but most of it comes through Germany."

"That's to be expected," Bradley said, his eyes watching Peter's face, his expression judgmental. "Mostly Germany?"

"Yes."

"You know that, or you're guessing?" he said impatiently. "It's important; don't dither around, Howard."

Peter hesitated only for an instant. "We're waiting for the proof."

"Proof of what?" Bradley was motionless now, frozen. A cloud drifted away and the sunlight streamed through the windows. "What kind of proof? Word of mouth, or actual records? What is this Fatherland Front I hear of? Is it serious? Or don't you know?"

Why should Peter be so reluctant to trust him? He was letting personal dislike take control. That was an error. It was not only unjust, it could eventually be self-destructive. And it would give Bradley grounds to fire him. He himself would not work with a junior who did not trust him, especially one treading on his heels in rank. Did Bradley think Peter wanted his job? *Did*

111

he? Was Bradley right?

"The Fatherland Front is a pro-Nazi group. Paramilitary, of course —"

"Of course! What else?" Bradley interrupted. "Is the money going to them?"

Peter forced himself to relax, even smile slightly. "I'm hoping my contact is going to supply proof of exactly who is backing the Fatherland Front, and to what degree. When we know that, we'll be in a far better position to judge the issue."

Bradley's eyes narrowed. "What are you looking for, Howard? Arrests? What can they tell you that you don't already know, or deduce? What sort of money? Thousands or millions? We don't want this getting to Churchill, the scaremongering old fool. We'd be playing right into his hands. This doesn't go beyond my office, you understand me? You tell Standish any of this and he'll tell Churchill. He thinks the daft old man walks on water!"

Peter chose his words very carefully, aware of how deeply Bradley feared Churchill's influence. That was another reason Bradley hated Lucas: because of his long and deep friendship with Winston Churchill. He was one of the very few who believed Churchill's dark fears were only too well founded.

"No, sir. Not amounts. I was more concerned with where the money came from."

Bradley frowned. "You mean . . . who."

"No, sir, I do mean where."

"Like?"

"The United States." He saw Bradley's eyes widen. "If it's from Britain, sir, that's one thing. But, for example, if it's from the United States, that's quite different." He saw the light change in Bradley's eyes. "At the very least, we need to know."

"Indeed, we do," Bradley said softly. "Do you think this Fatherland Front is influenced by the Americans?"

"Not the government. But if the Fatherland Front wants continued money, they'll be careful not to offend them. It's got to be worth something. Nobody gives away millions expecting nothing in return. I'd like to know who from, how much, and where."

"So would I, Howard, so would I. Keep me informed. I hope you've got a good man working on getting your man out."

"The best person I have, sir, for this job. Contact has been made already. We have to go carefully, because we want to know how much money is involved, and from whom."

"Yes, of course. Good work, Howard."

"Thank you, sir." Peter pushed his chair back and stood up.

He took the train home early and walked from the station to his house. He was inwardly far less certain of his own convictions than he had implied to Bradley. In the fifteen years since the armistice, a new generation had risen up who knew only the stories. But almost every family had lost someone, either to death or to disability. Who could blame anyone whose fortitude now and then took a turn away from any path that led to war?

Peter had hoped that the millions of lives taken or ruined in the trenches, the sight of so much wasted blood, would have driven home unforgettably the lesson that one man's blood is no different from another's. Yet here we were, dividing ourselves into Christian or Jew, British, French, or German, Catholic or Protestant, persecuting the different, Gypsy or homosexual or Communist. All over the place, people were setting up barriers to keep others in . . . or out. The Germans had already built vast camps to hold "unsuitable" people apart from the rest of society. Labor camps. Effectively, prisons. A life sentence for the crime of being different.

Germany had lost its balance. Italy was fast going the same way under that grandiose clown Mussolini. Austria was caught between the two. A buffer? Or a piece of living flesh, to be torn apart, dismembered, and swallowed piece by piece?

Peter crossed the sunlit road. The wind was blowing dust about.

The Austro-Hungarian Empire had been something of a mongrel beast anyway. Would the new republic be strong enough to stand in its place? Was Dollfuss going to help it or harm it? Would the British Foreign Office effectively feed it to the Germans, simply by standing by and doing nothing . . . until it was too late?

Yes. Probably.

Aiden Strother had been well placed when he was in Austria. It had taken years to get him so close to the people with real power and information. What he had sent back, carefully and infrequently, was vital to decisions made by the Foreign Office, and then by the prime minister.

They were lucky to have kept him there so long. It was a risk, but it was a judgment call. This money, raised to fund the Fatherland Front, directed into the right hands, might even be enough to support Dollfuss and an independent Austria until it had the strength to stand alone. It would definitely change the balance of power between Hitler and Mussolini.

It was a pity Aiden had to come out of Trieste.

And by a twenty-eight-year-old, sixteen years younger than Peter, a girl. But twenty-eight was old when compared to the young men who had gone to war. Elena had damn well better be up to the job of getting Aiden Strother out! What the hell did anyone's vanity, or career, or hurt feelings, or broken heart matter, compared with peace?

He reached his home and went through the gate. He put his key in the door, turned it, and let himself in. The hall was the same as always, except there was no post on the hall table. Had Pamela already taken it inside? The house was quiet, with no aroma of cooking or, better yet, baking.

He called out, "Hello!" He wanted her to be home, simply to have someone to demand something from him, to momentarily forget his fears for Elena, and Lucas's anger, Bradley's criticism.

"Pamela."

No answer.

"Pamela!" His voice sounded sharper than he had meant it to.

He opened the sitting-room door and

went in. The glass doors onto the garden were closed. He walked across to them, where he could see the lawn and flowerbed beyond. Pamela was standing near the rosebushes, a woven raffia flower basket in one hand and secateurs in the other, the sun at her back, bright on her hair. She was carefully selecting the bronzes and the reds and laying them side by side, watching the mound of brilliant colors grow.

She had always had a good eye for putting together surprising blends and mixtures. It was the one thing about her that had startled him with joy. Why did he not share it more often?

He opened the door and went out.

She looked up. "You're early." She frowned slightly.

He had no answer that he was prepared to share. It would worry her. She had always been secure in his income, because he worked for the government. Like the families of many MI6 officers, she had only the vaguest idea of what he did. If she had any curiosity, she was far too well versed in expected behavior to ask. Their roles were complementary, but quite separate. He did not tell her how to organize the house or manage the domestic finances; she did it well. Everything worked, always. That was enough.

"I went in early this morning," he replied, although she had not asked. "I think I'll go for a walk over toward the fields. I've been sitting all day."

"Dinner's at seven," she said briefly. She hesitated as if she was going to add something but changed her mind. Then she picked up a yellow rose and put it in her basket. She glowed, as if she had turned a light on inside the petals.

He went to the telephone and made the usual brief call to Lucas. It was time he faced the issue. Then he walked to the garage and drove his car out. Even that small act gave him a sense of freedom, since he went to work on the train. He could have walked to meet Lucas, but he lacked the energy and he needed to be there soon, as the sun was lowering already, spreading a patina of gold across the land.

He parked the car in the lane at the edge of the woodland and went on through the gate, closing it behind him. He walked the slightly winding track, which in spring was carpeted with bluebells and where one could hear the calling of new lambs. Now there was silence, except for the wind stirring the leaves far above him, the occasional early yellow one drifting down from its

118

branch. Autumn was on its way, evident from a cooling of the air, the sun reaching the horizon earlier each evening, a swirling of small birds returning home. He was going to the usual place, where he always met Lucas in these woods. He had first found it without conscious thought. Habit was dangerous in his profession. The last thing he should be was predictable, but everyone needed some certainties in life, something to rely on, without having to think first.

Lucas was waiting for him. Peter had let the peace of the woods wrap around his mind, and he had not thought what he was going to say. Not exactly. And "exactly" mattered.

The sun shone through a break in the branches and caught Lucas's face. He had been smiling until he heard Peter's foot break a tiny twig and he turned. The light made him look older, as if a weariness inside had ceased to be hidden. Was that his anxiety over Elena?

Peter envied him that. He realized that there was no one he loved so deeply that their absence would leave that type of hole. He knew how great the loss would be if Lucas were absent because he chose to be, and not because he could not help it.

He reached Lucas and stopped. "Thought

119

you might like some news, even slight," he said. Why did he begin with banalities? Because it was somehow indecent to begin with the emotion burning inside, like stripping off one's clothes. You left the other person with no way to retreat.

Lucas understood. He was the same: understated, subtle, emotionally aware. Very English.

They walked slowly, side by side, down the path beside the stream. It was almost silent, with too little water in it to rattle on the stones.

Toby was standing in it up to his chest. He had seen a water rat go down a hole in the bank, and it was obvious he was waiting, watching for it to reappear.

"I heard from Elena that she's found Strother," Peter remarked.

"Good," Lucas answered. "That was quite quick."

"She didn't need a lot of training: details rather than principle," Peter observed.

"It's dangerous, though," Lucas added. He did not turn to look at Peter but rather kept his eyes on his feet to avoid tripping over the big roots that erupted from the soil, breaking the smooth track.

"Yes, she knows that. But this information is vital."

Lucas smiled with a downward twist to his mouth. "And not Strother's life?"

"Only to him," Peter replied. He knew now what he was going to say. A part of him hated it. "The information is unique, I think. We'll lose agents sometimes, that's understood. If their lives mattered more than what they can tell us, we wouldn't send them. You've seen enough to know that. They weren't your grandchildren, like Elena, but that's hardly relevant. If it is, you're not fit for the job."

"Feelings and thoughts are not the same, Peter, and *you* know that," Lucas replied quietly. "What's more to the point now is that Elena knows it, too. She would hate it if you gave her special treatment."

"It wouldn't be for her, it would be for you," Peter said honestly. "But I did send her . . ."

"And?" Lucas knew there was something more. The heart, perhaps, of what Peter had come to say.

Peter walked a few steps further. The sunlight and shadows moved on the ground, as the branches overhead were stirred by the wind. A few more amber leaves drifted down.

"I think there will be an attack on Dollfuss," he began, trying to find the right

121

words to say, maybe too carefully, although he had not arrived at this thought with any major evidence.

"What sort of attack?" Lucas asked. "There've been all kinds of accusations and —"

"No. I mean physical," interrupted Peter. "It could be done in the open, or more likely secretly, and he would simply not appear at a meeting, an event. There would be excuses: he's ill, injured, whatever seems most believable. In time someone would replace him . . ."

"Nazism in Austria, and rooted in Germany?" Lucas asked grimly after another few moments of silence, broken only by Toby still splashing around in the stream. "Toby, come on!" he called. There was more splashing, then Toby came charging along the path, stopping beside Lucas and shaking vigorously, sending water all over the place. Lucas was about to tell him off when Peter started to laugh.

"What on earth is funny?" Lucas demanded.

"It's absurd." Peter controlled himself with an effort, ironing the panic out of his voice. "You are annoyed because the dog you love shook himself and got you wet, at the same time that we are debating whether the Austrian National Socialists are in the pay of Hitler yet. It's only a matter of *when,* not *whether* it will happen or not. It will."

"You think so?"

"Of course. If we prevent this attempt to spread Nazism, there'll be another, and not only in Austria. All the borders of Germany are at risk, and then the borders of those other countries. The question is whether it's worth another bloodbath to prevent it. I need to be certain that the only thing worse than another slaughter all over Europe will be to find Hitler's values in every country, every town. To find Brownshirts, or worse, Gestapo, in the streets of London. But am I right?" He looked at Lucas and waited.

Lucas remained silent for several moments. At last he spoke . . . quietly. "Yes, I think you're right. War decimates a generation, perhaps even two. But as long as we are alive, there will be a third and a fourth . . . and so on."

"For some, but the price is terrible, and we didn't pay it, you and I. We fought our fight, and our weapons helped win, but we didn't pay in blood. We didn't suffer those wounds to the body and the mind that don't heal, the ones we pretend we don't see." He was thinking of the blank-eyed soldiers he had seen for whom the horrors were all inside and would be until they died.

"Peter?"

"I know." He jerked himself out of his thoughts. "We're in a minority, you know. There are a lot of people who think we're warmongers because we're stopping what peace there could be, if only we just swallowed our pride and minded our own business about Germany."

"And there are others," Lucas argued, his voice dropping even lower, "who say we created this with our destructively harsh demands in the treaty after the war. We made another war inevitable."

"What should we do?" Peter raised his eyebrows. "Pray for peace, and expect God to bring it? While we prepare for war?" It sounded more bitter than he had intended.

"Are you preparing for war?" Lucas stared upward at the leaves as they rustled softly in the sunset breeze. The fading light caught the apricot and pink in their dying shapes.

"No, I'm just trying to see what direction the blow will come from first. I don't actually fight; I tell other men where to . . ."

"Did she say anything else?" Lucas asked.

"Who?"

"Did Elena say anything else?"

"No, and she can't force him to leave if he won't. She's only getting information,"

Peter replied.

"From a spy whose cover is blown, and whose handler may be alive and on the run . . . or dead. Murdered by whom?"

Peter raised his head sharply to meet Lucas's eyes.

Lucas shook his head. "No, you can't go and look; you'd only make it worse," he said sharply, as if reading Peter's mind. "But you'd better make sure you've got good people in Vienna already. And Berlin. Don't disturb them by sending anyone now. Just wait. And, for God's sake, don't go yourself! I've learned the hard way. Somebody will send word you've gone. If they capture you, they can ask their own price. And torture the hell out of you while they wait. Use a little sense. Leave it alone and wait. It's the hardest thing you'll ever do."

Peter closed his eyes and felt the faint warmth of the sun on his skin, the whisper of the wind in the leaves, and Toby crashing around in the undergrowth, chasing the scent of a rabbit. "Yes," he said, not sure if he had said it aloud or not. "I know."

CHAPTER 7

Margot left home soon after lunchtime and was driven to the airport for the brief flight to Paris. She had flown before, but it was still an amazing experience, like a step outside life into a bird's-eye view of the patchwork blanket of autumn fields, copses of trees turning color, villages like a child's toys. She found herself smiling without knowing quite why. It was an absurd sense of freedom, of being almost untouchable by ordinary cares. Of course, one had to come down again!

Once she was in Paris, she spent a very comfortable night in one of her favorite hotels, near the Luxembourg Gardens, then went to the railway station early and caught an express train to Berlin. It was expensive to travel first-class, but it was very much worth it. She had a considerable amount of luggage, filled with clothing carefully chosen for every likely event. She did not want to have to worry about it. She would arrive safe and rested.

She found a comfortable seat and opened her book, but was unable to concentrate on the adventures of fictional characters when there was so much drama ahead of her in Berlin. She had not read much about politics, until her sister's experiences in Berlin — not that Elena had spoken about it so much to Margot or to her parents. What concerned her, and drew her in reluctantly, was the fact that Elena hardly spoke about it at all. That was more powerful than any words would have been.

Elena had always been the quieter of the sisters, a follower rather than a leader. She tried to follow Margot in style, but Elena's fashion sense was about as interesting as a kitchen apron! She wore bland colors, ordinary styles, nothing that attracted the eye, and certainly nothing that startled.

But that had been before Berlin.

When Elena had returned in a scarlet silk dress that fitted her like a glove, it had drawn the eye . . . and comments . . . and she appeared not to care in the least! And her hair, which had always been a bit too long — wavy, which was good, but light brown with a glint in it, as if there were possibilities of glamour never realized — was now a casual, fashionable bob, still with the wave, but pale, Swedish-looking: blond. Enough to catch everyone's eye: men with admiration, women with envy.

The scarlet dress was gone now, and no one would explain why, although Margot was certain Josephine knew. It had been replaced by more dresses that fitted very well, with skirts that flared when she moved. They were in gorgeous colors of hyacinth blue, iris purple, pale primrose yellow. And green, lots of green, always leaning a little toward the aquamarine or teal. Plus smart, sophisticated black, which her fair skin and pale blond hair lit up like magic.

Margot's first thought was the obvious one: Elena was in love. But no new man had appeared.

That was all on the surface, just a symptom of what had changed inside. Her ambitions were less easy to read, but possibly deeper. Something had happened to her that week in May that had tested her to her limits and beyond, and she had not found herself wanting. There was now a certainty in her.

Grandfather Lucas knew what it was, but Margot had realized lately that there was an infinity of things that Lucas knew and never discussed.

128

When the train pulled into the station in Berlin, Margot faced the immediate practicalities of making sure she had all her luggage. She had a case of gifts for Winifred Cordell and, of course, for Cecily. She had taken a great deal of care to bring things that would cause pleasure, and show her affection, without drowning them in a sense of gratitude or, worse, inferiority.

She found a porter to help her get a taxi and ensure the luggage was all packed in. She sat back and stared through the taxi windows at the streets, the traffic, and the people.

Margot put from her mind the terror for Elena that had crushed out everything else the last time she'd been here. This time, she was here to support a friend, and she was determined to act as if she believed this was the beginning of a happy new life for Cecily.

Berlin looked better than it had only months earlier. It was early autumn now, a touch of winter in the air. There was more color in the women's dresses, the occasional bright stands of flowers for sale, a little more in shop windows. But there were also more groups of Brownshirts, young men armed and empowered, with almost no supervision as to how they exercised their will. Twice she saw them stop a crowd of startled pedestrians whose faces reminded her of cornered animals.

Sharp memories came back of her own experience of fear. Roger Cordell had told her that her presence could not help Elena if she drew the attention of the police or even the Brownshirts. It could only endanger Elena even more. Hitler's grip had grown firmer in these past four months. That much her father knew from his own work in the Foreign Office. He believed that the worst was over, that there was more work for people to do, a change toward stability, even a beginning of prosperity. There were claims that all conflicts were under control, and people began to hope again.

Could she see it in the streets? Perhaps. Or was it her imagination, because she wanted it to be true?

The taxi pulled up at the Cordells' house. Memory flooded back of all the times she had shared events with Cecily. There was a difference in their ages, but it had never mattered. They were both English girls, with fathers in the British embassy, in a strange, exciting, and disturbing city. Of course, Cecily and Margot had found a natural ease, quick laughter, a taste for the same music, fashion, and adventure that Elena did not join in. The ten years between Cecily and Margot did not matter.

"Oh, yes, thank you," she said to the driver when he broke her reverie to ask her if this was the right place. He got out to fetch her luggage, leaving Margot to open her own door and climb out onto the footpath.

"Thank you," she said again. She fished in her purse for the fare and a generous tip. He set her cases on the path and turned to her. He did not meet her eyes but nodded his thanks, took his fare, and climbed back into the vehicle.

A moment later, she was alone in the afternoon sun. There was a slight chill in the air here, too, just as there was at home. But then, this had been home, or almost home, years ago.

The front door flew open and a figure appeared. "Margot! You're here!" Cecily cried, running down the path so familiar to her that she avoided the broken edges on the steps without thinking about it. She looked wonderful, her dark hair flying, her face flushed.

Margot put the cases down and caught Cecily in her arms, hugging her fiercely.

Then Cecily stepped back, smiling. "Come in, you must be tired. Did you have a good journey? Let me tell you about all

the arrangements and who will be there."
She barely drew breath. "You'll have to meet
Hans, of course, but there are other people
as well. He's terribly well connected, you
know. But that's all by the way. Come, let's
put your things in your room. You'd like a
cup of tea, wouldn't you? Have you had
anything to eat? Railway food is pretty
ghastly." She picked up one of the cases,
with an effort, and carried it up the path.
She was wearing a floral silk dress and it
moved fluidly with her, showing how very
slender she was.

Pre-wedding nerves? With a sharp stab of
memory, Margot thought of her own excitement before Paul's last leave. Their wedding
so brief: a flurry of white roses, petals falling; their one week together and then good-
byes that turned out to be forever.

She picked up the other case and followed
Cecily.

Winifred, Cecily's mother, stood in the
hall, smiling. She was a pretty woman in a
fragile way, her hair still richly colored, with
natural curls, her eyes wide and clear blue;
her skin without blemish. Cecily went
straight past her and put the case down with
a gasp of relief.

Margot hugged Winifred, feeling her
respond gently.

"So pleased you could come, dear," Winifred said warmly. "Difficult to travel at the moment, so we are grateful you made the time and the effort. But things are really beginning to look better and this is a wonderful event for our family. We are so happy." She stepped back for a moment and gazed into Margot's face, her look absolutely candid. "We are at the beginning of hope." There was a flush in her pale cheeks. "It makes all the world of difference to Cecily — to all of us — that you are here." She looked past Margot at Cecily. "Leave that at the bottom of the stairs, dear. Ernst will take it up, and the other one." She turned back to Margot. "Go up and see your room, and then you will have tea in the sitting room and we'll tell you all the plans." She stepped back, as if cueing Margot to leave temporarily.

Margot smiled back at her. "It's lovely to be here, and to see you again for such a happy occasion. The beginning of new times." She turned and started upstairs, wondering if she should not have made that last remark. She so badly wanted it to be true. Perhaps she was helping paint a mirage, but it was too late to take it back.

Cecily followed her upstairs, led her across the landing, and opened the guest bedroom door. She turned, smiling.

Margot walked in. It had been arranged especially for her. The things she had loved years ago reappeared. Thin, soft curtains that moved with the breeze and brought back a sharp memory of going to see a desperately romantic musical drama with Cecily. Margot had been old enough to know how unrealistic it was, but it was an escape from the practical. Looking at the curtains now, the whole atmosphere of that dreamy evening returned. White curtains, stirred by the breeze, revealed so much, and hid all the framework that separated the real from the dreams, the present from an imagined future.

There were flowers on the dressing table. Not roses — that would be too ordinary. These were daisies of some sort, shaggy with loose, careless petals; some kind of chrysanthemum. Cecily had remembered those, too, and for Margot a memory danced just out of reach: the smell of damp earth, laughter, leaves turning gold on the trees.

The wardrobe door was half open, showing enough space for all the dresses Margot had brought for parties, for afternoon walks, and of course for the wedding itself and the dinner afterward.

Margot turned and saw Cecily in the doorway, her face eager to know if she had got everything right, if Margot remembered all the same things, despite the difference in their ages.

Margot felt tears prickle in her eyes. "It's beautiful," she said with intense feeling. "Nobody else could have brought it back, never mind so delicately. Thank you."

Cecily smiled happily and looked a little embarrassed that Margot had accurately recognized her feelings. "Tea downstairs," she said quietly. "You must be gasping."

"I'll be there," Margot promised.

As soon as the door was closed, Margot let out her breath. She was pleased to be here; it seemed almost immediately to have proved its worth. And yet she began to appreciate that the visit was going to be even more weighted with emotions than she had foreseen. Was she the only British friend to come? Or perhaps just the longest known, the only one who had shared briefly some of Cecily's girlhood, allowing herself to relive her own? Maybe she was the only one to have any understanding of the deeper situation, both their fathers having served in the British embassy in Berlin. Perhaps they had seen the changes in fortunes in Germany, felt the despair, the anger, and the hope. And now, also, the fear?

She stood up and opened the first of the cases in which her clothes were packed. She took out a comfortable dress, a dark, dramatic floral, one of her favorites. And after giving herself a brief wash in the bedroom basin, she put it on. She hung up the suit she had worn for two days of travel. She would brush it and freshen it later. Now, to put on new makeup. She had arrived, she was safe and comfortable, but this was still a performance. Not only might every word she said be weighed and remembered, but so also would be her expressions: the momentary smile or hesitation.

Winifred and Cecily were both waiting for Margot when she knocked on the sitting-room door and went in. It was at first glance so much like the way it used to be years ago. The carved fireplace was polished, but the fire in it was smaller than she remembered, although there was an autumnal nip in the air. The long curtains drawn back from the windows were the old ones, rich velvet, but carefully tied to fold over the places where she guessed the pile was worn. The same pictures were on the walls and she found herself smiling at the familiarity of it.

"I always liked this room," she said to

Winifred. "One of the good things that's still here."

Winifred smiled quickly. "And it's going to get better again," she promised. "More people are working. There is order. Buses and trains are running. Of course, you know that. You came by train, didn't you? How was it? Was it clean? On time?" There was an eagerness in her eyes, as if she knew the answer.

Margot felt a rush of relief. It was a question she could answer honestly. "Yes, exactly on time, and it was clean. A bit worn, but perfectly patched. Someone took care."

"Exactly," Winifred agreed. "So much has changed under the surface, like a tree when you can see the buds swelling and you know there will be leaves soon. I have great hopes . . ."

Cecily looked at her mother, and for an instant Margot saw the intense affection in her, even protectiveness. "Don't try to hurry it, Mother. They'll get it at their own pace. When the new take the place of the old, they have to do so with a certain hesitancy . . . gentleness."

"I know, dear. I'm just telling Margot what hope there is."

Cecily looked at Margot. "We can see so much more of the new government because

137

of Hans." She smiled a little self-consciously and glanced down at her slender hands folded in her lap, the diamond engagement ring prominent on her left hand. It was clearly still new to her and she was always conscious of it. She looked up and saw Margot's eyes. "He's rising quite quickly . . ."

"Very quickly," Winifred affirmed. "It's early yet, of course — we all know that — but he has caught the attention of the authorities with his intelligence, and the speed at which he sees the bigger picture."

"Of what?" Margot asked. "Germany's future?" Then immediately she wished she had not spoken. She was tired from the long journey, and now she was with people who had become partial strangers, old friends who had had different experiences from hers and had seen the reflection from the other side of the glass. Too much was reversed.

Margot spoke again, this time very carefully. "I haven't met your Hans yet. Tell me all about him. I feel almost as if he is going to be part of my life, if he is already part of yours."

Cecily blushed.

Margot knew it was part self-conscious pleasure and part embarrassment. She could remember feeling just that way when people asked about Paul.

"What else do you like about him?" Margot asked, prompting her and knowing exactly what she would say if someone asked her about Paul now. *He was wise, had an honest gaze, he never evaded the truth, even if he had to tell it gently.* She recalled it now as if the intervening years had not existed.

Cecily was still thinking. Winifred drew in breath and then thought better of answering for her. "His loyalty," Cecily said at last. "It takes courage and honor to be so loyal, not afraid of what other people think of you, or —"

"It is what he truly believes." Winifred could not resist speaking.

"Loyalty is a great quality," Margot agreed, maybe too quickly. "You can trust him completely. What do you enjoy doing together?"

"We . . . we haven't been alone together a lot," Cecily replied. "But he has introduced me to some marvelous friends." She smiled and looked down, as if not wanting to seem to boast. "Some of the people who are going to make this country great again. Such vision, such belief, is a little overwhelming."

"He is proud to show her off," Winifred

cut in, to say without immodesty what Cecily could not.

Margot felt a sudden chill, there and then gone again. Could it possibly be envy? Paul had not shown her off. He had wanted to be alone with her, to talk about what they would do together when peace came. He had thought it would not be long. He was right about that. It came soon, very soon. But he did not live to see it.

"Of course," she answered in response to Winifred's remark.

Cecily looked up, her eyes full of pain. "I'm sorry," she whispered. "I know you were here, where I am, once and . . . and had only a week. I shouldn't be going on."

Margot reached across and put her hand over Cecily's. "Yes, you should. No one knows what the future holds, and you can't carry the pain of someone else's loss. And I can be happy for you, without a shadow crossing it. I promise you, this is your time, and I am here to enjoy it with you. In the future, we will both be able to look back on it, and I can say . . . I was there. So tell me more. Has he brothers and sisters? What kind of music does he like? What makes him laugh? What is your dress like? No, I'll wait to see it. It's not what your dress is like that matters, it's you, and what you look like

140

when you're wearing it. You will look beautiful because you are beautiful. But sophisticated or innocent? Simple or ravishing?"

Again, Cecily started to answer and then changed her mind. "Traditional," she said instead. "He comes from a very prominent family, you know. His mother is quite a fashion icon."

"Is she beautiful?" Margot asked. "Be honest, not polite."

Cecily smiled. "Not really. She's . . . flawless, but there's nobody in there."

"Cecily!" Winifred said quickly. "That's . . ."

"What is she like?" Cecily said directly to Margot. "Enamel. Perfect. Not a mark or a chip in it. But slightly out of proportion; there's something wrong with the balance of it."

Margot was not sure whether to laugh or cry. Was it fear speaking, or was it the flash of perception she recalled in Cecily: the artist's eye. Cecily liked to draw. She never needed to rely on color: the art, the inner truth, was all in the line.

This felt suddenly too close to their current situation. "Then you will have to be everything in contrast," Margot said. "Vibrant, warm, imperfect, as true beauty always is."

"I don't know what you mean," Winifred said with a frown. "How can imperfection make beauty?"

Both Winifred and Cecily were looking at Margot, waiting. She had to say something. "I'm not sure. Maybe it gives it character, reality, a life instead of just art. A cry for you to meet it. I'm not sure what I mean."

"I know what you mean," Cecily said quickly. "A place where you can touch it, where your worlds meet."

Winifred still looked puzzled.

In her mind's eye, Margot caught a glimpse of two separate orbs, touching and then parting again.

Before she could think of it further, there was a noise in the hall outside, footsteps, and the door opened. Roger Cordell came in, saw Margot, and walked to her immediately. She stood up and, without thinking, gave him a hug. It seemed so natural, but it was only when she stepped back that she realized she had not greeted Winifred with such an enthusiastic embrace, and she felt self-conscious.

"Did you have a good journey?" Roger asked. "How is your family? Your father?"

They spent a good amount of time exchanging friendly and polite inquiries, and all the news. It was easy, comfortable, and needed no thought. They remembered old jokes, happy times, perhaps happier in the remembrance than they were at the time. It was the experience shared that mattered.

Dusk settled over the garden. Roger rose and pulled the curtains closed. They put more coal on the fire.

It was only after dinner and well into the evening that Margot excused herself, saying she wished to be fresh for all the events that were to come.

"Of course," Winifred agreed. "You must be tired from traveling." She rose also, accompanying Margot to the door. She hesitated when they were outside in the hall, as if she wanted to say something but could not find the words.

Margot did not know how to help her. Winifred was smiling, but there was uncertainty in it, even fear.

"Thank you for coming," she said awkwardly. "We've been friends for a long time. Your parents were the closest we had to family."

Margot nearly made some appropriate remark, but she realized Winifred had something for which she was trying to find words, something that mattered to her intensely.

"You may find Hans's parents a little . . .

I don't know the word I'm looking for . . . harsh? A little too forward in their opinions?" She blinked several times. "Perhaps it comes from having lost the war. It scalds the pride. They can't bring themselves to admit that they were in any way wrong. Their history books omit all of their invasions, their occupation of other people's lands and towns and villages. It seems to be difficult sometimes . . ."

"I understand," Margot cut into the awkwardness. "I don't like to admit some of the things that England has done, particularly when speaking to one of our victims."

Winifred looked puzzled. "Our . . . victims?"

Margot realized her mistake. Winifred could see only this war; nothing else was material now. "I was thinking of the past," she explained. "European wars, that kind of thing. I'm sorry, I'll be courteous, I promise you. If they make Cecily happy, that's all I care about."

Winifred's eyes filled with tears. "Thank you, my dear. It's all I care about, too. Happy and safe. Roger and I, we can't do that for her, not now. She loves Hans, and I'm sure he loves her. She's so . . ."

"She's lovely," Margot said firmly. "She was always charming, and now she's positively beautiful. He's a very lucky man, and I'm sure he knows it."

"Yes," Winifred agreed. Now she could not stop the tears running down her face. "I hate to let her go, but we have to keep her safe."

Without thinking, Margot put her arms around Winifred's shoulders and held her tightly for several moments. When Winifred finally walked away, her back was straight, her head high. She was ready to face her family again.

CHAPTER 8

Elena was restless all night after having found Aiden and spent the evening dining near him and his friends, as if they were total strangers. She had imagined it before, of course: how it would be, how they would address each other, and how each of them would feel. First, she had loved him, then she had believed he was a traitor, and loved and hated him at the same time. Then Peter Howard had told her he was loyal all the time!

Now it all fell into place. She should have trusted her instinct and known there was an explanation. He had not betrayed her; he had followed a higher loyalty. At what cost to himself? She might never know. But now that she had found him, it was different. A few moments alone and he could have healed so much of the wound she had merely covered over. No wonder she could not forget him! In her heart she must always have known. It was her turn to be loyal, even to save him.

She lay in this narrow, hard bed in the strange apartment in Trieste, staring up at the patterns on the ceiling made by the streetlights. The shutters were open, since closed they made the room completely airless, and she could hear the noise anyway: people's footsteps, now and then a car's engine, someone calling out "good night" in Italian or German or Serbian.

So many nights she had lain in his arms. How was it even imaginable that he wouldn't recognize her, however much she had changed? Her hair had been light brown; her mother had called it "honey-colored," which sounded so much more attractive. The heavy wave was natural. In May, in Berlin, when she was running away, she had cut it much shorter, level with her jaw, and dyed it pale blond. That was only months ago, although it seemed in another life. Half grown out, it had looked such a mess. She had it colored again, that luminous Scandinavian blond tone, and Margot had laughed at her. Elena had to admit she actually liked it. It made her look very different. She had kept it like that as a promise to herself that she *was* different, braver, a player and not just a watcher.

147

Elena was dressing more fashionably, too. She had disguised herself, when she needed to, not by melting into the background but by standing out against it. Bold and different. Strikingly dressed, so people remembered her clothes rather than her face. She had not admitted it until now, but this pleased her. The new self was who she wanted to be. It felt natural, true, as she imagined herself to be.

There was no time to waste. This was urgent. Time to dream later. Peter Howard had told her only as much as she needed to know. She could not find Aiden's handler, Max Klausner, and she had to warn Aiden and convince him to leave.

She got up fairly early, and, as she had done in the few days since she had come to Trieste, dressed, and went out for breakfast. The street was cool, and busy already. There was a café around the corner where she could buy newspapers in English, Italian, or German. She could not read the Serbian, so she left them. The German newspapers were best. They were actually from Vienna and gave a little bit of the news she most needed, specifically stories of unrest and criticism of Chancellor Dollfuss. It seemed whatever the poor man did, people were displeased. He was too autocratic, changed his mind too often; there was too much he was still learning and too much he didn't know. He was certainly heavy-handed — but then, so was Hitler in Germany, and there was nothing but praise for him. And Mussolini in Italy? Pompous, ridiculous man. Apparently, he had been a pretty good journalist before he became Il Duce. What had happened to him? Power was like that: enough of it and it strips you of the inhibitions that keep you outwardly sane. But inwardly? Judgment is affected and eventually you become dangerous and absurd.

She enjoyed her freshly baked rolls and two cups of coffee, then read the political articles in the Viennese newspaper and made her plans for the day. These included one last look around at the restaurants where Max had served. Then, if she did not find anyone who had seen him this week, she would go to where Gabrielle had said they would be this evening, a public place with delightful music. Gabrielle had mentioned it with an invitation to join them. Elena felt it was brash to accept, and in a way rather pathetic, but that was immaterial now. She must speak to Aiden alone and warn him, however it appeared to others.

She found no trace of Max this morning,

149

either. She came as close as she dared to questioning openly without attracting too much attention, then gave it up and went back to her apartment. She hated making a fool of herself and appearing desperate, but defensive feelings were self-indulgent now. In fact, when she thought about it, they were just a pathetic vanity.

How should she dress? Conspicuously, of course! If there were questions, the answers would be of no use. *The blonde in the scarlet silk dress, what was her face like? No idea. Would you know if her eyes are brown or blue? No.*

How was she going to approach Aiden? He was bound to be with other people. Gabrielle, at least, and from the way she had spoken, others as well. It didn't matter if she embarrassed them or what they thought of her, except that they must not know she was MI6, or whatever they thought the British Secret Service was called. She must look casual, harmless, even socially inept, or desperately lonely. No, that was galling. She shivered at that thought. It was the ultimate humiliation. She should have a life, a purpose that would make her seem more like everyone else. It was not hard to create.

Might one of them be the person who had killed Max Klausner? They might be shal-

150

low, trivial, or even absurd on the outside, but underneath, desperately serious. It was literally a matter of life and death. And not only for them, but perhaps for many others. She had seen that in Berlin. One minute she had been on the street, the next in a Gestapo prison. She had been rescued, but others had not. To hell with embarrassment!

She put on the scarlet dress and surveyed herself in the abbreviated mirror in her bathroom. The space was too small to get a full impression, but maybe that was just as well. Her appearance was eye-catching, but not necessarily the way she wanted to look. Or more honestly, the way she dared to look. She would be noticed, that was certain. She had gained weight in one or two places she had not realized. She had been a bit boyish at sixteen; there was nothing boyish about her now! Margot would be amused.

She put her cape around her shoulders and felt a good deal less conspicuous, then went downstairs to the street. She was tall enough to be elegant in fairly low heels, which was just as well, in case she needed to walk any distance. Or even to run.

She found a taxi in the first main street she came to and asked the driver to take her to the address Gabrielle had given her.

The journey was not long enough to sort out her thoughts. It seemed like they had barely navigated the busy street when the driver pulled in at the curb and told her she was there. She paid and thanked him, then stepped out, forcing herself to walk inside casually, as if she had done it a dozen times before.

"Have you a reservation, signora? Or perhaps there is someone expecting you?" the man at the desk inquired. He was charmingly polite, but there was a steel in him that said he did not allow unaccompanied young women into the establishment. She knew exactly what he was asking and what he suspected might be her true business here.

She smiled with all the confidence she could fake. "Madame Fournier invited me to join her. I'm sure she will say so, if you ask her." She wished she were as sure as she sounded.

"Of course, signora." He inclined his head. "Madame Fournier is over there," he indicated, with the slightest turn of his head.

Elena followed the line of his glance and saw Gabrielle immediately. She was unmissable. She was not quite Elena's height, but one did not compare Gabrielle with anybody else. She was elegant, slender, yet also voluptuous. Her dark hair was coiled at the back of her head, sleek and shining. She wore a gown of gold lamé that caught the light and would have exposed even the slightest flaw, had there been any. One looked at nobody else.

Elena took a deep breath and let the cape slide off her shoulders and trail from one hand. Then she walked over toward Gabrielle as if she did this every day . . . and had all the time in the world. She heard, rather than saw, a slight movement, the scraping of chair legs, as people turned to watch her. She took no notice.

Several people were staring, but the only one she cared about was Aiden. She noticed the light on his hair as he turned, and then the look on his face, almost instantly masked. She stopped in front of Gabrielle. "You were kind enough to invite me," Elena said calmly, although she felt as if her whole body was shaking with the beating of her heart. "So, I accepted. It looks as if everybody who matters in Trieste is here." She did no more than glance at the nearby tables and the two couples nearest to them, whom she recognized from the previous night.

Aiden covered his surprise immediately. "I'm sorry, signorina, at first I did not recognize you."

He smiled the same wide, charming smile she remembered from years ago. She refused to let it turn her heart over again. It did not matter what she felt, only what she did. Was there time to be subtle? Even slightly?

"May I get you something to drink?" he offered.

"Yes, please," she accepted, looking straight at him. There was no recognition in his eyes, not even a flicker. Apparently, she was infinitely forgettable to him. She could remember every gesture, every intonation, as if it had been a month ago, not years. She could remember his laughter, the long holiday they had taken together on the coast of Northumberland, exploring a hundred places. She remembered the rising sea thundering up the pale sand, and Bamburgh Castle towering above them, its battlements seeming to guard the whole coast from invasion. She could picture exactly how the sun fell on his face and the feel of his body that night as she lay listening to the roar of the surf as the tide came in.

She jerked herself back to the present. They must play this game now! Their lives and others' depended upon this. What should she ask for? She wasn't going to drink much of it anyway. "Whatever you think best, but not too sweet. You know the region, any white wine," she said, staring back at him. "You've forgotten my name. It's Elena."

"Elena," he repeated. "Good name. It's a version of Helen, isn't it? Legendary, quite something to live up to."

She recalled how he loved the Greek classics. Not just the romance of them, but the whole structure of the myths, the tragedies, and how, if you looked at them properly, they contained such wisdom. "There are quite a lot of us," she agreed. "Mothers with dreams we can't live up to."

"Dreams to reach for?" he suggested. And then he added, "I . . . I'll get you some wine." He turned and took a step toward the nearest waiter.

He might take the opportunity to speak to her alone, but he might not. Was he afraid she would give him away? Make a scene? That would be hideously embarrassing, and more to the point, it would endanger both of them.

She turned to Gabrielle. "Excuse me, I think perhaps I would prefer a red."

She took a couple of quick steps and caught up with Aiden. She gripped his arm to slow him before he could reach the waiter and they would no longer be alone in the crowd.

155

"Aiden."

"Anton," he said harshly under his breath.

"I won't forget," she said, her smile twisted this time. "But I have to speak to you."

"It's over." He swung round and stared steadily, his eyes angry, cold. And yes, frightened.

She met his gaze with perfect clarity. "Yes, it is. Max Klausner is missing, very possibly dead, and your cover is blown. You must get out of here as quickly as you can. With grace, that is."

"*Vino,* signor, signorina?" the waiter offered. He must have seen they were talking, but so was everyone.

"Thank you," Aiden accepted, barely looking at the man. He took the two glasses from the tray and passed one to Elena.

"Thank you," she smiled graciously, taking a sip.

As soon as the waiter moved on, Aiden turned back to her, leaning closer, so as to be certain no one else could overhear them. "Keep your voice down," he warned. "How do you know this . . . and who the hell sent you?"

"MI6, of course," she replied evenly, so quietly he had to lean over to hear her.

"You're hardly MI6 material." His voice was hard. "This is no time for playing stupid

156

games, Elena, or for personal emotions. This is —"

"This is not personal, Aiden. I know you by sight, and that's why they sent me. It's important."

"How did you find me? You haven't the . . ." He stopped.

"Brains? Seems I have! It took me only a couple of days. You weren't difficult to find. Anyway, it doesn't matter now, you have to leave."

"Why should I believe you?" he asked.

All sorts of arguments came to her mind, rational in many ways. But it would mean explaining things to him that he did not need to know. And as she thought that, she realized she had not believed everything unquestioningly that Peter Howard had said. There was still a dark shadow of doubt in her mind. Was it personal? Only because Aiden had betrayed her? How petty. Hurt feelings had nothing to do with this. What if he had cared for her to begin with, and then her devotion to him had cloyed? She had been too young, too naïve, looking for passion where all he wanted was fun.

"Why should you believe me?" She repeated his question, not looking at him, but looking at Gabrielle and the light catching her gold lamé. Gabrielle had already begun

157

making her way over toward them. She would be here in less than a minute. "Because without Max Klausner, you can't get in touch with England. You can't get funds. You can't get your reports back safely."

From the moment Gabrielle was beside them, his attitude changed utterly.

"Elena knows several of my favorite places in England," he said, pleasure suddenly back in his voice, a lightness of tone.

"How fortunate!" Gabrielle smiled. "For a relatively small country, there are so many places of beauty and history. I'm always amazed by the variety." She looked genuinely interested, not merely polite. "And you are looking for historically notable places in Trieste? Places most people would not know of, or perhaps that are related in history to other places. There are a lot of those here. We are a kind of crossroads for many things." She spoke clearly, above the babble of other voices and the clink of glass and china.

"History?" Aiden asked, with slight mocking in his voice.

Was this a warning not to get too deep into the conversation? What was his relationship with Gabrielle? Personal? Or something to do with the dangerous and complicated recent political history? There were so many strands at play: Austrian occupation of the whole Trieste area; Serbia; the rising intrusion of German interest and power in Austria; even Mussolini's growing power.

"No," Elena said with a slight smile. On the surface, this was polite interest and must remain so. "I'm sure there is plenty, but there are also more knowledgeable people to admire it than I. I think I want to concentrate on the smaller streets. I know they are far less spectacular, but they have their own beauty." She saw boredom in Aiden's face and a struggle to keep interest in Gabrielle's. But this part of her cover, at least, would be honest. "I did not realize it until I got here, but the light is unlike anywhere else. Not just beautiful, it's . . ." She struggled for the word. "It's as if it were all backlit in gold. That's —"

"Do you paint?" Gabrielle asked suddenly.

"No."

"Perhaps you should. You have an artist's eye." Gabrielle smiled. "I should be interested to see what you create."

"Reflect," Elena said modestly. "I'm a photographer. I don't create beauty, but I try to catch an element of it that people might not notice, or see from a different and less interesting angle. It's mostly in the light. Or should I say, in the shadows and

159

the light, and the change of emphasis?"

"Really?" Gabrielle seemed genuinely interested, but Aiden was beginning to move his weight from one foot to the other, as if he was bored.

This was slipping out of Elena's control. At least Aiden knew why she was here and she had passed him the warning, but that was only the beginning. She had money to give him, in case he needed it. She could fly back to England if she needed to, but she had to be sure he was safe first, and that, if he was not leaving, he gave her the list Peter Howard thought was so important. She wondered how well Peter really knew Aiden. Was he only relying on other people's beliefs?

She had believed Aiden once, everything he said. She again recalled their time at the seashore, and how he had shouted into the wind, "Elena, I love you!" a smile on his face, that charming smile that made her heart beat loud enough to choke her.

Perhaps he had meant it . . . for that day.

She turned to him. "Maybe you could suggest some places for me, Anton. You know the city quite well. What is unique, beautiful? Not too crowded: Somewhere I can set up a good photograph? And what time of day do you suggest for the light to be at its best?" She meant to ask when they could meet. He must realize that, surely. "The light makes all the difference."

She waited.

"That depends on what kind of effect you're looking for," he said, as if choosing his words carefully. "What are your favorites? Your signature images? Cloud effects? Patterns of shadows? There can be a lot of them."

He was looking at her curiously, analytically. There was nothing in his eyes but slight, cautious interest. Was he so good an actor? Had he always been? Why her? She had been of no particular use to him years ago. She wasn't senior enough in the Foreign Office to have known any secrets worth his while. His own were far more valuable.

"Light on water," he suggested, watching her. "Sunlight, moonlight, lamplight, the sea. Or, better for a close-up, a canal."

She could not meet his eyes. He was remembering those images she had thought most lovely, and what she had said to him about them, her most vivid dreams, sleeping or awake. She felt the heat burn up her face at the memory of where and when she had told him of those things. She had even told him the vision that went with them in her heart, the hope, the momentary belonging to the whole realm of things composed of light. They had always been the most magical of images for her: light of any sort, on water in any form; clouds, soft rain, a puddle in the grass, moonlight on surf . . . ice. She did not know whether it was with pleasure or pain that he remembered it; he quoted it back to her without any expression in his eyes. As memories jostled her mind, she drew a darkness over them deliberately, protective of herself and of them.

"Yes," she replied, forcing a smile of her own. "I think any kind of light on the canal water, and stones, of course. They give it weight, character. Where do you suggest? And what time for the best effects?"

"You could begin on one of the old bridges, and this time of the year sunrise could be good, if the sky is almost clear," he replied. "And you'll try sunset, too, of course. Midday, the light is a little hard. You get too much glare and too much clarity to do anything clever."

"Thank you." She tried to smile, but he had to be specific. Didn't he realize that? She felt the certainty that he had been in her hand a few moments ago, but then slipped out of her grasp like a dissolving cloud. She must not look desperate.

"You might try the wharf at sunrise,"

Aiden suggested. "There will be plenty of boats to see by seven o'clock in the morning, if you can be bothered to get there so early."

"Thank you," she said, nodding slightly. "I can probably manage that, it's not too far from where I'm staying. That's very good advice. I will take it." She gave him a quick smile, glanced at Gabrielle, and then turned and walked away into the thickening crowd.

She went toward the ladies' cloakroom. She would leave when Aiden and his friends were absorbed in their conversation. He knew she had come specifically to meet him. Surely, he would not be rash enough to ignore her arrangements to accomplish that? His life depended upon her help, and there was no time to waste in games.

Elena slept uneasily and then, finally letting go of the anxiety, slipped deeper into the peace of unconsciousness. When the alarm clock shrilled, she awoke with a start. She sat up and felt chill air touch her skin as the bedclothes slid off. It was still dark, and it was a moment before she remembered why she was getting up. She reached for the alarm, then found the light and turned it on. There would be no time to stop anywhere for breakfast. She must brew coffee

163

here and at least eat a breakfast roll. She did not feel in the slightest like swallowing food. Her throat was tight and the morning still chilly. She was going to be alone with Aiden after all these years.

She went barefoot and shivering into the kitchen and put the coffee on, then washed and dressed in her tiny bathroom. She put on a little makeup for pride's sake: she would not look as drawn as she felt. She was going to tell him the truth about the situation here and in London, as far as she knew it. But she certainly was not going to tell him anything about her own feelings. First priority was getting the details to him of her own situation, then making a plan to leave without alerting whoever had broken his cover. They would try to stop him or, at the very least, take from him the papers, the list, or whatever it was that Peter Howard wanted so badly. It was the fruit of Aiden's work here at these crossroads of Mussolini's Italy and Dollfuss's Austria, which was first cousin to Germany, and all that that meant. Although, of course, cousins could hate each other, as could brothers, for heaven's sake.

And she had to get some decent pictures. It was her cover. If she were stopped by anyone and the photographs were found to be amateur — memories of Berlin in May came back to her — she would be caught in an obvious lie.

The coffee was ready. She drank it while she ate a second roll. They had been fresh yesterday and were still good. It didn't matter what she felt like, she must keep her strength up. It was nerves that were making her stomach clench. Hunger would only make it worse. She remembered their parting: he to escape, she believing he was a traitor who had left her behind to take the blame. She had looked like a stupid, starstruck girl in love with an older man who had betrayed not only her, but his country as well. Which was the truth?

She took her coat — it would be cold on the water — along with her large handbag and her camera, checking that she had extra rolls of film. Then she went out of the door and along the street with a firm, brisk step. She knew precisely where she was going.

Aiden was not there. She looked at the heavy, black mass of the bridge spanning the water, the light already seeping under the arches, the shining wet steps.

Did she have the right place? Yes. She had double-checked. There was a cold sunrise wind coming up the canal, but the light was beautiful. Most photographers would have worked with the color and glory of sunrise, catching the faces of the classically beautiful buildings. The architecture of Trieste had a lot to be proud of. In ways, it was perfect, and yet it was the imperfections, the irregular frontages, that made it so achingly lovely. The simple boats on the water gave it reality, coming out of the shadows and down the shining surface, a reality beyond artists' dreams.

Not all the lines were unbroken. Here and there, wraiths of mist dimmed a palace façade or veiled a knot of moored boats into no more than an impression, as if the artist's attention had slipped for a moment. A lone boat sculled across the shining patch of water, its oarsman unaware of his own grace.

Elena took picture after picture as the light broadened and the pastel colors became deeper. When the sun rose above the skyline, spilling color across the water, she closed her lens, snapped on its protective cover, and put her camera in the bag. She found herself smiling as she climbed the steps to the bridge and was at street level again.

Aiden was there, waiting for her. He held out his hand to balance her up the last, steep step. He had a coat on, too, and the wind tugged at his thick hair, the sun making it seem fairer than it was. In the harsh, clear light, he looked older than he had in the kinder artificial lamps of the restaurant. He was over forty now and it suited him, gave character and depth to his smooth features. Perhaps he knew pain far better than she understood, engulfed in her own self-absorption, as so many of the young can be. How childish to expect to be anyone's whole world.

"Sorry," she said, when she stood beside him. "The light was quite different from the way I expected it to be, much subtler. Everyone does the sunrise."

"So, you really are a photographer." He smiled. "I didn't even know you were interested in it."

She allowed herself to smile back, as if it were a small thing. "I had to change my direction." He must know she had been dismissed in disgrace when he had left the Foreign Office as a traitor. That her father had been an ambassador, a senior one, was the reason for her escape from prosecution, and it was not something she was proud of.

"Only partially, it seems," he replied, without any loss of composure. There was not even a flicker of shame or embarrassment in his eyes. "Did they send you out to

167

rescue me?"

"You exaggerate," she replied. "All I can do is pass extra money to you, if you need it. And warn you of all they know in London, which is that Max Klausner has disappeared, and that things are apparently growing worse in Vienna. But I imagine you know that."

"Yes," he agreed. "Do you want a cup of coffee? We might as well be comfortable while you tell me whatever London wants me to know."

"Yes, it's cold here." She realized how cold she really was. Concentrating on the light on the water, she had been largely motionless, unaware of the increasing chill that seemed to have locked her joints and penetrated her flesh. She gave an involuntary shiver.

"I haven't seen Max for days," he remarked as they turned onto the pavement and began walking toward the lit doorways of bakeries and cafés. "But sometimes he goes to Vienna. We contact each other only if there's something to say."

"London can't reach him by any of the usual ways," she said, keeping step with him. The smell of fresh baked bread drifted out to mix with the faint odor of wet stone and the stale water of the canal. "And I can't find him here."

"Do you know where to look?" he asked with amusement.

She heard the note of disapproval in his voice and suddenly the years between telescoped in her mind. Only this time she knew he would not laugh at her and then touch her gently to temper the sting of it. How young she had been, hungry for his attention, satisfied by so little that would matter now. She looked away so he would not see the emotion in her face. She answered casually, "Oh, I thought about it, considered what he would have to do. It took me nearly two days."

"You found him?" he said incredulously.

"I found where he worked," she replied. "Before he disappeared. Of course I didn't find him, he's gone. None of his usual places have seen him for nine or ten days. I don't know where he lives. The important thing was to find you, causing as little stir as possible."

"So, you came into an expensive nightclub alone, in an expensive and almost indecent bright red dress, not to draw attention to yourself. Brilliant."

"It was the dress that got the attention, Aiden," she corrected. "If I walked down the street as I am now, in old trousers and a peacoat, camera on my shoulder, I'm not that woman. It was the dress they remember, not my face or my hair."

He was silent for a moment or two, matching his step to hers. When he spoke at last, his tone was quite different. There was urgency in it, and even respect. "Have you any idea where Max went?"

"No, have you?"

"I'm afraid I think he's dead. His job was here, and I don't mean his cover job, I mean his real one. He was a good man, clever and loyal."

For a hundred yards or so they walked in the broadening light without speaking. With a flash of memory, she was going with him, along the quay beside the North Sea, the tide low, and in the early light, the marble-pale sand stretched between the shore and Holy Island, a brief pathway until the tide returned. Its very fragility had made it magic, a dangerous thread across the sea to an island not only holy in name, but in character going back over a thousand years. She could remember standing by the stone wall with grasses all over it. It had been covered with wallflowers, gold and scarlet and blood red, and a sweet, almost overpowering perfume.

"Elena." Aiden's voice was sharp, jolting

her back to the present. This was business.

"Did you discuss a possible route out of Trieste, in an emergency?" she asked.

"Of course," he answered briefly. "But we don't know what has happened to Max. We can't afford to assume he remained silent about our plans and —"

"That he wouldn't betray you," she interrupted. "You didn't trust him."

He stopped, his face bleak and angry. "Don't be such a child, Elena. Grow up! They'll have tortured him for everything he could tell them. This isn't a game!"

She looked up at him, at his face, which was almost beautiful but for the anger in it. "I know that, Aiden," she said with icy calm, although she was raging inside. But a show of temper was precisely what he would want. Contempt, a perfect control, would be far more effective. "We knew each other years ago, or thought we did. You've changed since then, or maybe not a lot. But I have, too. Don't jump to judgment. It's stupid and it's dangerous. I've been caught by the Gestapo and tortured — not for long — but I'll have the scars always. There were those who were not so lucky. I'll get you out of here if I can, but don't you bloody patronize me."

He stopped exactly where he was, in the

morning sun on the stones of the quayside. He let his breath out slowly. His eyes were bright. "You're right, you have changed."

She should not have told him. It might have been better if he had not known. Peter Howard had always said, "Don't tell anyone anything you don't have to," but perhaps she did have to, or Aiden would not trust her. That could be fatal. Too late to do anything about it now. "We need to know what plans you had with Max," she said, "because we'll have to avoid those things and think of something else. I can't do that if I don't know what they are."

For a moment his face was closed, unreadable, as if they were strangers. Then it vanished and he glanced back at her. "We'll have to avoid the airfield and the railway station," he said with a tight little smile. "Can you manage that?"

"I'll have to," she replied. "Pity about the railway. I'm rather good on trains."

He opened his mouth to say something, then changed his mind and increased his pace along the stones, and she kept up with him.

CHAPTER 9

Margot slept restlessly. There was only one way for her to behave at this wedding, but it was going to be an effort to keep up the front of optimism and happiness. She was glad she had come, but not for the reason someone might suppose. No one here, save her parents, had known Cecily as long as she had and she felt a fierce protectiveness toward her friend. Roger was going to walk Cecily down the aisle and put her in the arms of a man Winifred did not like. She masked it well, and she would always do so. She had little choice.

Margot was angry with herself. She was tired and perhaps, at heart, also still grieving. She had been so sure of her own marriage: happy, secure in her decision, and certain of Paul's love for her, as she was of her love for him. They had had one perfect week.

She must pull herself together and be

happy for Cecily. If she loved this Hans, then Margot could at least like him.

She got up, washed, and dressed in the most casual clothes she had brought. She chose a summer dress in a dark brown that one would never have thought could suit her, yet it was marvelous. It was cut to skim the lines of her body, and on anyone less slender, less graceful, it would have looked severe, even dowdy. On Margot, it was both sophisticated and dramatic.

A hot cup of tea would make all the difference. There was bound to be a maid or a cook in the kitchen. She would sit in a corner to drink it, then perhaps go for a walk in the garden. It was small — the house was near the center of the city — but big enough for grass, flowerbeds, and what looked like a fruit tree of some sort. The first leaves were beginning to turn from green to gold, touched with pink.

But the kitchen was not empty. Roger Cordell was sitting at the scrubbed wooden table with tea, toast, and a boiled egg. A row of gleaming copper saucepans hung on pegs on the wall above him. There did not appear to be anyone else. Had he made his breakfast himself?

"I'm sorry," Margot said. "I didn't mean to disturb you."

He rose to his feet, an automatic courtesy. "You didn't sleep?"

She sighed. "Yes, I did. I just felt like a cup of tea. Please don't let me spoil your breakfast." She sat down opposite him so he would continue with his meal.

"Tea? Is that all?" he asked.

"Yes, thank you. I can wait for breakfast later, with Winifred and Cecily."

He stood up and fetched a clean cup out of the cupboard, then sat down again and poured her tea. He did not ask her how she liked it. It appeared he remembered from the past. He put it beside her and resumed his seat. "What are you going to do today?" he asked casually, but with interest, even a trace of anxiety.

"I'll be careful," she promised with a wry smile. "I know it's unwise to be too inquisitive, and certainly to criticize."

"Very," he said levelly, meeting her eyes over the rim of his cup. "Margot —"

"I will be very careful." She looked at him more closely. "What is it? I'm not Elena, you know. I don't have an instant reaction to injustice."

"Yes, you do, my dear," he said gently. "She is more like you as time goes by; she's growing up, if you like. What happened in May was a very profound experience for

175

her. She was badly hurt, you know, and it forced her to face a kind of reality she'd held at arm's length until then. She's a dreamer, she'll probably never lose that. It's what makes her such a good photographer. She sees things in a different light, and not necessarily a softer one."

Margot drew in her breath to say she knew, but she wondered if she really did. Habit was strong, and she had expected Elena to tell her more about her experience here, in Berlin, in time, but her sister had mentioned it only in passing and quite skill-fully had changed the subject. And then there was the extraordinary revelation that Grandfather Lucas had been head of MI6 during the war. She had asked him to explain, and after a few long, charming, interesting conversations, she felt happily closer to him. There was a warmth and a real understanding between them for the first time that she could remember, although she realized afterward that she knew very little more. But now she understood why: it was a subject that could not be discussed, for her sake as much as his. The stories he had told her were old, the issues long settled, the people concerned no longer alive. Elena had been sweet and friendly, and far more skilled than she expected in telling her nothing she did not already know.

She looked across the table at Cordell. "Yes, I'm beginning to realize that. Perhaps I've changed, too."

"Not too much, I hope." He smiled as he said it.

"If you judge Elena fairly, then you must be clear-eyed with me, too."

"What have I got wrong?" He suddenly appeared quite nervous.

It made her think in a way she had not intended. "Not the outside, for a start," she began. "I'm quite skilled at painting my face on and choosing carefully what I wear. But that isn't all of me."

He raised his eyebrows. "Do you think I don't know that?"

"Yes," she said honestly, "I do think exactly that."

"Margot, my dear, I've known you since you were a girl at school, with ink on your fingers, rather than nail polish. I've watched you grow up, both inside and out. I've seen you deal with grief, and watched your patience with Elena as she grew up, too."

She found herself blushing. "Really? Has it been that long?"

"Since your father and I have known each other? Yes, in fact longer."

He was looking at her gently and she

found it a little disturbing. Had he really seen her so clearly, and for so long? It was uncomfortable to be perceived so well, and yet it seemed he still liked her. There was affection in his eyes, even a degree of pleasure. Or perhaps it was because she had come to support Cecily with her friendship, and not many others had. A wave of pity overtook her for a moment. Were there friends who had abandoned her because she was marrying a German soldier? A Nazi? Cowards.

"Do you like him?" she said suddenly.

In spite of the fact that she had not mentioned any name, Cordell's eyes lowered to gaze somewhere toward the oven spreading warmth into the room. "No."

The thought hung in the air, unfinished.

She was more aware of the daylight creeping into the corners of the room, showing details of shelves and cupboards in sharp outline, and cold still from the night.

Cordell looked up. "But if he makes Cecily happy, then I shall learn to. Winifred worries so much less now, and I could like him for that alone." He looked rueful. "I suppose every father thinks that no man is good enough for his daughter, especially an only child." The color washed off his cheeks. "I'm sorry. I'm sure . . ."

She smiled genuinely. "It's all right. Whatever my father thought, it wasn't the time or place to show it. Paul was only home for a week or so on leave. You don't tell a soldier home from the battlefront that he isn't good enough for your daughter; he's good enough for anything."

"Of course. I'm . . . sorry."

"Don't be." She meant it. "It's natural you should worry about Cecily. Times are difficult. And although you know Germany well, you are English all through, and so is Cecily . . . in her own way. Although she knows Germany better than she knows England now. The only thing that matters is: Does he love her?"

"Didn't Pilate say, 'What is truth?' " he asked. "Does it make sense if I say, 'What is love?' "

"No, but we're not twenty-three; Cecily is. Falling in love is still magic for her. It can overcome all sorts of things."

"And does that stop?" he said ruefully, but the amusement did not fade from his eyes. "Don't give up, Margot. You're still in your prime, if you are even there yet. And don't expect anyone like Paul Driscoll to cross Cecily's path. Young men aren't like that anymore, but there's room for a different kind of heroism: quieter, perhaps, and

179

in many instances unknown. But of the highest order nonetheless."

"Are you thinking of Elena and —"

"All sorts of things," he cut across her. "Nothing in particular. Times are not as quiet as you think. Just enjoy the wedding, and be there for Cecily . . . and Winifred." He touched her hand lightly, just with his fingertips. "You make a great difference."

She was saved from having to think of a reply by the maid coming into the kitchen and offering to make Margot breakfast.

The morning passed pleasantly. Cecily, rather shyly, showed Margot her wedding dress, uncertain if she should or not. She knew Margot had had little time to prepare her own, and with wartime rations and restrictions, extravagance had been impossible, and, anyway, would have been in poor taste when there was so little to go around. Cecily's dress was simple: plain white silk with a little lace appliqué at the throat.

"It's absolutely gorgeous," Margot said sincerely, surprised how happy she was to say that and mean it. "I hope the photographer is good. You will be one of the loveliest pictures he has taken."

Cecily blushed with pleasure, then modesty made her bend her head. "Do you think so?"

"I do," Margot said. "I really do."

"Mrs. Beckendorff, Hans's mother, is coming for luncheon. I can't call her mother-in-law yet. My tongue slipped, and I did once. She gave me such a look. You won't like her, but please try to see the best in her, for my sake. I dare say no one would be good enough for her son, but certainly not someone who's English . . . and dark-haired."

"I dislike her already," Margot agreed, "but I will not show it, I promise."

"And don't make me laugh," Cecily added. "She thinks loud laughter is vulgar in women."

"She doesn't strike me as a woman with much to laugh about," Margot replied.

Cecily was right. Frau Beckendorff arrived exactly on time for luncheon. She had a striking appearance, but only because of the beauty of her gleaming halo of pale hair, her perfect complexion, and the art with which her linen suit had been tailored. It was the color of tomato soup, a little harsh for a woman of her bleached-out coloring.

Winifred introduced them in the hall and Margot was instantly aware of Winfred's in-

181

ner tension, though only because she knew her. It was the pitch of her voice, higher than usual, that gave her away, as if her throat were tight. Naturally, she spoke in German.

"How do you do?" Margot replied with a smile. "It's a pleasure to meet you, Frau Beckendorff." She looked at the pale blue eyes and thought of jumping into iced water. It was supposed to be good for your health, if it didn't kill you.

"I believe you have come for Cecily's wedding," Frau Beckendorff observed. "I'm so glad she has someone here from her home country."

It was a double-edged remark: nice at first, with a bitterness inside, as it reminded Cecily that she did not belong here. It was on the tip of Margot's tongue to say, "We are here because we conquered you," but of course she bit it back.

She was aware of Winifred's stiffness beside her.

"Do come in and sit down," Winifred insisted. "Luncheon will be in about fifteen minutes." She turned and led the way into the sitting room, and they all followed her.

Frau Beckendorff sat down, started to speak, and then bit it back.

Margot knew that Winifred would have

182

practiced something to say. She was an ambassador's wife, for heaven's sake. She had a lifetime's experience of being charming to people she did not especially care for. Now, however, she remained tongue-tied.

"Obviously, you care for fashion, Frau Beckendorff," Margot plunged in. "That suit is most beautifully cut. It becomes you very well, and it is not in the least ordinary."

Frau Beckendorff looked Margot up and down, noting the equally fashionable cut of Margot's dress. "Thank you," she replied, a little less stiffly. "One has to find where to shop. There is a lot of rather poor taste around." She carefully did not look at either Cecily or Winifred. "I hope you enjoy your stay in Berlin. It is a little battered still, but we are rising to our feet again, and there is much to see." Her voice was polite, even warm, but her face was expressionless.

"I'm sure I shall," Margot replied. "Do you travel much, Frau Beckendorff?"

"To Salzburg, occasionally, of course. To Vienna, one of the most beautiful cities."

"I don't know it," Margot admitted, although she would have pretended not to even if she had known it as well as she knew London. "What would you recommend?"

From there, the conversation went quite well. Winifred knew Vienna also, and Cecily was content to listen. She shot Margot a quick glance of gratitude.

The maid announced lunch and they went through to the dining room. Frau Beckendorff looked at it briefly, but neither smiled nor made comment. It was a pleasant room, meant for family life, with photographs of places in England they could barely remember now, and ornaments of value for the memories more than for their intrinsic worth.

Margot hardly knew what she was eating; she had to look at it in order to compliment Winifred on the meal.

"Thank you," Winifred murmured, looking at Margot to see for herself if she meant it. Satisfied that she did, she nodded her acknowledgment.

After several mouthfuls, Margot turned her attention to Frau Beckendorff again. "I've not yet had the pleasure of meeting Hans," she said with feigned interest. "And I'm keen to learn something about him."

That was sufficient to animate Frau Beckendorff, who regaled them through the rest of the meal with Hans's achievements, all his life to date. It was a momentarily chilling thought to Margot that this woman knew the list so intimately! Never once did she hesitate. It was a dance she had choreographed.

"I'm sure he has a great future ahead of him," Margot said with as much enthusiasm as she could, to keep out the sarcasm. She was not a natural sycophant. She turned to Cecily. "It's going to be a great adventure."

Winifred looked at Cecily with a smile and an intense hope.

Suddenly, Margot felt tears in her eyes and a wave of hatred for Hans Beckendorff, his mother, and all his family and friends. It was ridiculous. This woman was arrogant and insensitive, but neither Margot nor any of the rest of them knew what grief or pain lay behind her.

It was Frau Beckendorff who broke the silence. She turned to Cecily. "I think Hans planned to take you out this afternoon," she said. Then she turned to Margot. "It's a lovely day for a walk in the park. He would be happy to show it to you, I'm sure. Any friend of Cecily's is a friend of his."

It suddenly occurred to Margot that Frau Beckendorff, too, was nervous. Instead of making her tongue-tied, it had affected her the other way. She was mounting a defense, almost in expectation of attack. She was old enough to have been an adult all through the war. What loss of family, shame, and grief had she known? And perhaps at the

185

hands of British soldiers. And now her only son was going to marry an English girl.

"How kind of him," Margot said back to her, and then to Cecily, "If you don't mind my coming along, I should like it very much. In fact, I can't think of anything nicer."

Winifred settled further into her seat, relaxing for the first time.

Margot disliked Hans on sight, but she masked it for Cecily's sake. He was everything that set her on edge in a young man: the pale skin, tidy hair, a handsome enough face, but with no lines of laughter, or of pain. He was a little taller than Margot, which gave him two or three inches over Cecily. He was slender in build, but he had been trained militarily and was obviously strong and graceful. He had a faint dueling scar across his cheek, which, to a German soldier, was a mark of honor. Margot could make believe she saw imagination in his face, dreams of achievement to come. What she did not see was humor. Somehow, she found that chilling out of all proportion.

Perhaps it was the change she saw in Cecily that was the real measurement. As they walked in the quiet sunshine, along the graveled path in the park, trees in full leaf, only a few of them turning gold, Cecily kept glancing at Hans, even when she was pointing out to Margot her favorite places. There was no trace of Cecily's usual wit, just pure admiration for Hans. Did she think Hans would not understand her dry, self-deprecating British humor and would mistake it for criticism? Or was it that her thinking had so changed in his company? Was he so sensitive? Was the stiffness she had taken for arrogance really shyness?

Margot walked and talked automatically, finding something pleasant to say about everything that was pointed out to her. She saw how Hans looked at Cecily when she was unaware of it. There was a tenderness in him, even moments of awe, as if he could hardly believe his good luck that she had chosen him.

To her surprise, Margot felt a wave of sympathy for him. What was it like to be the only son in an ambitious family? A ridiculous thought occurred to her: Did his parents' prosperity, even their safety, depend on him? What a burden. Of course he did not trust Margot. The only person he could trust was Cecily, and maybe that was only partially. If she was naïve and put her trust where she felt she should, rather than where it was wise, then she could betray them all without knowing it.

That was absurd. Margot was letting her imagination run away with her. She turned to Hans. "How old do you suppose that tree is?" she asked, pointing to an ancient cedar. "It must have seen so much history."

He responded immediately with a long and unexpectedly interesting account of Berlin's history through the last 150 years. His observations were cleverer than she expected, and at times drily amusing. By the time they arrived back at the Cordell house, they were conversing with pleasure.

The evening party at an excellent hotel was a different matter. It was very formal, and while the wedding itself was Cordell's responsibility, this dinner was hosted by Hans's family and most of the guests were from their social circle.

Winifred had prepared Margot for the event and its formality. Margot was tired from travel and all the new experiences of the last two days. She would have chosen to have a quiet evening and early night, but she was not offered that option. She was there to support Winifred and, more than that, Cecily.

And perhaps she was there to help Hans himself stand firm against his parents' gentle but powerful insistence on his path upward, and all that it involved.

She hesitated among the gowns she had brought with her. Finally, she selected one that was more daring than the others. It looked at first to be only mildly sophisticated, a heavy black silk. Her arms were covered, and it was modest at the front. But when she turned, the whole impact was stunning. The skirt swung wide, the sleeves were broad and cut off at the elbow. The bodice commanded the eye, cut so low at the back that it was very nearly to the waist. It was a dress for a young woman, a bold and daring woman who would know that her figure benefited from a suggestion, rather than anything obvious. It was all subtle . . . and outrageous at the same time. It might not please Frau Beckendorff at all, but no one would forget it. And it was so utterly elegant that any criticism expressed would seem mean-spirited and, from a man, cause laughter and a vague pity for someone so lacking in art or humor.

When Margot came down the stairs, Winifred's eyebrows rose. Roger Cordell's rose even higher, but his expression was impossible to read.

"*Brava!*" Cecily said with laughter. "That's the Margot I remember! Whatever I wear, I will appear unforgettably modest."

Margot flashed her a wide smile. "As long as you're unforgettably lovely, my dear, as modest seems to be the excellent thing for a bride. In fact, perfect. Hans will never forget it, and who cares what anyone else thinks?"

Cecily shook her head, but she was blushing with pleasure.

The party was already in full swing when Roger, his wife and daughter, and Margot arrived. An instant silence fell over the large room, almost a lull, then after the noise resumed, a longer hush as Margot turned to Winifred to say something and her startling silhouette was observed. Whether it was awe or not, she thoroughly enjoyed it.

Frau Beckendorff came forward to welcome them. Introducing Margot to their friends, she had a change of expression, which Margot found amusing. She caught Cordell's eye and a brief laugh in it, before he was instantly sober again.

Margot accepted a glass of champagne and drifted from one group of conversations to another, all of them in German. The room was packed with people: women dressed gorgeously, men in formal black or military dress uniform. The noise was often punctuated with laughter. Several times

Margot found herself with the same half dozen officers as Hans, and he seemed hesitant to introduce her. But it was his social duty to make everyone's name known. It was his parents' party, but he was, in a sense, the host, and there was a look of pride in his face as he introduced Cecily to many of his friends from society and from the army or associates of his parents.

Several times, Margot found herself standing next to a man named Berthold. He was handsome, in a bold way, strong, and yet he moved with the grace of an athlete. She thought his sport might well be dueling, more likely with a saber than an épée.

To begin with, the conversation was bland enough. He inquired where she lived. He was interested in the time she had spent in Berlin when her father had been ambassador, and he asked her about it with curiosity. They had memories in common, and it was easy and natural to share them. Only gradually did they include older memories, things said and believed by the generation earlier, recollections of times before the war, at the beginning of the century.

At first Margot did not find it uncomfortable. Those were the days when at least the aristocracy of both countries mixed with pleasure and ease. She did not expect mention to be made of Germany's defeat at the end of the war, but it lay just beneath the surface of their remarks, and the bitterness was unmistakable.

She made a sudden decision. "It was a political mistake," she said quietly, and could hardly believe her own voice speaking the words. "And one for which we will all have to pay."

Berthold froze, but only for an instant. Then he gave a small smile, only a tightening of the lips. "You see that?" he asked softly. "But Britain does not suffer."

"We will," Margot replied, meeting his eyes candidly — or at least she meant it to be. If you are going to lie, do it wholeheartedly. "Germany is our natural ally, don't you think?"

His eyes widened a fraction. "Natural?"

"You want me to start as near as I can to the beginning?" she asked, the first thing that came to her mind. She was in dangerous territory; one step had taken her there — it was as easy as that — but she felt impelled to seize the chance.

Now Berthold was intensely interested. It showed in the rigidity of his shoulders, the fact that his arms did not move at all, even to set down his glass. "And what do you consider that to be?"

"The origin of our language seems the place to me," she replied, making it up as she went along. She hoped her racing mind did not show in her eyes.

"Yes," he nodded so fractionally as to be barely visible. "They are two trees from the same root. But you were conquered by William of Normandy in 1066. Now you have more French than we do. They were your overlords for years," he said bleakly, "as were the Romans before them. Hence, all the Latin among your words." He was smiling now. A petty nationalist victory.

She smiled back. "And we have collected thousands of words and ideas from having an empire that stretches around the earth, but we're happy to share them."

There was a flash of appreciation in his eyes. She had been right; he did not respect an easy victory.

"Do you think there are many English who think that Germany is your natural ally?" It was a question to which he wanted an answer. She could tell in his carefully affected disinterest.

"Not so many," she replied equally levelly. "But they are all in very interesting places."

"Such as?"

"For example . . ." Her mind raced. "One cabinet minister is worth more than a thousand agricultural laborers."

He breathed out in a gentle sigh. "I think you are unusual in your understanding, but not unique."

"I hope not," she said, suddenly earnest. The instinct was too deep to deny. "It's a bit like a river, don't you think? It starts with a spring bubbling out of the ground, far from the sea. Other streams join it. It gets bigger, deeper, maybe faster. By the time it reaches the sea, it is scouring its way through valleys, over waterfalls, until it is an irresistible force."

"Frau Driscoll, you are a remarkable woman," he said softly. "I hope you stay in Berlin after the wedding. There are people I would like you to meet, interesting people I think you would like; and I'm sure they would like you."

There was the opportunity, right in front of her. Had it been like this for Elena when she was in Berlin? She never spoke of it. In fact, she very obviously had avoided it. There had been a loss there, but perhaps many other things, too. There was a big change in the pattern of their relationship. Margot was four years older, and she had always known Elena well. Elena kept very few secrets, until now, and Margot was just beginning to understand that they were deep. Held because of their nature — not for power, but for safety. "How interesting," she murmured. "How . . . encouraging."

"Hans never mentioned you, so I conclude that you have only just met."

It was a delicate compliment. She smiled, appreciating it. "Yes, I have known Cecily since we lived here years ago. My father was a friend of her father's so it was natural we should meet."

"We?"

Had that been a mistake? She should not tell him too much. She might make a slip she could not cover. What did he know of Grandfather Lucas?

He was waiting.

"My family," she replied. "My sister was closer to Cecily's age."

"She is here with you?"

"No, her job would not allow her."

"But yours?"

"I'm a widow." There was no point in denying it, it would seem dishonest.

"I'm sorry," he said with apparent sincerity.

"England and Germany have so many." She seized the chance. It was open right in front of her. "Yes, we must never, ever let that happen again." She put all the grief of her own loss into her voice, her face, even the tears that came into her eyes. "Not ever."

He raised his glass. "Here's to you, Frau Driscoll, and all who have the courage and wisdom to think like you."

She lifted her own glass and touched it to his, then took another sip of her drink, although it nearly choked her.

She might learn more about their beliefs, who supported them, and how, if she practiced patience and stifled her own emotions.

CHAPTER 10

Margot woke up on the morning of Cecily's wedding day with emotions choking her so much she could barely breathe. She wanted to weep for all that had been hers for a moment and then lost. She turned over and felt her pillow cold on her cheek. It was wet with her tears.

Paul! Paul, why did you have to go back there one more time? There were only weeks left, and the war would have been over.

But Paul was dead years ago and time was rolling on inexorably. The year 1918 seemed like another lifetime. She must pull herself together, bathe her face in cold water, and go to breakfast with the family. They would expect it of her. This was Cecily's day, not Margot's. She must help make it happy. God knew, nothing was guaranteed.

Margot wished Cecily were marrying anyone but Hans.

How must Winifred be feeling? Her only

197

child slipping out of her protection and into a big, noisy, deaf, and dangerous world. There was nothing Winifred or anybody could do to protect Cecily — or anyone else. "You can't fight their battles for them, only give them armor." Who had said that? Grandfather Lucas, to Josephine.

And pray, of course. You could do that. You would feel as if you were helping. But what was God going to do that would help? Make Hans good? Make him love Cecily so much he would turn out to be a good man? What did that mean? In this context, it meant not a Nazi. Not an admirer of violence, oppression, the belief if you won, you could justify whatever you had done.

Would God soften this young man's heart so he did not break Cecily's? Find a way for him to serve his country, other than by becoming one of Hitler's acolytes? *"Ja, mein Führer. Nein, mein Führer. Heil Hitler!"* Reject all of that and still survive, even prosper?

Wasn't it the ultimate hypocrisy to pray for something you would not work for yourself, sacrifice for yourself? Rather like giving the servants a list of things to do for the day.

Get up, Margot! Go and do all you can for it yourself. Make Cecily's day one to remember all her life, whatever happens afterward.

She washed and dressed carefully, putting on new underwear, lace and silk. She had washed her hair yesterday evening. Now it was silky soft and shining. She wound it up carefully, sleekly, into a chignon, held together by a forest of pins. She made up her face lightly, complexion perfect, eyes wide and dark, lashes black. She stopped and looked at herself. There was no slackness in her jaw, no severe lines on her brow. Where was the wear and tear of time? She was now comfortably over thirty. In her eyes, she saw a certain immobility to her smile.

Now she must go downstairs looking happy and confident, and give all her attention to the Cordell family.

"Good morning, dear," Winifred said, as soon as Margot came into the dining room.

The table was set as usual, but no one except Cordell himself seemed to be taking a proper meal. Winifred was looking after everyone else, including the staff, at the expense of herself. Cecily was sitting at the table in her glistening white petticoat, trying to force herself to eat some scrambled eggs on toast.

A maid came in with a flat iron in her hand and tears on her face.

"What is it now, Greta?" Winifred asked

with careful patience.

Greta explained in German that she did not trust the electric iron. The old flat iron did as you told it, and she was so scared of scorching Miss Cecily's dress, she couldn't do it.

"Then don't worry." Winifred took the iron from her. "I'll do it. You get Miss Margot some scrambled eggs from Cook. Go on, now, there's a good girl."

Greta handed her the iron and disappeared into the kitchen.

"Can I help?" Margot asked.

"Yes, please. Eat your breakfast and see that Cecily eats hers. We want her radiant, not looking like a ghost and fainting in the aisle," Winifred replied. "Please." She was wearing some kind of a robe that covered her, but clearly she, too, had all but prepared herself. Her hair was coming out of its pins. Margot would have liked the opportunity to fasten it for her and make sure everything was set, before they finally departed for the church.

She glanced at Cordell. He was immaculately shaved, and his thick, slightly graying dark hair could have been a barber's advertisement for its perfection. He was dressed, ready to leave, but for his jacket and his expression. He might have been going to

200

his own execution, judging by the tension in his shoulders and the muscles of his neck.

Margot sat down and poured herself a cup of tea. It would be a few minutes before her eggs arrived. She was not at all sure she wanted them. She did not usually eat much at breakfast, but this was not a day to upset their little routine.

Cecily was watching her, a hesitant smile on her face.

Margot glanced out of the long windows onto the garden. They faced east and caught the first light. A good piece of planning. No one cared so much about last light at dinnertime.

"Going to be a lovely day in everything," she said, smiling back at Cecily. "Are your flowers here yet?"

"Oh, yes," Cecily replied, easing a little. "September roses, lush pink, so they can be seen, not lost against the dress, and framed with a little greenery . . ."

"Perfect," Margot said, although she would have said that if it had been a bunch of asparagus. "And from the look of the sky, no chance at all of rain."

Cecily picked at her food, as if her throat were closed and she could not have swallowed it.

"I probably won't know many of the

guests," Margot went on. "I may know some of your friends, if they were here when I was."

"Not many of them are coming," Cecily said hastily.

Margot could see from her face that it was an apology.

"I . . . I've lost touch with many of them," she added.

Margot wondered what that really meant. Did she not want to introduce them to Hans because they would not approve? It might even endanger her. Many people would surely prefer that the Gestapo did not know their names, see even their smallest mistakes or disloyalties. Or was it that Hans might not approve of them? At least in the past her friends were an eclectic group, rejoicing in their differences and conflicting ideas. That was a dangerous occupation now, but it was hard to give up the ideas of a lifetime — even a short one.

Did she miss them? Had everybody changed a little with hunger, despair, and then this new order? Everyone had hostages to fortune: family, friends, teachers, priests, simply the vulnerable. Were the circles getting smaller?

The silence was deepening over the breakfast table. Cecily took a mouthful and swallowed it with difficulty.

The maid brought Margot's breakfast, and Margot thanked her.

"I expect Hans has many friends," Margot remarked. "There must be some you particularly like and they will be so happy for him."

Cecily smiled. "Yes. Some of them are really nice. Especially those he has known a long time."

"Tell me about them."

The rest of the meal passed more easily. Cordell did not interrupt, but as Margot rose to leave, he gave her a quick look of gratitude. He had not spoken, but the warmth in his expression was unmistakable.

Margot found Winifred and helped her, mostly by taking her mind off the details, which had already been dealt with. The cars were ordered and checked on. The invitations to the evening's dinner were all sent, acknowledged, and replied to. The meal was catered and really more to do with the groom's family, the Beckendorffs, than with the bride's.

Winifred would go to the church early. Cordell would bring Cecily at the appointed hour. Margot would wait with Cecily, to make sure everything was perfect and that she was not alone in attending to the small details.

They had plenty of time. Margot went to the library beyond the study to fetch a book Cecily had decided she wanted to take with her on the honeymoon. She had just found it and was going to leave again, when she heard voices in the study: Roger Cordell and another man. They were speaking in German.

What an odd time for anyone to visit! The wedding began in less than an hour. Odd, certainly, but also a time when someone could be sure to find Cordell alone! Accident, or intention? She could not leave now without calling attention to herself. She had already heard too much.

"Are you sure about this? Once started, you know, there will be no going back," the stranger said.

"Do you think I haven't thought about it, weighed it again and again?" Cordell answered, his voice urgent, even frightened. "It always comes back to the same."

"I can't make promises," the man replied.

"For God's sake, do you think I don't know that? I've watched the bloody thing take form, grow like some sick incubus, feeding on the weak, the vulnerable, the frightened, until it can consume anybody . . ."

Margot stiffened. What on earth was he talking about? His voice grated with emotion. It reminded her of people during the air raids, during the war. There was a deep, devouring fear.

"I know. I know!" the other voice replied. "And you know what the cost will be, if we do this, and we're caught?"

"Of course I do," Roger said tartly. "But have you thought of the cost if we don't?"

"Nothing's guaranteed. The Fatherland Front has a lot of power and it's growing."

"Yes. And I think of the cost if we don't even try. But it will be paid, sooner or later, by everyone. Not only by us or our children, but their children, too."

"Has Cecily any idea . . . ?"

"For God's sake, of course not!" Cordell's voice was almost strangled in his throat.

"If you're sure . . ."

"Of course I'm not sure! I'm not sure of anything, except that to stand apart and not even try is the one thing that's wrong. I'm going to give my daughter away to that ambitious would-be dictator today and there's not a damn thing I can do about it. My wife thinks it's the surest way to keep her safe . . ." His voice cracked and he clearly struggled to keep it level. "She could

205

be right. I . . . I can't bring myself to tell her what I believe . . . what I've seen. But you need a bloody long spoon to sup with the devil. I can only hope that in poisoning myself, I'll poison him, too."

There was silence beyond the door. Margot waited. There was nowhere in here to hide. No cupboards. No curtains heavy enough to conceal her. She could feel the sweat trickling down her skin, inside her glorious, rust-colored silk dress. It was as close fitting as it could be, without vulgarity. It felt like a cocoon now, something she wanted to break out of.

"Then I'll begin," the man said from beyond the study door.

She heard Cordell say something, then footsteps, one set of them going to the door to the hall. There was a rustle of paper. Cordell was still in the study. What was she going to do if he stayed?

She had to get out! Cecily would be looking for her. If she insisted that she had heard nothing, he would know she was lying. She could hardly say she'd fallen asleep. At this time in the morning? Today, of all days? And standing up!

She looked at her watch. She had only a few minutes before she should go to check if Cecily was ready. And she had to get into

206

her own car to follow them. That driver would soon be here, too.

There was nothing for it but to face Cordell honestly. She turned the handle and pulled the door open. It squeaked faintly on its hinges. She had not even noticed it when she came in.

Cordell swung round to face her. The color drained out of his skin. For a moment, he fought for words, even as he knew they were pointless.

She was overwhelmed with pity for him. He struggled, and the net tightened. Everyone he loved could so easily be hurt, even destroyed. She walked forward without even thinking. It was the only thing she could bear to do. She put her hand very gently on his arm. "Be careful, Roger, please."

"Margot . . ."

"Don't try to explain," she said quickly. "I understand what I can see, and a few things that Elena told me. There are things of which we see only bits and pieces, and we can only guess what the rest is, or could become. I'll look after Cecily and do all I can to make this a wonderful day. What happens after that . . . nobody knows."

"Winifred . . ." he began, then stopped, his face filled with distress.

"I know," Margot said quickly. She gave

him a quick smile. Then she turned away and walked to the door, opened it, and went through without looking back.

The wedding itself was beautiful. The church was not a large one and was filled with people, even spilling out into the warm sunshine in the street. The families of the bride and groom and all their close friends were inside. Margot just managed to be at the back, on the aisle, as Cordell walked slowly past her, with Cecily on his arm. Whatever Cecily felt — tension, fear, just nervous excitement on the brink of what might be the most important decision of her life — she looked beautiful, vivid and confident, even through her light veil. She walked with her head high and with an extraordinary, almost regal grace.

Again, Margot found the tears prickling in her eyes, but it was not from grief for the past, for all the people who could have been here, if they had come home from the war. It was from emotion for Cecily: hope, courage, trust that fate would be kind to her, that she would find all the strength she would need.

Margot glanced toward the front of the church and saw the back of Winifred's head, the elegant tilt of her hat. It was blue-gray;

its sweeping brim would reflect the color of her eyes. Winifred was still beautiful in a luminous, fragile way. And she was prepared to pay any price at all to protect her only child.

The organ music swelled, filling the huge vault of the ceiling with a happy, glorious sound.

Cordell and Cecily were almost at the altar.

Margot was too far toward the back to recognize particular people, but she saw plenty of gray or balding heads above military uniforms. And there was a gorgeous array of hats: white, pale pink, blue, red, green, decorated with feathers, flowers, silk, velvet ribbons, with brims of every width and at every angle. Margot imagined what kinds of faces were beneath them and why they were here.

She watched Hans. He stood very straight. His uniform was immaculate, his thick, fair hair shone under the light. He stood with his back to the body of the church. She tried to imagine his expression. What was he thinking? Was he listening to the words? Did he believe in the God to whom he was giving lip service in the promises he made? Or was Adolf Hitler his god in this world?

She forced the thought out of her mind,

lest she have to face the fear that the essence of it was true.

The vows were complete, the sermon over, and organ music filled the air with elation and joy. Hans and Cecily turned and walked back down the aisle, smiling at friends and semistrangers alike, radiating happiness.

Margot found herself smiling, too, as widely as if she had no chill of doubt at all, as if the music took her on its wings and carried her along.

The meal was lavish, elegant, and in excellent taste. The triumph of Frau Beckendorff or Winifred? Or an uneasy alliance of the two?

Margot moved with ease among the guests, most of them speaking to each other in German, but also finding many British, from the embassy in particular. They were there as a courtesy to Cordell, and perhaps out of affection and loyalty for Cecily herself. It would not do to have an English girl marry a German and her own people not turn out in elegance and charm to support her, to pretend they were delighted and there was nothing to disturb their equanimity and self-assurance.

The clothes were gorgeous. Critical as she was, Margot was impressed and delighted beyond merely the styles; it was the confidence reflected in the women themselves, in their identity with the new Germany. Even possibly the alliance between Britain and Germany? It was more than coincidence that the bride was English. It was she who was now a member of the Beckendorff family, with its name, its heritage. She had promised to love, honor, and obey Hans, and he had promised to cherish and provide for her. But her worldly goods had become his.

Margot pushed that out of her mind and disposed herself to be as charming as possible, to speak to everyone, perhaps just a little bit, to make sure that all her old friends continued to keep in touch with her, invite her to their social events, keep the connections alive.

It was not difficult. Few people had forgotten her or failed to recognize her now. She kept the smile on her face wide and bright to fend off any attempts at sympathy. No one would inquire if she had married again.

It was, of course, easier to avoid the subject with strangers, such as Hans's friends and family. She was used to polite and relatively meaningless conversation. It was part of her family's life, her father's professional skill, to seem to be interested,

211

well informed, impressed by other people's lives and cultures. She could do it; her knowledge of German served her well, allowing her to pick up the undertones as she watched faces. The thought flickered through her mind that had she been male, she might have followed in her father's footsteps professionally. The new freedoms since the war, would they eventually extend so far as to let women be ambassadors?

She joined a conversation about current politics with Cecily's new father-in-law. She offered no opinions, although there were questions she would like to have asked, questions to which the answers would have been very revealing, but they would have told her things she could not listen to without betraying her own beliefs.

"Of course, there would have to be some," one elderly man observed.

The several moments Margot had been there, he had hardly moved position. It suddenly occurred to her that he was wearing a corset! Vanity? Or, far more likely, a serious back injury. She watched him as if she were listening to him intently, and saw the occasional wince of pain.

"Of course," Herr Beckendorff agreed. "The one at Dachau is only the beginning. It is all part of finding our identity again."

Margot opened her mouth to speak and changed her mind.

Herr Beckendorff saw and raised his pale eyebrows. "You were going to say something, Frau Driscoll?" His expression was courteous, but there was an expectation of criticism in his eyes.

Margot's mind raced to find something to say that was not critical. She knew what the camp at Dachau was for. Cordell had mentioned it. What could she say that was not offensive to the three men around her, and yet not a betrayal of herself? "It is a task so vast, I cannot see the end of it," she answered with a very slight smile. She bit her lip. "I hope Hans will not have to . . . spend time involved in that. I can see that it is socially necessary, but not the occupation for a brave soldier." Had she said too much?

Herr Beckendorff lifted his chin a little. "Of course. You are very perceptive, Frau Driscoll. Hans is an excellent soldier. The army knows that. I think he's due for a promotion quite soon. I think being in charge of camps like Dachau is a good position for those who have no actual military ability, not the courage or the decisiveness for leadership. Don't you agree, Gustav?"

"Or someone retired from active service," Gustav replied, easing his back a little by moving his weight from one foot to the other and wincing very slightly.

It was on the edge of Margot's tongue to suggest that they move to one of the tables surrounded by chairs, so he could sit, but she thought he might take it as an insult to his dignity, and she said nothing.

The conversation moved to the possibilities of honor in active service, now that there was no serious fighting.

Margot remained silent, listening to the pride in Herr Beckendorff's voice, the stiffness as he stood a little straighter and spoke of his hopes for Hans. She pretended to be listening to him and discreetly studied the other guests standing around with wineglasses in their hands, many with plates of food. Everyone seemed to be engaged, animated, many of the men in uniform, the women in the height of fashion, quite international. There was nothing provincial about the lines or the colors of their clothes. London, Paris, and Rome were all represented.

Cordell joined them, perhaps doing his duty as host. This was, after all, his daughter's wedding. He was welcomed, thanked for the excellent hospitality, and complimented. As far as Margot could judge, it was all completely sincere.

"The most beautiful bride I've seen," Gustav said.

"Indeed," Herr Beckendorff agreed. "They make a perfect couple."

"Indeed," another young man concurred quietly. His name was Stephan; he appeared to be a friend of both Cordell's and Beckendorff's.

Cordell followed Stephan's eyes, but Margot was looking at him and not the rest of the room. She saw perfectly controlled politeness, a gentleman caring for his guests on a happy occasion. She glanced down at his hand and recognized the clenching fingers too stiff to move. How far was he from breaking? Was it all because Cecily was marrying into this family, this culture, where he could no longer protect her from the day-to-day barbs and the unthinking cruelty of those who believed themselves superior? Or from the major tragedies that he feared — believed — might be ahead.

She looked beyond them to where Winifred was talking to a small group of people. She looked lovely, gentle and happy, a mother who had succeeded in marrying her daughter into a proud and privileged position, to a young man who loved her and was already several rungs up the ladder of success.

Cordell was speaking and Margot had missed what he was saying.

". . . to the cart," he finished.

She wanted to ask what they were talking about, but it would betray an interest she was not supposed to have. She stood there silently, being polite, decorative, and aching with fear of a future of which she could see only shadows. She was deeply afraid of what the darkest parts were hiding.

"Of course, Dollfuss is useless," Gustav said, shaking his head. "Poor little beggar, he's bitten off more than he could ever swallow."

"That'll be taken care of," Herr Beckendorff said, dismissing the subject.

Cordell put his hand on Margot's arm, outwardly a gentle touch, as if to guide her, but actually his grasp was hard, a warning not to say anything.

She was standing quite near to him, close enough to smell the faint bittersweet aroma of his aftershave and be aware of his warmth. She smiled and hoped he was aware of it. The last thing she intended was to make anything worse.

"What do you think, Cordell?" Gustav said sharply.

"Reluctantly, I agree with you," Cordell answered. "A man overtaken by history. At

216

another time, perhaps . . ."

"I told you!" Herr Beckendorff said. "He's perfectly sound, as the British would say!" He made as if to put his hand on Cordell's shoulder, but Margot was in the way. "A good word, 'sound,' " he repeated.

Cordell winced.

Margot put her hand over his on her arm. Only afterward did she realize what a possessive gesture it was.

CHAPTER 11

When he had first retired, Lucas had been delighted to have time to use in whatever way he wished. Even waste it, if he wanted. There were rows of books in his study that he had never had time to read, and they still called to him. But now that there was no urgency, the thought held far less interest for him. Even the philosophers he had believed he wished so much to study seemed either so obvious as to be tedious, or so abstruse as to leave him uncertain that they meant anything at all.

He sat down. His latest book of choice was on the table, its place unmarked because he knew perfectly well he did not intend to go back to it.

Beside his feet, Toby stood up and wagged his tail hopefully.

"All right," Lucas yielded without a fight. "We'll go for a walk."

Lucas had said the magic word and Toby

began to dance impatiently from one paw to the other.

At that moment, the front doorbell rang. Josephine was in the back garden, so Lucas walked out of his study to answer it, Toby pattering behind him. He opened the door and faced a uniformed policeman.

The man stepped forward a bit. "Good morning, sir. Are you Mr. Lucas Standish?" He looked very grave.

Lucas felt the first twinge of alarm. Police were connected with crime and tragedy. "What has happened?" he asked automatically, his mind going to Charles and Katherine.

"I'm very sorry to have to tell you, sir, that Mr. Gladstone Canning has passed away. It appears to have occurred sometime yesterday evening." He looked profoundly uncomfortable. He was a young man — at least, compared to Lucas and Stoney — perhaps in his late thirties. "The postman found him this morning. He had no near relatives, but there was a reference to you in a note left on his desk, on top of everything else. I don't know if you are related, sir, or just a good friend, but the message said we should contact you should anything happen to him."

"I see," Lucas said slowly. "Thank you."

Stoney had been an old man, older than Lucas, and yet he had seemed so alive, so full of thoughts and feelings, ideas and knowledge amassed in a lifetime of observation. It was a violence to the mind to think that he had ceased to exist, just like that! Yesterday, he was; today, he was not.

"Are you all right, sir?" the policeman said with concern. "Can I call someone for you?"

"No, thank you," Lucas answered, finding the words difficult to say. "I am perfectly all right and my wife is at home. Stoney was an old friend."

Of course he was all right. People did die, God knew, far too many of them before they'd ever really tasted life. He shook his head. He should be used to it. He hadn't seen Stoney for several months, and then saw him just days ago. He hadn't observed that Stoney was ill. Why hadn't he said anything? He tried to recall if Stoney had seemed pale, lost weight, appeared to be in any kind of pain. Nothing came to him. He had looked older, but everybody looked older.

The policeman raised an eyebrow awkwardly. "Stoney?"

"Short for 'Gladstone,'" Lucas said briefly.

"You knew him a long time, sir?"

"Fifty years, or about that." It was an amazing thought: so long, and yet seeming now much too short.

"I'm very sorry, sir. Do you think you will be well enough to come and identify him?"

"For heaven's sake," Lucas exclaimed incredulously. "Aren't you sure who he is?"

"I think we'd prefer to do better than just the postman's view, sir, despite the fact that he was found in Mr. Canning's house. If you don't mind. And we have to put his affairs into someone's hands. If you are not —"

"Of course I am able, damn it!" Lucas snapped. "I am not on my last legs, or anywhere near it."

"You looked a bit shocked, sir," the policeman said apologetically.

"I *am* shocked. I've known him a long time. Was it a heart attack?"

"No, sir, he fell and hit his head."

Suddenly, Lucas's attention was total, thoughts whirling in his mind. Hit his head? Violence, accidental or . . . "I'll come. I must tell my wife." He turned away, leaving the man on the step. Hospitality did not even enter his mind. He headed back into the kitchen. "Josephine, where are you?"

She came in from the garden at the sound of his voice. She saw his face and her

221

expression changed. "What is it? What has happened?"

"The police. Stoney's dead. They want me to go and identify him and . . ." He saw the surprise in her eyes turn immediately to grief. And then sympathy.

"I'm so sorry, Lucas. I didn't know he was ill. At least —"

"I'm not sure that he was," he cut across her. "He fell. The postman found him. They want me to identify him officially. And it seems he left a letter naming me as the person to be informed."

"Of course." She undid her pinafore and hung it up on the nearest hook, revealing the blue and white dress she was wearing beneath it.

"Do you mind coming with me?" he asked.

"Really, Lucas." She gave him a glance he was not sure how to read, but he was extraordinarily grateful. This news had shaken him more than he would have expected.

The policeman was still waiting a little awkwardly on the step. It must be one of his most difficult duties, and at another time Lucas would have been sorry for him.

"How do you do?" Josephine said politely. "We will take our own car."

222

"Ma'am, there is no —"

She fixed him with a steady stare. It was not unkind, but it froze his remark, whatever it had been.

"Yes, ma'am."

It was not a long drive, about thirty-five minutes, but neither Lucas nor Josephine spoke, filled with memories, each concerned for the other. There would be enough to say later. They were on the edge of the city and they moved quickly in the opposite direction from most of the traffic. The trees in the small copses of wood were just beginning to turn color. The chestnuts like liquid amber deepening here and there; willows still trailed streamers of green. The wild roses in the hedges were long finished, and they showed bunches of orange hips where flowers had been.

Lucas thought of blackberries; they would be ready, but he did not say so. "Why does loss make you notice the beautiful things so much more?" he said instead.

"Because you don't know if the dead still see them," she replied. "I like to think they do."

"Do you believe that, Jo?"

"I don't know, but I don't dare disbelieve," she replied.

He smiled and said no more. He knew

what she meant. As he grew older, life became ever more precious. He took it for granted sometimes. He lifted his hand off the steering wheel for a moment and touched hers, where it lay in her lap.

They reached Stoney's house behind the police car. The policeman got out and led them in through the big oak front door and into the hall. It had not changed since Lucas had been there seven or eight years ago. There were the same familiar pictures on the wall; he remembered the carved newel post at the bottom of the stairs, and he recalled with a sudden clear ache how Stoney had loved its lines, and must have run his hand gently over the curves a thousand times.

A man who appeared to be the local doctor came out of a side room and the policeman introduced him. "Dr. Hardesty, thank you for waiting for us. This is Lucas Standish and Mrs. Standish."

"How do you do?" the doctor said, nodding grimly. He was a lean, dark man with an intense face. "Sorry to have to inform you of Mr. Canning's death. We presume it is Mr. Canning, but we need a formal identification by someone who knew him, if you would be so kind? I understand that there is no close relative to take care of his affairs."

"Not in England anyway," Lucas replied. "He lost most of his family in the war; the surviving ones are pretty distant, both emotionally and literally. Australia, I believe."

"It happens," Hardesty replied. "This way. However . . ." He looked at Josephine, as if to bar her way, his face showing a sudden pity.

"I was in France during the war, Doctor. I have seen at least as many dead men as you have," she replied with a sad shake of her head.

His hand, which was stretched out to hold her back, fell to his side. "I doubt it, but of course you may, if you wish. Sometimes it helps . . ." He did not complete the idea.

Lucas knew that she was going in to help him, not Stoney and not herself. He said nothing, but he followed the doctor silently into the smaller room.

Stoney was lying on his back on a stretcher laid alongside the dining-room table. Underneath the light, he looked smaller than he had standing up, and he was fully dressed, except for his shoes. His hair was ruffled. He looked as if he could have been asleep, apart from the large and bloody bruise on his temple.

Lucas stared at him in silence, remembering the things they had endured together: a jumble of victories and losses, laughter and pain, sudden surprises. But most of all there had been a deep loyalty that had tied everything together. Perhaps that was what friendship was.

"Is this Mr. Canning, sir?" the policeman asked quietly.

"Oh, yes," Lucas said as he turned to Hardesty. "What was it? A stroke? A heart attack? Or did he hit his head on the way down? That looks like a hell of a blow." He frowned. "I presume you've looked at that pretty carefully."

"He was found at the foot of the stairs," Hardesty explained. "If he had the attack somewhere near the top, he'd have fallen the rest of the way hard, but there aren't any marks that we can see, apart from that one. The dead don't bleed; I dare say you know."

"But he bled," Josephine pointed out.

"Not badly, really," Hardesty replied. "We'll see if there are any other bruises or injuries when we examine him more closely, but I don't see that it makes any difference. The police say there's no sign of anyone else having been here. There's definitely no indication of a break-in or a struggle." He turned back to Lucas. "I'm perfectly sure of that. Don't distress yourself. It's a shock to his friends and family, but it's a very quick way to go." He gave a rather stiff smile, not out of lack of sympathy, more probably because he had had to say much the same to many people, and he knew it was little enough comfort.

Josephine said only what was necessary to be polite. But after the doctor and the police had gone, taking Stoney's body with them, she and Lucas were left in the house to go through his papers and make any notifications that might be necessary. They also had to inform Stoney's relatives, find his will, and perform all the other duties following a sudden death.

They heard the car pull away and silence settled again. Lucas turned to Josephine. He wanted to determine if anything about Stoney's death made her uneasy, or if it was only sadness that took the light out of her face. If it was as the doctor and police had said, there was no proof that this was anything other than an ordinary domestic death, inevitable at some time. And Stoney's death had been comparatively easy. No fear, no indignity, and possibly only a moment's pain.

He looked at her to read her face. Was it just grief, or was there something else?

"I'm so sorry, my dear," she said quietly. "It's a shock, even though he was old. Pieces of our lives being chipped away reminds us of our own fragility, and how precious life is." She moved closer to him and touched his arm very gently. "What is it? Don't let guilt eat at you. You were kind to him; and you could not have prevented this."

He put his hand over hers. "I suppose not, but when he came to me he was seriously worried about a lot of figures he'd collected. He thought there was something badly wrong. I agreed with him, but I didn't do anything about it."

"What could you have done?" she asked reasonably.

"I don't know." Still, he had the feeling he could have done something.

Josephine was waiting.

"He had a lot of figures," he told her again. "He said they showed some pretty large movements of money. It seems he kept detailed records of the amounts, as well as their transfers to unknown destinations."

"Theft," she said.

"Stoney didn't know, but that's not what he thought." Lucas tried to remember exactly what Stoney had said, but the words eluded him. Only the impression was sharp in his mind, the worry and the fear. "I think he suspected the money was being hidden in some secret fund."

"Belonging to people we should be afraid of?" Her eyes were very steady, her face pale now.

He looked at her and saw a shadow cross her eyes. "Yes," he agreed. "Very probably Nazi money. But precisely who and what for, I have no idea. He was going to follow it up." It was barely a question now. In his own mind, he was certain of it.

"Yes, of course," she said with a tight smile. "What else could he possibly do? And he told you because he wanted to see if you shared his fears." She bit her lip very slightly. "And he was right, and that is why he is dead." That was now her assumption, and it was up to him to deny it.

"I can't argue with that," he said. "I'm trying, and it doesn't work."

"I have to know," she insisted.

"Of course you do, my dear. It was unfinished business. If you are right, then there is someone guilty of Stoney's death. What greater and more dangerous purpose had he begun to discover that whoever is behind it had to kill him?"

229

"What do you think we should do?" she asked.

"We?" He felt his throat tighten at the word.

"Of course *we,*" she said tartly. "I suggest we search the house, in case he left you some kind of message, or at least evidence we could follow. And we had better do it now, in case other people come to the same conclusion as soon as they hear of Stoney's death."

"You don't think there might be someone responsible for it who knows far better than we do exactly what happened?" he asked, thinking aloud. "I am afraid I do."

She looked doubtful. "In that case, they will already have searched. If we can't find proof of that, I'm not sure what there is left for us to do." She looked around the room, seeing shelves and shelves of books until there was hardly any wall space left. The few pictures were landscapes, with high views from the Pennines, smooth water in the Lake District, always a sense of space and memories. And imagination. "I see nothing disturbed here," she added.

"They wouldn't leave it disturbed," Lucas answered. "If they did, the police might take it for a burglary, and that would mean a lot of further investigation . . . and a likely assumption of murder. Although Stoney was untidy — or looked it to others — he always knew where everything was." He gazed around with an overwhelming sense of loss. Without Stoney's presence, it looked chaotic.

"What will it be — this evidence of a secret fund? Papers? Figures? Names?" Josephine asked.

"Almost certainly figures." He stared at the shelves, seeking a pattern, but they looked in order exactly as he would have expected them to be. "We could search through this lot for the rest of our lives."

"He would expect you to look for it," Josephine said quietly. "So he would have put it somewhere you would look, but other people would not. How well did you know him, Lucas, really? Memory and sentiment aside."

"Lately, not so well," he answered. "But ages ago we were close. He was an odd duck, eccentric, good at conversation — sometimes he was very funny — and he was always kind." He heard again the sound of laughter from so many evenings long ago on the river, cricket games won or lost, but played hard, all with an innocence that they would never see again, that the next generation could not even imagine. It tore away part of your own life when those who remembered the same shattering events, the victories and defeats, were no longer there, no longer survivors but part of the vast bank of memories . . . Now there was an aching space where Stoney had been.

"Where would he expect you to look?" Josephine asked again. "What was important to him that only you knew?"

"Not in the pages of a book," Lucas said with certainty, thinking as he spoke. "It's such an obvious place, and easy to search, if tedious. All Stoney's books would have been read. It's not as if you could look for uncut edges."

"His papers?" she suggested. "Not behind a photograph or a painting, that's obvious, too."

"We'll start with his papers," he agreed. "I might recognize something."

"What would you like me to do?" she asked.

"Make sure there isn't anything in the places we've ruled out, just to be sure."

Reluctantly, he turned to Stoney's desk: the drawers, the piles of papers, letters, old diaries, and photographs. He sat in Stoney's chair and started methodically, looking through one after another. He felt uncomfortable about it, but it must be done. He had not intended to read the letters, only to see if there was anything added or concealed in them. Mostly they were from old friends. He ended by reading them all. He realized that Stoney had observed far more than Lucas had imagined, and that he was funnier. In the diaries, Lucas recognized himself in Stoney's view of him, standing on a punt in a summer evening, feeling awkward and afraid of falling in, and believing he looked dashing. Stoney had made fun of him gently. "Standish is so terribly clever," he had written, "and yet unintentionally so funny, I sometimes wonder if he knows it."

Lucas knew it now, looking back, but he had not known it at the time.

He skipped down the rest of the memories, tears coming unbidden to his eyes. Stoney had thought better of him than he deserved. It was clear in his choice of words, his gentleness. Lucas wished he had lived up to it. He was tempted to linger over each page; it was like having Stoney back again yet just out of reach.

He read pieces about Peter Howard that he had not known. Vulnerabilities he had hidden from others that, strangely, Stoney had seen. They had not been intellectual so much as emotional. Lucas had never appreciated how much Peter had grieved for his elder brother. He had tried to live up to their father's hope for both of them, and his father had not allowed him to. Reading it in Stoney's words, Lucas could see it for himself now. How had he missed it before?

"I think he's given up at last," Stoney had written in a diary a year ago:

The gap in friendship has been partially filled by Standish. And he'll be gentle, even if he has no idea why. Howard's father will have lost both his sons, the fool. One to war, one to indifference. Peter is a good man. He might even become a great one. But like everybody else, he needs to be loved by someone, or at the very least to have been loved, and to know it. To walk entirely alone is to endanger your balance, to lean too far one way, in circles, without realizing it, until it is too late. I think Standish knows that instinctively, if not in-tellectually. We'll see.

Was that true? At least, in part? It felt right. It brought brief memories to mind, sharp and cutting with truth. He had no idea Stoney had seen and understood so much.

Stoney also mentioned Jerome Bradley, who was now head of MI6, and Peter

Howard's immediate superior, whom he disliked intensely. Of course, he did not say so to Lucas, but it was in his omissions, the tightening of his mouth when Bradley was mentioned, as if he did not intend to betray it. Emotion in such relationships could be dangerous: they should be soundly based on loyalty, respect, trust, but also judgment, the ability to stand apart and see both sides of any decision, or however many sides there were, even an unthought-of third or fourth alternative.

It was beginning to grow cooler as the sun's warmth faded when Lucas at last found the information he needed. It was quite easily seen, but not so easily recognized. He had discarded most of the papers as unimportant calculations that Stoney had forgotten to dispose of. Stoney had been something of a squirrel. Then Lucas looked at them again and realized they were not as casual as they had at first seemed. The more he followed the figures, disregarding the signs of addition and subtraction, the more he saw a pattern in them. They were not calculations, as he had first thought; they were lists.

Josephine came into the room without his noticing. He looked up to find her sitting in the chair opposite him, waiting.

"What is it?" he asked, noticing that the light was deepening on the floor and shadows were encroaching further. "Have you found something?"

"I think so, but so have you," she answered. "What is it?"

"Lists, but disguised as calculations," he said. "Carefully hidden. They look crazy, full of error, until you try altering the pluses and minuses, and then suddenly it makes sense. I'm not a mathematician, but I can see the patterns. I think it's money transferred secretly, well covered, but big amounts and over quite a few years."

"Embezzlement?" she said incredulously.

"It's a hell of a lot, if it is. I think there would have been a fearful stink if it had been known. There certainly would have been a crisis somewhere."

"Then what, if it's not stolen? Why did Stoney care? And even more than that," Josephine added, "why was he killed? It's got to be something more than a hidden embezzlement, to murder for it. Are you certain he was killed?"

Lucas did not want to say so, as he was wondering if the crisis was all in their imagination, or rather in Stoney's. And because they cared for him, they were looking for some answer to his obsession, and to their own grief. It hurt like a knife turned in a wound to think that a magnificent mind could have drifted into such a loss of reason in his old age. Or *was* it possible that hundreds of thousands of pounds were being embezzled and laundered through MI6? Whose money? And why secretly, if it was empowered by the government?

"What, then?" Josephine pressed.

"I don't know yet."

"You didn't answer me," she pointed out. "Do you think he was killed? Or do you think he had a heart attack or stroke sometime late yesterday evening?" She made it only half a question. Clearly, she intended to answer it herself. "He was still dressed, so say it was before eleven at night, definitely before midnight."

"Possibly," he conceded. "Go on."

"And hit his head when he fell at the top of the stairs?"

"Yes, you can see slight scrape marks. And it would perfectly explain his bruises and the faint mark on the wallpaper at the side. I did notice it," he admitted.

"And the smear of blood on the bottom step," she added.

"So?" Lucas was not certain what she was driving at, but it chilled him to think there was anyone else involved in Stoney's death.

"I know." She bit her lip. "But it would not explain the blood marks in the potting shed."

"In the potting shed?" He was lost. "What are you talking about?"

"Haven't you noticed how beautifully Stoney's garden is kept? He did it himself. Haven't you looked at his hands? No matter how many times, no matter how hard he tried to clean them, the earth stayed in his fingers."

He looked at her more intently. Her face was creased with sadness. He knew her so well. She was seeing in her mind the care a lonely man gave to his flowers, the beauty he had a part in creating.

"He cut himself." He offered the obvious explanation. "He probably put a plaster on it, so there's no blood in here. I've seen enough of the papers. I'd have seen any blood."

"Unless it was dark," she said.

"Stoney wouldn't have been working in the dark," he argued. "There's no lighting out there, not unless he's put it in very recently."

"He hasn't, I looked. He doesn't have anything tropical, and there's no heating."

Lucas thought for a moment. "Then he

cut himself on whatever it was before dark."

"And if he has no cut?" she asked.

"What? You think he hit his head? You think the blood in the potting shed was from his head wound?"

"Yes, I do." Josephine was quite certain. It was unmistakable in her face. Dr. Hardesty would have noticed a cut. "To bleed this much — and scalp wounds do bleed badly. It was a hard abrasion that we saw, bad enough to have killed him. We are only assuming it was a heart attack, and that the wound was a result of his fall. Lucas, what if he was attacked out in the potting shed and carried inside, cleaned up from the earth and compost he had been working with, then thrown down the stairs?"

"Aren't you bending the facts to fit the pattern you imagine?" he asked, but gently. She looked so earnest.

She was not fazed in the least. "A theory has got to fit all the facts, Lucas. The blood in the shed has barely congealed. It's from, at latest, last night; it certainly wasn't several days ago. And it has to be from before dark, because he wouldn't work out there after dusk. There's nothing else there with blood on it. I looked. But there are certain tools you'd usually expect to find in a potting shed, and they aren't there. Particularly, a small spade."

"Perhaps he didn't have one."

"Yes, he did. Apart from the space where it would have been hung on the wall, and two empty rails it would hang on, the kind of garden work he did would need one. I have one myself and I know what I use it for, which jobs. It took me a while to work out what must have happened. Someone hit him with a spade pretty hard. It probably killed him outright. They carried him inside, washed his hands, changed his shoes to indoor slippers. They probably took the spade with them."

"Why not simply wash it?" he asked, playing devil's advocate, but he knew the answer.

"Not easy in the growing darkness to be sure of washing off every speck of blood, not if they were in a hurry. Blood seeps into a wooden handle, between the cracks. It would seem unnecessary to them for it to be spotlessly clean if it was found in a week or so. Who would be surprised? Gardeners get all sorts of cuts and bruises and scratches, and it would be too late to look at the body for the wound."

"Wouldn't Hardesty have noticed that the body had been moved?" Lucas persisted.

"It had fallen all the way down the stairs,"

she pointed out. "The one thing it couldn't have done is carry itself from the potting shed to the back door, through the kitchen, and up to the top of the stairs, ready to be in the right place to fall."

"Are his boots at the back door?" he asked.

"Yes." Josephine did not take her eyes from him. "But there are no tracks of them back from the potting shed to the door, though there are some on the way out."

He stared at her. Her gaze was direct, troubled. She was waiting for him to reply.

"You are sure?" It was not really a question, just a delaying of the moment he had to acknowledge it. He stared at Josephine. She had seen something she understood and could not deny.

"I'm sure there's something wrong." She bit her lip. "Lucas, he went out, but he did not walk back, not on his feet. Can we look the other way and still face ourselves? Exactly what were we all fighting for in the war? Not for another war, God knows, but not to avoid it using any means, including joining the enemy or becoming him."

Of course, she was right, but *exactly* right? He could not answer that because he could see so little ahead of him.

She waited for him.

"We must tell the police that they should

241

investigate Stoney's death, because it's murder." He stood up slowly. He was stiff. There would have been no crick in his knees ten years ago. His mind would have been quicker. He would not have seen so many clouds of obscurity ahead, uncertain and full of the possibilities of war. Was he wrong then . . . or now?

Josephine went with him to the police station. It was at least half an hour before the inspector came out to see them. He was clearly tired at the end of the day, and was straining his patience to deal with two elderly people whose grasp of reality seemed tenuous, at best. It was only because they were obviously grieved and completely out of their depth that he exercised as much patience as he did.

Josephine explained what she had seen in the potting shed.

"And did you see this lost spade, sir?" he asked Lucas.

Lucas kept his temper with difficulty. "Do you mean on another occasion? No, we did not meet in the potting shed. We sat in Mr. Canning's study."

The inspector's face showed his rapidly shortening temper. "Did you find Mr. Canning quite well?"

242

"Yes," said Lucas. "I've known him since we were both students in Cambridge and that was approximately half a century ago. And on and off, all the years between. Better during the war, of course."

"That was a long time ago, sir."

"Fifteen years. Blink of an eye in history," Lucas dismissed it. "Most of us alive now can remember it. We still have our scars, and our losses."

"Yes, sir. I lost my father and I'm in no hurry to see the signs of violence again, especially when it is no more than the sad death of an old man who had a heart attack and fell down the stairs. I'm sure he had a great record during the war, but he's lucky enough to die quickly in his own home, and at a good age. Go back to your house and take your wife with you. She has had a long, sad day. Don't look for violence and crime where there isn't any."

"But —" Lucas began.

"Take an honorable retirement, sir," the policeman said patiently. "And let Mr. Canning be buried in peace and dignity. Do you feel well enough to drive home, or would you like me to have one of my men drive you?"

Lucas felt as if someone had closed black curtains all around him, shutting out all the light. He stared at the younger man for several seconds before he spoke. "Mr. Canning served in MI6 during the war and after it, right up until his death. He risked his life in high and dangerous causes, without ever asking for or expecting any recognition. I know that because at one time I was his commanding officer. I owe him this much, at least. And I will see that you accord it to him." He stood up and took Josephine by the arm.

"You were . . . MI6?" The policeman appeared stunned, and then his expression reflected profound awe and respect.

"And I'm trusting you to keep that between us," said Lucas.

With that, he and Josephine walked out into the gathering night.

CHAPTER 12

"There's no point in going back," Aiden said grimly, as he and Elena walked along the quayside and turned sharply down one of the narrower streets, the alley walls closing in on them. He was slightly ahead of her. He stopped suddenly and caught hold of her elbow, pulling her to a stop. He leaned forward, and for a moment, she thought he was going to kiss her.

"Look at me and listen," he said quietly. "You brought me a message. London may not be certain that Max's cover has been blown, but I am. I can't rely on him. In fact, he may already be dead." He went on quietly, urgently, "You can either go back toward the center of the city — I'll take you until you're safe, and you can make it the rest of the way — or, if you come with me, you do as I tell you. It's dangerous . . . very dangerous. If they killed Max, they'll think nothing of killing either of us, or both. Body into the canal. One more suicide . . ."

Elena looked at him, puzzled. It was not
that she doubted what he said; it was his
emotion that confused her. Did he want her
to go or to stay? His voice was scraping with
the intensity of his feelings, but was he
scared, angry, or horrified that this should
all happen here, in this beautiful city, where
the light was so pure, touching the ancient
stones so tenderly? Did Aiden even see that?
Had Max been a friend, as well as his
contact with Peter Howard, his only link
with England and any of the things he was
risking his life to save?

"Of course," Elena said as levelly as she
could. "We have to find out if Max is alive
or not, and if he isn't, then who killed him.
And if possible, how much he told them. It
would be foolish to go back to any place
they know to look for us."

Aiden let his breath out slowly, and his
lips curved in a very slight smile. "You could
behave like a fool with the best of them," he
said. "It was your saving grace, because you
were insufferably clever . . . at times. I don't
know whether you have the courage or
not . . ." He let it hang, waiting to see what
she would do.

Or was it to see what she felt, if she had
the nerve, even the loyalty? Did he wonder

if she was still in love with him? Did he care? She had made such a fool of herself over him and yet, in a strange way, she was right: he had been loyal to England. She could not pretend that she had known that.

It was irrelevant now. She was a photographer! She needed none of her university education, nor the languages she had acquired, unless she used them as a spy.

It was at once absurd and, in the end, the only reality: a matter of life and death. "Doesn't your survival depend on being able to judge who to trust, and who not to?" she asked. "Can't you think of a way to use me? That's unlike you." She kept the bitterness out of her voice . . . didn't she? Why was she even allowing it into her mind?

He started to say something, then changed his mind. "If we get into trouble, I might not be able to save you."

She laughed outright.

"I mean it!" he said sharply, a flicker of anger in his eyes.

"Of course you do," she agreed. "I realized that quite a while ago. Really, Aiden, do you think that Peter Howard would have sent me if I were that half-witted?"

He hesitated again, carefully searching her face. "Right! We are looking to find Max, if we can, or at least discover what happened to him. But that's secondary. We've got to get the list out of Trieste and back to Howard." Suddenly he smiled; it lit his eyes, changing his whole aspect. "Like old times," he said softly.

For a moment, she was in the past again, as hand in hand they had raced along the narrow spit of sand between Holy Island and the mainland, the tide closing in on them from both sides, swiftly, with ocean strength. They had made it with nothing to spare, feet wet in the first waves that joined to cut off their path. They had fallen on the dry sand, in the sun, holding on to each other, laughing, gasping for breath.

"What are they playing for, Aiden?" she asked.

"Austria," he replied, meeting her eyes, then slowly smiling. "You don't see that?"

"Not yet . . ." she admitted.

"You'll see. Austria to begin with anyway . . ." He did not finish the sentence.

She nearly asked what was next, but she did not want to know, at least until she understood what he meant. "Does Peter Howard know that?" she said instead.

"I never know what he knows and what he doesn't," Aiden answered. "But this I haven't yet told him. I want to understand it better first. That's what I want you to help me find, before we get out of Trieste."

"Then we have to play harder, more cleverly," she said, without the slightest waver in her voice or her look.

He bent forward and kissed her slowly, gently, on the mouth.

She returned it, also gently, with no gasp, no momentary loss of balance. His respect, her self-respect, depended on keeping her balance completely, both physically and emotionally, no matter what feelings surged up inside her. She could not afford to let anything blur her judgment.

"Right," he said, pulling away. "Ready?"

"Yes," she answered without hesitating. There was no doubt in her mind. She must get him out, with whatever knowledge he had. And, of course, the all-important list of names of those secretly involved.

She walked quickly, keeping up with him, her arm linked through his.

They went to the restaurants where Max had worked. Aiden knew the chefs and the managers. He used Elena as a reason: the long-time friend he wanted to take to the very best places in Trieste.

He asked about Max casually, while she took photographs of the most attractive aspects of the restaurants, or the old buildings nearby, hoping to catch the unique character of each. Sometimes people gathered round her and were quite willing to pose, adding color and life to an otherwise purely architectural scene.

Outside the fifth restaurant they had tried, she waited for Aiden to emerge. When he did, his smile faded as soon as they were across the narrow street.

"What did they say?" she asked.

"Keep walking," he ordered.

She glanced at him. His face was grim, and a small muscle was ticking in his temple. Tension. She remembered it from years ago. It had been there when they were driving high over the moors in County Durham: bare, wind-scoured, great shoulders heaved up from land. The brakes had failed. He had barely managed to keep the car under control, until he had swung it round through an open field gate and finally run to a stop in the deep grass.

She remembered the terror and exhilaration. Her heart was pounding and she could see again the flush in his face, the victory! They had made love that night in some small inn, in what seemed the end of the world, near a place called Pity Me. Aiden had said it was a corruption of *petite mer,* but there wasn't a sea for miles around, large or small.

The wave of memory ebbed and left her wondering what peril Aiden had avoided this time, or thought he had. When they slowed down a little, she asked, "What did you learn? Have they seen Max?"

"Not for nine or ten days; I've seen him since then myself," he answered. "Come on, we can't hang about here. I'll be getting noticed soon. No one's seen him in over a week. At least, no one who's admitting it."

Elena considered that while he turned a corner and went north again. The day was getting colder, the narrow roads shadowed. The buildings were high and old, paint peeled off in places, and there were stains from damp and unmended roofs. This was one of the older parts of the city, where centuries of Austrian occupation had left less of a mark. There were no elegant and spacious buildings here; this quarter could be part of any old city that poverty had beaten to its knees.

"There's one last place to look," Aiden said after another five minutes of silence between them. "I can't very well leave you here, but if you come with me, you'll have to keep your mouth shut. Do you think you can do that?" He looked at her dubiously.

"I can be agreeable in English, German,

Italian, and French," she replied firmly. "I can do the silent bit in Spanish as well."

He gave her a sudden brilliant smile with a flash of white teeth. "Good, I like your style — stick to Spanish!"

They had to hurry in order to make the gathering that Aiden said they needed to attend. When Elena told him she needed something to eat, he agreed reluctantly.

"I need more information before we leave," he said with his mouth full. They were in a small restaurant off a side street, eating a quick meal of pasta with an unnamed meat sauce. Seated on stools crowded close together, they had to lean forward until their heads were nearly touching to be sure of hearing each other, and not being overheard by anyone in the crowd around them. They looked fully engaged in their own gossip, quarrels, and making up, but as Aiden warned her, a spy or provocateur with any sense would appear to be just that. "We should look like a courting couple," he said, with another sudden, broad smile.

All sorts of thoughts raced through her head. Is that what they were? At one time, she had believed that totally. Had he always known otherwise? Was she his excuse, his cover? An unintended informant? Of course, he could be more than one thing at a time. So could she! Anything they said might have two meanings, or three . . . or four.

She smiled her agreement, sweetly, straight into his eyes.

She saw only a momentary flicker in answer. Humor? Regret? It didn't matter now. "What do you need?" she asked him quietly.

He looked down for an instant, and then back up again. "I need to get more information for my list, and I need to know for certain if Max is alive or dead, and if they caught him, and I believe they did, how much he told them."

"What could he have told them?" she asked, a chill of fear running through her at what the answer might be.

"I can't see that far," he began, then gave a sharp movement of one shoulder. "About a violent takeover of the Austrian government." His eyes were intent on her face, watching for the slightest shadow of fear, or disbelief.

"By whom?" She managed to keep her voice level, but she knew the answer already. It had to be the Nazis.

"The Fatherland Front," he replied, unhesitating. "Or perhaps a splinter group.

That's what I really need to know. At the moment, it's only a feeling I have . . . a sense of a splinter force within the main body." He was watching her suddenly more closely.

She knew very little of the Front, only the scraps Peter had told her before she had left England. She needed to know who they were and, possibly just as importantly, who Aiden believed they were.

Before she could ask, he understood her thoughts. He had always been quick to read her. At times, it was very comfortable to be so well understood. She used to believe it was because their thoughts were the same, and because he cared. Now she made no judgment, except to be careful and not to try to deceive him, unless she was sure she could succeed. She must trust him only where she had to.

"A group of Germans who believe that Austria's natural place is with Germany . . . as part of it," he was explaining, watching her face. "They are decidedly German in language, culture, and a lot of their heritage."

"So do they want to take over?" she asked very softly. "Or to betray Austria to Germany? What happens to Hungary?"

It was a few seconds before Aiden replied.

She tried to read his face and failed. "I don't know about Hungary, but Austria's fate seems inevitable. I don't think Germany can digest Hungary at the moment . . ."

"Later?" she asked.

His steady gaze did not leave her face. "Perhaps."

"What about Chancellor Dollfuss? Is he in on it?"

"That's what I want to know before I leave Trieste," he replied. "If I can find out . . ."

"How? Who knows?"

He hesitated.

"Wouldn't Peter Howard have someone in Vienna? How would they know more here, in Trieste?" She stopped abruptly. One answer at least was obvious. The main conspirators had to be here. This part of Italy had been Austrian for centuries. It had Italian nationality, but one had but to glance at the great buildings to know that they were not the same in character as those of other Italian cities. It was hard to describe but easy to see, a different kind of beauty that was northern, not of the Mediterranean. It made sense now. No wonder it was important.

"When will it happen," she prompted him. "How soon?"

"Much too soon," he replied. "Maybe in

255

four or five weeks."

A knot tightened inside her. "That soon — really? What is the information you must get back to London?"

Again, he hesitated.

Was she asking too many questions? Should she pretend it did not matter? But it was said now; she could not take it back. Why was she being so cautious, as if she did not trust him? "What can we do about it?" she asked. "What will it help if we know?"

He reached his hand across the table and touched hers. "You're learning, aren't you?" he said wryly. "Perhaps I'd better tell you, just in case I don't get out."

"Aiden! Don't say that."

He smiled with what seemed real pleasure. It brought back memories she would rather not have seen again.

"It's the truth," he said grimly, bringing her back to reality. "Grow up, Elena. That list is dynamite. It has the names of most of the major financial contributors to the cause of the Fatherland Front. I don't mean the odd pound or dollar here or there. I mean millions."

She felt her insides clench. "You said pound or dollar, not mark?"

"I meant it." He leaned forward again, removing his hand from hers. "The names

256

of people who contribute to the cause or invest in it. Even some with investments in both sides, or just in war itself. It's not only valuable, it's dangerous. It holds immense power. What do you think would happen if these names were made public? Or even passed secretly to those in office? The foreign secretary is quietly funding Hitler's overthrow of Austria . . ."

"What?" She froze as if ice had gripped her body.

"Not actually!" he said sharply. "But it could be made just as important. Do you understand now? It's power, even if it isn't used. Knowledge of the list's existence and the threat of exposure would be enough. A small act at first, and they would use it —"

"I see!" she cut him off. "You don't have to paint pictures."

"Howard's a clever man, Elena. Don't ever forget that. And ruthless, if he has to be. All brain, no heart. And believe me, I've known him longer and far better than you have. He told you to get me out. It's good policy to get your people out alive, if you possibly can. But, above all, get the information. He will expect you to take it back to him, whatever happens to me. And to get yourself back, too, if possible, but that list at all costs."

257

She felt as if an iron hand had closed around her. Was that really what she had become part of? Was that who Peter Howard was? And behind that, far bigger, was that who Lucas was? How had she seen nothing of that? Had they — her grandparents — protected her, even Grandma Josephine?

She felt very small, and blind.

She withdrew her hand from the table automatically, then realized too late how it gave her away. "Then, when it is the right time, you had better give it to me," she said, trying to control the wobble in her voice. "I'll hide it not too obviously. Then we'll go and see if you can get the dates right, and if they really matter more than simply taking the list to Howard."

"War is dirty and expensive, Elena," he said softly. "Too often it's about killing. And believe me, dying in the trenches isn't any better. At least there, you are betrayed only by incompetence, not by one thing deliberately pretending to be another. And I don't think you even have the delusion that you are safe."

"But there you have some people you know are your friends, who would save you if they could and die beside you if they had to," she said with an edge of bitterness she would rather not let him hear.

"You have that here, too." He smiled with a downward turn to his mouth. "Even if they are far more difficult to recognize. Howard might just be right about you. We are about to see. There are some people you should meet . . ."

CHAPTER 13

Margot gave herself one last quick glance in the bedroom mirror. She looked almost as she had wished. There were always slight imperfections, but perhaps that was Nature's way of keeping her from too much arrogance. Her next really big birthday would be forty. She was more than half a decade off yet, but it would come soon enough. The faint lines on her face would be harsher then, if she was not careful. She remembered Grandma Josephine telling her that at twenty, or even thirty, you had the face Nature had given you, but at sixty, you had the face you deserved, the one you had made for yourself. Maybe that was why Josephine looked so good: all the lines in her face went the right way.

Margot laughed a lot, but did she smile? To be honest, possibly not.

Tonight, she wore a russet-gold dress that had cost a fortune, and it had been worth it. She was not meant for pastel shades. The burning bronze and gold and brown, close to black, were perfect. She had an ideal figure, and she moved with the grace of a dancer. All those lessons in deportment and etiquette had not been wasted.

This was to be a celebration dinner for Cecily's wedding. When it was over, Cecily and Hans would leave for their honeymoon. It would be short, of course. The demands of duty bent for no one. Their honeymoon would be in a hunting lodge in the Black Forest, lent to them by a man in very high office. That was an honor in itself.

Margot went down the stairs to the main room, where Roger and Winifred would be waiting for her.

Roger was standing, as if he knew exactly when she would appear. For a moment, he was speechless, eyes wide.

Margot smiled, then looked at Winifred, who wore a gown in that shade exactly where green turns to blue, of silk, which made it look almost liquid. The two women could not have been more of a contrast. Margot wondered if that had been simply an accident of natural coloring, or if perhaps they were equally different in nature.

Today, Winifred had handed over her only child to the care — or lack thereof — of an immature young man already destined for high office in Hitler's army. But whatever happened, whether Cecily remained close to her or not, she would still have Roger. Margot had no one on whom to lavish her emotional care. Except, of course, Elena, but that was no substitute.

"You look wonderful," she said to Winifred.

"Autumn and winter," Cordell said, and then, as if he thought better of it, quickly added, "The fulfillment of the year."

Margot smiled widely and caught his eye. "Well rescued, sir," she said very softly.

His mouth tightened in an instant's amusement and acknowledgment. "The season when you reap what you have sowed," he said under his breath.

They went out to the waiting car and were driven through the dusk of the early evening streets, as the lights came on, and stopped at the hotel where the reception and dinner had already begun. This was hosted by Hans's parents, as the wedding itself had been by Roger and Winifred.

Their arrival caused a slight stir, even in so distinguished a crowd, full of women wearing the latest fashion. Margot guessed that many of the gowns were imported from Paris.

Margot understood that it took more than money to carry off style. One needed a figure, grace, and above all, flair. It would be false modesty to pretend she did not have all of them. This was reinforced when she felt everyone's eyes on her as she moved forward to meet people, to be charming, to remember that this evening, of all evenings in her life, belonged to Cecily.

Cecily stood beside Hans and waited for Margot to join them. He was in full dress uniform. Whatever Margot thought of Hitler's soldiers or police, their uniforms were splendid. Hans would never look better. And he was smiling. Cecily wore a shade of rich apricot, which only someone of her vivid coloring could carry off. Margot decided she must try it herself sometime.

"Thank you so much for coming," Cecily said softly, when she kissed Margot on the cheek. "You made the day for me. The best of the past, with the best of the future." She touched Hans lightly with her other hand, without turning to look at him.

For a second, there was a shadow in her eyes, then gone again. Had Margot imagined it?

They were greeted by his father, his fair coloring faded, almost nondescript. His mother stood like a wedge of ice in ivory-colored lace, which was no doubt expensive, as were the diamonds at her throat.

"So nice of you to have come, Mrs. Driscoll," she said with a faint smile. "We have several of your countrymen here. You might know them. Or . . . perhaps not. Lord Wolstenholm? Lady Wolstenholm is quite charming. Her father was, I believe, something to do with the Foreign Office."

"Then my father might know him," Margot replied, wondering if her smile looked as artificial as it felt. "He was ambassador in Berlin for several years."

Frau Beckendorff's fair eyebrows rose. "Lord Wolstenholm? Really? How modest of him not to have mentioned it."

"I'm referring to my father," Margot corrected her. "But he probably wouldn't have mentioned it, either." She deliberately left her expression blank this time.

That seemed to kill the conversation, which prompted Margot to walk away, not needing to pretend interest. She kept smiling as she walked toward Hans. He had moved on and was speaking animatedly with a group of young men in uniforms like his own. They were joined by an older man, far more highly decorated. They treated him with obvious deference. Naturally enough, considering the occasion, most of this man's remarks were directed at Hans. He nodded and smiled, then continued his conversation with some intensity.

Margot listened, but she caught only snatches, as she was obliged to speak to others. She made a few flattering remarks, expressed interest, and sipped her wine.

". . . and a fine future ahead of you," the man in the senior uniform was saying to Hans.

"I shall do everything I can to serve the Führer, sir, and the Fatherland," Hans replied.

It was an ordinary enough response, but it was the underlying emotion in his voice that caught Margot's ear. It was more than a polite reply, more like the fierce reiteration of a vow, an oath of dedication. On his wedding day, it struck a jarring note in Margot's mind.

The older man was saying something enthusiastic. The others joined in with earnestness.

What did it bother Margot if Hans was speaking to a senior officer in his own chain of command? Of course he would use all the enthusiasm he could. Today, of all days, he must feel as if his whole life were before him and all things were possible.

She moved on again and caught sight of

Winifred, who beckoned her over. There were more introductions and polite, optimistic conversations. One of the other women, about Winifred's age, had a son in the diplomatic service. They spoke of recent postings to Vienna. There were comments on the quality of music, the rich culture he was experiencing.

"Well, after all, the Austrians are our natural cousins," someone replied.

"More than that. They are Germans, really," another put in quickly. "They should lose Hungary and come back into a greater Germany. They'd be far better off."

There was a brief exchange of opinions about that, which Margot was careful not to join. It was an idea she had not heard before. But then, in England she would not have.

"They may not be worthy, at first," one of the women said. "But they will see the sense of it."

"At least the ordinary people will," another agreed. "The Führer will accomplish it, you'll see."

"You think so?"

"Oh, there are things ahead we can't imagine," the first woman replied. "This is going to be a great country again. It's our destiny."

Margot opened her mouth to say something, and then changed her mind. She had spoken only German, and no doubt they took her for one of them. It would be a disservice to Cecily to stand out in their company in anything other than glamour.

"You make it seem inevitable," one of the women said.

"It is," her companion replied. "The question is only how long — and, of course, who will prove to be brave and loyal, and who might not. There will be sacrifices . . ."

"There always are, for anything worthwhile."

"Loyalty does not come cheap," another woman agreed, her voice trembling for a moment.

Margot wondered who she had lost in the war, its ashes of ruin still warm.

They went on talking. Were they comforting themselves with delusions?

Margot drifted from one group to another, stopping longer with some. She found herself lectured to enthusiastically on the hopeful and positive things that were on the brink of realization in Germany. These hopes for the future, not only of the people gathered here, but of the whole country — indeed, of all Europe — were part of the optimistic air of a wedding. If there were dark undertones, Margot tried to ignore them, put them down to the ambitions of young men, perhaps a little drunk from the very excellent wine. All German, no French champagne here.

A little while later, she found Cecily again. She looked flushed and excited. Margot was happy for her. Her own wedding had been nothing like this but all memories of Paul were happy, filled with hope of good things. There had been no greed, no desire to dominate, only to build a life for themselves and others, to heal and do it without hate or blame.

She would not have changed places with Cecily and have to spend tonight, and all the nights after it, with Hans, with his ambition, his hunger, the fear she thought she glimpsed in his eyes just for an instant. Everyone in this crowded room expected so much of him. They were here to rejoice, but so many of them were also here to keep him on the narrow road to success, especially in the favor of Hitler.

Did Cecily see that?

"I wish you happiness," Margot said with intense feeling, although she touched Cecily's arm only lightly.

Cecily gulped. "I know you do." She blinked rapidly. "In spite of the fact that you don't like him."

"Cecily . . ."

"Don't," Cecily said quickly. "I know what you're going to say. You are not as hard to read as you think. Be careful, Margot. This is not a time for selfishness. We have to think of our families." She gave a dazzling smile to a senior officer passing by, and he acknowledged it warmly. Her smile vanished as she turned toward Margot again. "Don't say anything to my mother, or I'll not forgive you . . . not ever. Father knows some things more than I do, other things less, but we don't speak of it."

"Did you have to marry Hans?" The instant the words were out of her mouth, Margot regretted them, but it was too late. "I'm sorry," she whispered. "That was cruel and none of my business."

Cecily met her eyes. "I love my parents very much. My mother has invested everything in me, all my life. It's time to give her something back. The illusion of safety, at least. Maybe the reality. If you question my choice of Hans, you'll break that. You won't do that to me."

"No," Margot said vehemently. "Of course I won't."

Anything further was interrupted by Hans joining them and putting his arm around

Cecily protectively. His eyes met Margot's with a candid smile, as if for an instant they really knew each other. "It was so generous of you to come all this way to wish Cecily well, Mrs. Driscoll. It was a kindness we shall not forget. Now, if you will excuse us, I have some very important people eager to meet Cecily." And without waiting for an answer, he moved away. Cecily went with him, close to his side, and she did not look back.

Margot stood stunned. Suddenly, the nightmare was so much clearer, and it made hideous sense. She had no idea how long she stood motionless. Other people swirled past her, full of chatter, laughter getting louder as the wine bottles emptied. Perhaps everybody had their own memories of weddings, theirs or somebody else's. The beginning or the end of happiness. Change, always change.

"We'll miss her," Winifred said from beside Margot. "But it's important."

Margot was startled. "What is?"

"Peace," Winifred said so quietly even the nearest group of people to them could not have heard. "It doesn't happen by itself, just because you've stopped shooting each other at some borderline. We have to forge links that both sides believe in. We have to forget what we lost and start thinking of what we can still keep and build on. You might have to swallow your words sometimes. Roger is good at that, and he's taught me how to do it. Cecily will . . ." She stopped, unable to say the words.

"She'll make a better man of him than he would be without her," Margot filled in quietly. She had no idea whether she meant to say these words or not, but something like that needed to be said.

Winifred gave Margot's arm a little squeeze, then disappeared into the crowd to speak to someone else she knew.

After that, Cecily and Hans left to have their first night in an expensive local hotel and set out in the morning for the hunting lodge. At this time of year, it was still mild, but autumn was coming and the trees were turning color. Occasionally, there would be a nip of frost in the air. For the newlyweds, the honeymoon in the countryside would feel like being on an island away from the world, drenched with beauty. Too short a time, but idyllic. One they would not forget. Margot hoped that, at least for a few days, they would utterly ignore everything to do with the political situation in Berlin, Vienna, or anywhere else. They had so much to learn about each other, day-to-day things that would be woven into the rest of their lives. They could weave memories to carry them through the bleak times of illness or anxiety, the habits and minutiae of daily life.

Margot could have envied Cecily that, but there were also dangers in it. The first tide of magic did not last. Reality could be as gray as a fog-ridden dawn. There were icy mornings when one could not see a single step ahead. You needed courage and good manners to sustain you then. Her memories of Paul had never been marred by a later reality. There had been none, at least not together. Paul had never disappointed, said or done anything shabby.

She suddenly became aware of a man next to her. He was speaking and she had ignored him completely. "I'm so sorry," she said, embarrassed at her own unintended rudeness. "I was . . . daydreaming . . ."

He smiled. He was quite tall, standing very straight in his German army officer's uniform, and it was a moment before she even noticed that his left sleeve was empty, folded back on itself and pinned. He had lost an arm at the elbow. He seemed almost her own age. There was a touch of gray in his dark hair, but many more lines on his face than on hers. Perhaps she had misjudged his age? Or, more likely, he had seen harder times; more physical pain, at least.

"Konstantin Buresch," he introduced himself, with an inclination of his head, rather than a bow, and a silent clicking together of his heels.

"How do you do, Major Buresch?" she said, reading the marks of rank on his uniform. "Margot Driscoll."

"Driscoll," he repeated. "I met a man named Driscoll once. Perhaps I can recollect where. It seems to me it was a good memory, or at least there was good in it."

Margot froze for an instant, then recalled it was not an uncommon name entirely. "Have you spent much time in England?" she asked. It sounded a harmless enough question. There were plenty of Germans in England, as there were English in Germany, and just about everywhere else!

"A few years," he said quietly. "But they treated me well . . ."

She felt clumsy. She should have foreseen that possibility. So, he had been a prisoner of war. She looked at him frankly and saw no anger in his face.

"You are surprised." It was not a question, but an observation. "Actually, it terrified me."

Now she felt a chill settle over her. What

273

was he going to say? It was too difficult to think that her own people were capable of the atrocities she had heard of, but history is written by the victors, not those who lost. Except that, in a sense, everyone who fought had lost. The real winners were the ones who stood apart and then fed on the pickings of the dead of both sides.

She felt a gentle touch on her arm. He had put down his glass and used his one hand to reach out to her.

"We all lost people, we have that in common."

It was as if he had read her mind and the confusion in it. Maybe she was more transparent than she thought. "And yet we learn so little," she said quietly. "We have a generation rising now who knows only the stories of war, not the taste of it, the exhaustion and the loss. I look sometimes, listen to what they are saying — hatred, excuses, blame, solutions that will only make it worse — and I am ashamed. If we do it again, we will all be ashamed."

"Fifteen years. See what another five will bring. But I have found the memory. It was the fifth battle of Ypres. It started in September. I remember it was dark. Mist and smoke drifting across no-man's-land. I was lying in the mud. My arm hurt unbelievably. I had never felt anything like it before, although it was not the first time I was wounded."

Margot forced herself to listen. "But you were rescued." She made it a statement. He was here, he had survived it, he was home.

"Yes." His smile was distant, far away in time and place. "By a British soldier. I must've been making a noise, crying out, because he told me to shut up or we'd attract attention and get shot at. He half carried me and half dragged me, until we got to a trench. We practically fell into it. He went first and caught me, so I didn't fall on my shoulder." He gave a short, sharp laugh. "We both thought it was a trench with people in it, and help."

"Wasn't it?" She couldn't imagine the pain and the fear. He was safe now, although perhaps he would always have pain in his arm, and always dream about what had happened to him.

"No, it was just a really big shell hole," he explained. "I remember he swore dreadfully, strings of words I barely knew, but I knew the intonation and the meaning didn't matter. I joined him, in German. It became a competition. He wasn't hurt, but I knew he was as exhausted and frightened as I was. But he didn't leave me. I don't remember it all. I was in and out of consciousness, and after a while I couldn't think of anything but the pain."

"But you got out? Both of you?" Now she had to know.

"Yes. I couldn't go any further, and he realized that. He left his water bottle with me and went to look for help, just as another volley of shots came over. In the light of the flare, I saw the terror in his eyes . . ."

"But he wasn't hit?" Her voice was nearly strangled.

"No. He took a long swig of the whisky he was carrying, then gave me that, too. Then he scrambled out of the hole and disappeared. I never saw him again, but he must've found someone because a couple of Brits came and got me. They said he had sent them. It seemed he'd got lost, no sense of direction. He rejoined his men. I don't know if he survived or not. I'd like to think that he did."

"What made you think of him tonight?"

He looked around the room. "Well, I believe his name was Driscoll. We sometimes forget that good men fought on both sides."

Tears filled Margot's eyes and she could not stop them. It took a moment before she could force out the words. "Yes . . . indeed."

"I'm sorry," he said with instant remorse.

"I've upset you."

"My husband . . . he died in that battle, the fifth in Ypres. Along with my brother."

His voice, too, was thick with old, deep grief: "That is why we must never, ever do it again. Whatever our differences . . ." He trailed off, staring around the room.

Margot looked at him, then away, and over to where Cecily had gone with Hans, where Winifred, clinging to hope, was doing her duty. Roger must be somewhere. She could not recognize his head among all the others. How many of them were clinging to the coattails of peace and felt anger or shame for what their allies and enemies alike were doing? Above all, their fellow countrymen? What was patriotism compared with humanity? They were busy with avenging old wounds, rather than preventing new ones?

"Thank you for telling me about this," she said, swallowing hard and managing to keep control. "It makes my husband more . . . real. I tried to imagine how he could not be afraid, and I never really succeeded. It took him away from me somehow. Can you understand what I mean?"

"Yes. Tales of courage, rather than the real thing, fragile and very mixed. Real courage is being terrified and doing it anyway. Sometimes, it's just because letting everyone else down would be even worse than being shot. Certainly than losing an arm." Konstantin smiled at her, and this time there was nothing in it but the gentleness of memory shared for a moment.

She turned away before emotion overcame her. When he departed she brought her mind back to the present.

Behind her, two men were talking, their heads together, wineglasses in their hands, almost touching. "Dollfuss won't bend," one of them was saying. "He's got a taste of power and he's going to run with it. You think he'll listen to us? You're whistling in the wind. You'll be overtaken. Believe me."

"It's for the greater good," the other man said with certainty.

"Whose greater good?" There was derision in his voice. "Ours? Austria's? Europe's?"

"Europe's, of course! Can't you see that?" the second man said sharply. "Think what we could accomplish in a hundred years of peace! A thousand!"

"Don't be so bloody ridiculous! Hitler's lifetime, at best."

"By then, people will have come to accept it. England's coming around already. Did you see who was here tonight?"

"Yes, of course I did, and it's a start, but

we must be careful about Austria."

"Dollfuss will crack like an eggshell, you'll see."

"He could surprise you!"

"He'll have to be got out of the way, that's easy enough. The Fatherland Front is very strong; their victory is inevitable, and soon. Don't be so damned lily-livered . . ."

"More wine?" a voice said at Margot's side.

"What?" She turned and saw Roger Cordell. She was unreasonably, overwhelmingly pleased to see him. "Oh! I'm sorry, I was watching —"

"Two rising soldiers of the Führer's new army," he answered, so quietly she barely made out the words.

"They were talking about Austria," she began.

"What about it?"

"Something to do with getting rid of Chancellor Dollfuss." She stopped, seeing the shadow across his face. "Roger, you don't . . ." She had been going to ask if he believed there was anything in it, but that seemed a facile question now. He clearly knew what she was talking about, because he had not asked her to expand.

"There's only so much we can do," he said quietly. "I feel as if we have one finger in the dike, but there are more holes springing up all the time."

She looked at him and saw more clearly the tiredness in his face, so evident now, this close to him at the end of a very long day in which he had said goodbye to his only child. He did not believe that it would be all right, and neither did she.

CHAPTER 14

"You can't go like that," Aiden said when they had left the café and walked half a block along the road, then into a third narrow street and finally into a slightly better district. "You look too casual."

"So do you," Elena replied, regarding his old trousers of indeterminate color, so well worn were they. His sweater was a heavy fisherman's knit, equally faded. One could only guess that once it had been blue.

He smiled. "We're going to Gabrielle's apartment. Just along this way. I keep clothes there." He did not explain. "You can borrow something of hers. We don't want to look as if we've come to deliver the food."

She looked him up and down. "You look more as if you'd come to sweep the pavement. And I don't think Gabrielle lends her clothes to relative strangers, even in the unlikely event that they should fit."

They were stopped on the narrow footpath

281

at the end of the street, waiting for a break in the traffic. He looked at her carefully, slowly, his face touched with amusement. "A bit more on top, perhaps, but I dare say Gabrielle can arrange it so you don't actually fall out. Come on, don't stand there, we must get changed and ready. It's late . . ." He took her hand and pulled her forward, into the street, and quickly to the far side, too rapidly for her to argue. He led her to the vestibule of an apartment building and into the rickety-looking elevator. The door closed and the whole contraption jerked and rattled upward.

Elena drew in breath to say something, then realized that she had nothing to say.

They stopped at the fourth floor. Aiden led the way toward the back of the building, then knocked on the door of the last apartment. It was opened after a few moments and Gabrielle immediately looked beyond Aiden to Elena.

"Come in," she said with perfect composure, as if she had been expecting them. She stood aside for them to pass. She was wearing a simple, dark dress, but it still managed to look elegant. Aiden seemed to know where he was going. Gabrielle did not ask him; instead she looked briefly at him — his face, not his clothes — then followed them both to the large sitting room.

The view was magnificent. Nothing blocked it at this level. A panorama was spread out in front of them, over rooftops at all angles, some softened by trees, others cut by the shining waterways that the setting sun caught like scarlet ribbons carelessly thrown.

Elena stopped, ignoring both Aiden and Gabrielle, and reached automatically for her camera. Then she froze, realizing what she was doing, taking for granted someone else's home. "May I?"

"Of course," Gabrielle replied, laughter in her voice. "As long as you do not name me or give the address."

Elena stood absolutely still. It had not occurred to her that Gabrielle might also be dangerously involved in secret information. She had supposed the woman was exactly what she appeared to be.

"Thank you," she said, remembering herself and where she was. "I will put no names on it, should it be accepted." She turned round and spent the next ten minutes taking photographs at different angles, with different views and exposures. Perhaps one of these would be her defining picture of Trieste? Not the magnificent white castle over the sea at Miramare, or the sunrise on the canal with all its boats, which could so nearly have been Venice, except that the light was different.

When she was finished, she turned back to face the room and saw that Gabrielle was alone.

"I've got a gray dress," Gabrielle offered. "That sounds very drab, but it isn't. Sequins really lift it. I think a bright color would stand out too much. Make you more visible than you want to be. Don't worry, the sequins aren't everywhere. Come and try it on."

Elena followed obediently. It sounded like nothing she would ever wear, but she had little choice, and making a fuss would be absurd.

Gabrielle led her into a charming bedroom. It was feminine, but oddly severe for such a glamorous woman. What was most surprising was a second bed too small to be hers. It was in the corner, neatly made up for use, and a little rumpled, as if someone had been in it recently. There was a teddy bear on the pillow.

Gabrielle saw Elena's glance. "My son's," she said very quietly. "He has a nursery to play in, but I like to be close to him at night. He's . . . only four . . ." She stopped explaining, emotion powerful in her face,

284

obliterating the sophistication Elena had seen before.

"Your son?" Elena asked, then wished she had not. There was no evidence of a man in this room. It was classic, but very definitely feminine. And the main bed was made for one, two pillows piled on top of each other instead of side by side. One bedside table of fragile glass, and a small bunch of late roses.

Gabrielle walked over to one of the two large wardrobes and opened its door. She reached in and took out a dress on a hanger. It was gray, as she had said, but not a dense or leaden color. There was nothing heavy in it at all. It was more like a veil, and where the light fell on it, it shone a moment of silver, like streetlamps reflecting on mist.

Gabrielle was slender, dark, and genuinely beautiful. What on earth would Elena look like in it?

Gabrielle did not wait for Elena's consideration. She held out the hanger. "Here, put it on. You don't want to stand out as being different." She gave a smile of gentle amusement. "At least, not as if you don't mean it."

What has Aiden told this woman about me? Elena had a sudden chill, thinking about it. For that matter, what did Gabrielle know of Aiden? She had a momentary vision of Trieste full of spies, all watching each other and pretending they were not. Watchers and listeners, all trailing each other through the narrow streets and the elegant promenades.

"Thank you." She took the garment. There was nowhere separate to change, so she hesitated only an instant before taking off her own clothes and slipping on the gray dress. Gray dress? What an inadequate description! It was a gown, not a mere frock. It was so light, she barely felt it slip over her shoulders and down almost to the ground. It was obviously silk. Nothing else felt the same on the skin.

"Oooh!"

She turned round. It was not Gabrielle who had spoken, or rather sighed with wonder. It was a small boy. His hair was soft and fair, his eyes blue, his skin blemishless, as only a small child's can be. When he smiled, he showed milk-white teeth.

"You like it?" Elena asked him.

He looked up at her through his eyelashes, embarrassed now that she had noticed him.

"Do I look nice?" she asked. "It would be good to have a man's opinion."

He gave a tiny little giggle.

"Tell her, Franz," Gabrielle said softly, her voice filled with tenderness. "Do you think she looks nice?"

He nodded. "Yes, she's pretty . . ." Then shyness overcame him and he went to Gabrielle to stand just touching her, where he was safe.

"Thank you," Elena replied. "Then I shall definitely wear it. If your mother is kind enough to lend it to me."

He bumped up against Gabrielle, but his smile widened as he gazed at Elena.

She turned around slowly, then reached for the zipper to fasten it at the side. It was, as Aiden had suggested, a little tight across the bosom.

"Excellent," Gabrielle approved. Then she turned to the child. "I think you had better go to bed, now that you've seen us off. Marta will read you a story."

He held on to her a little more tightly.

"I'll say good night to you when I come home," she promised.

For a moment, he looked like refusing, but a young woman appeared in the doorway and held out her arms.

Elena bent down toward the boy, careful not to lean on the soft fabric of the dress, which spread around her. Out of the corner of her eye, she caught the light flashing on sequins, just a few. "Thank you, Franz. Now I can go, feeling beautiful." She kissed her fingertips and touched them to his cheek, which was as soft as the silk of the gown.

He smiled at her, then after the briefest hesitation, turned and went to Marta to hear his bedtime story. Only once did he glance at Gabrielle, as if she might change her mind. It was a routine he was used to, if unwillingly.

Elena looked at Gabrielle, at her rich, dark hair and brown eyes and, most of all, the warm tones of her skin. She had never been blond, even as a child. And yet Franz had the same smile, the same delicate brows, even if his were no more than a suggestion as yet.

There was nothing to say. It was all in Gabrielle's face. Whatever she said or did, or whatever other loyalties she had, Elena understood that Franz was first.

"Thank you for lending me the dress," she said with a straightforward smile and an even voice, although her heart was beating hard, almost in her throat. Why? Because in the middle of all this lying and pretending, there had been this intrusion of something real, whatever else happened.

"It suits you better than I expected . . ." Gabrielle began. Then, as if she realized Elena was not really listening, she changed the subject. "Shoes. You need shoes that go with it." She glanced at Elena's feet, and her face expressed her opinion of the shoes Elena was still wearing. She went to the wardrobe and brought out a pair of sandals, so constructed that a size or two one way or the other would make little difference.

Elena put them on. "Thank you," she said with a smile.

Gabrielle regarded her. "You need a little more lipstick," she decided. "You look pale, sort of unfinished. Try the top drawer on the left," she said, pointing to the dressing table. "And take a dab to touch your cheeks. We're going to face the enemy."

"Oh . . ." But Elena obeyed, even as she said it.

"I don't know who they are," Gabrielle said with laughter and apology, even regret, in her face. "I just know that they will be there. And don't look like that. We are probably all wasting our time if they're not." She walked over to the wardrobe and took out a heavy purple satin gown, held it up for a moment, decided it was right, and changed her dark dress for the purple. She looked at Elena inquiringly.

"Let's go and find the dangers," Elena said. Her voice was higher pitched and tighter than she had meant it to be. Gesturing toward Gabrielle, she added, "They will give up without a fight."

■ ■ ■

Aiden had changed into a dark suit that he'd kept at Gabrielle's apartment. Neither of them explained, and Elena did not ask.

They took a taxi. After twenty minutes or so, driving through heavy, noisy traffic, Elena had completely lost her sense of direction. When they got out and Aiden paid the driver, she had no idea where they were, except that it was clearly in the older and generally poorer quarter of the city. They went down steps, gaslit from a single lamp, to a door well below street level. A small window allowed someone inside to check who was at the door.

As soon as Aiden knocked on the window, it opened.

"Yes?" A man's face appeared and he looked at them critically.

Aiden stood so the light was on his face. "Anton Salinger, and my guests."

"Good evening, Signor Salinger. Ladies. Come in."

The window closed. There was a second or two of silence, then a click and the door opened.

Gabrielle went first, clearly knowing the way. Elena followed and Aiden came last.

They walked a lengthy corridor before double doors opened into a large, cavernous space, transformed with lights and music into a Viennese nightclub. Elena had an impression of lilting voices, a singer in a scarlet gown, people laughing, and the clink and gleam of raised glasses. From the dark narrow street above, it was unimaginable.

Quickly, they melted into the crowd, watching, listening, offering the occasional comment or appreciation for a joke. What could Elena do that was useful? She was here merely to stay with Aiden, and to be safe. But there might be something to learn. Several languages were spoken around them: Italian, German, Hungarian, Serbian, French, and now and again Elena heard a word or two of English.

There was music, and dancing in the pocket-handkerchief of a floor in the middle of all the separate tables. There was room for perhaps a half dozen couples, if they were careful.

Elena spoke to people, but only in Italian. The interesting conversations to overhear were in German. She danced with Aiden a couple of times, close, because there was no room to do anything else.

"You all right?" he asked quietly, his head bent to her ear.

"Fine," she replied. "I don't understand the Serbian or Hungarian . . ."

"They're not part of this. It's strictly Austrian . . ."

"And German. I've heard a lot of German accents. Munich, Berlin, Hamburg, some from further north."

He hesitated a moment, then asked, "Are you sure?"

"Of course I am! My German is pretty good," she reminded him. "How could you have forgotten that? They were being secretive. They stopped speaking when I passed close to them . . ." She recalled the surreptitious movements, the hostile eyes, but she did not mention it to him. Possibly it was her imagination and her intense discomfort at being here at all. This was not a time for self-indulgence, let alone complaint. Her job was to get Aiden and his information out of Italy. Never forget that. And also to learn about when, or from whom, or where the Fatherland Front's blow would come!

"The wicked flee where no man pursueth," he said quietly. "That's a hell of a dress you have on."

"Hell of?" she said defensively.

"It's exquisite, very un-English," he explained. "It's not even French. I don't know what it is, but it's gorgeous."

292

"Should I thank you?" she asked, moving closer to him, but stiff-armed. "Or look for something a little more ordinary next time?" She shouldn't let that hurt her, but nothing that was suitable for Gabrielle would ever be natural for Elena.

"Less conspicuous, perhaps," he replied, his voice muffled by her hair.

That stung. "Do you think anyone will remember me after I've gone from here?" she asked.

"In that dress?" His voice rose in disbelief.

"Oh, they'll remember the dress, but me? If I put on something different? More . . . ordinary."

He held her away from him for a moment, looking at her face, her neck, which was quite bare of jewelry, and then down at her body. "No," he said with surprise. "I see that Peter Howard has taught you a thing or two. How interesting. I wouldn't have thought he'd have it in him. I wonder what he intends to do with you in the future. I don't suppose he's given you the faintest idea."

"Actually, I didn't learn that from Peter Howard," she reminded him a little tartly. "I learned it when I was trying to escape from the Gestapo, in Berlin." She could not so easily dismiss the question as to what Peter might have planned for her.

"Really? You shouldn't have told me that. Don't tell anybody anything they don't need to know."

"You need to know it," she replied immediately. "Because you don't trust me to have any idea what I'm doing."

He pulled her closer again, and reluctantly she yielded. "I apologize. And you're right about the Germans: there are certainly a lot of them here tonight."

"Men," she agreed. "I haven't seen any other women here at all." A sudden thought occurred to her. "Are they soldiers on leave or something like that?"

He stiffened, missed a step, and then caught the rhythm again.

"Aiden?" she said in a fierce whisper. "What? Is that what they are?"

"Don't say that again!" he hissed.

She did not reply. If they were German soldiers, army or ex-army, here in Trieste, why were there so many? "What are they here for?" she said in a low, urgent voice.

He pressed her even closer so that he was breathing through the softness of her hair. "I told you — a plot to make Austria a part of Germany. They are blood brothers, just under the skin. Common language, common culture, heritage, and philosophy."

Then he added, "And above all, music and art. There's no greater music in the world than German and Austrian."

Elena wondered if he was mocking her, but his face was perfectly serious.

"That's not the point!" she said tartly. "You've been working on this for years! Tell me the whole truth, or nothing at all, and let me work it out." That sounded desperate, but her mind was racing, trying to think of anything that made sense.

"Fatherland Front," he whispered. He kept his voice low so even those closest to him would not hear his words. But people seemed to be watching, assessing all the time.

Her heart was beating as if it were in her throat. So Trieste was where it was all starting from. It was absurd that such a plot should be moving so fast. Germany conquering another country, fifteen years after *the war to end all wars*? Germany was barely climbing up onto its feet again. Yet there was a hideous sense to it. Pictures came back into her mind of the arrogant Brownshirts in Berlin, forcing Jews off the pavement into the gutter so the bullies could pass four or five abreast. All this talk of Jews and Communists being enemies of the people. It would not be hard to persuade some Austrians of that. Hitler himself was Austrian, as were quite a few of his right-hand men. That the Fatherland Front planned to seize power in Austria, this she believed. And that they would give it to Germany she also believed. But that they should be doing it now, here . . .

"Elena!" Aiden said sharply.

"Yes, yes, I heard you."

"Then pull yourself together. There could be a splinter group here in Trieste, whatever the risk. Where are they going to strike, and above all, when?"

She pulled back and stared up at him. She breathed the words. "And whom?"

"Probably Dollfuss himself, in Vienna."

"You mean . . . murder him?"

"No, probably take him captive and dictate what he must say, with a mixture of threats and blackmail, physical violence toward him or his family. He has a wife, you know. Very pretty woman. It will all look peaceful. He'll announce some sort of alliance with Germany. To be led entirely by Hitler, of course."

"Damnation!" she whispered.

"Pretty close," he agreed. "Now come with me and meet my friend Baldur Wass. He has the final piece of information from which we can pretty accurately work out

296

where they'll strike. Then all we need to do is find out who killed poor Max, if he is dead, and what he told them before he died, so we can leave without running straight into their trap." He held her a little more tightly and put his lips to her hair. "Or I could give you a copy of the list for Howard, and you could leave straightaway; make sure the list gets to London."

"My job is to get you out." She did not even have to think of her answer. "We don't leave people behind, if we can help it. It's bad for recruitment," she added wryly.

"Very funny," he said with a catch in his voice. "I've got the list with me. Can you hide it anywhere in that impossible dress? And not down your bosom. That's the first place they'll look. In fact, they'll probably be looking at it anyway, if they're halfway normal men."

She stared up at him sharply.

He was laughing.

She felt a sudden sting of tears in her eyes and looked away, but she allowed him to pull her back a little closer. Any more, and she would risk falling over his feet.

They found Baldur Wass with a couple of other men, apparently friends or at least acquaintances of Aiden's, in a nearby room.

297

They had long ago lost sight of Gabrielle. Perhaps they would go home by her apartment so Elena could return her dress. One day, she would have to see if she could find one like it in London. Did MI6 provide a suitable wardrobe for necessary occasions? Probably, but not like this!

Elena was introduced to the men by name, and she tried to remember them. She had agreed with Aiden that she would speak only in Italian, and she had kept her own name, Elena, simply taking on an Italian surname.

Baldur Wass was tall, almost Aiden's height. Wass was as fair as his one friend Marek was dark. To judge by their accents, they were from southern Germany.

They all spoke companionably for ten or fifteen minutes, then suddenly Marek said something in what Elena took to be Hungarian, and the air in the room seemed to freeze.

There was a brief knock on the door and it was pushed open. A thin man strode in. He was beautifully dressed in dinner clothes and had a large, curled mustache.

"Hello, Ferdie," Wass said tersely, in German. "You're late. What have you got to say?"

"You're still going ahead with your plans?"

298

Ferdie asked, his eyebrows raised, his expression sarcastic.

"Why?" Marek asked immediately.

"Careless! Careless!" Ferdie said mockingly. "One mistake is enough. One could kill all of us."

"What the hell are you talking about?" Wass looked from one to the other of them.

"Ten men arrested! That's what I'm telling you about. Ten!" Ferdie whipped around and stared hard at Aiden. "You! I trusted you, you bastard." He swung back to the other two men, entirely ignoring Elena, as if she had been no more than an ornament on the table. "Ask our friend here," he said, indicating Aiden. "He went to the old Front deliberately and told them about us! Now we've lost that moment of surprise! You tried to fool me," he said directly to Aiden, "and that is betrayal."

Aiden's face was white, but he stood his ground. "Liar! I told no one. If anyone is trying to sabotage us, it's you! Why? Who are you working for? Are you loyal to the Front . . . or . . . my God, Ferdie, who is paying you? Are you siding with the splinter group?" He looked at the others. "All of you?"

Elena looked at Ferdie and knew that his confused expression was forced, insincere.

Baldur Wass produced a small black handgun from his pocket. He pointed it not at Ferdie, but at Aiden. "Clumsy," he said with a slow smile. "Been wondering about you. Were we moving too fast for your people, our little . . . what do they call us . . . splinter group? Why? Because we want to get the job done now, and not wait for the old order, the plodding old Fatherland Front, to make its move?"

They were still ignoring Elena. She saw a couple of long-stemmed wineglasses on the table. She moved very slowly toward them, and toward Aiden.

"Keep away from me," Aiden said softly. "You'll only get in the way."

She kept moving, as if to be closer to him.

"Very touching," Ferdie said with a raw edge to his voice. "Not like you to let a clinging woman stop you, Anton."

Ferdie was watching Aiden. So were the other two men, waiting for him to move or try to talk himself out of it. Wass, with the gun in his hand, was the closest to Elena.

She picked up the glass slowly, as if looking for water in it. Or better, wine. Then, in one move, she struck it against the table and it smashed into jagged, dagger-like edges. Without more than glancing at it, she lunged at Baldur Wass, aiming for the wrist

300

of the hand holding the gun. She caught flesh. Immediately, there was streaming blood.

Wass gave a high-pitched shriek and dropped the weapon.

Aiden dived for it, catching it as it hit the floor and exploded with an ear-splitting shot.

Elena glanced at the far wall and saw how the bullet had buried itself in the plaster.

The door to the passage burst open and Gabrielle stood there with a short-muzzled gun pointed at Ferdie. Wass was ashen, blood gushing out of his slashed wrist. Marek was trying to stem the flow.

"Come on!" Gabrielle said to Elena, then to Aiden, gesturing toward the door. "We've got to get out of here — now!"

"Where?" Aiden demanded. "There's no way, except through the club."

"Follow me!" she ordered.

"They'll corner us," Aiden replied. "Better to fight."

"You can stay and fight if you want to," Gabrielle said in a low, clear voice. "I'm taking Elena with me. It's narrow, but she can make it."

"She's scared of heights," Aiden said. It was true.

"She's still got my dress!" Gabrielle

replied, raising her eyebrows and smiling. "Do as you damn well want." She turned to Elena. "Come on!"

Ferdie made a move toward her.

Gabrielle raised her gun. "I'm a very good shot," she said levelly. "I can shoot you where it will not kill you, but you might wish it did. Want to try? I've nothing to lose if I do, but a lot to lose if I don't get away. Come to think of it . . ." She lifted the muzzle to take a perfect shot at his crotch.

Aiden looked at Marek. "Shut Ferdie up before he talks us all into a gunfight." As if Marek had agreed, Aiden walked over to Elena. "Go with Gabrielle. I'm coming right behind, when I've made sure these idiots don't come after us. Wass will be useless, but Ferdie just might try." He put his right arm around her, and she felt him push a folded piece of paper into her dress, at the side so it was under her arm. The list? No time to look now.

Elena was shocked when Gabrielle shot Ferdie, the bullet grazing his shoulder, enough to hold him from climbing up to the roof. Then she swung round and went straight out the door without looking to see if anyone was following her into the passageway. There was nothing she could do if they had.

302

Elena went after her. She should have been shaking with fear at the thought of scrambling along the roof's edge, but she was not. Aiden was right: she was afraid of heights, but her real fear was falling off the roof in sheer paralysis and letting them all down.

She followed Gabrielle out of a trapdoor at the end of the corridor and onto the roof. She could only just see her in the dark, no more than a dense shadow ahead.

"Go straight after her, follow her," Aiden said from behind. "Stay in the middle, then if you freeze, I can at least prod you forward."

"I'm not going to freeze!" she lied. She could already feel herself losing control. Her stomach felt sick. She was dizzy, and she had not even reached the ledge. She tucked Gabrielle's dress up around her waist and tied the flowing skirts into a bunch, then caught up with Gabrielle.

"Don't let the bastards beat you," Gabrielle whispered. "My father always used to say that!" Then she stepped out onto a ledge less than a foot wide and walked along it, as if she did it every day.

"Please, God!" Elena whispered into the near darkness, then followed after her.

CHAPTER 15

Margot arrived back in London tired but unable to relax. She could not let go of the thoughts that had been whirling in her mind during her journey home from Berlin. It was the emotions that overcame her most powerfully, though they were not all troubling. In fact, the story that the German soldier, Major Buresch, had told her about the British officer was overwhelming, but it was, in a way, also liberating. She realized that over the years of grief she had allowed Paul to become of almost mythic perfection in her mind. She remembered the good things — the intimacy, the courage, and the laughter — but they had become so large that he had grown to dwarf everyone else she might have cared for. No one could measure up to him. In fact, no one could make her feel anything, other than that to love again would be a betrayal.

The more she thought of it, the more she

brought back the reality of Paul: the humanity, and the fallibility that makes people real. He would have shown the same kindness, even fellowship, to a fallen enemy. He had admitted to dulling the edges of fear and pain with whisky. He had shrunk from superhuman to very human indeed, and she loved him the more for that.

She also grieved because he had felt it necessary to be a hero for her, instead of sharing with her what he really felt: the deep, wounding pain of horror and fear. It was the culture of the time not to tell those at home the truth about the realities of war. But that was fifteen years ago, and it was a different world. Naïvety was dead and cynicism was acknowledged. Perhaps too much, but who could blame anyone? It had been called *the war to end all wars,* and here they were, possibly on the eve of another. Their leaders made the same mistakes over and over again. The victims learned, but those in power either did nothing or forgot because something else had become more important. Like German expansion into Austria on the heels of assassination, and then the Fatherland Front taking over the government? It was all too believable. Or had she misunderstood the bits she had overheard and pieced together? Was she running from phantoms? Defeat does strange things to people. And she had certainly seen the utter devastation of defeat in Germany when her father had been ambassador. She had seen it every day, in Germany's hunger and despair. Men begging for work, women starving themselves to feed their children. Had they a choice in any part of this?

But the humiliations of defeat bred something far worse than poverty, hunger, or loss of both the past and the future for the enemy. It bred humiliation, which sometimes turned into rage. Too many had nothing left to lose. Anyone who offered a renewal of hope had a ready audience of millions. Should anyone be surprised that Hitler was gaining so many followers?

The word about Austria was only a whisper, but did people like her father know how deep it was, that it was turning into action? She wished she could do something more useful. Parties, theater, even time spent with friends seemed devoid of purpose now. She must at least tell her father what she had observed. Tonight would be good.

It was still daylight when she was in the taxi and heading home, not too late to have the driver take her to her parents' house. She found herself smiling as she redirected him. She would tip him well for his trouble.

Katherine was delighted to see her. "Margot, darling, come in, come in! Tell me all about it," she said eagerly, hugging her daughter, her face alight with pleasure. "Have you eaten? At the very least, have a cup of tea. Stay here tonight; your old room is always made up."

Margot hugged her back, harder than usual. Cecily was too young to remember the war as Margot did, but perhaps she would lose her husband in a long, drawn out, and far more terrible way. That is, he would still be alive, but altered until the good she had seen in him was fragmented into a thousand pieces, none of them big enough to matter anymore.

Margot let go of her mother and stepped back.

Katherine stared at her. "What's the matter?" she said. "Was it painful for you?" She went straight to the point, asking if Margot's going had awakened her grief and sharpened her aloneness.

Margot smiled. "No, in fact I met a man — a German officer — who had been saved by a British officer, and what he said made me think of Paul. It made me see him again in a good way. It reminded me of what he was really like, not just a frozen memory."

Katherine's face registered her emotions sharply. Margot saw suddenly far more than an ambassador's wife's usual smooth concealment of all personal thoughts. It was as if, for an instant, all pain was allowable . . . then it was gone again. "But . . . ?" she asked.

Margot decided in that instant she would not tell her mother more than the happy things, the social things: who wore what, what the celebration entailed. "I would like to talk to Father about one or two things." She saw her mother frown. "Just messages from people he knew," she lied. "Before I forget what they said." She smiled quickly. "And thank you, I'd love to stay here tonight and have a good meal. I have had excellent restaurant food in Germany, and I ate some marvelous meals, but I'm looking forward to something comfortable."

"Yes, of course." Katherine led the way through to the sitting room. "I'll tell your father. He will be delighted to see you safely back."

A moment later, Charles came into the sitting room smiling widely, clearly with relief.

Margot felt a moment of emotion sweep over her. She'd always been her father's favorite, and she had known this growing up. She had used it to her advantage, and she was not proud of this now. But recently she had felt grateful for their closeness, in spite of the extreme difference in their personalities. Above all, she was filled with an unusual wave of gratitude that she was not in Cecily's position and that Charles was not in Roger Cordell's. How painful for Roger to have to watch his daughter walk off into a dark and unknown future with a man he did not like or trust. Although he dared not show it, Roger was bound both by nature and by honor to protect those he loved. And Charles did not have such a fragile wife. Heaven knew, Katherine was every bit as strong as he, and possibly as astute an ambassador. Actually, she was not nearly as emotionally damaged by her experiences of loss as Margot had thought. And although Margot herself had suffered the death of her husband — a blow that perhaps had killed part of her — she definitely was not a fragile woman, either.

She went quite naturally into her father's arms and hugged him, and she felt him hug her warmly. "You weren't worried, were you?" she said with a smile when she stepped back.

"Of course I was. It's my job," he replied.

"Every decent man worries about his daughters. You may be braver and more competent than most, but you also get yourself into bigger messes."

"Then you must adore Elena," she replied instantly.

"Never more than you," he said in sudden gravity. "And she's only been daring since May, and that was forced on her. Not to diminish the fact that she handled it very well." He looked at Margot with pride.

Margot had sometimes wondered if he saw an echo of Katherine in her: the elegance, the individuality. Perhaps that was partly why she dressed outrageously sometimes: just to be different. But she must not waste this chance.

"Before Mother comes back with food for us, I have to speak to you."

He frowned. "Sit down and tell me how Cordell is. Is it about him?"

She sat in the big armchair opposite his. "Yes and no. I overheard something at the wedding party: German army officers talking. There were a lot of them there. I know it's . . ." She had been going to say *a proactive safety measure, get in on the ground floor,* but that was unnecessarily unkind.

He was waiting, dark eyes troubled. They were so much like her own.

310

"It's probably a good future for Cecily."
She narrowly evaded the point and then
hurried on. "I overheard two regular army
officers talking about German influence in
Austria. They mentioned a group called the
Fatherland Front. It seems violent. Have
you heard of it?"

"There are a lot of groups here and there,"
Charles replied, "and there's unrest all over
the place. I wouldn't take them too seriously. Young men indulge in all sorts of wild
talk." He shook his head a little, smiling at
some inner thought. "Most of it is just
daydreams. Add a little boasting and I dare
say they had more celebratory champagne
than they could well handle." He smiled at
her. "I'll look into it, I promise, but don't
worry, put it out of your mind. If you
believed every wild tale from a man who is
too young to have fought in the war, but
longs for a part of the heroism without having any idea what a real hero is like, what
real war is like, you would live in a state of
constant anxiety." His face tightened a little.
"Don't mention this to your mother. She
would only worry to no purpose. There are
enough strange things going on in Washing-
ton, according to her parents. I think it
would be a good idea if she took a trip out
to visit them in the spring or summer,

perhaps? Would you go with her?" There was a look of hope in his eyes. "I doubt I will be able to come, and you haven't seen your American grandparents for far too long."

"I'd love to," Margot said immediately. She could not refuse him, and it would be something to look forward to, a wonderful change after Berlin. "Yes, please. But you won't forget about Roger Cordell, will you?"

"Thank you, my dear. And of course I won't forget about him." At last the tension in him eased, and his tight muscles unknotted.

In the morning, as well as she had slept, Margot felt unsettled about the powerful memories that still hung heavily in her mind. After breakfast, she thanked her parents and left for home. But when asked, she told the taxi driver to take her to her grandparents' house.

As she rode, she thought about sharing her fears, her impressions of what was brewing beneath the polite chatter, and talk of the future. Her father had dismissed it, but she knew that, even had he taken it seriously, he would not have wanted to alarm her. But it made her feel as if he did not believe her — or did not trust her. It was no comfort; it was the opposite, although she had long grown past the need for comfort rather than truth. Perhaps she had not shown him that? She had accepted his protection rather than his support in facing hard truths. That was her fault at least as much as his. She hoped her grandfather would listen.

When she was outside the familiar gate, she climbed from the taxi and paid her fare. The driver put her suitcases on the ground just as Lucas came out of the front door, Josephine on his heels. Margot's heart sank. She should have telephoned. It had never occurred to her that they might not be in, and now here they were, clearly on their way out.

Lucas took one look at her face and told the taxi driver to put her cases in the hall.

"I'm sorry," Margot said, suddenly aware of how much she took them both for granted. She had come to Lucas because, since May, she had learned so much more about him, and her respect had taken wing. But it was still largely based on his work during the war, even if he discussed so little of the details. State secrets lasted a lot longer than a mere fifteen years. What did she expect from him?

"Come inside," Josephine directed her.

"We have no appointment; we always have time to see you. Tell us about your trip to Berlin."

Margot followed her inside. Without her needing to explain, Josephine went into the kitchen and Lucas took Margot into the sitting room. He left the French doors closed. Autumn was in the air; there was a certain chill.

"You look worried," he observed, indicating the chair for her to sit down, then sat opposite her. "Was it the wedding itself, or is there something amiss with Roger Cordell?"

"Not really." She found herself equivocating, even though she had not intended to. She was not used to total honesty with her grandfather. She had never felt at ease with him, as Elena had for as long as she could recall.

Lucas was waiting for her. Was he used to listening to confessions? Tales of spying, of fear, suspicion, or danger? She knew now that he had worked for British Military Intelligence, but not any more than that. And it had been her father who had told her, not Lucas himself. Charles had only discovered it in May. It had revealed to him an entire side of his father's life, his work and his experiences, even his very nature, that Charles had not known. In one hour, the disrespect he had shown his father, when he believed Lucas had sat out the war pushing papers in some government office, had been transformed into profound respect. It had thrilled him to see his father as a hero, but it was also disturbing. Decades of perception had to be changed. Some things vanished at once, others, woven through tiny memories, shedding light on things he had taken for granted all his adult life.

Some of that had rubbed off on Margot, but it was now peeling back like layers of skin.

Lucas was still waiting. Josephine would arrive in a moment, probably with tea and biscuits.

"I overheard a conversation at the party, after the wedding," Margot began. "It was between army officers, and they were talking about a group of people calling themselves the Fatherland Front." She stopped because she saw in his face a flash of recognition. "You've heard of them."

"Yes, Cordell has already told me of his concern. But this is important. Margot, I want your opinion, too. Cordell was very brief, and of course the information was encoded. Please try to remember what they

315

said as exactly as you can."

"Then it's true." It was as if the door to the garden had been opened and the cold air let in.

"Yes, but exactly what they are planning is not yet known. Tell me what you overheard as exactly as you can recall," he repeated.

"I didn't hear much."

He sat still, silently waiting.

Her mind was sharp on one thing, blurred on others. "They were talking about Chancellor Dollfuss and Austria becoming more or less part of Germany, and it being for everyone's good and . . . inevitable."

Lucas sat motionless. "In what way? Try to think . . . Be precise."

The chill bit deeper.

He leaned forward. "Margot —"

"I'm thinking, trying to get it exactly. They said Austria was culturally the same as Germany in all that was important, and together they could be the strongest power in the world . . . for an indefinite period of time."

Lucas asked, without a shred of humor, "Led by whom? Not Dollfuss, I presume."

"No, they said he would argue with them or . . . I don't remember exactly, but if he disagreed, he would crack like a chicken's egg."

316

"Did they mention Hitler?"

"Yes." She found she was shivering, as if there were no warmth in the room. "Yes, everyone spoke of him. Sooner or later his presence was there with the young men, almost as if he were there himself."

"Did you hear anything about money? And please be careful; I don't want you to say anything but what you are certain of. It matters, Margot."

She looked at his face, its ascetic lines, the steady calm blue eyes. She had known him all her life, loved him and trusted him, certain that he loved her. And yet, at this moment, she was deeply afraid of what she believed he could see, and what she had newly glimpsed. She had respected Paul as a soldier, and her brother also, of course, but this side of Lucas was a previously undiscovered territory. He knew the secret war that had begun before the soldiers mobilized and that continued, even now, after it was over.

"Yes," she whispered, her voice dry in her throat. "Do you know about this already?"

"A little. I'm learning more." He put his hand out and covered hers for a moment. "Don't talk about this to anyone at all."

"I told Father a bit about it, but he said not to worry. I don't know whether it was

317

to comfort me or that's what he really believed." She stopped, hoping he would tell her, and yet dreading it. "I think Hans Beckendorff, Cecily's new husband, belongs to an elite group, maybe even the Gestapo. I'm not certain. I . . . I think Roger suspects it."

"Very possibly," Lucas agreed. "I don't know, either," he added. "There are things we try not to know. People tend to believe what they need to, what will keep them safe and support all the things they love and want. We're all like that. Somewhere inside ourselves we will fight to believe the world is as we thought. Please tell me, but stay safe. You must go home and carry on with your life. Don't try to find out any more, please." He was very earnest. "Your grandmother and I lost a friend a couple of days ago. We have to take care of his affairs. He had no one else."

"Can't I . . ." she began. She saw the refusal in his eyes and suddenly she felt included, a Standish, like Elena, trusted. "I will, Grandfather," she promised.

His smile softened and he sat back in the chair just as Josephine came in carrying a tray of tea and biscuits.

CHAPTER 16

After the escape from the club, across the rooftops and eventually to the ground, Aiden and Elena parted from Gabrielle. Hers was the hardest and most dangerous lot, but she had no choice. Perhaps she would have gone deeper into the slums, where it was easier to hide, but for her child. She would never leave him, unless it was to save his life. She did not need to explain that, at least not to Elena. She trusted that Aiden understood it, too.

"Be careful," Aiden warned Gabrielle. There was a momentary tenderness in his face. It flickered across Elena's mind to wonder if Gabrielle and Aiden had once had a different kind of relationship, and if Aiden was Franz's father.

"You, too," Gabrielle murmured in the darkness. She touched his cheek and then turned to Elena. "Safe journey," she whispered, and then she was gone as silently as one of the shadows across the street.

"Come on," Aiden said briskly. "She'll probably be all right. She's good at this, and there's nothing we can do to help her anyway. We need to disappear. We're a danger to others, as well as to ourselves." He took her arm and pulled her along the pavement at a brisk pace. An actual run might draw attention to them.

"Where are we going?" Elena asked, struggling to keep up without breaking step. She had on higher heels than she usually wore, and the silk dress was designed with dancing in mind, not racing along a dark street with uneven cobblestones and occasional heaps of rubbish.

"Where they won't look for us," he replied, without turning to face her. "The splinter faction in the Fatherland Front is going to strike before the main group can. Ferdie's part of them and they won't let us live to tell anyone. We would have been shot and dumped if Gabrielle hadn't rescued us. Whoever the other players are, they'll be mad as hell."

Elena slowed down, trying to think. What Aiden had said made only partial sense. Which side was he on? Or was he on neither? It was not the time to ask. And more than that, she could not disentangle the lies from the truth, if there was truth in any of it.

"We'll have one more chance to find out about Max," he said. "It would help to know if he's still alive, poor devil. And on the practical side, what he told them. But we must get the information back home. It's urgent," he said. "At least, you must. Gabrielle is French, so God only knows which side she is on, if it comes to the pinch. Her own side, I suspect: anything to protect Franz. I wish to hell my mother had cared that much about me." There was pain behind his voice when he said it.

At another time, or another place, she would have liked to comfort him, but now it would risk both of their lives. And she was not sure she could even reach whatever the pain was, never mind actually help. He had never spoken of his childhood to her. But no one wanted pity, least of all Aiden. He had probably not even meant to let that slip.

She turned all her attention to keeping up with him, avoiding the chipped cobblestones and concentrating on not breaking a heel or twisting an ankle on the curb.

Once or twice he stopped to check which way to go. She thought they were moving steadily inland, away from the harbor and all the main canal outlets to the sea. The alleys were getting narrower and were smelling less pleasant.

"Who betrayed us?" she asked, trying to catch up as she struggled to keep pace.

"Maybe Ferdie, maybe Marek," he answered.

"Why?"

"For God's sake, Elena," he said impatiently. "Every man's got his own reasons. Money, love, hate, patriotism to anywhere — Italy, Serbia, Austria, Hungary. Maybe a hostage to fortune, fear, bloody stupidity? None of us knows what we'd do with a knife at our throat. The only one who's got any right to say is the man who's got a stake in this. I'm still trying to work out exactly what stake Gabrielle has."

"Who is Franz's father?"

"God knows. I don't." He stopped suddenly, halfway along the street. "It's not her who betrayed us, Elena. She got us out."

"Does that count?" she asked. "As you said, she'd do anything to save Franz. So would I, if I were his mother." She realized that this was true. If your child trusted you, loved you, how could you do anything else? Or perhaps it was also Franz's father she protected?

"It's not Gabrielle," he said again, quietly,

and there was something like admiration in his voice that Elena had never heard before. "She does what she does for Franz. She won't betray us."

"Is there anybody else we can trust?" Elena asked, trying to ignore her aching feet.

"No," he said. "No. Save your breath, and keep moving."

Finally, Aiden stopped outside a shabby wooden door in an alley. He gave a brief rhythmic knock. After a moment or two, the door opened and he exchanged a few words with someone Elena could not see. They were speaking neither Italian nor German. Elena thought it might be Serbian. Then the door opened wider and they were let in.

She had no idea where they were, but the man who stood in the small, stale-smelling passage was pleasant enough. "Not long," he warned in English, shaking his head.

"Gone in the morning," Aiden promised.

"One room."

"Whatever you've got." Aiden did not even glance at Elena.

The man nodded and led the way along the corridor for only a few yards, then opened the door to a small room. A single bare bulb showed it was furnished with two mattresses on the floor and a pile of sheets and blankets. He said something in Serbian, which sounded to Elena like instructions. Aiden translated, explaining where the toilet was and a basin. A bath was out of the question.

After the door closed and the man's footsteps had faded down the passageway, Aiden looked at her. "Take off that dress," he said. "It's great, but you can't wear it anymore. It's too memorable. If anyone asks, 'Did you see a woman in a gray dress?' they will be able to say 'yes' without doubt. And apart from that, no one wears such a thing in daylight. And you can't run at all in those heels."

"So, what will I wear?" she asked, confused. Now that she had stopped running, exhaustion overtook her.

"Marco will find you something. It won't be to your taste, but it'll be comfortable and inconspicuous. Now, get a few hours of sleep. We'll resume our search for Max in the morning." His face looked grim in the patchy light, strained and robbed of color.

"Where do we even start?" she asked. The momentary elation she had felt earlier had gone. She was tired and had no idea what they could do that was anything but pointless. "We need to get out of Trieste."

"Hang on to the list and go as soon as you can," he retorted, his voice harsh.

324

"I'd be happy to, if those had been my instructions!" she snapped back. "But they weren't. I work *with* you Aiden, not *for* you."

"Anton," he snapped. "As far as you are concerned, Aiden is dead. Don't forget that. You're more of a liability than I can afford."

She felt as if he had slapped her, but another thought came to her mind. How could it all unravel so quickly? Only an hour or two ago they had been allies sharing the danger, the excitement, and then the relief. Had he always been so sudden to bite back, and she had just forgotten? Did she selectively recall only the good times, the exhilaration, the excitement, the laughter, and the tenderness — a little like when someone dies and you weed out all the bad bits and wipe them from memory?

She took off the gray dress and draped it over the back of the only chair. Then she removed her underwear and went to bed with only her slip on. It was as good as some nightgowns, although she was aware of being too near naked for emotional comfort. There had been times when that would have led to intimacy, even passion, but that was in another life. Had he meant any of it? Or had he been that way in order to keep her loyalty? She would never betray a man she thought loved her, and he knew that.

■ ■ ■ ■

She slept far better than she had thought she would. She was a little cold, but not enough to keep her awake. In the morning, Marco brought her a very plain brown dress. It was unflattering, to say the least, but it was warm enough, and with a rough shawl it was sufficient to keep her sheltered from the worst of the weather outside. He also brought a pair of brown shoes. They were a little large but that was better than too small. He offered socks, too. She was about to decline, then realized she might have to walk a long way, and they would at least make the shoes fit her better. She thanked him and took them.

Aiden, too, left his good dinner clothes behind and took rough work clothes. They instantly changed not only his appearance, but his manner. He set aside the grace and arrogance that usually made him stand out. He was fair-haired and fair-skinned, but here, in far northern Italy, this was not so remarkable. In what had previously been Austrian-occupied Trieste, there were plenty of Germanic-looking people.

They ate a brief breakfast of bread and salami, with a little cheese and good hot coffee. It was still early, before nine, when they set out. No shops were open, but at least it was a mild day.

Elena walked along the pavement beside him.

"You surprised me last night," he said after a while.

She had no idea where they were going, nor, for that matter, where they were now, but she was quite sure what he was about to say. She did not ask. Silence was, she decided, the better choice.

"I didn't think you'd make it along the ledge," he added, the shadow of a smile around his lips.

"But you had me walk it anyway," she said, trying to keep the emotion out of her voice.

"Better to fall into the stream than into the hands of those men, I promise you." His voice was strained, tight in his throat. "They would have killed you, but had their fun first."

For an instant, she did not believe him, but a glance at his face quickly convinced her. In the morning light, clear, cold, without the luminous softness that comes later in the day, he looked older and far more worn by constant danger and pain. She felt a wave of sorrow for him. He was risking his life every day, in a country not his own. He could never forget the part he was playing. If even one of the men from whom he gathered his information suspected him, it would cost him his life, and probably in the most unpleasant way they could devise. They would want every word of information they could get.

Whatever else she did, Elena knew she must not endanger him. No careless or selfish word or thought, no slip of concentration. She must be worthy of his trust. To be less would be childish, even shameful. She changed the subject.

"Have you thought where we should start?"

"The last place I saw Max," he replied, "is about half a mile further this way." He did not add any more and they walked in silence, him ahead of her, as the alleys grew narrower and the traffic of carts and bicycles careered down the middle.

It was a long morning. They gained information about Max's movements only bit by bit: where he had been seen, who had spoken to him, and as much as they could learn, what they had talked about. People were reluctant to speak to them. Everybody had their own secrets. It was the middle of the afternoon before they found sufficient pieces to put together most of Max's last days.

They sat in a small restaurant, more to share their ideas and rest their feet than for any food. But the food was surprisingly good, and they were hungry. The pasta was cooked to perfection and contained a little fish. They were wise enough not to ask what kind it was.

"This was the last place he was seen," Aiden said when they had finished their meal, paid the bill, and were back outside in the street.

"Are you sure?" Elena asked, looking at him doubtfully.

"I spoke to the owner and he said Max was here. Max was your lover." He smiled bleakly, but the thought clearly amused him. "And he's left you pregnant and I am determined to find him."

"Why?" she asked with interest. "Are you my father?"

He winced. "Oh, Elena, that was unkind." But he laughed in spite of it.

She remembered with a sudden ache how he'd always preferred her fighting back to her being passive.

He stared at her steadily. "Did you know that that last man was lying to us?"

"No," she answered, "but I do know he's

following us now."

Aiden stiffened. She had caught him by surprise. "Are you sure?"

"Yes. He looks different, but it is the same man."

"How do you know that, when I didn't see it?" He did not seem annoyed, not this time. He needed to know.

"His jacket is different, and his hat, so we don't know what his hair is like," she replied. "And he has whiskers now. But his shoes are the same, even the same scuff marks. And a cut in the leather, on the left side, roughly where his little toe is. And his ears . . ."

"What about his ears?"

"Ears are so individual. Did you know that most people don't think to disguise their ears? He has a mole, a very small one, just on the curve of his right ear. You can't really cover that up unless you wear your hair very long, which he doesn't."

"And he's following us?" He was utterly serious now.

"Yes, I noticed him about a half mile ago, and again just now. We can't afford to believe it's a coincidence."

He did not argue. "We'll separate and meet up again outside the bookshop. It's called Via Rosario. The name's on the front in red letters." He told her how to find it. "I'll go a different way and see if he follows. But, Elena . . ."

"What?" She felt a chill already. What if they missed each other? He could take the opportunity to get rid of her and she would have no way of finding him again. But then, he could have done that at any time. She was being ridiculous, exactly the sort of amateur he abhorred.

"Be careful," he said gently. He reached out and touched her cheek. It was a common enough gesture, but it brought back a rush of old memories, old partings, when they had always met again. "This is a dangerous game." He smiled. "We need to win. And that means finding all the information we can, knowing how much the enemy knows, and getting out of here alive." And with that he turned away and, within a moment, was lost among a group of people waiting to cross the busy street.

Was the man close behind?

Elena shook away her fears and walked on, following the directions Aiden had given her, but already her mind was racing. She had the list hidden as well as she could, inside her clothes, but there was nowhere that was really safe, not if they took her prisoner and stripped her. In fact, she actually had not accomplished anything at all, except to tell Aiden that Max was probably dead, and it seemed that Aiden had worked that out for himself. To know what part of Max's information was compromised was important, but was it worth their lives? It definitely was not worth losing Aiden, and the information for which he had risked his life . . . and now hers, too. She could not consider her task a success until he was safe on British soil, with all that he knew.

A van rumbled down the narrow street, rattling on the cobblestones. It was packed with soldiers. There were a dozen or more of them, all with rifles. Where were they going so quickly? It must be some emergency, or they would never have used so narrow and twisting a way to get there.

Elena hastened her step, not looking back to see whether the man was following her. She hoped he was not, because if he was, it would mean it was she he was trailing. Did anyone other than Aiden know who she was? That thought sent another ripple of coldness through her. Had a mistake she had made given her away? Or had they always known who she was? That would mean a traitor somewhere further back — in England.

Where was this bookshop? It ought to be

here, but she could not see it.

Then she realized she was still a block short of where Aiden had said. She bumped into a young man and apologized. He looked at her too closely and she hurried on.

Elena reached the bookshop at last. It was exactly as Aiden had described it, but he was not there. She felt panic rise inside her and swallowed it down, as if it had been a bolus in her throat threatening to suffocate her. She must look as if she were waiting for someone, not trying to pick up anybody, like some prostitute.

Really! She must get a grip on her imagination!

Still, Aiden was late.

Someone touched her and she turned sharply, ready to strike out if necessary. It was Aiden, laughter in his face.

"Looking for business?" he asked.

She was furious with herself. "No," she replied. "But if you've got the money, I'd consider it."

"Touché," he answered, the smile still on his lips. "The man with a mole on his ear followed me, but I lost him. That's why I was a bit late." He put his hand on her arm and, holding her firmly, guided her away from the bookshop and back in the direc-

tion from which they had come.

"Where are we going?" she asked. "Did you find anything?"

"I started adding things up in my mind," he replied. "I think I know where Max might have gone, because I have an idea of who he was looking for."

"Will he be there now?" she asked, with a sudden upsurge of hope. Then, as instantly, it died. Why had he not mentioned it before? She pushed it out of her mind. She could not afford to doubt him, or ask questions.

"Not unless he's dead," he answered, without turning to look at her.

She could think of no reply to give, so she stayed silent. She wondered how well Aiden had known Max, and whether they had been friends or merely contacts. Either way, Max was the only person Aiden could trust, which meant he was more than just another acquaintance, someone he had known. She tried to remember other friends he had had in the past, people he had liked, shared jokes or memories with. No one came to mind. Had he deliberately not shared them with her? Had he been protecting her?

It was nearly half an hour before they reached the shed beside the house Aiden was looking for. He stood outside on the narrow pathway, his face somber in the late afternoon light. The sun was just above the rooftops and the shadows were dense. West-facing windows were sheeted in gold with the light on them. It was what Elena would have called a slum. Surely, this was not where Max lived? Maybe it was where he had run to and been cornered.

"Let's get it over with," she said, then saw an expression on Aiden's face that she could not read but made her wish she had not spoken so hastily.

"You can stay out here if you want." His voice also was unreadable, except that he was not gentle, nor was he afraid. Perhaps Max was not the first contact Aiden had lost.

"I'll come." She made the statement and moved forward as she spoke.

He met her eyes briefly. "Right," he said more gently. He led the way through the shed and down a narrow walkway between the buildings, then into a larger yard. There was timber stored there, and huge rainwater tanks, several bits of wood and coal, and an additional lean-to shed. Aiden stood still, looking around. The dustbins were too small to hold anything the size of a human body. He took the lid off the coal bunker. "Empty," he said briefly. He looked behind it, against the wall, and finally in the shed.

Elena went with him. It was obvious that Max was not there, but somebody had been. There was a straw-stuffed mattress on the floor, torn and spilling pieces of itself. Food wrappers had been half eaten, probably by foraging rats. There was a lingering foul odor. The light was pearlescent, almost luminous, fading the walls' colors and hiding their ugliness.

"He's not here," Aiden said slowly. "But it looks as if someone has been living rough, and probably hiding." He seemed to struggle for the word he wanted and did not find it in any of the languages he spoke. He turned slowly and his eye caught the water butt, as if he had not seen it before.

Elena said what she most feared. "We didn't look in the water barrel."

Aiden stared at her. He understood.

"Help me up," she said. "I'll take a quick look. If we don't, we'll always wonder." She met his eyes, dark blue in the waning brilliance of the air.

Aiden shrugged and moved beside her, next to to the barrel that was sitting on a wooden platform, raising it so that water could be drawn into a bucket from the tap at the bottom. Without speaking, he lifted her until she was head and shoulders above its rim. Carefully, she raised the lid, but she

336

pushed it too far to one side. It fell, clattering to the ground.

She saw it immediately: a man's head with the strings of hair floating on the surface. The rest of him was a dim and distorted shape impossible to distinguish beneath the dark surface of the water. His limbs had to have been bent or even broken to force him into the barrel. Judging by the shape of the body and the smell of the bloating flesh, he must have been there for a week or more.

She swallowed and felt her eyes blur and her stomach lurch.

"What is it?" Aiden demanded, gripping her harder.

"He's here," she gasped.

He let her down gently, then turned her to face him. "Are you sure?"

"I'm not sure it's Max, but somebody is there, and I'm guessing he's been there a week at least, from the way his flesh is —"

"All right," he said. "There's nothing for me to identify him by even if I climb up, but it all fits. I think we can assume the worst, and we should get out of here as fast as we can." He bit his lip. "Sorry, but we need to avoid all connections he had, and not go by any of the ways he might have arranged for me in the past. We're really on the run now."

"Shouldn't we call the police?" she asked.

"No!" The cry was torn from his lips. Then he spoke again, more softly. "No, I'm afraid that might be exactly what the Fatherland Front wants us to do. It would be an ideal way to get rid of us. Clever, really." He looked at her with a wry, twisted smile.

The Fatherland Front again. Was he for them or against them? Or neither — just using them for information?

"But the police can't —" Then she stopped. She had no idea if this was true or not. But both she and Aiden were foreigners with no help they could turn to. They could disappear into the police system and no one would know. They could not appeal to the British ambassador in Rome. That would ruin her cover for any future use. And in Aiden's case, he had not even used his real name. They were alone. "There's nothing we can do, is there," she said aloud. It wasn't a question.

"Get out of here," he replied. "And not the way we came in. Something is brewing. There's been more movement of armed troops lately. Events have been canceled unexpectedly. We're foreigners, and they'll know that as soon as we start asking. I've got a German passport, so they will not bother me, but you've got a British one, I

338

presume."

"Yes."

"Then you're not safe. Neither of us will be, if we get caught here with an obviously murdered body. You'd be the perfect person to blame," he went on. "They'll need to blame someone. I imagine Howard will not be pleased with the notoriety! Case closed . . . the less said, the better." He stopped abruptly, as they both heard shouting along the street. "The police. Come now," he said in a low, urgent voice. "Other side. Come on, we'll go down the alley, then out in the next street." He took her hand and pulled hard.

It would have been stupid not to obey. Struggling a little, she followed in his path over a broken fence and into another deserted back garden, along a couple of houses further from the shouting, then out between two more houses and onto another street.

They slowed down and he put his arm around her, changing his step to seem casual, as if they were just two people taking a sunset walk. The air was still warm and the sky glowed with waning color, delicately shadowed with shreds of cloud drawn out, as if the wind were combing it across the sky above the setting sun.

"I'd love to photograph that," she said quietly. "I'd love to have the balance of such an achingly lovely sky above the awakening violence."

He tightened his arm around her a little more, as two people passed on the other side of the street. "There's nothing up there but space, and space is unaware of us. One way or the other, we light fires to make our own warmth, and tell each other stories to create a reason we can believe in."

"You sound very sophisticated when you say that," she responded, keeping her voice far lighter than she felt.

"But I don't impress you."

"Not really. It takes courage to shrug off all belief, but it takes a lot more to hang on to it in the hard times."

"And blindness."

"I thought you were going to say 'illusion,'" she retaliated. "That would be better, wouldn't it? Hallucinations? We people the darkness with other beings, either good ones or bad. The bad ones are easier. They let us live as we like, and say either that it doesn't matter, or that it's somebody else's fault anyway."

"You really have changed," he said, glancing at her with a puzzled frown. As if he half wanted to mock her, but the words

340

eluded him.

"So have you," she answered. "I'm not sure yet whether I like it. Not that it matters, of course. We have to get out of here either way. That's pretty obvious."

He stared at her, this time saying nothing.

"You play to win," she stated. "You always did. I didn't know that then, but I do now."

He laughed a low, rich sound of pleasure.

A warmth blossomed suddenly inside her.

"Halt!" A voice came sharply out of the darkness and soldiers stepped forward. Light gleamed on the barrels of their guns. "Identify yourselves."

Neither Elena nor Aiden had seen the soldiers at the side of the street, and now they were suddenly surrounded. The pressure of Aiden's fingers on Elena's arm tightened until it hurt.

Aiden gave both their names.

"Where are you going?" The soldier in command spoke abruptly as he held a light up to Elena's face.

"I'm taking her home," Aiden answered. "She shouldn't be out alone after dark. I'll see she doesn't do it again; it's not safe around here."

"Do that." The soldier shone the light on Aiden's face. "Do I know you?"

Elena felt Aiden stiffen, and then hesitate,

341

even though he was touching her nowhere but on her arm.

"I went out to see my boyfriend," she answered the soldier. "But I won't do it again, sir. My brother," she indicated Aiden, "came to get me home before my father finds out."

One of the soldiers laughed, then another joined in.

Elena said nothing but smiled as if she were shy.

Aiden jerked her arm not very gently and pulled her a step or two.

"I'd keep her at home for a little while, a week or two," the commander said. "If your father can't keep her in order, then you'd better. It's not a good time to be around alone."

"Thank you," Aiden replied. "Good advice." He said that to Elena, rather than the soldier.

They walked away, around the corner, and a hundred yards along the next street before they spoke again.

"Where are we going?" she asked a little breathlessly.

"Somewhere safe. I haven't decided where yet."

"Safe . . . for how long?"

He did not look at her. "Until I can work

out how best to get out of here. I was hoping against hope that Max was still alive, but there's no getting round that he's been murdered. They're after us, Elena, or at least after me. I'm afraid this is real, it's a matter of survival. Have you still got the list?"

"Yes, of course I have. But it's my job to get you out, not to get out without you." As soon as she said the words, it sounded final, an irretrievable commitment. How much did she mean that, and why? For Aiden? Or because it was her promise to Peter Howard or, really, to Lucas?

She glanced at Aiden. He had the same expression he had had in the past, when they would have an adventure together. Daring, imaginative, with that touch of real danger that made it compelling, a beat in the blood that would remain long after the reality was lost.

"I suppose you have something in mind," she said, staring straight back at him. "This is no time for games."

"I do," he said softly. "But you won't like it."

She swallowed hard. "Does that matter?"

"Not really. Come on." He pulled her forward, off the street and into an alley. Just as the sound of marching feet echoed twenty or thirty yards away, he slammed

343

her up against the wall of one of the buildings and pulled her skirt up, then lunged toward her, holding her by the hair. He forced his face close to hers and began to move rhythmically against her.

The marching men went past, calling out crude remarks. One of them asked for the next turn. Aiden ignored them all, as if he had heard nothing. Their footsteps faded away and he stopped and let her skirt fall back in place.

Elena gasped and tried to control her shock.

"If you didn't like that, you'll hate this," he said. "We need to take the alley down to the water. There's a small canal that goes through this part of the city toward where we need to be. We can make our way to it along the back streets. It's narrow and steep, but it's not the end of the world. We can go along — it's not so very deep — and if we fall, the water will be cold and filthy. God knows what's floating in it, but probably nothing alive to do us any harm." He waited, almost as if he expected her to refuse.

Was he doing it to test her? *Don't be stupid,* she told herself. *He needs to escape as much as you do.* To her own ears, she sounded as if she meant it.

Without hesitation, he led the way through the alley to the edge of what was little more than a large ditch. There was a narrow ledge above it, then steep sloping sides without anything to hold on to or climb back up if she fell in. He turned around once as she hesitated. She must be easily visible in the glimmer from the end of sunset. She could see him clearly, too, like a figure of bronze. He made as if to take a step toward her, to come for her or perhaps even to turn back.

She stepped forward, slithering a foot or two on the wet stone, then finding her footing and walking along the narrow ledge, six inches at a time, after him.

He turned, no longer watching her, and went on ahead.

It was a nightmare walk. The slimy stones beneath her feet, the crumbling wall on the right, and the dark filthy water to the left. But she made it all the way to where the ditch emptied into a narrow black-surfaced canal. Now what?

She was standing beside him, and she could see in the fading dusk the curve of his lips. The image was almost clear in the soft graying light. He held out his hand.

She placed one foot on the stones, then the other. He dropped down into the water. It came almost to his chest and he was five inches taller than she.

For an instant she froze, then she forced herself to slide off, a little clumsily, and the cold water came up to her neck. She found it difficult not to shiver. It was harder still to take the steps forward and down even further, until the water lapped her chin. If she lost her footing, she would go under. She could already feel the gentle pull of the moving water, sucking her into one of the real canals and then the bay, and then out to sea.

For a moment, she panicked. What if he left her here, alone, in the black night with no idea of where she was going? She was an idiot! How could she have trusted him? Did Peter Howard have any idea what he was doing? Or, worse, had he sent her here to test Aiden, to prove finally whether he was for England or Germany? She was the sacrifice to find out!

She felt his fingers close over hers and she grasped them with all her strength. Then she thought that if he were going to drown her, this was the last thing he would have done. But she had no defense anyway: he was only a yard away and far stronger than she.

"Come on," he said sharply. "Elena! Move!"

She did not answer, but pushed her way closer to him in the black water, and her feet felt a muddy bottom hard enough to stand on. His grip was strong, pulling her forward until she was level with him. Then he put his arm around her for a moment. It was almost as if the past were back again. This could have been the clean cold water of the North Sea, off the coast of Northumberland, not a black canal running somewhere through the heart of Trieste. An adventure, not an escape.

A sudden thought rushed into her head. The list! Would the water destroy it? She felt it against her skin, the paper folded many times. Perhaps that alone would protect its vital information.

His fingers tightened around hers, and she gave an answering grip.

CHAPTER 17

Peter walked slowly up the slight incline of the path at the edge of the field. Not because it was steep, but because he was early for his meeting with Lucas. This was deliberate, because he wanted time alone, here in the early evening light.

The air was cool and smelled sweet. The sun was low on the horizon, making long shadows from the stocks of straw still uncollected after the harvesting. It was too early for the winter wheat to be sown. Then there would be new-turned lands waiting for it, good earth. It was one of the few things that did not change.

As he walked, the wind was gentle on his face, his eyes narrowed against the light tinged with red-gold as the sun sank toward the low cloud bank in the west. A flock of starlings rose from a nearby copse, black dots against the sky, all wheeling at once, as if a single mind were directing a thousand birds.

He found himself smiling for no reason. He was not particularly happy. Lucas had sent for him with urgency. In fact, he had said it must be today. Was he going to ask about Elena? Peter had not heard from her. As far as he knew, she was still in Trieste and had located Aiden Strother. But there had been nothing from her for almost a week. He should not worry. In May, in Berlin, she had proven herself brave and resourceful. She would not communicate unnecessarily, and above all, not dangerously. She had had a lot of training since then, but was she really cut out for this work? Had he taken her on simply because she was Lucas's granddaughter? Or because she knew Aiden Strother? Were those enough reasons?

He came to the end of the rise. The hedge beside him was full of orange hips where the wild roses had been, and darker red clusters of berries from the hawthorns, which had been covered with white blossoms, like snowdrifts in the spring. The perfume was almost too heavy. He paused and mourned its loss, but he acknowledged its glory was in its transience. It would come again another year. Would that everything

349

else could come so easily, or so surely, but each loss grew a little heavier, a little harder to deal with.

Lucas had called this meeting, but what could Peter say to him that would ease his mind, when he himself was anxious about what was happening in Trieste? He had other sources, naturally, but the word from Vienna, Berlin, Rome was all imprecise. It was Aiden who had worked his way to the core of the Fatherland Front conspiracy, after years of patient labor gaining the trust of the Nazis. But was there a split in the Front? A seed of something else hidden in the heart of it?

The shadows from the stocks were growing longer. A gust of wind blew straw dust in the air, giving it a sweet, clean smell. He was at a high point, only a slight swell in the land and yet, as he turned slowly, he could see for miles the gentle fields rolling away into the haze of the distance, and here and there a copse of trees, some of them hundreds of years old. He felt an aching love for it, the sight, the sweet-smelling wind in his face. He knew this was fragile; it could be broken like anything else.

The moment was shattered by the hard thump of Toby throwing himself at Peter's legs in total certainty of the welcome he always received.

Peter bent down and put his arms around the dog in a quick hug. He felt him wriggling, as if his whole body were made of muscle. He knotted his fingers in the thick fur, then let him go and stood up.

Lucas was still twenty yards away, but rapidly approaching. Even at a distance, Peter could see the weariness and a certain grief in his face. The lines from his nose to his mouth were deeper; he was smiling very slightly, but there was no sense of pleasure coming from him.

"What is it?" Peter asked, as soon as Lucas was close enough to hear him.

"Let's walk," Lucas replied, turning and beginning to go back in the direction he had come, toward the woods again.

Peter fell in step with him, and Toby — now certain of where they were going — bounded ahead of them.

"You know Stoney Canning?" Lucas asked.

Peter did not hesitate. "Of course."

"He's dead," Lucas said, eyes down at the rough ground. They were walking across giant roots protruding through the ground, the shape of claws grasping the earth. "The police say it was a stroke or a heart attack. I'm sure now that it was murder."

Peter felt the shock ripple through him, followed instantly by grief. He knew Stoney only slightly, but he liked him very much.

"The police called me because Stoney has no one else, and he left his affairs in my hands," Lucas explained. "Josephine and I went to his house immediately. He was found at the bottom of the stairs." His voice was level, as devoid of emotion as he could make it. "At first glance, it looks as if he had an attack and fell down, probably dead before he reached the bottom. But I think if the pathologist looks hard enough, investigating the bruise on his head, he'll find it didn't come postmortem but was actually the cause of death . . . and it happened in the potting shed, nowhere near the stairs. There were blood traces there; he had no other cuts." Lucas stopped, glancing at Peter and then walking on, his step slower, as though waiting for Peter's reaction.

"Did you say that to the police?" Peter asked. He felt the weight of something far bigger, far darker, beneath the surface.

When Lucas did not respond, Peter felt anger rise. "So, they told you to go home and they'd take care of it," he summarized, making a guess. "What do you think really happened and why? I mean, why did it happen?"

Lucas smiled briefly, a moment of light in his face, and then it was gone again. "Stoney came to see me a week ago. He told me he had sheets of figures representing money he believed — was sure — someone has been moving through MI6 accounts. It comes and goes. All appears fine . . . until you look more closely. You need a head for figures like Stoney's to understand it, and —"

"And you have one," Peter interrupted, knowing that Lucas did not need to be modest about it.

"I might understand the figures, yes," Lucas agreed. "But not the coding of it, nor the reason why the movement of the sums is hidden. And I mean hundreds of thousands of pounds, at least."

Peter felt a chill, as if the sun had gone behind the horizon, although actually it was still crimson in the west and staining all the clouds around it, as if dripping fire on the small patches of water, the ponds and streams, in the field. "Laundering money through MI6? For God's sake, why?" he asked, although a fear was settling at the corners of his mind.

Lucas looked at him for a moment and then far away across the fields. He could see Toby and called him several times, until he saw him running toward them and was satisfied.

"Funding for one of Hitler's schemes," he replied. "A very big one. I don't know which, but my guess would be the Fatherland Front, to squeeze Dollfuss until either he breaks or they kill him." Lucas paused for several moments.

Was he marshaling the reasons in his head? The evidence? Or was he wondering how much to tell Peter . . . or not to tell him?

"Margot went to Berlin for Cecily Cordell's wedding, you know," Lucas said at last.

There was silence for a few more moments. Toby arrived, running straight into Lucas, whose legs were, as usual, braced for it. He bent and patted the dog. "She overheard several conversations," he told Peter. "She told me about it after her father had dismissed it as nonsense, young men boasting and of no importance. At least, that's what he told her." He straightened up and met Peter's eyes frankly. He relayed what Margot had said.

"That's not nonsense," Peter answered. "I'm afraid it's true. It's a matter of exactly how and when. It looks like they're not quite ready yet, maybe sometime early next

354

year, but I've got other information that it could be sooner than that. There seems to be a splinter group within their own body, like a cancer eating the heart out of them. Likely to preempt them in late October this year." He was still debating telling Lucas the whole truth. Perhaps that would jeopardize a job, or worse, break a trust he needed to keep. Trust was the breath of life to a man who was alone and surrounded by enemies. That was one reason he had sent Elena to get Aiden Strother back alive. It was not just to show his whole support for Aiden, but for every other agent in the field. If you deliberately let one go, morally you have to let them all go. Trust was built up . . . or it went nowhere.

Lucas was waiting.

Peter made the decision. "That's why we have Aiden Strother in Trieste. He's sent a lot of good information back, but now we've got to get him out."

Lucas's face was tight. Neither of them mentioned Elena, but the fact of her mission was there between them, as if she were beside them in the field.

"You trust him?" Lucas asked quietly.

Peter could either answer honestly or commit a betrayal that could never be mended. "He's been planted deep, for years.

355

All his information — and there's been a lot of it — has been good."

"So far . . ." Lucas said. "Do you still trust him?" He waited.

A flock of starlings whirled up in the sky, curved, and came down again.

"I don't know," Peter said honestly. "I have no grounds not to. I just . . ."

"Did you send him to Germany?"

"I picked him out," Peter admitted. "But Bradley actually sent him. He denies it, which is interesting. But he has to have authorized continuing it, not to mention getting the reports."

Lucas's face was as tight and hard as Peter had ever seen it, and yet he understood perfectly. "Was it Bradley who used Elena in the original, pretended, betrayal?"

"Yes . . ." There was nothing he could add. It was six years ago.

"I see." Lucas did not make excuses. There was a world of knowledge unspoken between them. "When did you last hear from her?"

"Not since she found him. Pretty quickly. She's good."

"Don't make —" Lucas snapped, then broke off as quickly. "Good," he repeated. He looked away. "What now?"

"Strother has a list of the donors of money

collected in Austria, Italy, and America, all for the Fatherland Front. A complete list. Ours is good, but only partial. That's why we have to get him out, apart from the morality of not leaving him there, now that his contact has disappeared. Elena's instructions are to bring him out with his information, if she possibly can."

Lucas looked back at him at last. "That might make sense, of course. Stoney's list, that's the other half of it: the sums involved." He sounded as if it hurt even to speak, but clearly it was making sense to him.

A different thought was forming hard and deep in Peter's mind. Aiden Strother was Bradley's man, not Peter's. Bradley had contacted him only because he was interested in what Peter knew and Bradley did not. At least he said he did not, but someone here in London might be responsible for Stoney Canning's death, if Lucas was right. "Who do you think killed Stoney?" he asked abruptly.

"I don't know," Lucas replied, "but I mean to find out. That's really what I wanted to ask you."

Peter held up his hand. "If you were running an inquiry into European money given to Hitler to bring down the Austrian government, would you trust the murder of Canning to someone else? Leave it incomplete? Or give them that much power over you?"

Lucas did not have to hesitate. "One golden rule for anything: never involve anyone you don't have to." He drew in his breath, then let it out again in a sigh. "I have a feeling Stoney knew the man who killed him." A shadow crossed his face. "Perhaps even knew that he had come for that reason."

Peter winced. It was a sickening thought. "You're sure?"

"I believe so, but I need proof."

"Are you thinking of taking it to the police?" Peter began.

"No, of course not!" Lucas said sharply. His face twisted with bitter humor. "Apart from the fact that I'm not sure whom I trust, there are some very odd political opinions around now. God knows I don't want another war, but I think perhaps there are even worse things. Like slowly being eviscerated by lies and fear. Always being afraid and eventually losing your balance so that you don't know what you believe anymore. Thinking it will be all right if you do as you're told, until you believe any lie. Because you don't know what the truth is anymore, you wake up afraid and go to sleep afraid. You don't know who your enemies are when truth dies, and you are afraid of anything different. That's worse, the ultimate defeat, when you become indistinguishable from your enemy. You look in the mirror and you don't know who you see."

Peter was too horrified to argue. And, in truth, he had no argument to give. "If your enemy has turned you into a copy of himself, he has won everything," he said, as if perhaps he were repeating Lucas's words back to him. "Find out who killed Stoney Canning," he added quietly. "And you had better not trust anyone, even in MI6. It has to have started there."

"What are you going to do?" Lucas asked. His face was pinched with worry, and in the deepening gold of the light and the darkening of the shadows, he looked desperately vulnerable.

"I'm going to Trieste," Peter answered.

"Is Elena in danger?" Lucas's voice almost choked on the words.

"Not that I know of," Peter replied. "Although Strother is quick and highly intelligent, and very brave, he's not my man."

"He's Bradley's?"

"That's what I'm going to find out."

Lucas nodded, stood still, then turned and

walked toward the shadows of the trees, too choked by emotion to speak. Toby bounded after him.

When Peter reached his home, he found Pamela standing in the middle of the drawing room, facing him. She looked lovely, her fair skin flushed, her hair shining. She was wearing a plain white dress that was not especially fashionable, but so beautifully cut it would never date.

"I called your office. They said you'd left." Her voice was measured, quite soft. He knew she was holding in her temper with great difficulty. "I thought maybe you would remember that we had plans for tonight." She looked at his shoes, which were dirty, a piece of straw caught in one of the laces. "But I see you have been God knows where."

As always, he could not tell her. He should have been able to say something about secret work now, but he did not truly know her opinions. She had friends who believed cooperation with Hitler was the way to eventual peace. "I'm sorry," he said, knowing it was not enough. He always said it, and it meant less each time.

"You're always sorry," she snapped. "But not sorry enough to change. And don't tell me you had a late meeting! You've got straw in your shoes and dog hair on your clothes. I'll call a taxi. I'm going to the Rutledges' alone. I'll see you when I get back, assuming you're still here."

He had to make an effort now. She had a right to be angry, years of right. "Stoney Canning is dead," he said quietly. "I've known him since before the war. It looks as if he's been murdered, but it's not clear yet who did it."

"Oh." She looked bewildered. "I'm sorry." That was genuine. It was in her eyes, the tone of her voice, the way she stood.

"I don't think you knew him. He was a bit eccentric, very lonely, I think." He didn't know why he was talking like this. It didn't make any difference now, except that it was part of the reason he had to find out who had done this. Perhaps he wanted someone to pay part of the debt that he himself owed for the years of quiet duty of an old man, a man who apparently had no one in his life outside MI6. "He had no one," he said aloud.

"Is there anything I can do?" she asked, her voice softer.

"I don't think so, but you might . . ."

"What?"

"You might . . ." Should he ask her?

361

"Perhaps you would help Josephine Standish with organizing the funeral. Stoney had nobody. We should do it properly, with flowers and —"

"I will," she said immediately. "You can tell me something about him, what he liked."

"Thank you, Pamela."

"You can't know yet when it will be . . ."

"No. Lucas says he was murdered, but the police are treating the death as from natural causes." Already he had said too much. He could see it in her face. "I say that because it might delay things." He must say enough to explain. "I expect they just have to do a post-mortem to be sure. Apparently, he wasn't ill."

"Poor man" was all she said. "I'll wait until you tell me."

"No," he said quietly. "I have to go to Trieste tonight. I'm sorry. Someone else is in trouble." He stopped. There was really nothing more he could add. He was increasingly afraid of what he might find, and as always, he could not explain it.

"Be careful," she answered.

She meant more than that. How much did she know, or guess? How could he have been so blind as to think his own wife couldn't see what he was about? How could

362

he have underestimated her so badly? If only he could tell her more.

be have understand and not so badly it only
he could tell her more.

CHAPTER 18

Elena woke very late. She looked at the
small alarm clock on the table beside her
bed and saw that it was after ten. The first
thing she was aware of was that her body
ached. She remembered the previous night,
the bitter, perishing chill of black water.
Now there was daylight coming through the
wooden slats of the blinds and she recognized where she was. It was her apartment
in Trieste, but it was far from the comfort
of her home in London.

Then she remembered yesterday, finding
Max's body, or what was left of it. For a
moment, she was ice cold and nausea
gripped her, then it passed, or at least she
gained control over it. She recalled escaping
with Aiden through the streets and eventually into the dark water of the canal. She
could not remember ever having felt so
cold. But they were alive and, for the moment, no one knew where they were . . . or

who they were.

Aiden had seen her to the door but he, too, was soaking wet and the night had lost the balmy summer warmth of only a few days before. She had kissed him good night quickly and gone inside, locking the door behind her. She had stripped off her soaking clothes and stepped into the shower, as hot as she could bear it, and had run it until it was no longer any more than warm. Then she toweled herself down, rubbing hard to get her circulation going.

She had thought she would lie awake remembering the horror, the fear, even the feeling of Aiden supporting her physically for a moment, kissing her briefly but fiercely, like having the past back again — the exhilaration and the understanding — only wiser this time, more as equals than before. But surprisingly, she had slept. Even the dreams had been few. Few . . . and blurred.

Now she forced herself to get up, wash, dress, and begin the morning, although it was already half over. Would there be police looking for her? That brought back memories of Berlin, which was ridiculous. She had discovered the body of a man who had been dead since before she landed in Trieste, and whom she had never known. It was a dreadful sight, but she had had no part in his death. They could do nothing for him; she could never have helped. But would the police know that, or believe it if they recognized her from the brief encounter in the street last night? What sane, innocent woman goes looking for dead bodies in water vats in the slums?

Aiden had said they were in immediate danger. Perhaps he even more than she! Max had been Aiden's one contact with Peter Howard and, as far as she knew, with England. It was her job to get him out with his information. Was that more than the list of names of those who were collaborating financially with the Fatherland Front? It sounded innocuous enough, until you realized that its purpose was to extend Nazi power and possession over most of Northern Italy.

In a rush of panic, she retrieved the folded paper. Had the canal's water washed away the critical information? She unfolded it carefully and was relieved to find the writing legible. The paper was still quite damp, so she spread it across the bed, hoping the warmth of the sun would dry it.

She had no bread in the house, no fresh tea or coffee. There was jam, but no butter. She hated the way jam seeped into any kind of bread without butter to keep them separate, making the bread soggy. She needed several supplies, at least two days' more, in case it was that long until she could organize some form of transport. And it might be difficult to persuade Aiden that it was too dangerous to stay.

She thought of his face in the streetlight last night, his excitement. He was more alive than anyone she had ever known. He made others seem pallid, even bloodless. This rescue, the fight against the Fatherland Front, the whole visit to Trieste in its limpid light, all of it was like a new birth into another more vivid world — it all brought the past back again, but this time she was so much more aware of it, in control, almost as if she had at last found her real self.

But this was no time for considering the status of her life. She must make plans to save them both. And she must say goodbye to Gabrielle, even if Gabrielle did not know that it was indeed goodbye. And at least pay for the dress. She had taken it and lost it; there must be reparation.

She would have breakfast at one of the local cafés and then think of making plans.

It was half past one when she stopped by Gabrielle's apartment, much further inland than her own. Elena was pleased to find her at home. She had brought some fresh fruit as a gift. The room was small, but so cleverly designed that it did not seem so, and it was full of light at this time of the day. It took Elena a moment to realize that the light was thanks to a clever use of mirrors. She smiled at the skill of it. "It's beautiful."

"Illusion," Gabrielle said, smiling a little ruefully. "It's amazing what you can achieve if you know how. It's my old home in France, re-created with tricks of memory and imagination."

Elena looked at the porcelain and the glass and realized it was all French, as were the clock and the calendar on the wall, with pictures of the French countryside. She recognized the architecture, the deep fields and huge white Charolais cows. "Normandy?" she asked.

"Yes, do you know it?" Gabrielle's face lit with pleasure.

"A little," Elena answered, smiling at the memory. "My father was British ambassador in Paris for a short while." She unpacked the fruit and placed it carefully in one of the empty dishes. "I'll go back one day, but for now I will have to return to England. And I have lost your gray dress. I can't replace it, but I must make some recompense."

"You don't need to," Gabrielle said

quickly. "It didn't really suit me anyway." She dismissed it with a wave of her hand.

Suddenly, there was shouting in the street outside, high-pitched. Then a shot rang out, followed by more shouting.

Franz appeared at the door, eyes wide and frightened. His face was twisted, his fair hair tousled. "Mama, what's happening?" He looked at Elena, then went round the table to Gabrielle and she kneeled to take him in her arms.

"It's all right, little one," she said to him in French. "They're angry with each other, not with us. Stay in here, don't go to the window, and you'll be all right." She looked at Elena over the child's head. "They arrested several people last night. I don't know what it was about, but I can guess."

Elena said nothing but felt a sense of relief sweep through her. "If you were to guess," she asked, "would it be the Front, striking already? I thought they weren't going to act for weeks!"

"I don't think it is, but everyone is very tense," Gabrielle replied. She hugged Franz quickly, then let him go. "Would you like some of the grapes that Elena has brought?" she asked him.

He looked at Elena and then at the grapes on the table.

"Yes."

"Yes . . . what?"

"Yes . . . I would." Then he smiled shyly, sharing the joke with her.

"Yes . . . please," Gabrielle corrected him, but she touched his cheek so gently that he could hardly have felt it.

There was more shouting in the street, and several more shots, but Franz took the grapes and did not seem to be worried anymore.

"You had better stay here for a while," Gabrielle observed, standing up slowly. "Go home when it settles a bit."

"Do you know what's happening?" Elena asked, as there were more angry voices in the street and then another volley of shots, sounding some distance away.

Gabrielle moved out of the line of the windows, taking Franz with her. Not that she had to grasp him, the boy was so close he was now practically standing on her feet.

Elena heard the front door open and then close. Not loudly, but as if someone had come in with a key. They all froze, Franz twisting the fabric of Gabrielle's skirt with tight fists.

There were footsteps in the passage, then Aiden stood in the doorway. He was shaved, his hair tidy, and dressed with casual grace, but his skin was pale and his eyes shadowed. He took in Elena's presence with a single glance. Had he expected her to be here? "You've got to get out!" he said to Gabrielle. "All hell's broken loose. The streets are still safe, more or less, but they won't stay that way."

"What happened?" Gabrielle did not raise her voice, but it was hard-edged. "Did somebody jump the gun?"

"Looks like it," he answered, coming forward into the room. "Some Fatherland men have stormed the arsenal. Thought they were making a preemptive strike."

"Do you know who?" Gabrielle asked.

"What the hell does it matter!" he said sharply. "You've got to get out of here for a few days anyway. Get out of the city. You know where to go." He left the rest unsaid, as if it were a previously understood plan.

Elena wondered how long they had known about, or expected, this.

Gabrielle nodded a fraction. "We'll pack." She took Franz's hand in hers. "Come on, sweetheart, we're going to go on that trip I've told you about. We've got everything ready."

"Can we take the grapes?" he asked, looking at Elena, and then at the table where the grapes were still sitting.

371

"Of course!" Gabrielle took them up in her other hand. She looked momentarily at Elena, a question in her eyes.

"I'm going with Aiden," Elena said. There was no other choice for her, no matter what shadows of doubt were at the edges of her mind. It was even more important now that she get him out of the city. It wasn't only the list, which she had safely hidden now in her bag's side compartment. It was also the assumption that he would be adding to it.

Gabrielle stared at her for a moment, as if digesting what Elena had said. "Then I have a gift for you. Wait a moment." She turned, with Franz on her heels, and went into the bedroom.

Aiden's eyes followed Gabrielle. He even took a step after her, then changed his mind and turned back to Elena. "We must go," he said urgently. "We've got to get out of here, now." He lowered his voice. "We can't risk airports, even small ones. They will be watching every one of them. They can't afford to let us escape. We know too much . . ."

"Rail?" she asked.

"No, they can stop any train, and the nearest border is Austria."

"Road?"

"Where do we get a car?" He gave a tight

little grimace. "We have the best chance of escaping without being followed if we go by sea."

A ship. She tried to imagine going aboard secretly. How could they possibly manage it? They would be so obviously fugitives. And once they were aboard, they were trapped. No one gets off a ship at sea.

Gabrielle came back into the room holding out a small but beautifully ornamented hair comb. She met Elena's eyes, smiled, and put it into her hands. For an instant, Elena felt the handle was loose and might come open in her grasp. "Thank you." She smiled and put it in her handbag.

Aiden was increasingly impatient. "Gabrielle, please hurry. You and Franz have to go down into the city. If you try leaving, they'll be watching the roads. Someone has betrayed us again, and I'm betting it was Ferdie."

"Are you going?" Gabrielle asked, glancing at Elena, then back at Aiden.

"Yes," he answered. "As soon as I'm sure you've left, I'll lock up behind you." He leaned forward, brushed a stray lock of dark hair from her brow, and kissed her very gently on the cheek. "Go now." He turned and looked at Elena. "Are you sure? I could make my way out of here without you.

373

Maybe not as well, but you . . ." He stopped and gave a twisted little smile. "If you could go with Gabrielle, it would be safer. If we get out, it could be rough, even at best we —"

"I understand!" she said sharply. "You're wasting time." She gave Gabrielle a quick hug, then bent and kissed Franz on the cheek. "Look after each other," she whispered. "Goodbye for now."

"Goodbye," Franz whispered back, then he and his mother went out of the front door, leaving Elena and Aiden alone.

Aiden remained looking at the door for several seconds, then his expression changed, the gentleness vanished. "They may have found Max by now. There's no time to go back for anything."

"I've got no clothes or —" Elena started, then stopped. No one thought of anything as trivial as clothes when they were running for their lives.

Aiden took her arms and held her hard. "Elena, if you haven't the nerve to come with me, then you should have gone with Gabrielle."

"I have!" she said angrily. "I'm just trying to think a step ahead."

"Have you got money and your passport?" He glanced at her handbag. "And your cameras, of course. And the list?"

"Yes, of course I have the list!"

"Then come on!"

"Gabrielle wouldn't mind if I borrowed at least some clean underwear," she argued. "I'll be back in a moment."

"Hurry. I don't know how far behind us they are, and we can't go directly to the port. That's exactly what they expect us to do. We have to go the long way around, inland first, then back on the main thoroughfares, looking like tourists. We can't hurry. We must stop and look at shop windows. Anyone who runs, or rushes about in any way, or even looks frightened, will draw attention. We can't afford that." He gave a small, rueful shrug. "I can't. Howard won't be very pleased with you if you get me shot!"

"I won't get you shot!" she said tartly.

He gripped her arm hard. "The Fatherland Front is all through Austria, but this is the driving unit. If they begin, the rest will follow."

"Can we —"

He cut her off. "No, I've done all I can. We've got to get out. They know me, Elena! Don't argue, just do it!"

"I'll be two moments." She pulled away from his grasp and went swiftly into Ga-

375

brielle's bedroom. She opened drawers and found underwear that would do. She did not take the best. She preferred to believe that Gabrielle would come back. She opened the wardrobe and picked out the plainest dress and a heavy woollen jacket. She put the jacket, the dress, and the underwear in a small traveling bag.

Aiden was waiting for her. He looked her up and down. "Right." He gave a sudden, brilliant smile. "Come on, this is going to be tough. Are you ready?"

"Yes," she said with certainty. Not because she was sure they would be safe, but because she could not change her mind. She must go with Aiden.

They went out of the door, closed and locked it, then walked into the street. There was no shouting now, no gunfire. Aiden took her arm lightly, just enough to guide her to the left and then across the road to the opposite side. "Keep walking," he said softly. "Don't hurry; don't meet anyone's eyes."

"Are they looking for us?" she asked.

"I don't know, but Ferdie might well be looking for me. He has to get rid of me, because I know too much."

They walked for a little while, she thought

toward the docks, but she knew they were still miles away. They crossed another street. There were very few people out; the gunfire must have kept them inside, perhaps behind locked doors. That's where Elena would have been, had she the choice.

"Do they know who you are?" she asked quietly.

He glanced at her, then away again. "I think Ferdie does. He knows there's someone who's a British spy, because of the number of things that have gone wrong. Process of elimination, really. And our encounter in the nightclub was a bit of a giveaway. Couldn't last forever." He said the words as if they were both good and bad.

"Would you have gone earlier, if Max hadn't been killed?" The moment she put words to it, she wished she had not. Aiden was a very private person, in some ways. He had never told her of his family, his past, even his present feelings. "I'm sorry."

He looked at her, smiling. "Why? It's a shame about Max. He was a decent enough man, but it's the chances of the trade. He knew that." His lips tightened in a grimace, rueful, philosophical. "I just hope it was quick. I always hope it's quick. It's necessary sometimes that people die in this business. We're dealing with the rise and fall of rulers, sometimes of nations. Death is necessary, but cruelty is not."

"It attracts the people who enjoy cruelty," she argued. She was not thinking of Austria or Trieste, but of Berlin, of the students dancing around the fires as they burned books, as if they could also burn ideas. She had not talked about it with Aiden. Perhaps he didn't even know. Was that possible? Later, perhaps, she would tell him; this was not the time.

"But violence attracts those who like cruelty," he added, as if he could read her thoughts, or guess them. "When the fight gets tough, we use what we can."

Somewhere ahead of them there was shouting, but this time no gunfire.

Aiden pulled her to a stop. "That way." He pointed, and without saying anything more, he started out again. Not quickly, but at a steady pace, as if they were not fugitives. They must not attract attention by obviously heading somewhere. Anyone obviously fleeing would be noticed. They avoided all the main thoroughfares, rather seeming to meander as tourists might. Several times they circled round places where there were soldiers, taking the longer, more circuitous route, but always getting

378

closer to the docks.

They stopped for a break and something to eat. He looked at her anxiously. "Are you all right?"

Elena was tired. Her legs ached and she was glad to sit down, but she was no longer as frightened as she had been in the beginning. They had seen no more violence. They were in a better part of the city. It was almost as if nothing had happened, except that they were growing closer. The years apart had melted away, like a dream in the night, gone with daylight's return.

As if he recognized her thoughts, he said, "It's like old times, isn't it?" He put his hand out across the table, in the café where they sat, his palm up and open.

She reached out and touched his fingertips. It was a gesture of communication, rather than ownership. It was comfortable, as between equals. That was so different. She used to feel so much as if he were the leader, and she was privileged to follow. Now she kept up, she had her own value. She smiled back at him.

When they left, the sun was lower, the shadows longer across the pavement and into the narrow streets. Perhaps that was a good thing; they were definitely close to the waterfront now. This was the oldest part of the city: not the smart, rich area with the exquisite views, but the old industrial port.

They walked along a narrow pavement toward the dock. There was not far to go. It seemed that if anyone was trying to stop them, they had given up.

"This was a good idea," she said softly.

"Less than a mile to go and we'll start looking for boats waiting to take the evening tide."

"Do you know the tides?"

"Of course." He smiled with black humor. "I knew this might happen."

"What does the Fatherland Front want to do, other than have Austria join Germany? How is that not a political decision?"

"Big political decisions aren't made without getting the people on your side first," Aiden said with a laugh in his voice. "Sometimes it takes one decisive action, and then people accept it and follow. That's what the Fatherland Front wants, and Chancellor Dollfuss does not."

"And England doesn't."

"Of course not. England wants Hitler stopped wherever possible, or most of England does. That's why we have to get home. At least one of us must get this list of financial contributors to MI6. Given our experience, we know that wars are expensive. A waste of steel, of brick and stone. Above all, of lives."

They were in a shadowed alley. At the far end of it, a figure moved rapidly, then seemed to disappear.

Aiden pulled Elena to a stop almost roughly.

She did not move quickly enough to avoid being yanked, and almost lost her balance. "What is it?" she whispered suddenly. The calm was shattered, the momentary island of certainty.

"Someone at the end of the alley. A man. He moved as if he didn't want to be seen," Aiden replied, his mouth close to her ear.

"Maybe he's frightened, too," she suggested.

"I don't think so." His voice was low, tense. "There's not much difference between the hunter and the hunted, but it's there if you know. Stay behind me and be ready to move the second I say."

Closer to the wall now, they both moved forward, almost inching along the shadowed stone, occasionally glancing down at the chipped pavement.

A man moved across the street, the lowering sun bright on his face for a moment. Then he was gone. He did not even glance toward them. Were they invisible in the shadow of the wall? Or did he simply not care?

Elena stayed as close as she could to Aiden.

They were almost at the end of the street when the shot rang out, shattering the silence in the narrow space. It slammed against the stone wall above Aiden's head, just slightly too high to strike him.

He froze.

Elena stood half behind him, her heart thumping wildly.

"Keep still," Aiden whispered.

She touched his arm in acknowledgment.

He took a step forward.

She was engulfed by fear for him; it was like a wave almost suffocating her.

His right hand moved under his jacket, then came up. His answering shot was as loud and jarring as if it had come from her own hand. The gun was inches away from her.

"Keep back!" he whispered.

They were moving on now, slowly, very carefully.

Silence.

Aiden put his left arm out and grasped her, pulling her closer to him, and foot by foot, they came to the corner.

"Stop," he whispered. He bent down and

picked up a pebble and threw it ahead of him.

There was no answering sound, no movement she could hear. "Has he gone?" Elena asked.

"No. He has to get me. He won't stop until one of us is dead."

"Dead?"

"Or wounded badly."

"Would you leave him alive?" she asked.

He did not answer.

Silence.

Elena could hear her own heart beating.

Then there was a sound, like a tiny stone rolling, but she could not tell in which direction. Somewhere to the left?

Aiden froze.

Seconds ticked by.

Another stone rolled somewhere else, further away.

Elena looked at Aiden's face. Already the sun was lower, the light a deeper gold, catching the dust in the air like the patina of an old painting. She had an artist's moment of regret that she could not photograph it.

"Get behind me." Aiden did little more than breathe the order, but his hand on her arm was hard.

She obeyed.

He moved in front of her, one step forward, then another. They were very near the corner now.

Elena's heart was beating even more violently, making her feel as if her whole body were shuddering. What could she do to help him? Her mind was whirling, grasping at ideas, and none of them made sense.

There was another shot, then another, and more chips flew off the wall, but lower down, closer to them. Whoever was shooting at them knew exactly where they were. Where could they move to without breaking into the open?

Aiden turned, pulling Elena back, then swiveled around. They began to run along the pavement as fast as they could go. She could barely keep up with him, and was almost pulled off her feet. They swung around the corner and along the next street, back toward the place the shot had come from. Elena had to watch the street, the uneven stones, the broken curb, trying not to fall while keeping hold of the travel bag.

Then Aiden stopped. "Stay here," he commanded. "As close as you can get to the wall." He did not hesitate to see if she obeyed. He froze. For a moment, Elena froze, too. Then, as Aiden stepped forward, another shot rang out. This one struck the cobblestones ahead of them.

Aiden shot back.

Silence. Seconds ticked by.

"Don't move!" He turned to face her for an instant, looking straight at her, his eyes a brilliant blue in the fading light. She had never felt so close to him, so intimately bound. He leaned forward and kissed her softly on the lips. Then, before she could respond, he turned away and moved a step off the curb and into the street. He ran forward, to the opposite corner, hesitated a moment before stepping out into the open, then turned once more and fired into the darkness, his black figure silhouetted for an instant against the paler stone.

Elena followed as he started to run along the pavement toward the place where he had directed the shot. By the time she caught up with him, he was standing over the body of a man sprawled face-up on the stones, blood covering his chest and soaking his shirt. A revolver lay a few inches from his outstretched hand.

"Ah, Ferdie," Aiden said softly. "I wish you hadn't done this. I really didn't want to hurt you!"

It was Ferdie, from the club room. There was still light in his eyes, but it was fading. He tried to speak, sighed, and then he was still. The light faded, and his eyes were empty.

Elena felt a consuming sense of loss paralyzing her.

Aiden turned from Ferdie. He was looking at Elena, searching her eyes.

She could not think of anything to say.

Aiden stood motionless. Then he put his gun away somewhere inside his jacket and reached for her hand. "We need to go. We've got to get out of here before his friends come." He bent down, picked up Ferdie's gun, and slipped it into his pocket. "We've got to find a boat leaving tonight for anywhere, and get on it. We've got to get that list back to England."

"Yes," she said, almost as if she were speaking in her sleep. The street with the dying sunlight draining everything, as if the darkness absorbed it; the dead man lying at her feet, someone who had been uniquely alive. They were so intensely real that the rest of the world was a dream. And yet they were also separate from everything else, and she ached to get back to the familiar, any reality other than this. "Yes," she said again, following willingly as he took her arm.

They began to walk swiftly toward the dock, then turned the corner without looking back.

386

CHAPTER 19

Lucas and Josephine were at breakfast early, when the September sun was just over the horizon in the east and there was a hint of chill in the air.

"I've been thinking," Josephine began. "If Stoney knew anything — and we are almost certain he did — then he will have left clues of some sort."

"He did know something," Lucas said with absolute certainty. Thinking back on Stoney's visit, he remembered things he had barely noticed at the time: his choice of words, a sense of anxiety deeper than he was admitting to, an absence of his usual wry humor. Lucas recognized it now as controlled fear, perhaps sadness, even an understanding that they might not meet again. Why had he not recognized it at the time? Was he so long out of the game that he had become blind to shades and tones that he used to understand as second nature? Or was it that he thought Stoney was growing lonely, living in the past where he had had many old friends? Please God, Lucas had not condescended to him. Looking back on it, he could not be certain.

"Then he will have left a sign, such as he could," Josephine said. "Something perhaps only you would pick up, or see the meaning of. Lucas" — she put down her cup, as if it were of no more interest to her — "we must go and look further, before the police or anybody else comes and moves things. He may have left clues as to who the murderer was."

"You're right," he cut her off, rising to his feet. "We're going straightaway." He debated whether to tell her about meeting Peter Howard.

"What is it?" she asked. She could not read his thoughts, but she could read his face, and she knew when a new idea or memory had assailed him.

"Yesterday evening, when I took Toby for a walk, I met up with Peter."

"Has he anything to do with Stoney?" Her face suddenly grew more serious. There was a new anxiety in her eyes. She put facts together and made a story as easily as he did.

"Yes," he said. "I told him about it. He

believes Stoney was murdered. But he thinks that there is someone even higher in MI6 who knew about the figures Stoney discovered, and what they mean."

"The money," she cut in. "Where from, and more importantly, where to? Do you know . . . or do you have a guess? I can see it in your face. Why does it trouble you so much?"

"Because Stoney died for it." The initial reason was that simple, whatever complications followed. "Not only that, Peter has an idea where it's going, and so do I. After what Margot told me, I'm almost sure, but we must have proof."

"Margot?" Her face was troubled. "Then has this got something to do with Roger Cordell?"

"I am as certain as we can be of anything that it has nothing at all to do with him."

"Lucas."

"Believe me, Jo, this is far too serious to tell anyone comfortable lies, you least of all," he said quietly. "Margot told me she heard whispers at the wedding party in Berlin. A group calling itself the Fatherland Front is trying to annex Austria to Germany, as a cultural and political ally of the Germans."

"You mean consume it, conquer it without

a fight?" The sudden disgust in her face was so fierce it startled him.

"Yes, that's almost exactly what I mean," he agreed. "The money is for that cause, and the list of contributors would horrify us. That's what Stoney was working on. And the amount is vast, millions."

"And he was killed for it."

"It looks like it," he admitted.

Josephine frowned, her concern deep in the shadows of her eyes. "And there is something else. What more did Peter say to you? And how is it that he knows about it? Did you tell him what Margot told you? You did. Of course you did."

There was nothing to be gained, no protection he could give her from the reality. Now, of all times, he would have wished to, yet it was a relief to tell her, not to face the fear alone. "Peter has a man in Vienna and another in Trieste, where the root of this particular plot is planned. He's well established there, Peter says."

"The point, Lucas?" Her voice was brittle. She looked tired; she was too old to be frightened all over again for those she loved.

And he resented it profoundly. "The point, my dear, is that Aiden Strother is the man in Trieste, and has been for years."

She paled, but she did not interrupt.

"His cover was broken and Peter needed to warn him, in spite of the fact that his contact is apparently dead. He sent the one person who would know Strother by sight, and that he would trust."

"Elena. That's where she's gone!"

"Yes."

Josephine said nothing. For Lucas, this was worse than if she had spoken.

"He didn't tell me until after she had gone," he said. It sounded like an excuse. In fact, it was. "Not that I could argue with his choice. She can't join MI6 but refuse to do the jobs that are dangerous or distasteful."

"I know, I know." She almost choked on the words. "So, all we can do is sort out who killed Stoney Canning and take our evidence to Bradley."

"No, not Bradley." His voice was dry in his throat. "I don't entirely trust him. Nothing specific or I'd do something about it. But this stuff of Stoney's goes very high."

"I thought Bradley was head of MI6? How much higher can you get?" She blinked and shook her head.

"I don't know what more he wants. Maybe he's riding a tiger, and now he can't get off?"

"Oh, heavens." She closed her eyes, then seemed to have to force herself to open them and look at him. "Where the hell have we missed our way so badly?" Her voice cracked and she struggled to keep it level. She seemed to understand all the things he had said, and everything not said as well: the suspicions, the fear, the innate dislike, the disagreement that seemed fundamental. "How far back does this go?" she asked. "Do you even know?"

"I've been studying Stoney's diaries. I haven't read every word — God knows his handwriting is worse than Elena's — but I can trace this thread of thought back just over a year."

Her eyes widened. "That long?"

"Adolf Hitler didn't come to power overnight, Jo. He planned very carefully. He didn't tell people what he was going to do for them; he asked them what they wanted, then turned around and said that was what he would give them. Over forty percent of the people voted for him. It's not as if we couldn't have seen this coming."

"Stoney —"

"Stoney was far wiser than he seemed, but I can't prove anything because he was very vague in his diaries. I might be reading into it what I can see now."

"Then we must find the rest," she said quickly. "This isn't enough. We have to know who killed Aiden's contact, and how, and then why. If I understand all the things you've been saying for the last two years at least, and the things that tie them together — and they must be followed up, if you are right — then it is much worse than we think."

Lucas stood up. "We had better start. We haven't found much here. I've read all the papers we took and you've read most of anything else we could find. We need to look harder."

Josephine also stood. "I'm ready, but we must have a plan. Otherwise, we're going to miss the piece that matters, even if we have it in our hands."

They went out to the car and were several miles along the road before she spoke again. "You knew Stoney at university," she said.

"Yes."

"What did he study? And what else did he do, that you know of? Hobbies, interests, sports . . . ?"

He smiled. "Stoney? No sports, except it came as a surprise to me to learn that he actually skied quite well."

Josephine gave him a doubtful look. "I'm thinking about something the two of you shared. Do you know one end of a ski from the other?"

"I think the bit that curves up goes to the

front," he said with almost a straight face. "But I take your point. He would choose to communicate with me through something I would see, or at least understand when I saw it." He tried to think back to when he and Stoney had been young men, excited by the world of thought, the vast and ever-expanding exploration of the physical universe; by the beliefs of past ages, wonderful minds that embraced, that created the curious and the beautiful. At Cambridge, they had seen dawn over the River Cam, the spreading of light, both outside and within their minds. Lucas looked back on it and remembered the sense of brotherhood that had never completely left him. He remembered one clear night when the stars seemed close enough for him to stretch out and reap with a casual hand. How had he left Stoney alone when he so much needed someone who believed him, when he couldn't explain himself?

Something danced on the edge of his imagination, something only he and Stoney knew.

He pulled into the drive of Stoney's house, then put his foot gently on the accelerator and continued round to the far side of the garage, out of sight of the road.

Josephine glanced at him questioningly.

He knew what was going through her mind. "No," he answered. "I would just rather not explain myself to the local police, or have inquiries filter back to MI6."

She bit her lip but did not answer.

They had the keys now. Lucas was executor of Stoney's estate. They had been back a few times, but still, it felt strange to let themselves into someone else's house, as if they had the right to intrude without even calling out a greeting.

The hall was tidy, exactly as they had left it. There was no sign that anyone else had been there, until Josephine stopped suddenly at the entrance to the beautifully carpeted dining room. It was a formal room, probably very seldom used.

"What's the matter?" Lucas asked. The house was not cold, yet he felt a certain chill. "Josephine?"

"There's not a mark on the carpet," she replied. "Not a footstep, nothing. No one's walked across it since it was vacuumed."

"Well, surely, no one —" Then he understood, and the slight chill he felt turned to ice. "We were here."

She looked back at him. "I walked over to the side table. I looked in the drawers. It's a thick carpet; my footsteps showed, and they have been erased. That was yesterday, Lucas. Someone was here overnight, someone who removed all traces of themselves . . . and of us."

"It wasn't the police," he said, almost as if he were hoping she would contradict him. "No policeman would bring a vacuum cleaner with him."

"No one with any right to be here would," she added. "It must be worth a lot, whatever it is this person is looking for."

"At least to him," he agreed. "The question is, did he get it? Stay with me, Josephine. No wandering off alone."

"Do you think this person might still be here?" she said incredulously, but she did not move, and her hands were shaking very slightly. "There was no car anywhere around, and I don't imagine he came on a motorbike." She stopped.

Lucas smiled. "With the vacuum cleaner strapped to the passenger seat? No, neither do I. All the same, we'll do this together." He said it resolutely and was relieved to see that she understood.

They checked the house to make sure no one else was there, then began methodically going through all the places of easy access first, on Lucas's assumption that there was something that Stoney had intended him to find.

They searched slowly and carefully, piling things as they went, ready to move them. It made Lucas feel uncomfortable, even though he knew Stoney would mean him to do exactly this. It was still an intrusion into the man's life: all of his present-day habits and his passions of the past. He had been orderly in some things, those daily necessities that were important: his toiletries and clothes, the good tie he liked, his favorite jams and the Seville orange marmalade he always had with breakfast. The bills that were paid up to date.

Did he know that he would die soon, or at least believe it was likely? Had he even recognized his killer when he rang the doorbell and stood waiting on the steps until Stoney answered? It was a terrible thought, and Lucas did not speak it aloud.

Then there were things from Stoney's past, all of which Lucas had seen before. But had he seen all that they might mean? A couple of seashells, which were ordinary enough, but in this case absolutely perfect, still — pink shaded into blue and gray, washed by the sea, but unblemished. There were pebbles from a mountain stream, found when they had gone hill walking in Scotland. They were worth nothing, except the memories of laughter, endless windy spaces, and a horizon lost in shadows of a mountain shielded by mist.

On the shelf below were packets of loose photographs, black and white, an interesting evocation of what seemed another lifetime. Lucas picked them up and started looking at them. He could recall most of the places. Had anything happened there? Had Stoney told him something then that had bearing on the present? Lucas stood there, still holding them in his hands, trying to think. He turned one over and saw what must be the date it was taken written on the back. Except it wasn't a date, it was far too long. In fact, it was too long for anything he could think of. "Josephine."

She was on the other side of the room, leafing through books. She looked up.

"What do you make of this?" he asked.

She came across and took the photograph from him, looking carefully at both sides. First the picture, then the numbers. "Where is it?"

"Scotland, the Cairngorms. It wasn't one of the higher peaks, but much like that. What do you make of it?" he repeated, passing her the whole pile of pictures. There were about two dozen, many very similar.

She studied them for so long that he finally lost patience. "I don't think the place mattered, except to me," he said. "Nothing special happened there. It was just a particularly happy memory. We felt free, kings of the world." It sounded ridiculous now, but a shred of the old invincible feeling came back, even as he looked at what was a very ordinary hillside, rendered bland by the lack of space that the camera reflected, missing so much of the width of it. It was shades of gray, rather than the luminous veils of lavender, and indigo, white into silver that he could remember, or thought he could.

"Did you pick them out because of a memory?" she asked, meeting his eyes with startling intensity.

"I suppose so. When I try to explain, it seems so commonplace."

"But you do remember a profound emotion?" Her voice was urgent now.

"Yes," he said with certainty.

"Then that will be what Stoney meant you to see. The numbers must refer to what he was working on. We just have to figure it out. What does it all refer to?"

"I think we went there in . . . Oh God, it seems like another lifetime. It must have been in the early 1880s, or even before. I was young, I know that." He felt strange even saying it aloud.

The woman who had broken complicated

codes in wartime was staring at the figures on the backs of the photographs. There were twice as many on some, even three times as many. "It may not have anything to do with the photographs." She was thinking aloud. "He put these numbers on them because he knew the memory would catch you. They don't look like dates, but there's a group here that could be. See? Several that are in 1933 or 1932. They could be months, and these could be days."

"All in the last two years," he observed. "But everything put into numbers. This is what really matters. The other numbers we've seen as we've looked through Stoney's papers are just calculations. This is information."

Josephine thought silently for a moment. "These could be map coordinates, but they are all sorts of places far apart, hundreds of miles. Different countries even. But you could identify people by their addresses, I suppose. It seems a heavy-handed way of doing it, very approximate." She laid out four photographs and then pointed to the sequence of numbers on the back of each that could be coordinates. She was frowning. "But even if it identifies the appropriate place where someone lived or worked, without more it doesn't mean much . . . or even anything."

"Then the last figures must be something that explains it." He was guessing, grasping at straws. Had Stoney left him all the clues he had? There must be something else that he was missing.

Josephine was looking at him.

"What is it?" he asked, trying to keep the edge out of his voice.

"Lucas, we can't stay here much longer," she said gravely. "If the police come back, they'll take these from us, and neither of us has the ability to memorize these apparently random numbers. If he left anything else, we've got to find it and then leave, and quickly. Someone could easily return . . ." She did not bother to add what danger that would be.

Lucas nodded. She was saying it as if it were an apology. She knew him so well. No matter how he tried to disguise it or control it, she could always feel the distress in him as palpably as if it were electricity in the air. He thought it was one of the greatest gifts in life, to have someone know you so well and still love you. It was also a limitless responsibility.

"Yes," he agreed. "We'll take these photographs, give the house one last quick look around, and then leave. What are we going to do with Stoney's things? Who do we give them to?"

"That's tomorrow's problem, not today's," she said firmly. "They'll suit somebody. They're of good quality. Let's look around. If he knew this much, he knew the man intended to kill him, and that's a horrible thought."

"I know," Lucas agreed. He stared around the room with no idea of what he was looking for. If Stoney knew that, in a matter of minutes, he was going to be killed by the man who was with him, what sign would he leave? What would he expect Lucas to find, other than the little pile of photographs, which obviously had been placed here long in advance, in case this should happen? Stoney had known of the danger, even understood it. Lucas felt slightly sick at the idea.

Josephine was thinking aloud. "It seems there was no weapon, except something to hit him over the head, like the spade I thought of before. The assassin was probably younger and a good deal fitter than Stoney."

It was a terrible thought, walking around your own home with a man you knew was going to kill you. Lucas wanted to leave this place, at least get Josephine away from it. He was as cold as if the walls were made of ice. He was torturing himself, thinking of Stoney's last minutes, and he knew it was pointless, but he still went on doing it.

And then something caught his eye. "Jo, that pile of books on the floor: Did you put them there when you were looking for something?" He pointed to them, stacked as if waiting to be returned to the correct shelves.

"What are they?" And then she looked at them and read the titles. She looked puzzled. "They don't seem to have anything in common. What was he trying to say?"

Lucas kneeled down and studied them without moving anything. They were about all sorts of subjects: poetry, bird watching, a couple of novels, poetry again. What on earth had they in common? The first author was Robert Browning, the last William Butler Yeats. The rest were people he did not know: someone called Roland, others called Alan, Dawson, Lovell, and Evans. And Jerome's classic *Three Men in a Boat*.

Then he saw it, as clear as day.

Josephine was staring at him. "Lucas?"

He said nothing.

"Lucas? What is it?"

He turned his eyes to her, his face pale. "Bradley."

She looked confused.

403

"Look at the authors' names, Jo. It's not the subject at all, it's the first letter of each name!" He pointed to all the titles. "Look closely! What does it spell?" Before she could answer, he said, "Bradley!"

"But Bradley is —"

"I know, head of MI6." Lucas felt frozen in place. He forced himself to get to his feet and leave the pile of books exactly where it was. Not that it was proof of anything. There was nothing to show that Stoney had left them there, or that they meant anything at all, except that they were out of place. "Jo, we must leave. Take the photographs; we'll work on them at home."

"Are you going to tell the police?"

"No use at all. We have no proof, and even if they know it was MI6, they still think we are a couple of old duffers looking for something to do to make ourselves important again. No, I don't know who I'll tell. I'll have to think about this very hard. Surely, Peter first."

"But he's not here," said Josephine. "He's flown to Trieste."

"Elena," he said softly, and saw the shadows change in her face.

"Lucas, she doesn't know anything about Stoney," she argued.

"She knows about the Fatherland Front

and Aiden Strother, who is our man in Trieste," Lucas answered. "Strother is on our side. He was a deliberate deep plant in the Nazi side. She's gone to rescue him." He saw from Jo's face that she only half believed that. "At least that's what Peter thinks," he added.

"Then why has he gone to Trieste, too?" she asked.

"To get Elena out, and possibly Strother as well. I think the net is tightening. The Front is going to move sooner than we thought."

When Josephine spoke, her voice had a slight tremor that she could not hide. "And what are we going to do?"

"We are going home." He took her by the arm and, putting the photographs in his inside pocket, guided her to the back door, locking it behind him and walking toward the car. "And we're going to study those numbers until we know what they mean," he went on, as he started the engine and drove the car back into the road.

He thought about it all the way home, almost oblivious to the great sweep of clouds towering white into the blue of the sky. The avenue of beech trees burned bronze and gold with dying leaves. Three times Josephine had to tell him to watch the

405

road, mind the corners. The road held a beauty that usually seized his imagination and his senses, but today all he could think of was Stoney, knowing that he had minutes to live and leaving him the only clue he could: a pile of books on the floor that offered names that spelled out *Bradley,* and old photographs that almost certainly had no meaning to anyone else, taken over half a century ago, when the slaughter and ruin of the war was unimaginable. How impossibly young they were then. "We must find the places these references indicate," he said, as he stopped the car at their house, "and what happened there, on those dates. That will tell us something."

But it told them nothing. The dates covered almost two years leading up to the present day, and the places were cities in France, England, Spain, Italy, and the United States of America.

"I keep feeling it should be about money," Josephine said, her voice tired and a little hoarse. She rose to her feet stiffly. "I'll get us a cup of tea, and perhaps a couple of sandwiches. We forgot lunch."

He smiled at her bleakly. "I'm sorry, I . . ." But he did not know what else to say. "I feel as if it should be about money, too, but who donates odd amounts like 15,522 pounds four shillings and three pence? There isn't a round figure among them."

Suddenly, as if a dark cloud had been pushed aside, Josephine said, "Tea can wait, unless you want to make it. You'll find cold lamb in the pantry, and you know where the bread and butter are."

Lucas was suddenly alert. He knew that voice, the controlled excitement. "What?"

"And don't make the slices too thick."

"Jo! Tell me!"

She flashed him an almost mischievous smile. "Not the lamb, Lucas, the bread. Don't make doorsteps of the bread. Go on!"

It took him a quarter of an hour to boil a kettle, make the tea properly — heating the pot first, letting the tea steep — then cut the sandwiches by buttering the loaf and then slicing it so it did not fall apart, finally placing the meat carefully. He did not care in the least about making the sandwiches nicely, but he knew she did. And she needed time to follow through on her idea, without him breathing down her neck.

When he finally walked back into the sitting room carrying the tray, setting it down on the table, he found her scribbling lines of figures all over sheets of paper and smiling.

"Tea's up," he said, half expecting her not to hear him.

She looked up at him, her face shining with victory. "Thank you, my dear. And I know what it is! These are amounts of money from different places, the dates on which they were transferred in rounded amounts, and in the original currency." Her smile widened. "But when you exchange them into German marks, they come out odd numbers, of course, and slightly different amounts from day to day . . . as the exact exchange values go up and down. But they always start as round numbers. Here, look at this." She indicated the first one she had done. "This is thirty thousand pounds on the twentieth of January 1932. It's an odd number changed to this amount exactly, but it tallies precisely with the exchange rate that day, plus the cost of the transaction." She pointed to another set of figures. "This one is fifty thousand American dollars. It works out on this date, the fourth of February 1932, at this amount of money." She indicated another set of seemingly erratic numbers. "Lucas, they all work out to the penny, or whatever it is, when you know what you're looking at. It's exactly right, it's proof. There's no way on earth this could be coincidental, and it's an enormous amount. I am over halfway through, but the amounts are getting larger, and there is more than seven million here. Look." She turned the page round so he could see.

And he could. Once you knew what you were looking at, it was crystal clear. "I'll write down a copy of it," he said, "after we've had a cup of tea. And then, when it's all finished, I'll take it to Churchill, just to cover myself. We can't be the only people who know this, for our own safety as well as the survival of the truth. Then I'll take it to the home secretary."

He must be careful to whom he spoke, but he knew the home secretary, Sir John Gilmour, was trustworthy. Those who wanted to avoid another war at any price were easy enough to understand, even to sympathize with. The difference lay in what they believed the alternative would be. Lucas believed it would be a slow corruption, with people ultimately being consumed by violence and hysteria. He had no wish to die on any battlefield, but he preferred that to slowly giving in again and again, until you become so like the enemy you cannot tell yourself apart.

He went the following morning to the home secretary, whom he had met on several occasions. He gave his name to Sir John Gilmour's assistant as Lucas Standish, head of MI6 during the war and for some time afterward.

"Good morning, Standish, good to see you. How are you?" Gilmour said warmly. One glance at Lucas's face told him that Lucas knew better than to waste his time. This was not a social call.

"Gladstone Canning, who also worked for MI6, was very recently murdered, sir. He entrusted me with the work he was involved in. I have come to give you the result of it."

Gilmour took a deep breath. "Don't mince words, do you?"

"No, sir. It concerns funding for the new Fatherland Front created and supported by Hitler and the Nazis, for the purpose of overthrowing Chancellor Dollfuss and eventually annexing Austria."

"I presume you can back all this up, or you wouldn't have come to me. Why didn't you take this directly to Bradley at MI6?" He looked at Lucas very directly, his eyes narrowed.

Lucas swallowed. "Because Gladstone Canning believed Bradley was behind it, sir. Canning was murdered. I believe the medical report will confirm this — it certainly won't dismiss it — although his killing was

410

very cleverly done. I've known Gladstone Canning for half a century. He left clues that only I would recognize regarding the sources of the money and its transfer. My wife actually decoded it. She worked on decoding during the war."

"I know," Gilmour said succinctly. "And you think Bradley killed Canning himself?"

"I don't think he would trust anyone else with a job like that. I wouldn't in his place. Give someone else that kind of a hold on me? Unnecessary risk. Canning was an old man, no match for Bradley."

"And Peter Howard?"

"Gone to Italy, sir, to sort out that end of it. A lot of information is coming in about the Fatherland Front from Trieste."

"I see, and what is it precisely that you would like me to do?"

"Send the best police you've got, men you trust, to arrest Jerome Bradley for the murder of Gladstone Canning. Unless he has been there and moved them, there is a pile of books that Stoney left on his office floor. *Three Men in a Boat* by Jerome K. Jerome, and a pile whose authors' names spell out 'Bradley.' I can't prove that I didn't put them there, but I didn't. I should have seen it sooner. It wasn't until I went down and saw them sideways that I noticed."

"There will be hell to pay if you're wrong."

"Yes, sir, and hell we'll all pay if I'm right, and we do nothing about it."

"I miss you, Standish. You have an eye for the absurd that no one else rises to. God knows we're going to need it."

"There's hope for Peter Howard, sir," Lucas replied. "He has an eye for the absurd, too."

"He'll need it! Right, I'll do it and take it out of your hide if you're wrong. You'd better give my men all the details."

"Yes, sir."

When Lucas walked out of the office, he released a loud sigh, feeling the tension fall away. Gilmour believed him, and he was a man of action.

Lucas entered the office of MI6 quietly, like anyone else, an elderly man, still tall and with a slight stoop, the wind ruffling his gray hair, now thinning. He was accompanied by two policemen in plain clothes. It was a gift from the home secretary that he should do this himself, as if he still held office; as if he had never retired, never been told he had served well and the country was grateful, but he was too old now. Of course, it had not been put in such crude terms, but that was what it amounted to. This was a subtle

412

gift, to be sure, but it was also a way of accomplishing this decisively and without hesitation.

They went in quietly, without speaking to one another. It had all been said already.

At the outer door to Bradley's office they entered without knocking. The secretary had changed since Lucas's day, and she did not recognize him, but Lucas shook his head. "Lock the door," he directed. "Keep her here."

The men understood and obeyed.

Understanding also flared on the woman's face. Even unintentionally, she might warn others, perhaps call for assistance.

Lucas opened Bradley's door without knocking and closed it just behind him.

Bradley was standing in front of the window, staring out at the handsome view of the trees and the street. At the sound of the door, he turned sharply. For an instant his expression was blank, then it was filled with anger.

"This might have been your office once, Standish, but it's not now. You bloody well knock now, and you come in only if I say so!"

"Don't be an ass, Bradley," Lucas said quite softly. He was a man who spoke quietly when he was very, very angry. Bradley had betrayed an office that Lucas had held with honor, even reverence. And he had betrayed Elena, too, making her the goat when he knew that she was guilty of falling in love with Aiden Strother, but was innocent of treason. Everything Bradley had done was calculated to hurt Lucas, taint his reputation and his legacy.

Bradley saw a difference in Lucas's face. He recognized something that, under the bravado, he had feared for years.

Lucas saw the man's face turn pale. He knew. "This is the end of the road, Bradley. Stoney left your name quite clearly for us . . . before you killed him."

Bradley chose to bluff. "Stoney Canning? That old fool . . ."

"Has outwitted you," Lucas finished for him. "You can give up with grace, or struggle and be half carried out like some dangerous lunatic."

"Ha! You think you're man enough to do that?" Bradley laughed, but utterly without humor. "You're an old man, Standish. Past your time! Long past it. You're finished. Hitler is rising. You're a relic of the past, and too damn stupid to see it."

Lucas took a step backward and opened the door. The two policemen came in. The secretary was just visible, handcuffed to the desk. Her face was ashen.

Bradley looked at her, then at the unsmiling police, and lastly at Lucas. "You may have won this round, Standish, but this is far from the end. There will be no war, no battles, just a slow change, from the top, to join our natural allies, the Germans. Then you'll know what defeat really is." Suddenly he dived forward and lashed out at the nearest policeman, who staggered backward, and stumbled.

Lucas picked up the hard-backed chair, swung it high, and brought it down hard on Bradley's shoulders.

The man let out a cry and collapsed to the floor.

Two policemen picked him up, carrying him out of his office like a sack of rubbish.

Lucas stared around him. This was a sad and bitter victory. But it was a victory nevertheless, and the beginning of a new battle.

CHAPTER 20

They walked in silence toward the waterfront. Elena's mind was teeming with questions, but she did not know how to frame
them. What had happened so quickly that
they needed to escape immediately? And
now that Ferdie was dead, how long could
it be before the police found his body and
raised the alarm? Some of them, at the very
least, would assume that the people who
killed Ferdie, whoever they were, would
make for the port and the first ship out.
Ferdie had tried to kill them before they
could escape — and do what? Tell everyone
that part of the Front had splintered off and
struck early, preemptively? They would
know that by now. Know the chain of command upward, to whoever was the leader.
Was Aiden aware of that? Did it even matter anymore?

She was short of breath and her feet hurt,
but she matched Aiden stride for stride. It

was getting dark quickly; buildings were becoming black shapes without features, heavy blocks against the luminous embers of sunset in the sky. Did Aiden know where they were going? Had he thought of this route ahead of time, or could he be as lost as she was, just better at hiding it?

He had taken it for granted that she would come. Why? Now that she was on the run the police would suspect her of killing Max, or at least being the cause of his death. She had found his body with Aiden, and they had run away from the area together. And yet it had never occurred to her not to go with him. It was her duty to get him out. It was what she had come for: to save him, and to save the list, and then get it to Peter Howard. But she could not afford a confrontation with the police now, and the risk of being caught out in a lie.

She was holding the money for their passage back to England, for both of them. Aiden was relying on her. He had not questioned her. Could trust bind you to loyalty? Yes. He knew that it mattered to her. Trust must never be broken. The thought chilled her.

They reached a major intersection illuminated by streetlights and car headlamps, busy with bright sweeping movement and noise.

Aiden came to a stop, holding his arm out to keep Elena from moving past him. He glanced at her, and the light of the nearest lamp was faint but clear on his face. He seemed exhilarated, and more alive than she had ever seen him.

"Wait," he ordered. "We've got to get across to the other side."

"Do we wait till it's quiet?" she asked.

"No, the opposite," he told her. "We go when there's a group, but you've got to look like one of them. Can you do that?"

"Of course I can," she answered tartly.

He smiled, the lamplight gleaming on his teeth. It reminded her absurdly of *Alice in Wonderland,* in which the Cheshire Cat disappears until only his smile is visible.

They waited in silence, standing so close she could feel the warmth of his body and imagine his heart beating. Memories intruded: running ahead of the tide, across the fast-vanishing sandbar, feeling the water's power. Running the risk of drowning, and then collapsing on the sand just out of the tide's reach. Laughing for the joy of it. She had never felt more brilliantly alive herself. That was the first night they had made love. It had been years ago. She was so young then. She was older now . . . and the stakes were immeasurably higher.

Suddenly, Aiden moved forward, grasping her hand as he strode across the street, leaving the shadows on one side and making for the shadows of the other. They walked quickly, vulnerable out in the open. She turned toward him.

"Don't speak," he told her quietly. "Just keep walking. Don't stop, don't move suddenly. Don't do anything to attract attention."

"Is somebody following us?" she asked, a little breathlessly.

"No idea, but we have to assume they are, or at least that they are watching. They will have found Ferdie by now. He was against us, but we don't know who he was for. The Fatherland Front, yes, but perhaps somebody else as well."

As if to answer her question, there was a loud shout behind them, and another response over to the left, as if in reply. Aiden began walking toward the sounds.

"What —" she started to say, but he pushed her so sharply the words turned into a grunt of pain. She ran a little to keep up with his longer strides. Then, as they rounded the corner and saw a bunch of armed and uniformed men, she felt a wave of remembrance wash over her, and a fear she could taste, bitter in her mouth. They were exactly like the Gestapo in Berlin.

Aiden jerked her upright, then hiccuped loudly. "Sorry," he said to the nearest man. "Celebrated a little too well."

One of the soldiers laughed. "Go and sleep it off, brother," he said loudly. He looked Elena up and down. "Have one on me," he added with a lewd gesture.

Aiden guffawed, and promised he would. He gripped Elena at arm's length with one hand and used the other to push with a hard, even pressure on the small of her back.

She held on to him, even as they staggered past the soldiers and into a different, nameless street away from the harborside.

Aiden stopped. "Good," he said so softly she barely heard him. "They didn't suspect anything. We'll go another block this way, then straight to the waterfront and the first boat we can find going out on the evening tide. I'm afraid it doesn't matter where to; we've got to get out of here. Damn Ferdie! I knew he was getting close to me in order to . . ." He touched her head gently. He had often told her how he liked her hair, even when it had been an ordinary light brown. It had a softness that pleased him, the way it ran through his fingers like silk.

They moved past huge buildings, no more

than shapes looming in the darkness. By the time they had walked in a huge half circle and got back to the dockside, her legs ached and her heel had rubbed a blister. This was not where they originally intended to be, but it was a far less likely place from which fugitives would be trying to escape.

Aiden stopped on the road across the street from where fishing boats were tied up alongside small freighters and tramp steamers looking for any cargo to carry down the eastern coast of Italy.

"We're lovers escaping your jealous husband," he said, his face in the pale lamp bright with amusement. There was urgency in his voice, but also the edge of laughter, as if this new idea had added zest to the affair.

"Why not your jealous wife?" Her words were out before she thought about them.

He shook his head. "Wouldn't have to run away from a woman."

"She has a rich father," she shot back. "And brothers, very protective, family honor and all that."

This time his amusement was undisguised. "You chose me?"

Her mind raced. "No, you're probably right," she said straight back at him. "More believable that you stole me."

This time he laughed outright and pretended to wince. "When the chips are down, you will fight."

She opened her mouth to snap back, then changed her mind and started out across the street, and then down the narrow path toward a sailor who was standing and looking at the water, a cigarette in his mouth. She sauntered over to him with no idea what she was going to say.

Aiden caught up with her, slipping his arm round her easily, but his grip was strong. "Not him," he whispered, then laughed as if whatever he had said were a joke.

She forced herself to laugh as well.

They went another fifty yards until they were alongside a tramp steamer long enough to carry several tons of cargo, and possibly an extra passenger or two eager to travel discreetly and very suddenly and pay the appropriate cost. There was a sailor swabbing the deck.

Aiden pulled Elena to a stop. He leaned forward and kissed her again gently. He moved until his mouth was just in front of her ear. "I assume you brought all the money you have with you."

"Of course," she answered. "Not much point in freeing you if I can't afford two tickets out, or half a dozen on this crate, if necessary."

"Don't play it down, it floats," he replied. "Just . . . let's go and do our best. Let me do the talking, and for God's sake don't speak English."

She nodded and walked beside him down toward the stone steps of the quay. The sailor looked up.

Aiden spoke to him casually in Italian, indicating Elena beside him. The sailor laughed and looked at Elena with very obvious admiration.

Elena moved even closer to Aiden, as if they were longtime lovers. Weren't they . . . ?

Aiden went on, speaking quickly.

After a few more moments, the sailor invited them on board and they were conducted to the captain's cabin. He was a stocky man with thick arms, a barrel chest, and a wind-burned, crooked-nosed face that had seen its share of fights. He came straight to the point and asked for money.

Elena passed across most of what she had. She kept back only a few notes against the next part of the journey. Now she must think of immediate survival and escape from the militia closing in on them.

The captain looked at Aiden curiously. "What's to stop me taking this," he held up the money, "and then handing you over to this woman's husband?"

Aiden smiled. "I could say that you're an honest man, but you and I know that has yet to be proved." His smile widened. "On the other hand, I could tell the authorities that I paid you to take contraband for me and it's already in the hold. They could search it and see." He raised his eyebrows. "Are you sure that they won't find anything? I'll wager there's something there, and they'll search until long after the tide has turned . . . and it's too late." He shrugged. "And that's, of course, if they don't take the interesting things in your hold and the money as well."

The captain moved his weight from one foot to the other. A very slow smile grew on his face, which made visible a scar on his upper lip. "You're right, my friend, one course is bad for you and bad for me, good only for the police. I have no friends in the police and I want to catch this evening's tide."

"South," Aiden said, with barely a change of expression.

The captain held out his hand and Aiden took it and grasped it hard.

Elena knew that Italy lay to the west, Austria to the north, and Serbia to the east, so there was no other way to go but south.

They were shown to the cabin kept for the occasional passenger whose need the captain and his crew profited from. The first officer was willing enough to sacrifice it and take a smaller one. It was greatly to his financial advantage.

Aiden and Elena stayed below deck as the ship loosed its moorings and pulled away, riding the tide from shore and picking up speed in the dark.

Aiden appeared relaxed; they were almost free.

Elena looked around the cabin. It was small, cramped, with barely enough room for the double bed. A small chest of drawers stood in one corner. There were no chairs and only the barest facilities to wash, but they were at sea, moving down the Italian coast and away from Austria and the politics of Germany and the Fatherland Front. They hadn't enough money left to get to the British embassy in Rome, or even Venice, if that should be closer. Elena felt panic rising in her chest, then pushed it away. What mattered was that they were moving away from danger.

She turned to face him. He was watching her unusually closely. What for? To see if she would accept sharing a bed again? Of course she would. Her life might hang on it for successfully getting him out of Italy. Almost certainly the question was only how well she did it, how graciously, how much she behaved like the fugitive lover she claimed to be.

She did not know what was ahead of them each hour, each minute. Even one mistake would cost them everything. What she actually felt was immaterial; it counted for nothing at all. She could do it easily, because there was a part of her that wanted the passion and the intimacy as much as she ever had. It was not the wide-eyed infatuation she had had before, when she had been so naïve, so terribly young. This would be more like a love of equals. She knew and understood what he did; she was even getting fairly good at it herself. There was only the tiniest doubt, shadows, there and then gone again. She pushed them away.

"Can you make them believe it?" he asked very quietly. He did not need to whisper because the wood of the cabin creaked loudly with the movement of the ship. The whole thing shuddered as if it were alive, breathing, aware of the passion always in its body, the incessant flow of the current deep below the surface and above it; tides in and out of the vast curved coastline of Italy and

Serbia, waves constantly changing with the wind.

She smiled at him. "Of course. My life depends on it, and yours. And more important still, getting the list back where it can be of use."

"Did I do this to you?" he asked curiously.

"This?" she questioned.

"I know they gave you a hard time," he went on. "I'm sorry." He touched her cheek, his fingers unusually gentle.

She drew in breath to tell him she had succeeded very well. She had beaten the devouring self-doubt and regained faith that she was intelligent, brave, or valuable at all. But it was unnecessary to say; he already knew it.

He was waiting, the anticipation fading from his eyes, the edge of his smile.

"Everyone else seemed rather boring after you," she said, and she knew there was enough truth in that for him to see it in her face.

"Dear Elena," he murmured. "So safe in your own way, so . . . comfortable."

She would have liked to slap him, but she couldn't afford to. And what angered her most was that it was not true, not now. And he had not even noticed! Or had he? And he was pushing her to see if she would deny it.

"Do you suppose meals are included in that exorbitant fee?" she asked instead. "It seems like days since we ate."

"It's been a long time," he agreed, changing the subject as easily as she did. "The food may be pretty vile, but we should eat anyway." He offered his arm. "Shall we dine?"

They ate with the captain and some of the crew. There was no space for passengers to dine alone. It was a tramp steamer that took in the extra cargo of desperate passengers, or anything that stretched out the crew's meager financial reward for a hard and often dangerous life. The captain and five of the crew sat with Aiden and Elena around a wooden table that was fixed to the floor. It took up most of the floor space, and they were forced to sit elbow to elbow. Oil lanterns hung so they could see each other's faces and the surface of the table. Everything swayed very slightly with the movement of the sea, and there was a faint creaking of timbers all the time. It was a comforting sound. Elena found herself relaxing and enjoying the food, a stew of meat she could not identify and various root vegetables augmented with savory dumplings.

At the table they said they were fugitive lovers, and they had to keep up that story. It seemed to satisfy the crew, even amuse them, which was good since they had nothing else believable to offer.

They went to bed early. Aiden had been invited to take a drink with the captain but had declined with a wink and a smile. It made Elena uncomfortable, but not as much as the leers and sly remarks she had to contend with.

"Sorry," Aiden said when they were alone, the cabin door closed and the clothes chest pulled across it. "But if I leave you alone, one of the crew might take a chance or —"

"I understand," she cut him off with a shudder. The thought was repulsive, but the story was that she was a woman who would abandon her husband for a lover, so it made sense that she might extend that favor to include paying her passage in kind.

She prepared for bed, as much as their circumstances allowed, which was not a lot more than to sleep in her slip. It had been a terrible day; irrevocable decisions had been made. She was exhausted, but the idea of relaxing enough to sleep seemed impossible.

What did Aiden expect? They had been

lovers once. It seemed like ages ago, another life, another world, and a totally different kind of emotion between them. But was it so different? She wanted the excitement, the comfort. More than anything else, she wanted the tenderness — the elusive, aching, healing tenderness.

She got into bed and pulled the blankets up, glad of their warmth in the chilly air, glad of the gentle sound of the water and the slight rocking of the boat. She had no idea whether he was going to touch her or not. She lay still. Minutes passed. Could he be asleep already, without a word? She drifted off, not sure whether to feel relieved or disappointed.

The next day, they had breakfast with the crew. It was plain: bread rolls still reasonably fresh, served with a choice of cheese or jam, and surprisingly good coffee. They were out of sight of land now, the weather was pleasant, if a little windy, and they rode the waves easily enough. There was nothing for them to do, and the long empty hours stretched ahead. Aiden fell into conversation with some of the men. He affected interest in their lives. It might even have been real, perhaps a degree of friendship. Showing respect was a good idea.

Elena went down to the cabin and tidied up a bit. She could at least make it look cared for. She wondered what kind of people the passengers had been on other voyages. Nobody on holiday, that was for certain. Possibly fugitives of some sort, running from private enemies or the law?

She unwrapped the gift that Gabrielle had given her. She hoped Gabrielle was all right, and especially Franz. One of them would only be fine if the other was as well.

She looked at the comb, a generous gift. It was beautiful, made of polished and curved tortoiseshell. It was not for combing her hair, it was to wear as an ornament. But it required long hair, like Gabrielle's, while Elena's was little more than chin length. Gabrielle seemed to think she would need it. Why? How could she need an ornamental hair comb with her short hair? She turned it over and looked at the strong clasp. She unfastened it and found it unusually thick, with a section that jutted away from the shell. Carefully, she used her fingernail to dislodge it and found a very fine steel blade, its razor edge a good two inches in length.

She folded it again quickly, making it look like the ornament it had first appeared to be. She would have to be very close to someone, very close indeed to use that in an attack, or in self-defense.

What was Gabrielle warning her against? She couldn't know anything about this voyage.

Suddenly, Elena felt very cold. Was the danger coming from the Germans? Or was it . . . Aiden? She pushed the thought away. Ridiculous! He was risking everything to transport her to safety!

She slipped the comb back into her bag, along with her passport and the remaining money. They had a long way to go to reach the nearest British embassy, where hopefully they could get help. Tomorrow was the first day they would be able to get off the ship for a few hours. The ship was calling in at a small port to offload some cargo, and probably take on more. She was feeling more and more closed in by the tiny cabin, and she was still shocked by the way events had turned violent so suddenly.

One moment Ferdie was pro-Hitler and supported the Fatherland Front, and considered Aiden an ally in this cause. He had been alive, making sly remarks, some of them funny, others edged with a sarcasm that cut deeply. When he turned on them, she had not seen it coming. It had erupted out of an argument that seemed trivial. Was he with the Front . . . or was he part of the

432

splinter group? If the latter, and if he believed Aiden was loyal to the Front, that could explain the sense of betrayal. She, Aiden, and Gabrielle had escaped precariously, and from then on the whole atmosphere had changed. There was open violence in the streets. She and Aiden were truly running for their lives.

When Ferdie lay dying in the street, he had been unable to speak. What an appalling decision for Aiden to have to make. And yet he had had no choice. Ferdie had somehow figured out that Aiden was a British spy. One of them had to die.

Elena faced the thought she had been refusing to look at for the last twenty-four hours. It lay like a pool of ice around her heart. She really was not certain who was on which side, except that Aiden had given her the list that she was expected to pass on to Peter.

Aiden had infiltrated the Fatherland Front, a group that wanted to undermine the Austrian government and effectively annex Austria into a greater Germany. And now this splinter group wanted to make it all happen sooner, including the assassination of Dollfuss. So Ferdie was with them? It was so daunting! All of them were Nazis, but quick to kill their own!

She remembered the times she had spent with Aiden, both long ago and these past days in Trieste. The excitement, the exhilaration, the daring to do anything you could think of. Above all, the passion to live every last breath of it. Had he always taken such risks, she just had not known it?

What about Gabrielle? What was her part in this? Aiden had said they had worked together. Why, thinking now, did that seem strange? She tried to think back, but she could remember nothing meaningful, at least not clearly. Why had Gabrielle given her the comb? It was far more Gabrielle's style than Elena's. Did that mean anything? Affection? Or was it a warning?

She leaned over and took it out of her handbag again, then unwrapped it from the tissue. It was lovely, bright polished shell, beautifully carved. She fiddled with the clasp and slid it open. That blade was sharper than a razor, a beautifully disguised weapon. But why did Gabrielle think she would need such a thing? Who was going to attack her now, at such close quarters? Only Aiden, but that was absurd.

She thought back over all the conversations they had had, she and Aiden. Nothing came to her. Aiden had told Elena that Gabrielle was one of them. What had he told

Gabrielle of her? Of anything?

What did Gabrielle know of Aiden that Elena did not? Something hovered at the edge of her mind, half seen, and then pushed away. Aiden's laughter, his excitement, the vivid, pulsing life in him. The courage. His brief sense of loss at Max Klausner's death, and then Ferdie's. Had Gabrielle seen that, too, at some other time, but understood it better? Elena could see in her mind the excitement in his eyes, the flush on his face as he turned to the battle. But did he care who won? How would she know? Where was the vulnerability in him? She searched her memory and found only an emptiness where understanding should have been.

Elena felt suddenly alone on the ship. Only Aiden could protect her from the crew. They liked him, he saw to it that they did. What if she had to fight for her escape, her life? Would he be there for her?

One lie that he heard in her voice, and would she even make it to the shore, never mind back to England? Here she was again, questioning Aiden!

But why had he given her a copy of the list? That was a stupid question! What on earth made her think it was the true list? What better idea than to let her give a false list to Peter Howard, a list that might blame innocent people, people who might get in the way of an alliance under the Nazis? Clever. Was that why he wanted to be sure she got back to MI6? There were high stakes in this game, but Aiden had never shrunk from that.

Was there another list — a true one — the one Peter Howard had sent her for? Or had that never existed? If there was, did Aiden carry it on him, or was it hidden somewhere in the cabin, in his belongings, where no one else would recognize it? She tried to think what she would do if she found it, but her mind was whirling. The safest way would be to carry the names in her memory, but she could not afford to rely on that. No, definitely not. She would have to have something to remind her, perhaps not obviously, but something that would have meaning for her alone.

What did Aiden always carry with him or on him that was indestructible? It would have to be something that could take getting wet, that was of no discernible value for a thief to steal, or for authorities to confiscate if he was searched. The only things she could think of were his clothes, and he changed those every so often. Different shirts, different shoes, socks, underwear. And then she knew. The only thing he always wore was his leather belt. He wore it with everything. She went over all the times she had seen him since that evening in Trieste. Yes, there was always that thin, dark leather belt. The only time he took it off was at night.

Aiden slept naked.

The thought made her almost sick with revulsion. At him, but more at herself. She would have to get into bed with him tonight, into this same lumpy bed, even though everything was different. She could already feel his hands on her skin, the smooth warmth of his body, his strength and his certainty as she caressed him, moved her body so he could come into her easily, hold her close to him.

Could his gentleness turn to violence in an instant, if she gave him cause? How easily Aiden had shot Ferdie the instant he believed him to be on the other side.

But which side was Ferdie on?

And what about Max Klausner? Had he discovered something that had cost him his life? Had their discovery of his body been far from accidental?

Elena felt the chill around her. Was Aiden playing both sides, while working for the Nazis? Perhaps he always had been. Is that what she had feared at the back of her mind, and denied each time?

Whatever the cost, she must survive, get back to London, and tell Peter what damage Aiden could do, if they went on trusting him.

How could she get the belt, or at least see what she believed it hid? If she found the list and read it, could she remember it? Could she turn the tables and play him?

And then it settled in her as a deep, cold conviction, as she should always have known: Aiden Strother had no emotions, no real ones. Nor did he have true loyalties. What he needed was the constant thrill, the danger, the risk. The wild and heart-lurching exhilaration in the place of real emotions. He seemed so much more alive than other men, but perhaps that was because he was painting a patina of life over a dead heart.

She straightened up the bed and combed her hair, but not with Gabrielle's comb. That was for wearing. She would keep it close to her.

She went out into the cramped passage, then up the steps, clinging to the rails, and onto the deck. She must behave naturally, friendly, but not too curious.

"Hello, darling!" Aiden was there immediately. "Look!" He made a wide sweep with his arm, indicating the white wake of the ship and the wheeling gulls above. "Great unbounded sea. Not another soul on it. Except the gulls, of course. Do gulls have souls?"

She smiled. This was going to be the act of her life. "Of course they do," she answered. "Aren't they supposed to be the souls of lost sailors, or something of the sort? I can think of worse things to do than ride the wind and the sea forever." She smiled up at him and deliberately met his eyes.

He was surprised. It was clear in his face for an instant.

Mistake. She tried not to make him rethink anything. "I read that once," she lied, "and I remembered it. It was a good thought."

He relaxed. "Did I thank you for reminding me? It's good to be free . . . at last."

She linked her arm in his and they watched the gulls over the water, the ship's wake streaming behind them.

CHAPTER 21

The day seemed to pass on leaden feet, but
eventually it was dinnertime and then the
hour for bed. Elena had been dreading it,
but now it was here and she wanted to get
it over with. She smiled at Aiden deliberately, as if she were looking forward to the
night with more pleasure than before, now
that she was gaining confidence. Except that
she wasn't, of course. She was terrified,
revolted, uncertain what to do, how to
behave as if she were still in love, so pliant
and willing, aching for his touch. If that
were true, she would not be filled with
doubts that were hardening by the second,
lies dissolving into dreadful certainty.

Should she take it for granted that they
would make love? Anticipate him a little?
No, don't take it for granted. Don't assume
that he would want her. She wore her slip,
letting it slide over her naked body. She

brushed her hair to make it shine and swing loose.

She was waiting for him when he came in. He smiled at her and locked the door. She had expected that, but it still made her stomach roil.

He looked at her with appreciation. Did he mean that, or was it to keep her calm?

She smiled back.

"A slightly unorthodox cruise, but fun, don't you think?" he asked.

"Unforgettable," she replied, then laughed at his momentary confusion. Did he like that, or would he think she needed taming a little? Had she really been so naïve before, so dependent? Perhaps that was one reason he had never been in love with her. She was so predictable that he was bored.

Don't be a fool! How nearly she had slipped. Aiden Strother did not love anyone; he merely found some women less boring than others. Love was caring about someone, being prepared to sacrifice, to think of their good and their happiness, not always your own.

He was undressing. He took off his shirt and underwear, then climbed into bed naked. For a moment, she froze, then she moved toward him and into his arms.

"What?" he asked. "You're shivering."

"Hold me," she said.

"What is it?" he asked again.

"Making every minute count," she said. "It will never be quite like this again."

His arms tightened around her; he was already aroused.

She closed her eyes so that, even in the faintest illumination, he would not see the conflict in them. Whether he felt it in her body or not, she would have to pray that he read it differently.

In the morning, while he was out of the cabin at the toilet, she had two minutes in which to look in his clothes for any clue. There was nothing, just polished leather. She was at once disappointed and relieved. Could he possibly have committed a true list to memory? Or was there not one, apart from the one he had given her? His whole purpose was to incriminate the people most valuable, to destroy people's trust in even the best. A different kind of betrayal altogether. With shaking hands, she replaced the belt exactly.

She was brushing her hair when he came back.

"I hope your shoes are comfortable," he remarked. "We're going ashore." He glanced at her face.

442

It did not appear a very interesting port. It was in the center of a half-moon bay, with wharfs along the center and shipbuilding yards to the north. It seemed busy enough. There were five ships that Elena could see from the deck of their own, all loading or unloading cargo, and several heavy-duty cranes, some standing idle, others like long-necked dinosaurs bending and turning slowly. The town behind the harbor was small, but it would afford the only chance she had of escape.

"Looks all right," she answered with a smile. "And it will be good to get off the ship and be able to walk more than twenty feet in a straight line."

It was about half past ten when they were safely tied alongside the harbor, and they made their way past the piles of unloaded cargo to the street.

Elena had her bag with her passport and cameras, money and the comb. Her nerve might not hold, at least not well enough to fool him. She must not panic, but she had no idea of where the next port might be, or even if they would go ashore again. It must be at this one that she acted. She would walk with him as far as he wanted to go, making light conversation as naturally as possible. She would have to take her chance when she could, perhaps when they stopped at a café for a meal. She would go to the ladies' room, or whatever was provided. It was the only opportunity to be alone she could rely on.

Aiden walked close beside her, taking her arm occasionally. It was absurd. In the past, she would have been thrilled to have his undivided attention, his presence so close she bumped into him if he turned too sharply.

They looked in shop windows, stopped at stalls with all kinds of goods in them, but they both knew without conversing that they had no money to spare.

They had lunch at an outdoor café. The food was edible — fish and stale Italian bread, cheap house wine — but to Elena it all tasted like cardboard.

She was turning over in her mind where she would go. There would not be any kind of British authority here; the place was far too small to warrant even a consul. If she turned to anyone for help, what would she say? The crew already thought she was lightly balanced; Aiden had seen to that.

But if she didn't make a break now, what other chance would she have? She could not deny that Aiden would soon be on to her. He knew her too well. Her own body might

444

betray her at the next intimate touch.

He would kill her. He would have to. Otherwise, she could tell MI6 about his success as a double agent, and his life would be over. She had to do it. Now.

They were done with their meal, the sunlight bright on the floor and on his hair.

She pushed back from the table and stood up. "Excuse me, I must go to the ladies' room before we leave." She pulled out some money from her purse and put it on his plate. Without waiting for his response, she walked between the tables and across the floor to the passage leading to the toilets. Would he be watching to make sure she came back? How could she evade him?

She used the facilities quickly, not knowing when there would be another chance, then came out and glanced at the dining area. Aiden was talking to the waiter and paying the bill.

It was now or never. She stepped out the back door, ran across the yard with its rubbish bins and storage shed, and into the street. It didn't matter which way she ran, as long as it was away from here . . . and the front door.

How long would he wait for her? When he knew, he would be furious. It would all be in the open then, no more pretending about anything. Her life depended on getting away! She was shaking as the reality of it struck her, and she almost missed her footing on the cracked pavement. She must not run; it would attract attention. People would remember a woman running. One walking, they might not.

Elena had very little idea where she was going, or who she could ask for help. She still had some money left, perhaps enough to pay for lodging and a fare to somewhere else.

She crossed the road, hoping to lose herself in the crowd. On a side street, he would see her at a glance. This street was full of villagers, shoppers, women with children. For once, the blond hair was a disadvantage. The sun shone on it and made her stand out among darker heads. It was like a beacon.

She was nearly at the bus station when she saw him. Of course, he would have had the same thought: he knew her!

She stepped back into a doorway before he could turn in her direction and see her. But she also knew him. She must think. What would he do? What plans would he follow, what mistakes would he make?

What could she do that he would not foresee? What did he know of her? What might he have learned? That she was more resourceful than he had thought? Far braver than she used to be? But was she really any wiser underneath the brave new surface?

What choices had she? To stay in the crowd? Try to get out of the town on the first flight to anywhere? Or stay here overnight, sleep somewhere, and then try in the early morning? Nothing seemed any clearer. She went back into the crowd, bumping elbows with women who were carrying shopping baskets and overtired children, with many hours of work still ahead of them.

It was five minutes, ten, and then half an hour. She kept moving, although she was hot and tired, and her feet were beginning to hurt. Friction had rubbed her skin red and blisters would come again soon. She stopped for a little while and bought something to drink, all the time half watching over her shoulder.

It was late afternoon, the sun was beginning to sink in the west, when she saw him. He was only yards from her, the sunlight on his head. He was fairer and taller than most others around him, and she knew immediately, with an absolute certainty, that she was caught.

She turned to run, just as his hand closed like a vice on her arm. There was no point in fighting: he would only injure her. He could pull her arm out of its socket if he needed to. They were in the open, but she saw his anger, his contempt for her for having fooled him, even for a few hours.

Their eyes met. He said nothing, but it was startling how his face had changed. What was once almost beautiful now was frightening in its hatred. She thought of screaming but knew she would be dead before a sound came from her.

They went together all the way back to the port. People looked at them, but Aiden conducted a one-way conversation, as if she were arguing with him. He twisted her arm so she cried out. People were embarrassed. Some might have been sorry for her, but no one intervened. The more she protested, the more hysterical she seemed.

Before the sky was blood red in the west, she was back on the ship.

"Don't bother trying to persuade any of the crew," Aiden said close to her ear. "They've all seen how hysterical you are, how emotionally unbalanced. I've told them the truth about our journey: that I'm taking you back to England for a doctor to help you. They understand, most of them, and not one of them will listen to you. I think perhaps you'd better have your meal in our cabin. You don't want to embarrass yourself in front of those men."

She could not think of any reply. Everything was closing in, getting harder, in fact, impenetrable. By nightfall, there might be nothing left. Aiden could take her up on deck after dark and easily knock her unconscious and toss her body overboard. He would say in the morning that she went out while he was asleep. He had locked the door, but she had found the key. She had been threatening suicide for a while. He was distraught with grief.

There would be nobody to argue with him, no proof of anything different, no one to question him, no one to ever know where she was. Lucas would never know.

That was the essence of spying, wasn't it? Not being known? Utter aloneness? Disappearing without a trace.

Elena would not go quietly without leaving a mark. Gabrielle had given her a weapon. It might not save her, but she would damn well use it.

She dressed for dinner and, with some difficulty, twisted up her hair and fixed it at the back with Gabrielle's comb. She put hairpins close to it, to stop it from falling out. If a few strands of hair escaped, it hardly mattered. She looked good, wearing a dress with red flowers, cheerful, as if she were happy.

The door was locked, but Aiden came back to wash and change into his clean shirt for dinner. One of the crew members passed by; Elena took the chance. "I'm glad you've come," she said to Aiden. "I'll go up and keep your place for you." And she slipped through the doorway, almost touching him, but smiling at the crewman. It was all over in a moment. She put her hand lightly on the crewman's arm and walked with him.

Dinner passed with little comment. They talked about all manner of irrelevant things. Elena listened politely, as if she were genuinely interested. She asked questions.

The meal was over just as the sun's edge dipped below the horizon, the color deepening, staining the water as if it were spattered with blood.

Elena insisted that she be permitted to go up and look at it before the color died away. She asked Aiden to go with her to share the glory and make sure she did not slip or fall in.

He hesitated a moment. She saw the struggle in his eyes, and the second in which he took the bait. "All right," he agreed, "why not?" He smiled and offered his arm.

Elena looked away quickly. Was she afraid

she might read something in his eyes? What? Cruelty? Triumph? Even regret? *Don't be a fool,* she told herself. This was no time for emotion. If ever anyone knew that, it was Aiden.

They went up the main steps to the deck. None of the crew was visible. Did they know what he meant to do? Or did they guess and prefer not to be certain?

She touched the comb in her hair, Gabrielle's comb. She got rid of one of the hairpins so it would slide out easily. She was as ready as she would ever be. All doubt was gone. She knew it was her life or his.

They made their way to the stern, where they had a view of the blazing sunset, uncluttered by ropes or wires or any back railings over the path of fire across the water. The orange of the ball of the sun dimmed at the bottom, where it was already below the horizon. Gold was turning to bronze, scarlet, and crimson.

"I'm sorry it had to end like this," Aiden said quietly, gripping her hard. "At first you were a bore. Sorry, but that's the truth. No time for lies now."

She reached up, as if to push back a stray wisp of hair, and took the comb out. "I can see that, looking back," she admitted truthfully.

451

"It's a pity you became interesting too late." He looked away from the sunset and directly at her. "But you've outlived your usefulness. You're not so much fun."

He let go of her arm and she knew that this was the instant. She must use it; the next one might be too late.

"I'm sorry, Elena," he repeated.

She raised the comb, exposed its blade, and slashed at his throat as hard as she could, high up, just under his ear. Her aim was perfect. The blood gushed out in a fountain, as crimson as the dying sun.

He let out a gasp of surprise and put his hand to his neck. But the cut was deep and long; there was nothing he could do to stem the flow of blood. Rage twisted his face and he grabbed for her with his other hand.

She stared back and then hacked at his hand, catching his arm and causing another deep slash.

He dropped to his knees. There was blood everywhere.

Elena felt faint, as if she was going to be sick. Part of her wanted to help him, even though, in her brain, she knew that it was too late. In minutes, he would be dead. It was irrevocable. It had been either his life or hers. He would probably have broken her neck, as one twists the neck of a rabbit. One crack and it's done.

She looked at him. The light was gone from his eyes and he fell forward onto the blood-covered deck.

Panic washed over her like a wave. She had done it. She had struck first . . . and survived. But what was she going to tell the crew? She might be able to heave the body overboard, but she couldn't get rid of the blood. The first daylight would show it clearly enough. She had not thought of this, before the immediacy of surviving.

Then with a horror that almost stopped her heart, she heard movement behind her and turned slowly, as if she could not feel her limbs. There was a crewman standing six feet away. He must have come up to the deck only moments before. She did not recognize him in the dark. What could she say? What would anyone believe? She tried to speak and nothing came.

The man took a step forward. "We'd better get rid of him," he said in faultless English. "And then take the lifeboat. It's ready to go, such as it is."

She could not move; she could scarcely breathe.

"Elena!" he said sharply. "There's no time to waste! Somebody else could come on deck any minute. Take his feet. We've got to get him over the side." He moved forward and picked up Aiden by the shoulders and started to lift him. "Move!" he ordered again. "Time to think about it afterward."

She stared at him, unable to respond. At last she moved, bending to pick up Aiden's feet, using all the strength and balance she had, and together they lifted him over the rail and let him fall into the water. Within seconds, the white wake of the ship smothered him. When he reappeared twenty feet away, he was staining the water with blood.

The man's hand on her shoulder was gentle, but only for a moment. "Come on," he ordered. "It will take both of us to get the lifeboat launched. It's heavy, and if we get it wrong, we're finished."

"Peter?" she said incredulously, feeling as if her mouth were half paralyzed. "What are you —"

"Long story, tell you later. Now move." As he said it, he led the way back across the deck, toward where the single lifeboat was hanging on its davits. He started to work the winch that would swing the boat out over the side and let it down into the water.

She worked with him, with very little idea of what she was doing, only what seemed to make sense.

"It has to be simple," he told her. "And

quick. No, no, that one!" He pointed to a lever. "Now . . . down!"

It took them precious minutes before the boat touched the water. In a few more, they were in the boat and reaching for the oars. They sat side by side on the central bench, taking only two or three strokes to get into a steady rhythm.

There was still no sound from the ship.

"Elena," he said loudly, above the creaking of the oarlocks, "we've got a little while before help comes. With luck. I gave the crew a quick shot of brandy from my own flask. It was laced with laudanum, just to make sure they don't follow us."

"How . . . how did you get here?" She gasped for breath between strokes.

"RAF flight," Peter answered.

"But . . . how did you know?"

"Don't talk," he replied, "just row." After a moment, he said, "I knew it was all going south. I have other contacts, a few people who owe me favors. It all fell into place, once I realized that Aiden was a loose card . . . on nobody's side."

"How did you know that? And when?" she asked, ignoring his order to keep quiet. She had to know.

"A little before you knew it, I think," he replied. "I did a favor for a French agent . . ."

"What?" She was confused, her mind numb with fear and horror. Aiden's death, the sea full of blood . . .

"Gabrielle Fournier," he said, his voice barely audible.

"Gabrielle?" Elena was trying to make sense of this. "You . . . you knew he was going to kill me tonight? And you . . ." Further words escaped her.

"I thought it was likely. But I couldn't catch up with you. The first port, where the ship unloaded, I took a crewman's place. He's sleeping it off in the street behind the café. I trusted you would look after yourself. I cut it fine, I know."

"Is that an apology?" she asked in a shaking voice.

"No. I expect you to do your job well. But I do apologize for sending you to rescue a traitor. I believed him to be loyal, and for that I'm incompetent . . . and profoundly sorry."

"It took me until yesterday," she replied. "And I knew him better than you did." She missed her stroke and, catching a crab, the oar bumped over the water, soaking him with spray.

Peter laughed, his voice a little out of control with relief.

"I didn't do that on purpose," she protested vehemently, her arms feeling heavier than lead. "Are we going to row all the way back to England?"

"No, of course not. Stop a moment." He fished in his pocket and took out what looked like a truncheon.

"What's that?" she demanded sharply. Suddenly she was afraid again. They were utterly alone in the darkness. Nothing but the sky and the water, and enemies far too close by.

"It's a flashlight, what do you think?"

She could not see his face. The last shreds of light on the horizon were fast sinking into darkness, and there was no sound but the water slapping against the sides of the boat. Then she heard the sound of something high above them.

Peter lifted the flashlight and signaled.

She read the Morse code easily. It had been part of her brief training.

"GOT HER PICK UP PH"

He put the light away and took up the oar. "Row," he said. "The more distance between us and the steamer, the better."

"What good does a plane do us?" she asked. "We're in the middle of the sea!"

"Seaplane," he said patiently. "Just thank God it's a clear night."

They shipped the oars and waited.

The small seaplane landed a hundred yards away, then moved across the water until it was quite close. Elena and Peter picked up the oars again. She was surprised by how stiff she felt, her arms heavy and weak, even after rowing for such a short time, and she was cold to the bone. She struggled as she rowed against the current. When they were alongside the plane, she grasped the co-pilot's outstretched hand and stepped precariously into the cockpit, with Peter coming immediately after.

They took the seats behind the pilot and his navigator. Even before they settled in, the plane picked up speed across the water. Elena was clutching her handbag as if it were a life raft.

The plane lifted off, the sea dropping away below them, and then did a quick swing to head west over Italy and toward home.

"Just in case they have a machine gun on deck," the pilot explained, changing course again, although this time into a direct route.

"Good man," Peter said above the engine noise. "I think they're armed, and certainly any kind of bullet shot through the engine or the fuel tank wouldn't do us any good."

Elena refused even to imagine it.

Peter put his hand on her arm, his touch

amazingly gentle. "Are you all right?"

"Yes, thank you, I'm fine," she said with a very slight smile. Any more would have looked as fake as it would feel. "Aiden gave me a list of names. He said it was a copy of his, in case he didn't make it out of Trieste. I'm not sure it really was a copy."

"Let me see," Peter said.

She went into her handbag. The outside was wet and completely ruined, but the inside was waterproofed. She took out her passport with the list folded inside. She gave it to Peter.

He read it, holding it up to the dim cockpit light, then met her eyes. His own eyes revealed shock; they were almost hollow in the unnatural illumination. "Elena, these are people holding real power in England, good people, who are fighting the Nazis. If we had blamed them, we could have ruined some of our best." His face was ashen in the cockpit lights. "He meant you to give me this. Sweet God, that was close. If this had been given to Bradley, he would've used it to shatter any chance we have of stopping this horror. It's quite different from the list Lucas gave to Gilmour. Sweet God," he repeated, "that was close."

"Lucas? Gilmour?" She was confused. "Home secretary, Sir John Gilmour? What does —"

Peter cut her off. "Jerome Bradley is a traitor. How long he has been one, I don't know. Perhaps always. But Lucas had him arrested, discreetly. We don't want a scandal, or to give him the chance to talk to people." Before Elena could speak, he rushed ahead. "Many people who survived in the war don't want another. For them, it's peace at any price. That means even helping Hitler. Sometimes, it takes a hell of a lot of courage to see the truth and accept it."

Elena could not find the words. Bradley? Hitler?

"Lucas will tell you about it when we get you home." He smiled faintly, a rather lopsided smile, intense in the red light from the instruments. "One day, he might even forgive me for sending you to rescue Aiden. I only did so because I believed he was one of ours." He fell silent for a moment. "I think that's the worst mistake I've ever made."

"Me, too." She tried to smile and knew it was only half a success. "But I fixed it."

"You did," he agreed softly, and this time the smile was whole and bright and gentle. And filled with respect. "You really did."

ABOUT THE AUTHOR

Anne Perry is the *New York Times* bestselling author of two acclaimed series set in Victorian England: the William Monk novels and the Charlotte and Thomas Pitt novels. She is also the author of a series featuring Thomas and Charlotte Pitt's son, Daniel, including *Triple Jeopardy* and *One Fatal Flaw;* the new Elena Standish series, beginning with *Death in Focus;* five World War I novels; eighteen holiday novels, most recently *A Christmas Resolution;* and a historical novel, *The Sheen on the Silk,* set in the Ottoman Empire. Anne Perry lives in Los Angeles. Visit her website at anneperry .co.uk.

The employees of Thorndike Press hope you have enjoyed this Large Print book. All our Thorndike, Wheeler, and Kennebec Large Print titles are designed for easy reading, and all our books are made to last. Other Thorndike Press Large Print books are available at your library, through selected bookstores, or directly from us.

For information about titles, please call:
(800) 223-1244

or visit our website at:
gale.com/thorndike

To share your comments, please write:

Publisher
Thorndike Press
10 Water St., Suite 310
Waterville, ME 04901.